The Dead Soldier

THE DEAD SOLDIER

A Doherty Mystery

Sam Kafrissen

International Digital Book Publishing Industries
Florida, USA

First Printing
10 9 8 7 6 5 4 3 2 1

ISBN: 978-1-57550-148-2

International Digital Book Publishing Incorporated,
Clearwater, Florida

Cover Photo:
Château du Colombier, St-Malo, France

Printed in the United States of America

For
Jeanne,
Heart of my Heart

Chapter One

March. They say it's supposed to come in like a lion and go out like a lamb. Although it was nearly the end of the month the lion was still on the loose. The sky had been overcast for a week and temperatures were barely above freezing. The calendar said it was spring, but that season seemed intent upon staying in hibernation.

For the last five days Doherty'd been traveling all over Rhode Island looking for some teenage boy who'd stolen his father's car and taken off with his underage girlfriend. When the old man plunked down his fifty bucks to hire Doherty it was apparent he was more interested in getting his car back than his "good for nothing" son. Arriving back in town Doherty was hoping his secretary Agnes would not be in the office this late in the day. He wasn't looking forward to seeing the disappointment on her face after another day of fruitless searching. On top of that he hadn't been able to throw much money her way lately as business had all but dried up thanks to the bad publicity surrounding the Grimaldi case.

That job had left three people dead and Doherty looking like a chump for standing by while a woman he was supposed to be protecting stuck a kitchen knife into the chest of a guy who was trying to kill her. Since all this happened at night in her apartment, the press made it sound like Doherty was shacking up with this gal and had done nothing to protect her from her assailant. The

1

truth was more complicated than that, but the public wasn't interested in the truth; only the salacious accounts the papers spit out on a slow news week.

The scent hit him as soon as he passed through the door at Doherty and Associates. It was not the kind of cheap perfume they sold at the Woolworth's counter. This one smelled more like the stuff somebody would spend twenty dollars on in exchange for a container slightly larger than a thimble. She was dressed in a black-skirted suit with dark stockings to match. A white blouse and a pair of black stiletto heeled shoes completed the outfit. Her hair was dark and pulled back from a face distinguished by high cheekbones and red lipstick. She was sucking on a thin filtered cigarette with a hand that held a diamond ring not quite as big as the Ritz though bright enough to blind anyone who looked at it too closely.

She blew the smoke out of the corner of her mouth so that none of it landed on the young girl sitting in the adjacent chair. That one looked to be about sixteen and was wearing a parochial school outfit of Mary Jane shoes, blue knee socks, a plaid skirt, a white blouse buttoned to the neck, and a blazer with the school's insignia on the left breast pocket. She was doing her best to display the kind of bored attitude that teenage girls do better than just about anyone. She occupied herself by twirling some of her long brown hair around her fingers.

Agnes sat uncomfortably behind her desk. Before Doherty could remove his fedora, she said, "This is Mrs. Royal. She and her daughter have been waiting for almost an hour. I didn't know how to reach you."

This last comment was thrown out solely for the potential client's benefit. Doherty seldom checked into the office on a pay phone while he was out on a case. Since they had so few walk-in clients his presence in the office wasn't really required most days. When he did hang out in town it was because he had nothing better to do. Even then he spent a good amount of his free time downstairs at Harry's barbershop chatting with his barber pal Bill Fiore and lingering there just long enough to get under Harry's skin.

Doherty invited the woman and her daughter into his back office where he shrugged off his overcoat and hung it on the antler rack. He assumed his spot behind the big desk and offered the two chairs on the other side to his guests. The woman wore so much make-up her face looked like it would crack if she tried to offer up the smallest of smiles. Everything about her appearance wreaked of money, though there was something in her manner that told him she'd come up hard before marrying into wealth. Whatever the case may be, he was hoping she was prepared to wave some of that money his way.

"So, Mrs. Royal, how can I help you and ...?" he asked waving his hand in the daughter's direction.

"My daughter's name is Mary Margaret. My husband is Brayton Webster Royal. I assume you know who he is." She took a long drag on her skinny cigarette letting this last piece of information sink in.

Brayton Webster Royal, or B.W. as he preferred to be called, was the last son of Webster Royal Jr., whose father Webster Sr. along with his brother Richard once owned nearly all of the large textile mills in Rhode Island - including the Royal Mill at Riverpoint in West Warwick, where Doherty's father put in twenty plus years before his liver ate him up. The Royal family had made several fortunes along the way before the family-owned companies went bankrupt during the Depression. By then most of the textile manufacturing in New England had already begun to move down south. The Royals were forced to sell off a lot of their mill properties for pennies on a dollar to cover their debts. Some of their mills "accidentally on purpose" burned down, which left the family with a fair amount of money from the insurance settlements.

Less anyone feel sorry for the Royals' fate, not only had they worked hundreds of mill workers to the bone over the years, they still had some substantial land holdings throughout the state. One in particular was a large estate in the Natick section of Warwick just over the town line from West Warwick. Rumor had it they were about to sell some of that land to the state, which wanted to locate a junior college there. An adjacent parcel was supposedly being shopped to a developer who planned to build a gigantic indoor shopping plaza on it. Such a complex when completed would probably decimate the small shopkeepers in Arctic who had for most of this century kept West Warwick a thriving center of commerce. Whatever the current financial status was of the Royal family, and B.W. in particular, they were still one of the richest families in the state.

"We would like to hire you to find someone, or at least to find out about someone," Mrs. Royal began. "Mary Margaret will be sixteen soon and she has made an unusual request for her birthday present." The woman had the kind of voice that indicated she was trying hard to sound sophisticated and was only being partially successful.

"What exactly is the nature of this request that involves your hiring a private investigator?"

"I want you to find my father," the girl blurted out. These words left Doherty momentarily confused.

"I thought B.W. Royal was your father."

The girl looked at her mother before saying, "No, Royal's my stepfather." This explanation didn't come out smelling like roses.

"Perhaps I should explain," the woman said as she extracted another skinny cigarette from a gold case. Doherty tapped out a Camel and reached across his desk to light hers with his Zippo. She didn't see the need to thank him.

"I was married before I met Brayton. At the time I was barely out of my teens. I married a boy I'd been going with since high school. After he was drafted into the army, we were wed a few months before he was shipped overseas. Not long after that he was killed at some place in France following the Normandy invasion, or so the government told us. I didn't realize until after he left that I was pregnant with Mary Margaret. My first husband's name was John McDonald. John Stuart McDonald to be exact. He was a sweet boy, though my marriage to him now seems like ages ago." The girl flashed her mother a dirty look that the woman had no trouble ignoring. Doherty decided before he took the case, he needed to figure out a little about the relationship between these two.

"I'm assuming the war department provided you with some information about your husband's sad end."

"They sent us a telegram. By us I mean his parents and me. All it said was that he was missing in action. Then a few months later a more detailed letter came thanking him for his service and bravery. It said that his remains were interred at the American cemetery in Normandy. A few weeks later another typed letter came to us from his commanding officer saying that John had died heroically in combat. That was the last I heard about my first husband.

"A few years ago, at Mary Margaret's prompting, Brayton did a little more digging for us and found out they were only able to uncover some physical remains with his dog tags attached to them. That's what they buried at the cemetery." Doherty knew from experience this was a polite way for the military to tell them they only found parts of McDonald's body.

"That's what B.W. told you," the girl said in a frosty voice. "Why would he want to find out any more about my father since he was already married to his wife?"

"Please Mary Margaret, retelling this is hard enough for me. John was my husband; you weren't even born yet. You never knew him like I did."

"And now you're married to Mr. Moneybags. Why do you care what happened to my father? You're the rich bitch you always wanted to be."

Doherty felt the need to interrupt this little set-to before Mrs. Rich Bitch slapped her daughter across the face. "Look how about if you two gear it down a few notches. All of this is very interesting, but if I'm going to take this case, I need you folks to calm down and tell me what you want from me."

The schoolgirl sat up straight and said, "I want you to find out exactly what happened to my father. It's important that I know who he was when he died."

Doherty leaned back and scrutinized the mother who was nervously twitching in her chair. "Are you okay with this, Mrs. Royal?"

There was an uncomfortable pause. "I suppose. If this is what she wants as her sweet sixteen gift. Personally I had something more tangible in mind." Doherty figured she'd be happier buying her daughter some bauble along the lines of a lesser version of the rock that sat on her third finger or the gold earrings that dangled from her lobes. "We're hoping this will help improve Mary Margaret's relationship with my husband. It hasn't been good for a long time now and I'm at my wit's end as to what to do about it."

"How does your husband feel about you hiring a private investigator for this job?"

"He's very supportive of my daughter's wishes. He said he would be willing to spend whatever was necessary to find out the details of what happened to Mary Margaret's father over in France."

"In France?"

The woman smiled for the first time – and surprisingly her face didn't crack. "Yes, France. Brayton thinks the only way someone will be able to get to the bottom of the situation would be to go to France to find out for himself what happened to John."

"Does that mean you're expecting me to travel to France?"

"Why, of course, Mr. Doherty. Though first you'll have to meet with my husband to work out the details. We'll leave that up to the two of you. Here's one of his cards," she said as she extracted a business card from her purse. "You'll have to call to make an appointment. Brayton is a very busy man."

Chapter Two

After filling Agnes in on the Royal family's proposal, he told her she could pack up and go home for the day. He then locked up the office before taking a walk up Brookside Avenue to a place he always regretted visiting. The headquarters of the town's Democratic Party were located on the second floor of what used to be the Plaza Hotel. The building was now owned by Judge Martin DeCenza, the town's political boss. Although Doherty was no friend of the Judge, he needed some insight as to what B.W. Royal and his lovely wife were up to. And Martin DeCenza was the man who knew everything about what was going on in West Warwick and its environs.

He'd had some unpleasant dealings with the Judge a few years back that left them both in a position where they held something over each other. So, meeting at party headquarters with DeCenza was no longer an unbalanced transaction. Back when Doherty was a cop on the West Warwick police force, like a lot of other men in uniform he was required to do off-duty work for the machine. He chafed at the conditions of those jobs, which was the main reason he'd eventually left the force. Most of his fellow officers did them willingly for the extra cash it gave them to supplement their paltry salaries. Doherty liked to think he was acting nobler than his fellow officers. The truth was he did not like taking orders from anyone who wasn't technically his superior. He'd had the same problem when he was in the army.

As long as he could remember the political machine's business was conducted in the large room on the second floor that once served as the hotel's ballroom back when people actually went out dancing on Saturday nights. It had also been used for large gatherings like weddings, banquets, and christenings. DeCenza'd partitioned part of the hall into a glassed-in office for himself that looked out over the rest of the space. That way he could watch over his minions to make sure they were busy doing what he liked to call *the people's business*.

When he arrived at the top of the stairs Doherty saw that the smoke-filled office was already occupied by the Judge, his number one flunky, Angel Touhy, and to Doherty's surprise, his old pal Willy Legere. Willy was a navy veteran who'd been blinded during the war when his ship was sunk by some Japanese kamikazes. After he came home Willy spent over a decade supplementing his small government disability checks by selling pencils and begging for handouts on Washington Street in front of the Artic News. Using some inside dope he acquired on the Judge about a crooked real estate deal, Doherty pressured DeCenza into giving Willy a job in the town government. It was a form of blackmail on his part, though he figured it was an acceptable form. The last time he'd seen Willy he was working at the water department office in the building adjacent to the old Centreville Mill. His desk had even been outfitted with some specialized Braille equipment.

The men inside looked shocked when they saw Doherty knocking on the office door – all except Willy of course. DeCenza flashed his knowing grin before indicating to Touhy that he should usher their unscheduled guest in.

"Why, Hugh Doherty, this is a pleasant surprise," DeCenza said, though Doherty knew there was nothing pleasant about it for either of them, or for Touhy. "Willy here was just mentioning the other day that he hadn't seen you in a dog's age. Isn't that right Willy?" Legere swiveled his head around, not exactly sure what was going on.

Doherty settled things by taking Legere's right hand in a friendly handshake. "Nice to see you again, Willy boy."

"Why Mr. D. What're you doin' here?" Willy was obviously confused by his unannounced visit.

"Sorry, Willy. I didn't mean to shock you. I came up here to have a few words with Judge DeCenza. It's a bonus seeing you at the same time. How are things down at the water department? Still keeping tabs on everyone's water bill?"

For some reason this last remark seemed to make everyone in the room a little uncomfortable. There was an awkward pause that the Judge broke by coming out from behind his big desk and resting a hand on Willy's shoulder. "As a matter of fact, Willy here is now the head of the department."

Doherty looked in Touhy's direction, well aware that the water department had been Angel's little fiefdom for the past few years.

"I thought Angel ran the water department."

The Judge smiled, pleased that Doherty was uninformed about the inner workings of the town government that he almost single-handedly controlled. "I had to relieve Angel of some of his more pressing duties here in town so that we could get him up to speed for when he goes into the legislature next January." This last remark confirmed the rumors that DeCenza had decided his right-hand man and main gofer was going to be the next state rep for West Warwick and the surrounding villages.

"The voters might have something to say about that," Doherty tossed out.

"A mere formality, my boy. A mere formality." He knew when it came to elections, nine times out of ten whoever DeCenza decided should win, usually did. Even if it was necessary for new, unaccounted for ballots to miraculous appear. Or for others to disappear.

The Judge then turned his attention to the other men in the room. "Willy, I believe you and Angel have some business to attend to down in Crompton, don't you?"

"Yes, boss," Willy said as he rose and reached for his red tipped cane. It was only then that Doherty noticed that his blind friend was wearing a nicely tailored suit and some fashionable new dark glasses. Clearly Willy was moving up in the world. For Willy's sake Doherty hoped he didn't fly too high. Sometimes those that did in DeCenza's circle had a way of falling back to earth with a thud.

"I'll come by the department office to see you sometime soon, Willy. I promise."

"You better make an appointment with Elaine first. I'm not in the office much these days. I'm out a lot doin' other business around town." Doherty didn't want to speculate on what else the Judge had Willy doing on behalf of the machine. Nevertheless he gave Willy a warm handshake before he and Angel set off to do some of the *people's business*.

Once the Judge's two subordinates were on their way, DeCenza settled himself back behind his oversized desk. "Well, Doherty, according to the papers it appears you've gone from being a local hero to being a cad in a very short period of time. I suppose you can thank that girlfriend of yours who stuck a knife into someone's chest while you were snoring in the next room."

"She wasn't my girlfriend and it didn't happen the way it was reported in the news. But I don't suppose that really matters to you."

"No, it doesn't mean anything to me one way or another. Though I did enjoy seeing you get hoisted by your own petard. Judging from the pictures in the papers of the woman who did the stabbing I'd say you would've been better off sticking with that cute little Vitale girl you were dating at the Centreville Bank."

Technically Doherty was still dating Nina Vitale, though their relationship had cooled somewhat after his night at the murder scene in Doris Donahue's apartment. The main factor, of course, was the terrible way his role in that incident was depicted in the news.

Doherty took a seat on the other side of DeCenza's desk and lit up a Camel.

"You don't have to tell me why you're here. I suspected from the moment you walked in you came to talk to me about Brayton Webster Royal and the fool's errand his wife and daughter are thinking of sending you on."

"You don't miss a trick, do you?"

"Normally someone like B.W. and I don't travel in the same circles. People of his ilk tend to look down their noses at someone who's immersed in the grubby business of politics. I don't have to remind you of the many years our organization fought tooth and nail with the mill owners in this town to protect the workers whose labor lined their pockets and allowed them to live high off the hog."

"Yes, Judge, I'm well aware of your reputation for nobly representing the interests of the working men here in West Warwick. You've always been a regular Robin Hood - in a hundred-dollar suit."

DeCenza pounded his desk. "Don't think you can come into my office and sass me like some snot-nosed school boy. No one amounts to anything in this town unless I say so, and that includes you and your fly-by-night investigations agency. I could squash you like a gnat if I had the mind to."

The Judge had apparently taken it into his head that he could ignore the fact that Doherty was privy to some information about a crooked real estate deal that the Judge had pulled on some members of Rhode Island's gangster class. If Doherty ever fed that information to certain parties, it would be DeCenza who might end up as a squashed insect.

He cracked a grin at the Judge's last remark. "Well, I sure hope you're able to save West Warwick when B.W. Royal sells that big piece of land off East Avenue to the developer who's planning to build a shopping plaza on it. It won't be long that puts a lot of the shopkeepers in Arctic out of business. Sounds like it's going to be a big challenge to you and Touhy and the rest of your gang who are supposed to be protecting the working people in this town. First those rich wags pack up the mills and send them south. Now Royal will be providing the land that the mall developer will use to destroy the Arctic business community. Once that happens you and your political cronies may be put out to pasture."

DeCenza sat back in his big chair and for the first time in his dealings with him Doherty could see the Judge looked uncertain about his future.

"He called me about you."

"Who did?"

"Who do you think? B.W. himself. He told me about this harebrained scheme his wife and stepdaughter were cooking up to send somebody over to France to find out what happened to the girl's father during the war. He wanted to know if I knew someone local who was qualified the job."

"And you suggested me? Why on earth would you do something like that? Is this your way of getting back at me for the Soap Works business?"

"No, I did not suggest you as a possible person to send on this futile mission just to please my own perverse sense of humor. I recommended you because I thought you were the perfect man to accomplish whatever they wanted you to. Look, Doherty, I'll put my cards on the table. I don't like you. I don't like the fact that you go around thinking you have more integrity than the average person in this town; acting like you're holier than thou. But I've followed your career and I know you're good at what you do. To me you're like a dog who gets his teeth into something and won't let it go. In fact, that's exactly how I described you to Royal.

"If they send you on this mission, no matter how crazy it may seem, I know you'll bring back something of value. Besides, it'll be fun to watch Royal piss away a fair amount of his money just to find out his wife's first husband, his rival from the grave as it were, was nothing more than some poor sap who died in the war like thousands of other poor saps. The dead soldier probably wouldn't have amounted to much of anything if he'd survived and come home to his pretty wife and daughter. His death may've the best thing that ever happened to Mrs. Royal. Now she can be the queen of a castle rather than living out her days in some run-down duplex."

Doherty couldn't argue with DeCenza's assessment of the good fortune Mrs. Royal found herself in. The only reason then for her to propose this French mission to Doherty was to bind up whatever open wounds existed between Brayton Royal and his stepdaughter. He got the sense from their short meeting that the fissure between the two must be pretty extensive for the girl's parents to be willing to pay for Doherty to make a trip to France. Though the challenge of the investigation should have been his main concern, what was really troubling him was his own uncertainty about venturing to a foreign country he knew little about. He'd briefly been in Paris on leave during the war, but that was over fifteen years ago. Since then Doherty'd never been out of the U.S. not even to Canada. He wasn't confident about employing his skills as an investigator outside of Rhode Island, let alone outside of the country.

"Look, Doherty, I'm a busy man here. I don't have time to argue ethics or the future of West Warwick with you all day. Why don't you get to the point and tell me what you want? And don't deny that's why you're here. Nobody comes up those stairs to see me unless they're looking for a handout or a favor."

"Okay, you got me there. If I do agree to take this job the Royal family is offering me, I'm going to need a connection to someone over in France who can help me. Possibly at the embassy in Paris. Or short of that someone who at least can point me in the right direction. I was hoping you might know someone. Frankly I didn't know who else to ask."

"Well, well, well. The great detective apparently doesn't have a clue where to begin his investigation." DeCenza leaned back in his chair, clasped his hands behind his head and cracked a big smile. He was reveling in Doherty's having come to him with hat in hand. "I'd like to help you but I can't."

"Can't or won't."

This time the Judge laughed. "I wish it were the latter. The fact is I don't know anyone in either the state department or the department of defense. That's what they call the war department nowadays. All my work during the war had to do with procurement. Finding materials and civilian manpower here in Rhode Island to provide for the shipyards and whatever was needed at Quonset and Davisville. The diplomatic machinations during the war were outside of my purview."

Doherty stood to leave, realizing he'd hit a dead end. He was disappointed that the only person in town who might've hooked him up with a good source was unable, or perhaps unwilling, to do so. It was possible B.W Royal would know someone, but this meant he'd be going into his initial meeting with Royal empty-handed.

"Well, Judge, I would like to say it was nice talking to you. Hey, at least I got to see Willy Legere. He seems to be a rising star in your operation here."

"Oh, don't go away so downcast, Doherty. It doesn't suit you. I said I personally didn't know anyone who could help you in this enterprise. That doesn't mean I don't know someone else who might be of assistance."

Doherty hesitated before slipping his overcoat on. "And who would that be?"

"You're not going to like it."

"Try me."

"Your Uncle Patrick McSweeny. I have it from good sources that your uncle knows some people quite high up in the government. And now that he's a rainmaker for the Kennedy campaign, there's no telling who he'd be able to introduce you to. You should give him a call if you two are still on speaking terms."

Doherty didn't know if DeCenza knew about his or his uncle's role in the downfall of the big time Boston political operative Kevin O'Shaughnessy. Either way perhaps it was time for him to bury the hatchet with his only living relative within a hundred miles of West Warwick. No matter how unsavory that meeting might be, it could be the only play he had right now.

Chapter Three

Doherty stopped for a quick lunch at the downstairs counter in the Arctic News. He accompanied his grilled cheese sandwich and tomato soup with a copy of the morning *Providence Journal*. As usual he went first to the sports pages. There was a baseball story about spring training down in Florida. The article did not express much optimism about the Red Sox's chances of crawling out of the second division this year. They'd had only two real stars last year: Ted Williams, who at 41 was now on his last legs, and Jackie Jensen who is making noises about quitting. According to the papers, the Sox right fielder has a fear of flying in airplanes. With the league expanding out to Kansas City and soon to the West Coast, it won't be long before teams travel mostly by air.

After their disastrous performance in finishing third the previous season, the Yankees were retooling for the 1960 campaign. They had shopped their starting leftfielder Norm Siebern to the Kansas City A's in exchange for a kid named Roger Maris, who apparently has the perfect swing for Yankee Stadium's short right field porch. They threw Hank Bauer and Don Larsen into the deal, which upset many New York fans. Larsen had tossed a perfect game in the 1956 World Series, though he hadn't done much for the Yanks since. Bauer, on the other hand, had been a fixture in right field for the team since the late 40s. It appeared that the ex-marine was finally going to take a fall for

15

the infamous brawl some Yankees had gotten into back in 1957 at the Copacabana nightclub in Manhattan. The other players involved in that melee were Mickey Mantle, Yogi Berra, Whitey Ford, and Billy Martin. Martin had already been shopped to the Tigers, but Mantle, Ford, and Berra weren't going anywhere but to Cooperstown. No one in New York would miss the Siebern kid after he'd lost several fly balls in the sun during the 1958 World Series, thus doing his level best to hand the Milwaukee Braves back-to-back titles. The Yankees ended up winning the series, though by the end of '59 it was clear Siebern no longer figured in their plans.

Meanwhile fans in Boston still hadn't forgiven the Braves for leaving town just a couple of seasons before they became world-beaters. Now the locals would be stuck with a Red Sox squad that would slug it out with the expansion A's and the Washington Senators to see who could stay out of the cellar. No wonder so many Rhode Islanders were throwing their baseball allegiance to the New Yorkers.

Doherty spent the rest of his lunchtime perusing the news sections looking for any tidbits he could find about the budding Kennedy-for-President campaign. His uncle had given him a behind-the-scenes view of that operation in their discussions last fall. Back then his insights were mostly about how much money was being stockpiled by the candidate's father, Joe Kennedy, and other rich Irishmen; money that would be spread around by campaign operatives in primary states like West Virginia and Wisconsin. With the downfall of his boss Kevin O'Shaughnessy, who was on a permanent hiatus in Ireland, Doherty's uncle was now functioning at the highest level of the campaign's fundraising operation.

In the local races it looked like the Democratic Lieutenant-Governor John Notte was going to challenge the sitting Republican governor Chris DelSesto in November. Rhode Island governors served only two-year terms, so no sooner was one race over than the next one began. The last race had stretched out beyond Election Day so that the all-important absentee ballots could be carefully counted.

In 1958 the then-governor, Democrat Dennis Roberts, had used his influence with the state supreme court to have the absentee ballots suppressed so he could defeat DelSesto in a tightly contested race. That effort cost him the

16

governorship two years later when DelSesto prevailed in a rematch. Now Roberts was trying to resurrect his career by running for the open senate seat old man Green, who at the ripe age of 92 was finally vacating after representing Rhode Island in that body for 23 years. So far, the jury was out on who the Dems would choose to replace Theodore Francis. Whoever they chose he would be the favorite in the general election. Despite DelSesto's recent success, Rhode Island was still a predominately Democratic state.

With nothing else of interest in the paper besides the comics, Doherty left the folded-up *Journal* on the counter at the News for the next customer and headed back to the office. Agnes hadn't come in today. He couldn't blame her since he'd only been able to toss twenty dollars her way over the past two weeks. If he took the Royal job at least then he'd be able to share some of his retainer with her.

He puttered around the office checking the mail, all bills and advertising flyers, and the answering machine, which had no new messages. The phone call he had to make to his Uncle Patrick was weighing heavily on him. Since the sun was making a rare appearance today, he decided to go for a drive to think things over.

He drove north along the river and then through the backcountry into Cranston. It was surprising that much of the western part of that city was still occupied by dairy farms. He thought about the night he drove out this way with two of Frank Ganetti's thugs, expecting it would be his last night on earth. Instead of shooting Doherty, one of Ganetti's men, a fearsome character named Angelo, killed the other one, a young punk named Bobby Carnavalle, because he'd betrayed the Ganetti family. Outside of the war, that night was as close as Doherty'd ever come to dying.

He headed north and skirted the Providence waterfront and found himself driving east toward the Riverside section of East Providence. On impulse he pulled in at a spot where he could look down over Providence where the rivers intersected. Smokestacks were billowing white plumage into the first sunny sky the city'd seen in days. Standing by his car smoking a Camel Doherty wrestled with the idea of taking a case that would require him to cross the Atlantic to look for clues about a guy who'd been dead for sixteen years. Although the whole project seemed ridiculous, he was sure there'd be a generous remuneration from B.W. Royal regardless of what his search turned up. The other thing bothering him was the very notion of flying in an airplane across the Atlantic Ocean. Except for the few jumps he'd made in training out at Ft. Sill and his airdrop into Sicily, Doherty'd never been on an airplane – and never on a commercial flight crossing three thousand miles of open water. And on this trip he wouldn't have a parachute strapped to his back.

Another car pulled up about fifty yards away along the overlook and a girl jumped out as soon as it stopped. A teenage boy followed her and grabbed her by her wrists. The two were shouting at each other. They were too far away for Doherty to hear what the argument was about. When the boy slapped the girl across the face, he thought it would be a good time for him to intervene. While jogging over toward them he noticed their car for the first time. Damn if it wasn't the Ford Fairlane he'd been hired to find a week ago. It meant these two teens were his client's runaway son and the underage girlfriend.

The kids looked nervous as Doherty approached them. The girl was still struggling to free herself from the boy's grip.

"This ain't none of your business," the boy said to Doherty.

He stepped up closer. "I think you should let go of your girlfriend's wrists." The kid looked unsure of what to do next, still holding onto the girl as if she provided him some sort of protection. The car thief was tall and skinny and couldn't have weighed more than 130 pounds wringing wet. He had dark-ish skin, a short crew cut, and big ears that stuck out. The girl was short and a little bit on the chunky side. Her hair was strawberry blond and her cheeks were covered with freckles. She looked to be about twelve, though the father who hired Doherty said she was fifteen.

Doherty moved in and forcefully released the boy's hands from around the girl's wrists. The kid said, "Hey." But it was a weak hey. Otherwise he offered no resistance.

"Unless you two want more trouble I think we should have a little chat."

"Hey, I don't have to do nuthin' just cuz you say so." The boy's voice was irritatingly whiny. He was trying to regain his bravado, if only for the girl's sake. He wasn't being very successful.

"Yes, you do."

"Yeah or what?"

18

Doherty smiled at the feeble attempt the kid was mustering to sound like a tough guy. "I'll punch you in your smartass face and break your nose. Then I'll call the cops and have you arrested for kidnapping. That's a pretty serious crime. They might even charge you as an adult. How would you like to spend a couple of years at the ACI? You think you're tough enough to do time in an adult prison?"

"I didn't kidnap no one. She went with me cuz she wanted to. Ain't that right, Lorrie?" The girl was still rubbing her wrists where her boyfriend had roughed her up.

"What's your name, son?" Doherty asked, though he already knew from the father that his name was Russell.

"I don't have to tell you nuthin'."

Doherty slapped the kid hard across the face, though not hard enough to break anything. The girl let out a little shriek when he did this.

"Listen punk, I happen to know your name is Russell Minasian - Rusty to your mother. As it turns out you two stopping here is a lucky break for me. You see I've been looking all over the state this past week for you two. I'm a private investigator, Rusty. Your father hired me to find you. Then just like that," Doherty said snapping his fingers, "while I'm sitting here contemplating the state of the world, you two pull up less than a hundred feet away."

"Yeah, so what does that mean?" the kid said, rubbing the red blotch the slap had left on his cheek.

Doherty raised his hand again and Rusty cowered away from him. "Well this is how things can play out – that is if you don't want the police to get involved. So far, the only ones concerned about you two being missing are your families. Nobody's reported anything to the cops yet. I'll let you drive yourself home in your father's Fairlane while I take your girlfriend to her house. Once I'm there I'll call your place to make sure you've arrived home. You don't get there with the car by the time I call, I'll suggest to Lorraine's parents that they contact the police and have you arrested for kidnapping and statutory rape. Those, my friend are major league crimes. If I were you I wouldn't try to run again. You might've been able to elude me for a week, but you won't outrun the state police. So, what'll it be, Rusty, home or jail?"

The kid hesitated, looking at the girl and then at the ground.

"Please, Russ, do what the man says. I don't want any more trouble. We been sleepin' in that car for five days now. I just wanna go home and sleep in my own bed."

"What about your parents. What're they gonna do?"

"I don't know, baby. You know how my father is." She then turned to Doherty. "Do you think you can convince my parents not to call the cops on Rusty? It wasn't all his fault. I went with him 'cause I thought it'd be fun to run away from home. It was at first 'til we started runnin' outta money."

Doherty considered the girl's plea. "I'll do what I can. Given what you just told me, if they try to cause trouble for Rusty with the law, I'll tell them you could be charged as an accomplice. At least in stealing his father's car. That would give you a record – a juvenile one, but a record nonetheless. If I explain to them how things might play out for you maybe they'll decide to go easy on your boyfriend."

The three of them stood in silence as the two teens nervously tried to decide how they wanted their joyride to end.

"What do you say, Rusty? Why don't you take your father's car home while I deal with Lorraine and her folks?"

"All my old man cares about is his fuckin' car. He don't care nuthin' about me." Doherty chose not to respond knowing what the kid was saying was probably true.

A few minutes later Rusty drove off in his old man's Ford. After he left Doherty escorted the girl home in his Chevy.

Chapter Four

L orraine lived in Warwick on a side street off West Shore Road. The house was set back at the end of a long dirt driveway that looked like it would be hell to clear in a big snowstorm. The place was nothing more than a one-story makeshift cottage that had been built out on one side. In its present state it was sorely in need of a paint job. There were no cars parked outside, though the girl said her mother was probably at home since she didn't work and her father took the family car every day. She led Doherty through the front door where he was immediately hit with the sour smell of some un-appetizing food cooking in a kitchen somewhere.

The mother emerged from that room and stopped in her tracks when she saw her daughter accompanied by an older man.

"You're gonna catch hell when your father gets home," was the first thing out of her mouth. No warm welcome home or even concern as to where she'd been the past five days. The girl just snorted, no doubt expecting a whipping from her old man.

Doherty stepped forward and flashed his PI license. "My name is Doherty; I'm a private investigator. I was hired by Russell Minasian's father to find him and your daughter. I discovered them over in East Providence ear-lier this afternoon."

The mother didn't respond. She continued to look cross-eyed at her wayward daughter. "What the hell were you thinkin', Lorrie, runnin' off like you done with that boy?" The woman was short and a little on the heavy side like her daughter. She had close-cropped, non-descript brown hair that ended at her chin. Her face had that saggy look of a person whose whole life was dragging her down.

"I hate to interrupt this lovefest, Mrs. ..." At this point Doherty realized he'd never asked the girl her family name.

"Name's Beegan, Mr. whoever you are," the mother said in a voice as sour as the food smell.

"I was wondering when your husband'll be home?"

"What's that to you?" the mother snapped.

"I think we need to talk this out before you and he decide to do something you're going to regret later."

The mother looked confused. "Vincent should be here in about a half hour. I don't understand. What's there to discuss?"

Doherty ignored her question and asked if he could use their phone. She was reluctant at first but then told him it was in the kitchen hanging on the wall. She pointed toward the back of the house and then followed him when he made his way in that direction. The stale food smell in the kitchen hit him like a low tide on a particularly brackish day. He took out his little note pad and thumbed through it until he found the Minasians' phone number. He dialed it up and a woman answered after the fourth ring.

"Hello, Mrs. Minasian, this is Hugh Doherty, the private detective your husband hired to find your son and his car. I was wondering if your husband was at home."

The woman answered in the negative, so he asked if Russell had returned with the car. She told him he had and gone right to his room as soon as he showed up. Doherty told her he'd call later to touch base with her husband.

When he returned to the living room, Lorraine Beegan was standing in the middle of the room with her coat still on. Everyone looked uncomfortable. The mother broke the silence. "I just put up some coffee. Would you like some, Mr. ..."

"Doherty. Yeah, that would be fine," he said, though not sure he would survive anything that came from their foul-smelling kitchen. "I'll take it black."

When the mother disappeared, Doherty asked the girl if she was going to be all right.

"Yeah, I guess. After my father whacks me around some, everythin'll go back to normal. More of the same old crap." He didn't bother to ask what the same old crap was, though he had a pretty good idea what was in store for her. He handed the girl one of his business cards. "Give me a call if things get bad. Maybe I can help you," he added, though not at all sure how he could.

The mother returned with a cup of weak coffee and offered him a seat on a lumpy sofa. He found it curious that she did not ask her daughter anything about where she'd been for the past five days. Or why she'd felt the need to run away from home at the tender age of fifteen. An uncomfortable silence filled the room until they heard a car pulling in down the long driveway. Doherty stood, intent on taking charge of the next scene.

The door flew open and a worn-out looking man somewhere in his late thirties barged in. He was wearing dirty work clothes; the smell of booze combined with grease emanated from him. He had thinning dark hair that was matted across his scalp. His face was unnaturally red, probably from the liquor. For a few seconds he took in the scene in his living room then headed straight toward the girl. Without hesitating he smacked her hard across the face. When he raised his hand to hit her again, Doherty grabbed his arm and pushed him back a few feet.

"Who the hell are you to come into my house and…"

Doherty didn't let him finish. He stuck his index finger a few inches from the father's nose and said, "How about if you shut your yap for a couple of minutes so we can talk this out in a civilized manner." The father tried to push past Doherty, so he shoved him with more force this time up against a wall. A framed picture fell to the floor, its glass shattering into a number of pieces. The wife let out a shreik.

"We're going to have a little talk, Mr. Beegan. And if you try to hit your daughter again while I'm here I might have to hurt you."

"What do you know about this, Linda?" he yelled at his wife. "Did you let this creep into our house?"

The wife had withdrawn into herself. Apparently she too was a regular victim of her husband's rage. Meanwhile the girl was rubbing her face as tears rolled down her reddened cheeks. "He's a private detective," the wife said between sniveling. "He found Lorrie and Rusty and brought her home."

Meanwhile Doherty had positioned himself between the husband and the other members of his family.

"Why don't you sit down, Mr. Beegan, and cool off. We need to hash this out."

"What's there to hash out? I don't want my daughter near that piece of shit Minasian kid anymore. I hate them Armenians. All that greaseball wants is to get into my Lorrie's pants." Doherty didn't say anything, choosing instead to let the man of the house blow off some steam.

"Did either you or your wife call the police after Lorraine disappeared?"

The two parents looked at each other but didn't say anything for a few awkward seconds. "Minasian called me - said he'd give me fifty bucks if we kept quiet about the kids runnin' away. Hey, fifty bucks is fifty bucks."

"So, although you hate Armenians, there's nothing wrong with taking their money." Beegan didn't answer. He looked down at the floor instead.

"The kid's father gave me some sob story about how he loved that car and didn't want anything to happen to it if the cops got ahold of it."

"How did you get the money?"

"He brought it to me at work. I didn't want my wife to know about it. She kept tellin' me to call the police, but I'd promised Minasian I wouldn't."

"Before or after he gave you the fifty bucks?"

The father looked up at Doherty and gave him a nasty look. "What the hell business is that of yours? She's my daughter, ain't she?"

"Yeah I get it. For fifty bucks you were happy to have your daughter out there running around with some eighteen-year old kid who'd just stolen his father's car. Did you ever think something bad could've happened to the two of them?"

"Hey nothin' did, did it? Here she is now, safe at home." Doherty didn't know how safe the girl would be once he left. But there was only so far he could go to protect her.

Beegan stood up and reached in his back pocket. "Look whaddya want, a couple bucks for your troubles?"

"Keep your money. Minasian already paid me for my services. He's concerned that there not be any problems with the police for either him or his son. He's afraid if the cops get involved Russell might be charged with some serious crimes because Lorraine is underage. Since your daughter went with him of her own accord, she could be charged as an accomplice in the car theft. If you and the Minasians decide to keep this between yourselves that'll be the end of it."

"Yeah, and what should I do if that dirty Armenian comes sniffin' around my Lorrie again?"

"Thankfully that's none of my business. Now if you could move your car I'll be on my way." Doherty nodded at the girl before he left, though he was sure she'd be in for a beating not long after he was gone.

Chapter Five

The Royal family still owned enormous parcels of land in Warwick on either side of East Avenue stretching all the way to Tollgate Road to the south and the drive-in movie theater in Cranston to the north. One section of the land was about to be sold to the state where a community college was to be located; another portion, rumor had it, would be sold to a developer planning to build a major shopping complex on it. These massive constructions were now commonly referred to as *malls.*

Doherty turned off East Ave. and entered a world that felt like something out of another era. For the most part northern Rhode Island was a very densely populated area; that is except for the Royal estate. It was laid out as if it were an active farm from the late 19th century. The road through it was composed of finely crushed gravel with flat stone curbing fashioned by hand from individual squares. Before reaching the main house, he drove by a carriage house, a windmill, a large greenhouse, small buildings that looked like corncribs, and a cider mill. The entire estate was encircled by waist-high bluestone walls.

The main house was bordered by a variety of shrubs and bushes that would be bursting with flowers as soon as warmer weather arrived. The house itself was a low slung, rambling edifice with a wraparound porch. A series of wings had been added onto to it over the years that gave it the appearance of a country house that had sprouted appendages. The circular gravel drive allowed

Doherty to park his Chevy directly in front of what he took to be the main entrance.

Crossing over the wide porch he noticed a couple of double-seated swings, several high-backed rocking chairs and some small tables where the master and mistress of the estate could sit and drink mint juleps while the field hands tended to the crops. Of course, none of this ever happened here as the Royals made all of their money in the textile industry. This rural estate was nothing more than an affectation where a couple of generations of the family could play at farming when they grew bored with the grinding noise inside their mills. The place was referred to by most Rhode Islanders who were aware of its existence as a *gentleman's farm.*

He'd been summoned by B.W. Royal's secretary two days before to appear here at 2 p.m. She made it clear that Doherty should be prompt as Mr. Royal was a very busy man. As was his habit Doherty showed up fifteen minutes early, which gave him time to take in the whole of the estate. It was obvious the family was attempting here to recreate an earlier pastoral way of life.

There was no button for a bell or chimes on the main door, so he used the tastefully understated knocker to make his presence known. A middle-aged man in some sort of work clothes greeted him and introduced himself as Murray. Doherty was disappointed he wasn't being ushered in by a butler in full livery. Murray didn't say if that was his first or last name, so Doherty chose to avoid addressing him.

"Mr. Royal is on the phone. He's asked me to escort you to the library. Please follow this way."

They walked down a long corridor that had paintings of various scenes from the farm lining the walls on either side. Doherty tried to read the names of the artists but was unable to decipher the signatures scratched in the corner of each. At the end of the hall they turned left into a large sitting room with comfortable looking furniture and a stand-up piano against one wall. He was disappointed that the Royals didn't have a Steinway; perhaps there was one was in another part of the house. He could see that the sitting room had an exit out to a screened-in porch at the back of the house that overlooked at least an acre of orchards containing a number of different fruit trees. They passed through another short corridor and before Murray opened a heavy wooden door leading into a room he announced as 'the study'. It looked like the kind of room where Colonel Mustard would've bludgeoned Miss Scarlett with the candlestick.

"Please make yourself comfortable, Mr. Doherty. B.W. will be with you in a few."

After Murray departed Doherty took the opportunity to examine the numerous photographs mounted on the walls of the study. There were several of a young Brayton Royal in an aviator's outfit that included the requisite leather helmet and jacket along with a white scarf tied jauntily around his neck. He was standing next to a series of different small planes, a couple of which had double wings. It was Doherty's recollection from his time at Ft. Still that these particular models were called Sopwith Camels. Adjacent photos of Royal beside newer planes were apparently taken at Hillsgrove Airport judging from the backdrop.

Another wall was lined with photos of B.W. standing on a small boat decked out in scuba diving gear. In one he had his arm around the actor Lloyd Bridges, who starred as the underwater adventurer Mike Nelson in the television series *Sea Hunt*. Bridges had scrawled his autograph across it with a dedication to fellow diver "Bray". That picture was flanked by two underwater shots, one of a large shark and the other of an enormous stingray. Other photos on this wall showed a young Royal at national parks out west dressed in a variety of outdoor hiking, fishing, riding, and hunting gear.

A set of much older pictures were hanging on the wall behind an oversized hand-carved wooden desk with a green felt blotter atop it of equal size. Doherty took the liberty of slipping behind the king-size desk to get a better look at them. They were mostly old sepia prints of prominent Rhode Islanders standing in front of various Royal mill properties. There was a photo of the old Lippitt Mill, one of West Warwick and Rhode Island's earliest textile mills, when it was still in operation. Another photo was of an early version of the Royal Mill where Doherty's father had labored for a number of years. In addition, there were also photos of personages that Doherty assumed were progenitors of the current Royals, perhaps going as far back as B.W.'s grandfather and his brothers who bought many of their early mills as well as this land

28

where the farm now stood from the Sprague family. As Doherty learned last year while working a case in Cranston, the Spragues were one of the most important families in Rhode Island history, perhaps topped only by those of Roger Williams and Stephen Hopkins.

Like the sitting room the study was furnished with very comfortable looking couches and easy chairs. Most of them were dark brown leather that gave the room the air of being a place where men of means would smoke cigars and drink hundred-year old whiskey while making decisions about the future of Rhode Island. Sadly for them, the task of these old Yankee patrons in determining the state's future was much diminished now that Irish and Italian politicians and businessmen ran most things in Rhode Island. He wondered what the Royals and their ilk would think of an Irishman like Jack Kennedy becoming the next president of the United States.

Doherty's reverie about the state of Rhode Island's past and present was interrupted when Brayton Webster Royal entered the study. He was a man of substance, about Doherty's height but at least fifty pounds heavier. He kept his gray hair on the longish side slapped across his head from a part that was widened by his progressive balding. He fancied a mustache that made him look decidedly old school. B.W. was wearing an olive-green outdoorsman's shirt with breast pockets on either side and epaulets on the shoulders. His pants were stiff khaki and they met feet encased in what appeared to be work or hiking boots. He was garbed as if he'd just stepped out of an Abercrombie and Fitch catalog. Despite wearing his best suit Doherty felt distinctly underdressed for the occasion.

Royal stuck out his hand and said, "So nice to meet you, Mr. Doherty. My friend Martin DeCenza tells me you've become something of a legend in our part of the state." As they shook hands Doherty noted that B.W.'s welcoming remarks had contained two certifiable lies. DeCenza was hardly a friend of the Royal family and Doherty was anything but a legend. Nevertheless, the one-time textile baron had a strong handshake even if his paw was devoid of any workingman's calluses.

"I doubt legend would be the first word that comes to mind when people hear my name these days."

Changing the subject Royal said, "I understand your father Peter worked

29

in one our mills."

"Two to be exact. He worked in the Warwick until it closed down and then at the Royal until his health went bad. I believe you folks might've already sold the Royal by then." Doherty threw out this last remark to remind B.W. that his family went bankrupt in 1935 and had to sell the Royal property to the Seabrooke Company. By the time Peter Doherty's liver cancer had spread so that he had to quit working, the Royal Mill had already changed hands a couple of more times. It finally shut down all its operations over a decade ago. Now it was just a vacant hulk of a building whose windows the local teens used for target practice.

"Would you like something to drink, Mr. Doherty? I have an ancient bottle of Scotch here that I've been dying to find an excuse to open." Doherty wasn't normally a Scotch drinker but agreed to taste some stuff that might've been distilled when Rob Roy was running around the Scottish Highlands in a kilt.

Royal turned to a bookcase that held numerous volumes of hardbound classics that Doherty was sure no one had ever cracked open. He swiveled one of the shelves and a small bar miraculously appeared. Royal poured two tumblers from a bottle that appeared to be caked with 18th century dust. No ice or water was offered, as that would've offended the ancient spirits. The Scotch was indeed as smooth as silk and made Doherty reconsider his aversion to that liquor - if only he could afford a thousand-dollar bottle of it.

The two men sat down in easy chairs facing each other. "I take it you had a chance to get a good look at our estate on your way in. My Aunt Livinia was the last family member to live here before we moved in. She never married so there were no heirs on her side of the family. For a long time everyone called this place 'Livinia's farm'. She was famous for her flowers and shrubbery." Doherty wondered who this everyone was since most Rhode Islanders knew little or nothing about the Royals' private lives.

"My first wife Adelaide and I move in after Livy died, though by then our marriage was on its last legs. She never liked living on the farm, nor did our two sons, as much as they were ever here. By the time they were of school age she shipped them off to boarding school. One of them is at Harvard now and the other is doing something on Wall Street that I don't really understand.

He informs me that he makes a substantial amount of money from whatever it is. Charlene, of course, loves it here, which is not surprising given her rather humble background." Doherty figured Charlene was the Mrs. who came by the office to propose the venture to France.

"Her name wasn't always Charlene," Royal continued. "It was originally Cheryl but she didn't think Cheryl was an appropriate name for a Royal, so she had it legally changed to Charlene before we were married." Doherty had been right in his suspicions about Mrs. Royal's earlier life.

"What about your stepdaughter - does she like living here?"

An unpleasant look took hold on B.W.'s face. "At this point I don't think young Mary Margaret would like anything that has to do with me. She spends as much time as she can out at St. Mary's Academy at Bay View where she does her schooling. She plays field hockey and is on the swim team. I think she does both of those activities just so she can stay away from the farm as much as possible. At least three days a week I have to send Murray out at all hours to pick her up at school. She would like a car of her own but the school frowns upon student drivers. They send a motor coach around Warwick to pick up girls in the morning, but the drivers always complain about having to come up our drive, especially in the snow. Lord knows I give that school enough of our money. I'm not even Catholic and I'm still one of the largest donors to Bay View Academy. Charlene insisted that Mary Margaret continue her Catholic education so what could I do."

Doherty was already growing tired of hearing about the trials and tribulations of the idle rich.

Royal leaped from his chair and stepped behind his oversized desk. He opened a humidor that held a fistful of cigars. "Can I offer you one of Cuba's finest? I bought several boxes of Monte Christos in Havana last spring before the revolution."

"No thanks. I think I'll stick to one of my Camels instead." Doherty wasn't a big fan of cigars. His Uncle Patrick always smoked them, and he found their acrid smell distasteful.

Royal took out a cigar cutter and neatly snipped off the end of one before torching it with a stick match he ignited with his thumbnail. He took several long puffs before the cigar was burning to his satisfaction.

31

"Why don't we cut to the chase, Mr. Royal, and talk about this proposed trip your wife and daughter wish to send me on to France."

"Oh that," Royal said waving his hand in disgust while taking a swig of his ancient Scotch.

"Look, it's a pretty straightforward proposition. I pay you to go to France. You take a little holiday for yourself in Paris, then go out to Normandy, nose around a little, talk to a few people there, see what you can find out about John McDonald's time in the service during the war. Then you come home and tell my stepdaughter that her father died a hero in the famous D-Day invasion. And please, do your best to make his wartime experiences sound as glorious as possible. While you're explaining all this to her, I would appreciate it if you would emphasize my generosity in funding your expedition. At least that way maybe we can have some peace around here until she goes off to college - which, as far as I'm concerned, can't come soon enough."

Doherty sipped some of the smooth Scotch while contemplating if he wanted to take on this task or not. "It still sounds like a fool's errand to me."

"Of course it is. Thousands of men died on both sides in the Normandy campaign. Everyone knows that. Hell, half the graves in the cemeteries there contain little more than body fragments if that. I've been to Normandy myself on two separate occasions. I tried to explain this to Charlene and Mary Margaret, but the girls didn't want to hear what I had to say. Right now my wife is only interested in making peace between her daughter and me. What do you think? Do you want the job or not?"

"I've got to be honest with you, Mr. Royal, the only time I've ever been out of Rhode Island for any length of time was when I was in the army. I'm not sure I'd know where to begin with a case like this. I mean I don't even know how to get a passport or purchase an overseas airline ticket."

Royal chuckled at this last comment. "Of course, you don't. That's why I'm interested in hiring you. Look, I could've pulled some strings and maybe gotten an ex-CIA officer or someone high up in the military to dig into this for me. I could've sent someone like that to France, but maybe they'd find out something about this McDonald fellow neither my wife nor her daughter would want to hear. Like perhaps that Mary Margaret's father was not such a hero after all. I know you have a reputation for being successful at finding lost people, Mr. Doherty. But quite frankly, over there you'll be like a fish out of water. And that's what I'm banking on. As far as I'm concerned that makes you the perfect man for this job."

Chapter Six

Doherty caught the eleven-thirty train to Boston out of the big Union Station in Providence. He knew he could've driven or taken a Greyhound, but he preferred traveling by rail. On a train he could walk around, sit in the smoking section at the end of the car and have a cigarette, or go to the club car for a bite and a drink. He would've hated driving into Boston. Hell, he didn't even like driving into Providence if he could avoid it. When he called his Uncle Patrick for help, he felt like a beggar asking for a handout. But his uncle seemed genuinely glad to hear from him and invited him to come up to Boston for lunch. He even agreed to pick him up right at South Station. In his patented good humor Patrick said he didn't want his nephew to get lost in the "big, bad city."

Doherty had left things with B.W. Royal up in the air. He told the heir to the textile fortunes that he needed some time to think about his proposition. Royal acted disappointed, obviously used to having men jump at his offers when he dangled money in front of them. Doherty had never been anyone's patsy and he wasn't about to play that role for the Royal family even if it meant passing up a free trip to France along with some serious cash. All he knew about the French was that they made good fries, bread, and wine. He was concerned how he'd broach the possibility of this trip to Nina – though he'd gotten the feeling lately this might be a good time for them to take a little recess from one another. Before Doherty left the *gentleman's farm,* B.W. Royal gave him a week to make up his mind.

Much as he hated to admit it, his uncle was probably the only person he knew who could put him in touch with someone that could help him get a start on how to make this mission successful. Looking for missing people in Rhode Island, or parts of Massachusetts or Connecticut, was something Doherty could do in his sleep. In a foreign country it would be a different story. From what Royal had said this was clearly what Mary Margaret's stepfather was counting on. Yet Royal's smugness about Doherty's likely failure was making this offer a distinct challenge. Perhaps he could do this thing and turn up some information of value about the dead soldier. If he took this case he would work it as hard as he did for any other client. In the end Royal might not be happy about that, which would give Doherty some added satisfaction.

He parked his Chevy in a short-term parking lot by Providence's large railroad station. Next to the statehouse, Union Station was the second most impressive building in the center of Providence. In fact, while driving up to the station he could see the white dome of the statehouse with its Lady Liberty statue atop looming on the hillside just beyond it. Rhode Island's state capital building was designed to be a smaller replica of the U.S. capital in Washington.

The railroad station was a formidable looking edifice with a wide but not terribly tall clock tower at its center. It stretched a good city block covering most of the west side of the Mall in the center of Providence. A four-lane tunnel ran beneath the building with two outside lanes set aside for busses only. One could drive directly under the station and end up on the other side looking straight up at the statehouse.

Inside, the station's rotunda was covered by its own dome giving the space a vast open-air feel. He didn't know when the building was first constructed, though it was probably in the early days before widespread auto transportation when most people still traveled by rail rather than car. It was a symbol of a time when railroad stations were the vital center of every city and town where trains stopped.

On one side of the main hall there were curved one-piece dark wooden benches set in a line attached to the tiled floor. Along that same side against the wall were a series of small shops; one sold carry-out foods, another was a newsstand selling papers, magazines and cigarettes. Beside it was a small coffee bar with a few stools sitting out front. On the opposite side of the large hall was a line of ticket booths. Above them sat an electronic board covering nearly the entire wall listing the arrivals and departures of various New York, New Haven and Hartford trains along with their appropriate tracks. Beyond the ticket booths he saw the arched gateways that opened up to the four main tracks running in and out of the station.

Doherty had no problem locating the 11:30 train departing for Boston's South Station on the big board. It was an express with no stops until it reached Beantown. Anything heading south would be making multiple stops in Westerly, Bridgeport, New Haven, Hartford and other places in Connecticut before passing on to Grand Central Station in New York. From there several lines continued on to Philadelphia, Baltimore and Washington. He assumed anyone going further south would have to change trains in either New York or Washington. There were no trains going west out of Providence, not even to Worcester or Springfield. Anyone wishing to go on to say Cleveland, Chicago or Detroit probably had to take a westbound going out of Boston or New York. The first time Doherty had traveled by rail was during the war when his outfit was transported from here to Boston before being transferred onto a troopship in the Charlestown navy yard bound for England.

For four dollars he purchased a round-trip ticket to Boston on a train that would be leaving on track #3 in fifteen minutes. He used the wait time to buy a pack of smokes and the morning *Journal* at the newsstand. The fellow who waited on him was a blind colored man who didn't wear dark glasses like Willy Legere did. His glassed over eyes just stared off into space. Nevertheless, he took Doherty's dollar bill and made correct change without ever questioning what Doherty told him he was purchasing. It set him to wondering if some smartass travelers used the man's lack of sight as an opportunity to steal things from the stand like candy or smokes. While musing about this Doherty noticed two young sailors scurrying by toward Track #3 carrying duffel bags on their shoulders.

A Negro porter stood by the passenger cars looking bored since hardly anyone getting on the train here needed help with their luggage. The car Doherty mounted was half full when he climbed aboard. The two sailors were already sitting at the end in the smoking section puffing on cigarettes. Their duffels were stashed up on a shelf above some nearby seats. Doherty sparked up a Camel and took a seat across from them. He unfolded the newspaper and turned immediately to the sports pages.

Most of the stories had to do with basketball since the baseball players were still just going through their motions at spring training in Florida. The lead story was about the Providence College basketball team, which had reached the finals of the NIT tournament before losing in a squeaker to Bradley University of Illinois. PC's captain, Lenny Wilkens, was named the MVP of the tourney. This was the first time Doherty could remember the Friars performing so well in such a prestigious event.

On the second page of the sports section were stories about the pro league Boston Celtics battling it out in a playoff series with the Philadelphia Warriors. Most of the drama of that series apparently involved the titanic battle between the Warriors' giant seven-foot center, Wilt Chamberlain, and the Celtics big man, Bill Russell. Doherty had little interest in basketball because so few of the games were on television. Unlike baseball, he found it difficult to listen to basketball on the radio because the announcing was too rapid-fire given that the basketball changed hands so often. The Celtics announcer, Johnny Most, had the kind of gravelly voice that Doherty found grating over the span of a forty-eight-minute game. As a result, it was hard to leisurely follow the game's progress because it required more attention than he was willing to give it. Conversely, he found the casual rhythms of the baseball announcers more palatable to his ears.

Over the years he'd gone to a couple of professional basketball games with Benny O'Neil when the Celtics came to the Rhode Island Arena to play each year. They were always doubleheaders with some teams like the Minneapolis Lakers playing the Ft. Wayne Pistons in the first game and the Celtics taking on the Warriors or the New York Knicks in the second one. He mostly liked watching that Bob Cousy fellow perform magic tricks with a basketball. No one he'd ever seen handled a basketball or passed it like that little maestro did. He was also impressed with how the big Negro Russell would often appear at the last second to swat an opponent's seemingly wide open shot out of the air. The newspapers and sport magazines loved writing about the Chamberlain-Russell hard court battles. "Wilt the Stilt," as the papers called him, was the first seven-foot player to come into the pro league. Although Russell was somewhat shorter, he always gave the bigger man a challenging contest. When Doherty was finished with the sports section one of the sailors asked if he could have a look at it.

"Where are you fellows headed?" he inquired as he handed over the back section of the *Journal*.

"We're going to Portland," the one who'd asked for the paper said. "I got family up there."

"Are you stationed at Quonset?"

"How could you tell?"

Doherty smiled. "Why else would you be taking a train out of Providence? You might've come up here from New Haven, but I saw you two get on the train back there," he said gesturing at the station with his thumb. "I used to work at Quonset, in the aircraft engine division."

"How'd you get that job?" the other sailor asked. He had a noticeable southern accent. Doherty figured he was the Maine sailor's pal being taken home to meet the other guy's family. It reminded him of Nina's tale about her previous boyfriend, who she was supposed to marry until his navy buddy showed up for a visit. Once the friend was around them, Nina sensed that the two men were queer for each other. Doherty quickly pushed that story out of his head.

"I worked there before I got drafted. I didn't think they were going to call me up because of the kind of job I had. Later on, they needed more men in the ranks so you could say by then I was prime beef."

"What were you in?"

"The army."

"A doughboy, huh. Did you see any action?" the southern kid asked.

"More than I wanted to. I was dropped into Sicily. My outfit was in Italy and then part of the last push into Germany. I did and saw a lot of things I wish I hadn't."

"Bad, huh?"

"Yeah. I hope you boys never have to go through something like that."

"Hell, I wouldn't mind a little bit of action. All this sailin' around shit for no reason is gettin' on my nerves," the southern boy said.

Doherty leaned forward giving him a stern look. "Let me tell you something, son. I got a pal back in West Warwick where I live. He was in the navy during the big war. His destroyer went down in the Pacific in a kamikaze attack. Most of his shipmates who weren't killed when the ship exploded were eaten by sharks. My friend was lucky, he only lost his eyesight – blinded for life. If I were you, I'd be careful what you wish for. There's a lot of killing in wartime. I hope getting seasick is the worst thing that ever happens to you two."

The kid from Maine looked shaken. All his friend from down south had to say was, "Shiiiit." That seemed to be the extend of the kid's vocabulary.

.

Chapter Seven

After finishing his cigarette Doherty went back to a more comfortable seat to read the rest of the paper. He must have dozed off because the next thing he knew the conductor was walking down the aisle calling out, "Boston. Next stop Boston's South Station." When they pulled in under the station's outdoor canopy, he could see at least a dozen tracks heading in and out of the Boston depot. The building itself wasn't all that much bigger than the station in Providence, but the open space inside seemed a whole lot larger. The big board listing arrivals and departures of the New York, New Haven and Hartford line had twice the number of trains than the board in Providence. In addition, there were numerous listings for commuter trains going all over Massachusetts and into southern New Hampshire and Maine. Uncle Patrick was right, Doherty was now in the big city.

He exited the station and looked back at the building that bent around two street corners in a crescent shape. The façade had a number of pillars lining its second story. Pedestrians were hurrying along the big avenue that abutted South Station. It was lunchtime and everyone appeared to be on their way to or from their mid-day meal. For a moment Doherty was overwhelmed by the number of cars and people just within the few blocks he could see. He'd been in downtown Providence at lunch hour but had never seen this much activity there. It made him feel like a rube from the country.

40

A black Cadillac was parked in a No Parking zone by the curb. A large man in an ill-fitting suit and a gray fedora was standing beside it. As Doherty approached the big fellow stepped away from the car and said, "Are you Mr. McSweeny's nephew?"

When Doherty answered in the affirmative the big guy took his arm and led him to the Caddy. "My name's Murphy," he said. "I work for the organization." Doherty wasn't sure if he meant the campaign or some other organization his uncle was connected to. When Murphy opened the rear door Doherty peered in to see his uncle sitting in the backseat with his sheleighly lying across his folded-up knees.

When he slid in next to him, Patrick gave him a big smile and clasped his hand in a two-handed shake. Despite his age and various infirmities, Patrick McSweeny's hand still had a viselike grip. The result no doubt of all the glad-handing that was part of his stock-in-trade.

"So good to see you, sonny boy. Any problems getting on or off the train?" he asked with a twinkle in his eye.

"No, everything was fine. Met a couple of sailors from Quonset going up to Portland. One of them told me he wished he could get into some wartime action."

"Oh, the follies of youth," Patrick said with the little Irish lilt he put into his speech every now and then. "What do I owe the pleasure of this unexpected visit after so long an absence. As I recall we had not parted on very good terms when last we spoke."

"I believe it was that O'Shaughnessy business that caused the rift between us." As soon as these words were out of Doherty's mouth Patrick put his fingers to his lips and then motioned toward Murphy, the driver.

"Dennis, could you please drop my nephew and me off by the market and pick us up at say," here McSweeny looked at his watch. "Around two-thirty."

"Okay boss."

"Where are we going?' Doherty asked.

Patrick patted him on the knee. "My boy, I'm going to take you to one of Boston's most famous restaurants, where the drinks are strong, the food is delicious, and the waitresses are the surliest cusses you'll ever meet. You're in for one helluva dining experience. We're going to the world famous Durgin-

Park."

"It's a park?"

McSweeny laughed. "Don't worry, my boy. It's a fully enclosed restaurant. The place is called Durgin-Park because the two original owners were fellas named John Durgin and Eldridge Park. That was way back in the 1820s. Needless to say those men are long gone, but the place hasn't changed much since then – except for the prices, of course. Mind you, my boy, this isn't one of those snooty restaurants where the Boston Brahmins take their lunch. This is the kind of place the real people of Boston eat – except now it tends to attract many tourists. Fellow named Jimmy Hallett has owned it since the war. At some point he decided to make it a destination for visitors to our fair city on their way to the Old North Church and Paul Revere's House."

Murphy parked the Cadillac on the edge of what looked and soon smelled like the market district. Men were pushing wheelbarrows along the sidewalks carrying sides of beef while others hauled large sacks of potatoes and other vegetables with handcarts. It hardly seemed like the kind of area where one of Boston's finest restaurants would be located. Patrick had a little trouble getting out of the car, so Doherty helped his uncle and then handed him his cane, which he leaned on for a few moments while trying to catch his breath.

"It's just down here," Patrick said, taking Doherty's arm as they dodged between workmen hauling various foodstuffs here and there.

"What is this area called?"

"This, my boy, is Quincy Market. It's been the center of trade in this city since Paul Revere and the Adams boys were running around in knickers. Food is shipped in and out of here at all hours of the day. It comes in from farms all over New England and goes out to markets and restaurants everywhere. And that building over there," he said as they passed by a large classical style structure adjacent to the market, "is Faneuil Hall. That's where our revolution was organized. Without the rabble rousing of the Sons of Liberty in that building, Queen Elizabeth rather than George Washington would be on our one-dollar bills."

They ducked into a building that didn't differ much on the outside from the food markets either side of it. There was a line of people stretching down the long front hall. Patrick pushed his way through them to the front without offering any apologies. A man in a suit was standing behind a small rostrum at the end of the hall facing the line. Noisy kitchen sounds and smells came from the area just behind him. When he saw Patrick, his face lit up.

"Why, Mr. McSweeny. How very nice to see you. "

Patrick gripped the maître d' in his familiar two-handed shake and introduced him to Doherty as Robert. "This is my nephew, Hugh Doherty. My late sister's boy. He's come all the way up here from Rhode Island to indulge in your tasty victuals."

"Then follow me this way, Mr. McSweeny. I have just the table for you." Robert led them into a large, loud dining space that had picnic style tables running down the center covered in red and white checked tablecloths. Tables set for four lined each wall. On the way to their table Patrick glad-handed a few acquaintances.

Once seated at a table for four, his uncle leaned in and said, "I must warn you, Robert's kind words are the last ones you'll be hearing from the staff in this particular establishment." Doherty didn't know what his uncle meant by this comment; he soon found out.

A heavyset waitress with her head encased in a hairnet came over to the table to drop off two menus.

"Well if it isn't Patrick McSweeny hisself," she said in a voice heavily laden with an Irish brogue. "Who's this young fella with you here," she said referring to Doherty, "one of your flunkies?"

"Why Tessie, you old broad. This fellow is my nephew Huge Doherty, my late sister's boy, God rest her soul. He's come all the way up here from Rhode Island just to meet the likes of you."

"Isn't that the state that calls itself an island when it don't really have one?"

"Well, technically it does," Doherty said, "but that's a long story."

The waitress snorted. "All well and good, honey. You can save your story for your fat uncle here. I don't have time to listen to any stories, long or short. Would you boys like somethin' to drink to get your day started?"

"I'll take a whiskey on the rocks with a splash of water. And make it the good stuff, not the cheap slosh Hallett puts in the good bottles. The young fella here will have …"

"A Jameson, straight up."

"Comin' right at ya. And Patrick don't you get too snookered today. Last time you drank two whiskeys you took the liberty of grabbin' me arse."

"And a fine bountiful arse it is," Patrick said with his characteristic lilt as he gave Tessie' ample behind an affectionate tap.

After she was gone Doherty said, "Well I guess you were right about the waitresses not being your run-of-the-mill, yes sir, no sir types."

Doherty uncle patted his arm. "My boy, you ain't seen nothing yet. Wait 'til Tessie and I really get going."

Just then the maître d' Robert ushered a couple over to share the four-seater with them. He asked Patrick if everything was okay for him and his nephew.

"Not really. I think Tessie's in too good a mood today. She's been nothing but civil to us."

Robert smiled knowing that Doherty's uncle was putting him on. "I'll see what I can do to crank up the old battle-axe."

The couple next to them exchanged greetings. They then craned their necks around taking in the full ambience of Durgin-Park. The two were some-where in their late forties or early fifties. They were obviously tourists as he had a camera slung over his shoulder and she was holding a wad of brochures to various must-see spots in historic Boston.

"Where do you folks hail from?" Patrick asked putting on his lilt for their benefit.

The woman smiled at the two men and said, "We're from Peoria. That's in Illinois," she added.

"Yes I know where Peoria is," Patrick replied. Given his role in the Ken-nedy campaign Doherty figured his uncle already knew who the biggest Dem-ocratic donor was in that city. "First time in Boston?"

"Yes," the man said. "It certainly is a bustling place compared to our hometown. More like Chicago than anywhere else we've ever been."

Tessie arrived with their drinks, which she dropped in front of them mak-ing sure to spill a few splashes on the tablecloth. "Who are your pals, Patrick? They look like a couple of hicks from the country."

"Why, Tessie, these fine folks are from Illinois."

"Illinois, huh. Isn't that somewhere near Chicago?"

"Actually Chicago is in the state of Illinois. We live in Peoria which is a little more downstate," the woman said politely.

"Is that right. Where do you get your hair done, dearie? At Ruthie's bird-cage emporium?" It was only then that Doherty noticed that the Illinois woman's hair did sort of resemble a bird's nest.

"Well I never!" the woman said.

In order to smooth things over Patrick explained, "You'll have to excuse Tessie. She's just a cantankerous old broad." The waitress stood with her hands on her hips staring at her four customers. Finally, she said to Doherty and his uncle, "Are you two gonna eat or just drink yourselves silly today. This here is a restaurant in case you hadn't noticed."

"I will have a cup of your delicious clam chowder followed by the Yankee pot roast," Patrick said. "My young companion here will have the prime rib. How do you like your meat, my boy?"

"Well thanks for asking. I'll take it medium rare and I'd also like a house salad to start off - with blue cheese dressing if you have it."

After Tessie left the woman from Peoria asked if the waitress was always this rude.

"You should've read your guidebooks more carefully. The surly wait-resses are one of the attractions at Durgin-Park. Don't take it personally. I come here at least once a week and they still treat me like a stray dog who's wandered in off the street. Tessie is probably the worst of the lot, but the other gals aren't much better. It's what they serve here along with the best pot roast, prime rib, and Indian pudding you'll find anywhere in the city."

"So is that what you'd recommend?" the husband asked.

"Yes. And the clam chowder. You won't taste better chowder than what they have here."

"What do customers do if they don't like being insulted by the wait-resses?" the woman asked.

Patrick laughed at this question. "Why they go down the street to the Un-ion Oyster House. It and Durgin-Park are the oldest restaurants in the city – except maybe for Jacob Wirth, where the Yankee dandies prefer to dine."

The couple went back to planning their tour around Boston, which gave

Doherty a chance to ask his uncle how the campaign was shaping up.

"Well we took New Hampshire, though that wasn't surprising since young Jack being from Massachusetts made him almost a favorite son. The real test will be on the 5th when he squares off against Humphrey in Wisconsin. Hubert's from the neighboring state of Minnesota so he has a considerable amount of good will with Wisconsin voters. That's why Jack's old man is pouring a lot of dough into that contest."

"Then what?"

"After that it'll be clear sailing until the middle of May. We have Illinois, Pennsylvania, Indiana, and, of course, Massachusetts all wrapped up. We're letting Ohio Governor Mike DeSalle take his own state's delegation to the convention as their favorite son. Our thinking is that he's doing this so he can either be considered a VP possibility or, at worst, a horse trader at the convention. The next real test won't be until the tenth of May in West Virginia. That state is full of Bible belt hillbillies and coal miners. It's the one place our boy's Catholicism could prove to be a problem. If we beat Humphrey there or at least make it close, it'll be all over for Hubert. His money'll dry up making it sayonara time for him."

"Will a good showing there lock up the nomination for Kennedy?"

Patrick drained his whiskey and washed it down with a gulp from his water glass. "We wish. There are still a few wild cards we'll have to contend with."

"Like who?""

"A couple of governors like DeSalle want to take their delegations to Los Angeles committed only to them. They hope that'll give them some bargaining power in case the voting goes beyond the first ballot. Then there are always the dark horse candidates who are not running in the primaries. One is Adlai, though I can't see our party nominating a two-time loser for a third time. That would be like handing the presidency to that unscrupulous bastard Nixon."

"Are there any others you're worried about?"

"Well there's always Stuart Symington, who looks like a president out of central casting. At least until he opens his mouth. The other is the senate majority leader Lyndon Johnson. He's a wily sonofabitch that one. From what our sources down in D.C. tell us he has the book on everybody."

"Including Jack and his Hollywood girlfriends?"

Lowering his voice Patrick said, "Let me tell you something, sonny, it may be worse than Hollywood. I have it on good information that our boy has bedded down with some gal tied to the Giancana crime family in Chicago." Patrick made this last remark quietly, not wanting to pique the interest of the couple from Peoria. "He also had a dalliance with some bimbo connected to the Russians. The good news is that old Lyndon isn't too circumspect about keeping his own pecker in his pants. What we're really afraid of is that in desperation the tall Texan could resort to playing the Catholic card. There aren't enough of us papists down south to hold the line. No Democrat wins the presidency without taking a fair number of states south of the Mason-Dixon. We saw what happened when Ike carried a large percentage of voters down there."

When the first courses arrived, Patrick dumped some oyster crackers into his bowl of thick milky chowder. The soup even had a pad of butter floating on top. Doherty could see that the chowder was much thicker than the way clam chowder was served in Rhode Island. Doherty's salad was quite fresh with a generous helping of thick blue cheese dressing on top. The Peoria couple eyed their food while generally keeping to themselves. When Tessie took their order, the wife opted for chicken; the husband took their advice and chose the prime rib. The waitress made it very clear that she thought the woman with the bird's nest hair had made a poor lunch choice. Perhaps their travel budget couldn't bear much more.

The main courses soon arrived, and Doherty was confronted with the largest piece of meat he'd ever seen on a regular sized dinner plate. It hung off the edges and was cooked to perfection. It was so big that his side dishes of green beans and a baked potato were served on their own separate small plates. Patrick's pot roast was nearly as large. It was soaking in aromatic gravy. His sides of corn and mashed potatoes likewise came in separate bowls. Doherty ordered a bottle of Gansett to go with his meat while his uncle asked for another whiskey. Tessie's last remark to him was, "That lard'll put a few extra pounds on your expanding waistline, Patrick. I hope you don't bust out of your fancy trousers."

The two of them dove into their meals, suspending conversation while they ate. Patrick interrupted only to ask if he was right to order the prime rib for him. Doherty had too much meat in his mouth to offer anything but a nodded ascent. The waitress reappeared with the neighboring couple's food and all of their drinks. In time the second whiskey turned Patrick McSweeny's face as red as a stoplight.

Eventually he put down his knife and fork and looked at his nephew in a serious manner. "Okay, my boy, it's about time you told me why you came all the way up here to Boston after so many months of me not hearing from you. All this talk about politics wouldn't be the least bit interesting to you unless you're carrying water for Martin DeCenza. Please tell me that's not why you're sitting here with your uncle eating the biggest piece of beef you've ever had."

Doherty had to laugh. He hadn't thought that his uncle's old feud with Judge DeCenza still weighed on him as much as it did. "No, DeCenza is not why I'm here. I have as little use for the Judge as you. In fact, it will bring you great pleasure to learn that your old nemesis is backing Humphrey because he doesn't think a Catholic can get elected president. I'll admit one of the reasons I'm here is because DeCenza recommended that I consult with you about a case I'm thinking of taking on."

Patrick looked confused but motioned with his fork for his nephew to continue.

"I've been contacted by none other than B.W. Royal to undertake a missing persons case of sorts. It's actually his wife and stepdaughter who initially expressed interest in contracting my services, though it's Royal's money that'll be paying the bill."

Patrick gave him a sullen look. "For years the Royal family were nothing but a bunch of blood sucking bastards who made their money off the sweat of men like your father and hundreds of others working in their mills." The Peoria woman gave them a nasty look, clearly offended by Patrick's profanity. He bowed his head toward her as a form of apology.

Doherty spent the next fifteen minutes laying out the plan that Mrs. Royal and her daughter had presented to him. Then before Patrick could offer his criticism, he explained how Royal assured him that it would probably end up being a futile mission balanced out by a free trip to France.

Patrick gave him his best avuncular smile. "But you, my boy, are having other thoughts, right? You think you can go over to France and discover something the family has never heard before about this dead boy. Perhaps you'll find out he was a hero, or coward, in battle – or that he sold military secrets to the Germans."

Doherty laughed at this last comment. "I doubt I'll uncover anything as dramatic as that. Maybe all I'll discover is that this McDonald boy was an unlucky GI, who, like so many others over there, met his maker on the sands of some Normandy beachhead, or was shot by a German soldier a few days later in a place the boy couldn't even pronounce."

"What then, pray tell, do you need from me? I'm thinking you didn't take a train up here just to have a free lunch at this fine establishment?"

"Well one thing Royal said that was true is that I would be out of my league in France without some significant help. That's where you come in. As I recall you worked in the war department during the war. That makes you the only person I know who may have some contacts in France that could help me with this case. So, my question is, do you?"

His uncle spent some time cutting some pieces from his pot roast while mulling over this request. "Here's the deal: As you know we and our British allies caused quite a lot of damage in France and other countries trying to drive those Nazis bastards out of them. We may have been heroes in our eyes, but we left a hell of a mess in our wake. That, my boy, is what General Marshall's plan was partially about, and as far as I can tell, still is. We are trying to do our best to repair the damage we caused during the fighting. Not only have we lent our European allies a ton of money over the past decade and a half, but we've also sent a lot of personnel over there to help with the clean-up and rebuilding. Many of our engineers, military personnel, and diplomatic people are still working on one project or another. It takes but a few months to destroy things and many years to put them back together. That's why the Marshall Plan has cost our government so much money. On the other hand, as these countries have recovered, they've used that money to buy an enormous number of goods from us, especially building materials. In that way it's as if we lent the money to ourselves.

"What I can do is give you a contact with someone I know at the embassy in Paris. Through him you might be able to connect with other Americans working elsewhere in France. From what I heard some of these Americans fell in love with French mademoiselles while over there and have chosen to remain there. That's the best I can do – but it should give you a start."

"Does that mean you think I should take on this job?"

"Of course not. It sounds like Royal wants to send you on this worthless pursuit just so he can make up with his stepdaughter and get back into good graces with his wife. That said, anything you can do to take money out of the Royal family's pockets and put it into one of ours would certainly make it worthwhile. Maybe you'll even meet some cute mademoiselle over there yourself. You know what they say about French women."

Chapter Eight

He was early for the three o'clock train back to Providence when Patrick's driver dropped him at the curb by South Station. He thanked the big fellow but didn't bother waking his uncle who had fallen asleep a block away from the Quincy Market. He figured he'd call him sometime during the week to see what contacts he had in Paris that could be of use. Otherwise he left the old guy sawing logs in the back seat of the Cadillac. A three-whiskey lunch will do that even to the best of drinkers, and his uncle had always held his own with most tipplers.

About halfway back to Providence he fell asleep himself under the weight of the roast beef dinner, a whiskey, and a beer. When he got back to West Warwick he stopped off at the office. If Agnes had been in that day she'd already cleared out. The place was locked up tighter than a drum. He briefly scanned the mail and flipped on the answering machine that told him there were no new messages. Doherty flirted with the idea of stopping by the Centreville Bank to run the French trip idea by Nina; then realized the bank would be closed by now. He'd forgotten about *bankers' hours*. Without giving it much thought he called the number Royal had given him. Though her boss was out of the office, he told his secretary to pass onto B.W. that he was willing to take on the job in France.

51

The next morning he walked into town from the apartment without stopping by the office. He ducked in at the Arctic News and took his breakfast there for a change. He thought two eggs over easy with an English muffin would start his day off in fine fiddle. He liked the way Andy the grill man cut the muffins, slathered them with butter, and then tossed them face down on the grill. He would then put a heat weight on top of them to make sure they got cooked all the way through. After his second cup of joe, Doherty paid the tab and ambled down to the bank.

As usual Nina was parked at her desk behind the half barrier that separated the offices from the main floor. Behind her were the private offices of the bank managers including the president. On the other side of the hall were the teller windows where people made withdrawals, deposits, or paid off their mortgage bills. As he expected there wasn't a lot of foot traffic in the large building this early in the day.

When he approached her desk Nina was leaning forward in her chair closely perusing some documents. She looked decidedly professional with her reading glasses perched on the end of her nose. Her attention was so focused on the material that she was startled when he drew close to the barrier rail.

"Well, this is a pleasant surprise," she said. "What are you doing in the bank at this hour of the day?"

"Jeez, I hate to disturb you. Looks like you're reading some really important stuff there."

"Don't I wish. They're some new regs about deposit plans the bank is thinking of introducing. The main thing seems to be that we're thinking of paying more interest on accounts if people leave larger sums of money on deposit. Don't worry, this wouldn't apply to a pauper like you," she concluded with a giggle.

"I bet reading those regulations is not nearly as interesting as one of your women's magazines."

Nina gave him one of her better smiles. "No, they're not. In fact I had to read this memo three times before I got the gist of what they're proposing. I don't suppose you're here to check on your safe deposit box."

This last remark was a reference to a practice they had developed even before he and Nina started dating. He was working a case last year that required him to stash some evidence in a secure place so he rented a safe deposit box at the bank. The evidence had another purpose as well. For as long as it was in Doherty's possession it insured, he hoped, that no danger would come to him. And if it did, then the evidence put into the right hands would bring down some very powerful people. However, in order to activate this plan he needed someone else to be a co-signer on the safe deposit box. He considered Agnes, but she'd just had a baby and he thought it unwise to put her in any danger. Under most circumstances Gus Timilty would have been a logical choice, but he was out of the question because he too was implicated in the case and therefore at risk as much as Doherty. On a whim he asked Nina if she would agree to be a co-signer. He assured her she would be in no danger, which wasn't entirely true. After some hesitation she went along with the plan on the proviso that he treat her to dinner in return. By tying Nina into this scheme he had someone who could put the evidence into the hands of the proper authorities if anything were to happen to him. At the time, as far as he could tell, Nina wasn't on the radar of the people who were desperate to get their hands on this evidence.

To placate her Doherty agreed to take her to dinner. And that was how their relationship began. Every time he came to the bank after that he asked her if he could visit his safe deposit box. Once they were in the little room off the vault where the boxes were kept, they engaged in a little canoodling. However, now that most everyone who worked at the bank, including her supervisors, knew they were dating, they had to suspend their little trysts.

"How would you like to have dinner on Friday night. We could go to the Maryland Chicken Restaurant. I need to talk to you about something important."

"You're not going to break up with me over a pile of chicken bones, are you?"

"No. Nothing like that. Should I pick you up at six at your place?"

"Why don't you pick me up here when the bank closes at four? You know how my parents feel about you coming to the house."

He indeed did know that Nina's parents thought he was too old for her, being twelve years her senior. They also told her they didn't think he was the marrying kind. That was also true. In fact, he was thankful the marriage conversation had never come up between them. They did pretend to be husband and wife one weekend when they were down at Narragansett staying at a swell place called the Greene Inn. Technically, he was there on a case, though they still found time to eat some good food and engage in other pleasurable activities.

"Besides, if you pick me up at four, that'll give us a couple of hours to kill," she added with a sly smile. He knew exactly how he hoped they would kill those hours.

Chapter Nine

In the morning, before Agnes showed her face Doherty got a call from Royal's man Murray. He said he would drop by Doherty and Associates around three the next afternoon to go over the details of the trip. Fifteen minutes after he got off the phone Agnes strolled in for the day. It was unusual for her to arrive later than he unless she had a problem with her baby or a calamity with some member of her large sprawling family. With little or no business of late at the agency, she didn't bother to offer an excuse for her tardiness. Instead she just took her place behind her desk and began working on her nails with an emery board.

He heard her fussing around but didn't bother to appear in the outer office until he had what he was about to tell her well-rehearsed.

"I've decided to take that job in France," he said while stepping into the front beside her desk.

Agnes gazed up from her nails, gave him a disapproving look, though wisely did not say anything.

"Let's face facts, Agnes, we haven't had any new clients since that Grimaldi case left egg all over my face. I know this trip to France might end up being a waste of time, but at least the payoff sounds promising. Even if I don't find out anything of value for Mrs. Royal and her daughter, I'll do a thorough enough job that maybe her husband will find use for my services in the future.

All things considered this might be a good time for me to get out of town for a while."

Agnes looked despondent. "What about me, boss? What am I supposed to do while you're off gallivantin' around France lookin' for some dead soldier?"

"I don't know. It'll give you more time to spend with Justin. What's wrong with that?"

She shook her head. "I don't know. I suppose you're right. I mean what kind of a mother doesn't want to spend more time with her kid. It's just that…" She didn't finish the sentence.

"It's boring, right? You can admit it to me. Hell, Agnes, look at it this way, it's not like there's been a lot for you to do around here lately. There aren't exactly hordes of clients knocking on our door looking for my services. Plus, if I take this case, I'm sure they'll be some bonus money for you if the deal pans out. When I met with Royal it sounded like he'd be willing to pay almost anything to get on the good side of his stepdaughter."

"I know, I know. Right now, it makes perfect sense for our operation. And like you said maybe it'll lead to future work for Royal or some of his rich pals. I guess what I'll really miss is comin' in and havin' us talk like we do about your cases. This job adds somethin' more to my life than bein' a mother and a housewife. Maybe things would be different if Louie wasn't on cruises so much of the year. Even when he's home, he gets stir crazy after a day or two on land. Sometimes I feel like I'm married to an amphibian."

"Don't worry, we'll get through this. I'd like you to be here when Royal's man comes by at three tomorrow afternoon to go over the details of my trip. You know me, I'd probably forget half of what he tells me if you weren't here." Agnes knew this last comment was only intended to make her feel useful. It still drew a smile.

"Yeah, and who else is gonna be able to tell you how to pack for a trip that could take up to a week or two."

Royal's man Murray showed up at three o'clock sharp the next day. He was dressed neatly in a sport jacket, slacks, and an open collared shirt. No farm clothes today. Doherty ushered him and Agnes into the inner office where they both took chairs on the other side of his desk. Murray had come armed with a large briefcase that he began hauling items from. Agnes sat dutifully with a steno pad on her lap and a pencil poised.

"Okay, Mr. Doherty, the first thing you have to do is get a passport. I took the liberty of assuming you didn't have one already." Agnes shot her boss a smirk at this last remark. "I stopped by the post office and picked up a form for you to fill out. You'll have to mail it to Washington along with three passport photos. Mr. Royal has provided an address of someone in the state department that will expedite this process as quickly as possible. Otherwise it could take up to 3-4 weeks before you'd get an authorized passport on your own."

"Hold on for a minute. How do I go about getting these photos you just mentioned?"

"Mr. Royal has taken care of that too. Do you know the optometrist Maurice Lague here in town?"

"I don't know him personally. I've seen the signs for his office down on Main across from the old police station."

"Well Dr. Lague doubles as a photographer. He does a lot of weddings as well as family portraits. It's kind of a side business he has along with examining eyes and fitting people with glasses. Mr. Royal has already contacted the doctor. All you have to do is find a time to go into his office and have your picture taken. Lague promised he could have them developed by the next day. When that's done you just put them along with your application in this mailing envelope." Murray presented Doherty with a large manila envelope. "It's already addressed but we suggest you take it to Paul Kent at the post office. Do you know Mr. Kent?"

"Yeah, I know Paul."

"Good. Then just give him this envelope and ask him to send it out special delivery. I'm afraid you'll have to pay the passport fee and the postage yourself."

Doherty turned to Agnes and said, "Are you getting all this?"

"Got it, boss," she said as she scribbled away on her steno pad.

"Now the next thing I'm about to give you are your airline tickets. There are four them in all - one from Hillsgrove to Idlewild airport in New York and another from there back to Rhode Island. As of now they are not dated. Once you've determined the date you're ready to depart, call Mr. Royal's number and we will arrange for your reservations. The other two are for the transatlantic flights from Idlewild to Orly Airport in Paris and back to New York. We will likewise arrange those departures commensurate with your flight from here to New York. When you're ready to return from France you can either call us or the Pan American Airline office in Paris directly to arrange the flight back to New York. You will have no problem getting a flight from Idlewild to Hillsgrove since there are a few each day and none of them are ever full. Am I going too fast for you?"

"No, I'm sure my secretary is writing down everything in case I don't remember something." Murray gave Agnes a weak smile.

"Good. Now as far as your retainer is concerned, Mr. Royal has asked me to give you these packets of traveler's checks. They are all in denominations of twenty dollars. We are providing you with one thousand dollars in these checks. You must sign them at the top before you leave. When you desire to cash any of them all you have to do is date them and sign at the bottom when you present them at a bank or an American Express office in France. You will have to show your passport each time you cash one of these. I suggest you ask to have them cashed into French francs since dollars won't do you any good to you over there and the dollar exchange in foreign countries will not be to your advantage. They also take quite a bit out in commission fees when you cash them. Carrying travelers checks instead of dollars ensures that you will be reimbursed in case you lose them or they are stolen. I believe the current exchange rate is somewhere between 4-5 francs per dollar, though that can change at any time day or night. Mr. Royal has directed me to tell you that if you have any checks remaining when your trip is completed you may keep the balance as part of your retainer."

Doherty shot a glance at Agnes who now had a big smile plastered across her face.

"Can we continue?" Doherty nodded.

"We have booked you into a hotel in Paris for three nights. It is a modest hotel on the Left Bank called the Hotel Wetter. The address is attached to your confirmation form. Once you've decided on the exact date of your departure, we will ensure that a room is available there for you. Most transatlantic flights

58

leave at night so you will arrive in Paris the morning of the next day – keep that in mind when we finalize details. Have you ever flown across the Atlantic before, Mr. Doherty?"

"No never. The only time I went to Europe was when I was in the army and that was on a troop ship."

"Well, then I must warn you that you may suffer from a bit of what's called 'travel fatigue'. You will be crossing five time zones so your body's clock may be thrown off somewhat. Everyone responds differently to these time changes. My advice is that after you arrive in Paris you try to acclimate yourself to European time as quickly as possible, otherwise you may feel mentally strained and unable to perform the mission for which you are being paid." Doherty didn't appreciate the demanding nature of this last comment.

"Once you decide to leave Paris to meander through Normandy you may wish to rent a car or take a train and then hire a driver at your destination point. We've decided to leave that up to you since we do not have any idea where you might be headed. And I dare say, neither do you at this point. One final thing. Mr. Royal wanted me to give you this tour book," Murray said as he pulled a thick soft-covered book out of his case.

Doherty turned it over to look at the cover. It was titled *Europe on Five Dollars a Day*, written by someone named Arthur Frommer.

Murray explained, "Apparently this Frommer fellow was a GI stationed in Germany in the middle of the last decade. After being discharged he decided to take a personal tour of the continent before coming home. In his travels he encountered a lot of other soldiers doing the same thing. So, he published a guidebook called the *GI's Guide to Traveling in Europe*.

"Apparently the book was so successful that when he got home he decided to publish one for civilian travelers on the continent. He went back to Europe a few more times over the next two years gathering information on inexpensive places to stay and to eat. In the book he also suggests sights worth seeing while in Europe. I understand many American tourists, particularly young ones, now use this book when they travel on the continent. Mr. Royal highly recommends it for someone who will be traveling on a limited budget like yourself."

It didn't take a financial genius for Doherty to figure out he could travel in Europe on five dollars a day for two hundred days with the thousand Murray had just handed him. That, of course, did not take into account a train tickets, a rental car fee, his meals, or the number of people he might have to grease along the way to get information about John McDonald.

After Murray left Agnes looked at him with a silly grin. "Well, he was some piece of work, wasn't he?" Doherty joined her in a good laugh.

"And you know what's the funniest part of all this?"

"No, what?"

"I still don't know if Murray is that fella's first or last name. Did you get down everything he was telling us?"

"I sure hope so, boss. There's no way you would've remembered all the things he said. What's next?"

Doherty was considering the course of action he'd be taking to get the trip to France off the ground. "Well, the first thing I've got to do is contact my Uncle Patrick."

"Patrick? I thought you and him were on the outs?"

"We were – or at least I was. But after making some inquiries it turns out my uncle may be the only person I know who can put me in touch with some people in France that might be able to help me once I get over there. Otherwise I'd be flying blind – excuse the pun. The other day when you weren't here I took the train up to Boston and had lunch with the old fella."

"What was that like?"

Doherty was still trying to figure out that day's interactions for himself. "Well he took me to this famous restaurant where I ate the largest piece of prime rib I'd ever had in my life. Meanwhile my uncle had three whiskeys and then passed out on the car ride back to the railroad station to drop me off. But it wasn't a wasted trip. He said he could help me out with this France thing. And I guess you could say we kind of made up."

Agnes smiled, obviously pleased that Doherty had reconnected with one of his only living relatives. "That's good. I always liked seein' the old rascal whenever he dropped by here. Is he still workin' on the Kennedy campaign?"

"Oh yeah. He's become an even more important operative since last time I saw him. Or so he says anyway. That reminds me I should call the old boy before he passes out for the day."

Doherty retreated into his office and dialed up the number for Patrick's law office. A woman answered the phone and told him that his uncle was out of town and wouldn't be back until early next week. He asked if Patrick had left any messages for him. She put him on hold while she went to check. A few minutes later she returned to the phone.

"It isn't much. Just the name of a Michael Shanahan. According to Mr. McSweeny this Shanahan person can be reached at the American Embassy in Paris. He wrote that he would contact Shanahan himself before you left. There was no phone number attached to his name, though Mr. McSweeny left a personal message for you. It says, 'I'll leave it up to your great skills as a detective to find Shanahan.' I assume that makes some sense to you, Mr. Doherty?"

"Oh, yes. Perfect sense. Thank you for your help. Please tell Mr. McSweeny I'll try to contact him sometime next week when he comes back from … Where is he anyway?"

"I believe he's in Washington today, though I never know for sure with your uncle. He does travel quite a bit and doesn't always leave messages as to where he's going." Doherty thanked the woman once again and rang off.

Chapter Ten

D r. Lague's office was on Main at the corner of Weaver Street, right across from the town's large Greek revival post office. It was on the ground floor of a two-story building with apartments above that looked to be similar in size to Doherty's digs on Crossen Street. On the adjacent corner of Main and Weaver were Whitey's Fabric store and a millinery shop. Doherty had passed by this block dozens of times on his way to the Benny's further down Main. He'd seen the signs for the optometrist, but his eyesight was such that he never had cause to drop in.

He stepped through the front door into an empty waiting room. There was no sign of the doctor, so he spent some time looking around the space. There were some large black and white photos on the walls. They were not the kind of stock photographs one would buy at Woolworth's just to fill up wall space. They looked like ones taken by someone who knew how to work a complex camera. Several were of well-known buildings around West Warwick, including some of the old mills. Others were photos of prominent buildings and street scenes from downtown Providence.

The room contained a set of wooden chairs, a coffee table with some magazines and the doctor's business cards on it. On one wall was a display case with an array of the latest styles in glasses frames. Doherty was still perusing that set-up when the good doctor emerged from a back room, surprised to see someone in the waiting area.

. "I'm sorry, I didn't hear you come in. I assume you're Mr. Doherty," Dr. Lague said with a pleasant smile.

The doctor was of average size with a bald head surrounded by tufts of graying hair all the way around the sides and back. He was wearing a white doctor's smock with a pair of glasses hanging on a chain around his neck. He had a dark complexion and an agreeable smile.

"Nice to meet you Doc," he said offering his hand.

"Please call me Maurice," Lague said. "West Warwick is such a small town; I feel like we should all get to know each other like family. Who are your parents? Perhaps I know them."

"Knew would be more like it. They're both dead now. My father was Peter Doherty and my mother was Mary Anne McSweeny before she was married."

"She wouldn't have been related to Patrick McSweeny, would she?"

"She sure was. My uncle Patrick was her younger brother. He's my only living relative aside from my sister Margaret, who now lives in Minnesota."

"Your uncle was quite the character as I recall. He was involved in politics, wasn't he? Even took on the DeCenza machine at one point, if I remember correctly."

"That would be him. Now he's a big-time lawyer up in Boston. In fact, I just had lunch with him the other day. Lately he's been spending most of his time handling money for the Kennedy presidential campaign."

Dr. Lague shook his head in admiration. "Well, that's quite a step up from the political battles in our little town. Why don't we go into my office and get those passport photos taken? I got a call the other day from some fellow named Murray who said he works for B.W. Royal. Asked me if I could put a rush on your photos. I don't usually do passport work, but I've done quite a few family pictures for the Royal family over the years, so it didn't seem like such a big favor to take some for you. There was a time when the Royals practically owned this town."

"And a lot of others around Rhode Island. Are those your photos on the walls out in the waiting room?"

"Why yes. I dabble in photography as a hobby. In some odd way I see it as being connected to the work I do helping clients to improve their vision. I have a Telicord Reflex camera I like to play around with. And a photo lab I built in the basement of my house. I've just begun to experiment with color development. My wife Betty tells me I spend too much time down there," he said with a chuckle.

While the doctor was describing his camera, Doherty took the occasion to take in the large family photo sitting on his desk.

"You got a nice-looking family there. Your boys seem to be pretty hefty."

The doctor laughed. "They certainly are strapping young men. Practically eat us out of house and home. My older boy Larry is being recruited to play football at Holy Cross."

"I don't remember him on the West Warwick squad."

"No, he went to LaSalle Academy in Providence. His brother Dick will be going there in September. I'm sure he'll play football as well. Our daughter Louise is still at St. John's here in town. My wife wanted all our children to continue with their Catholic education."

"I bet Monk Maznicki isn't happy about losing out your boys." Maznicki was the longtime coach at Deering High in West Warwick. His teams had had great success over the years, especially for ones coming from a town as small as West Warwick.

"Now Mr. Doherty, most of my commercial photographic work is of family photos, wedding pictures, and things like that for people here in town. Let me fetch my camera. Then all you'll have to do is stand up against that white wall over there and I'll snap some mug shots."

Dr. Lague disappeared through a door in the back of his office that opened up onto an alley. There was a small attached building connected to this one that Doherty saw had a sign on it that simply said "Lena's." He soon returned carrying a large box camera and a folded-up tripod. He set the camera on the tripod and positioned Doherty against the blank wall. Doherty put on a half-smile and Lague snapped off about ten shots.

"Do you mind my asking where you're going?"

"Not at all. I'm off to France at the behest of the Royal family. You see I'm a private investigator and they're sending me over there to do some research for his wife and stepdaughter." Doherty felt that was all he should say

64

about his upcoming journey abroad.

"Now I know where I heard your name before," Dr. Lague said as he broke into a wide grin. "You're the fellow who killed that Nazi in Pawtucket a year or so ago. That story was all over the *Times*."

He was pleased the doctor hadn't referenced the more recent killing of Brian Willis by Doris Donahue where Doherty was present. That was one story involving him he was hoping everyone in West Warwick would forget. The *Pawtuxet Valley Times* had indeed made a big deal about Doherty's role in the death of the former Nazi collaborator Stanislaw Krykowski, whose real name back in Poland had been Antonin Bradz.

"Yeah, that was me. When do you think the photos will be ready?" he asked, purposely changing the subject.

"You know my family can trace its roots all the way back to France. To the town of Dijon, which is famous nowadays for its mustard. They emigrated from there to Quebec several generations back. We are one of the oldest French-Canadian families here in West Warwick. Fortunately, most of our ancestors never had to work in the mills. Do you speak any French, Mr. Doherty?"

"Not really. Just bits and pieces of the Canadian French I've picked up living here in town."

"My wife Betty teaches French as well English and math at the junior high. I doubt you would've had her since she didn't begin teaching until well after your time. Did you go to the junior high?"

"Just for a year and a half. I went to St. James' before that until my father took sick and couldn't pay the tuition anymore. To be frank with you, I liked the public schools better."

"I assume that means you also went to the high school. Did you play any sports there?"

"I was on the baseball team. I even got one of those major league tryouts. However, after my father died, I had to go to work to help my mother make the payments on our house. That was pretty much it for my baseball career. When the war came along any dreams I had of playing professionally came to an end."

Lague shook his head. "Yes, I suppose that happened to a lot of aspiring athletes. They had to put their careers on hold until the fighting was over. I hope our children appreciate the benefits they have growing up in a world at peace. It's too bad you don't have more time before your trip. My wife could give you some impromptu French lessons. I understand they don't like to speak anything but French over there."

"Yeah, that was certainly the case when I was in Paris on leave back in '44. I'm sure many of them had learned German by then, though no one wanted to speak it in front of us. Now, what about the pictures – when will they be ready?"

"I should have them for you by tomorrow morning. Feel free to swing by whenever it's convenient. Before you go would you like an eye exam – it'll be on the house."

It took Doherty a few seconds before he agreed. Why not, he thought. He hadn't had his eyes checked since he was in the army. The doctor had him sit in a chair that was similar to a barber's chair and then posted a chart with several lines of letters on the white wall where Doherty had his passport photos taken. Lague dimmed the lights and swung a contraption in front of Doherty and had him rest his chin on a holder while he looked through two lenses at the chart. The doctor asked him to recite what he viewed on each line that diminished in size as he read from top to bottom. First his right eye's sight was measured and then his left. Lague made noises that were sounds of satisfaction after each line reading.

"You have remarkable far-sighted vision, Mr. Doherty. 20-15 to be exact. No wonder you were a star baseball player. The pitches must have looked to be the size of grapefruits to you."

Doherty smiled. "I don't know about that. I did read somewhere that Ted Williams had exceptional vision which was one of the reasons he was such a great hitter."

"Well you obviously don't need glasses for your far-sightedness. What about closer vision? Do you have trouble when you read?"

"Sometimes. I read a lot of paperback books. If I read for a long time my eyes start to get tired."

Lague took out a little flashlight from the pocket of his smock and looked into each of Doherty's eyes. "What prompted you to become such an avid reader?"

"Well it certainly wasn't from school. I guess it started when I was in the service. They'd circulate these small paperback books among the soldiers called *Books for Victory* that had this flying eagle on them. Most of the guys preferred to look at pin-up girls and stuff like that. I didn't want to do a lot of that because I knew they would only make me horny or homesick," he said with a self-deprecating laugh. "Reading those paperback books was my way of escaping from all the blood and guts I saw over there. I kept up the habit after I got home mostly because I don't like spending a lot of time watching TV."

"Well said, Mr. Doherty. Well said. My wife and I have tried to instill the same love of reading in our children. Betty has always been an avid reader."

"Has it taken with your kids?"

Lague gave him a pleased smile. "I think so. It's hard to tell since they have so much reading to do for school. All three of them were schooled at St. John's so they can read and speak in both English and French. My daughter Louise already writes her own stories. I wouldn't be surprised if she ended up doing that as a vocation."

"Well you tell them reading and doing well in school is the only way to get ahead in life nowadays. Working in mills like the ones here in town is a thing of the past. From what I've seen it's a whole new world out there."

"So, Mr. Doherty, would you consider having me fit you with some reading glasses when you get back from your trip?"

"Are those the kind people wear sitting on the end of their noses?" he asked, thinking of how Nina's glasses were perched in that manner.

"They don't have to. I can cut you some very fine reading lenses that look just like regular glasses. And the best part is you don't have to wear them all the time, only when you're reading in the privacy of your home or office."

"I'll think about it while I'm in France. What do I owe you for the passport photos?"

"Oh, you don't owe me anything. Mr. Royal's already taken care of those."

Chapter Eleven

The next morning he picked up the three small, two-inch by two-inch photos at Dr. Lague's office and stuffed them into the manila envelope Murray had given him along with the passport application, and a check for twenty dollars. The post office building's design was a close match to that of the Centreville Bank building located a block away where Nina worked. He didn't see Paul Kent so he asked the woman at the counter if she could find him. Paul soon appeared from the large backroom where the mail was sorted, stacked, and put into large bins or on shelves to be placed into postal bags for the deliverymen.

Kent was a tall man with a shining bald head that was accentuated by the building's harsh fluorescent lights.

"Doherty, I've been expecting you. I got a call the other day from B.W. Royal himself requesting that I give you the VIP treatment when you came in."

"Hardly what I deserve, but I'll take the exclusive deal if that's what you're handing out."

The post office clerk leaned across the counter and said in a more serious tone, "That was some nasty business of the woman stabbing that fella up there in North Providence. Just between me and you, what's the scoop on that anyway?"

Doherty snickered. "I'd like to say it was pretty much how the papers reported it – but you know how the press boys get when they smell blood. The old adage in the newspaper trade is 'if it bleeds, it leads'."

"Did that gal really stick a knife right into the guy's chest?"

"She sure did, right up to the hilt - and without any hesitation. I would've stopped her if I could've. The whole thing started when I was fast asleep in the next room. Apparently, the guy she stabbed wanted to kill her 'cause she knew too much about what he'd done to that other girl down in South County; the one who was strangled and dumped into the ocean. To be honest with you, Paul, my role in the whole affair was pretty minor despite what they said about me in the papers and on TV."

"Whatever you say, Doherty. Still that was some bad business. I suppose you'd seen a lot of guys killed during the war. Everybody in town thought you were a hero when you came home."

"Yeah I saw a lot of killing over in Europe. That hardly qualifies me for being a hero. I just did what I had to do. Seeing somebody get killed here, up close and personal, is something else altogether. Look, Paul, can we get started on this passport business."

'Oh yeah, sure. Sorry about that. When I spoke with Mr. Royal he said we should send your passport application out special delivery directly to some big cheese he knows in Washington."

"Then we'll do whatever he said. He's hired me to go to France to investigate a case for him. It looks like I'll be leaving as soon as I get the passport back from Washington. This envelope," he said as he held up the one Murray had provided for him, "is addressed to some important honcho Royal knows in the state department. Supposedly he's going to put a rush on my application."

"France huh, that sounds like it's gonna be fun. You going alone or are you taking your girlfriend from the bank?"

"Jesus, is there anything about my life the people in this town don't know?"

"Hey, don't get all huffy, Doherty. The folks who work here at the post office are friendly with people over at the bank. And you know how women like to gossip."

"And the men too, huh Paul."

"You got me there," he said with a sheepish grin. "Lemme have that precious envelope so I can get your passport taken care of." Kent placed the packet on a flat scale and plugged some numbers into an adding machine sitting beside it.

"This is gonna cost you seventy-five cents. Baring incident, it should be in the hands of the fella it's addressed to by noon tomorrow. Out of state special deliveries are now flown out of Hillsgrove. We used to send them by train but there are enough flights out of the airport these days to send special deliveries by air. Is there anything else I can do for you today?"

"Yeah, you can tell the post office gossips that my girlfriend isn't going to France with me. This is a business trip. I don't think Royal would appreciate it if I took her along."

After her left the post office Doherty walked several blocks back up Main to where it turned into Washington Street. Three blocks further on was Ryder's package store. It was one of only two liquor stores in Arctic on the commercial strip where most of the drinking was done in the town's many taverns. A lot of West Warwick men, especially those who still worked in the mills, preferred drinking at taverns with their fellow workers rather than buying booze over the counter.

The liquor store was small and from what was on its shelves and in its cooler, it was apparent most of its business was done in pint bottles of whiskey or six-packs of beer. Finding wine bottles was not easy, particularly ones from France. Because he and Nina had agreed to spend a couple of hours at his apartment before they went to dinner, he felt the need to buy some wine since she wasn't much for drinking beer or hard liquor.

After perusing the shelves, he finally discovered a couple that held bottles of red wine. It was mostly the cheap stuff like Gallo and Napa-Sonoma-Mendocino blends in bottles or large jugs. They also carried the distinctly designed bottles of the Lancers and Mateus that were popular these days. On the bottom shelf he found some dusty bottles of French red that may have been there since Prohibition was repealed in 1933. One bottle had the picture of a French chateau on it and a label mostly in French. Remembering the night they'd had dinner at the Greene Inn where Nina ordered French wine to go with their meal, he hoped this bottle would do the trick. Since Doherty's typical purchase at this establishment was a fifth of Jameson, the store's proprietor, a fellow named Jack Hansen, gave him a funny look when he put the dusty bottle on the counter. The wine cost Doherty a healthy five dollars.

He walked home from the packie, not bothering to stop in at the office on the way. His plan was to get the apartment in shape before he picked up Nina at the bank. He thought about putting the wine in the frig, then remembered her telling him that red wine was supposed to be served at room temperature. While at home he made himself a bologna sandwich, which he washed down with some reheated coffee from the morning. After lunch he walked up to Lefty's Market a few blocks along Main where, along with Belanger's, he bought most of his paltry grocery needs. He exchanged some small talk with Lefty, who had his face buried in a racing form. Lefty was a big man in his forties with dark skin, black framed glasses, and a rapidly receding hairline.

Scouring the less than abundant shelves Doherty chose a box of Ritz crackers. From the cooler he took a block of Swiss cheese as well as a package of Laughing Cow cheese that held six individually wrapped triangles. He hoped these would pass as accompaniments to the red wine. For good measure he played a punch card number at the counter. Most people from the neighborhood came to Lefty's specifically to play the numbers or to buy a newspaper. From the shortage of goods on the shelves it was obvious that selling groceries wasn't much more than a side business for Lefty.

He spent the balance of the afternoon cleaning the apartment as best he could, trying to make it looked presentable to Nina. He knew she did her best to tolerate the messiness of his place, given that he was a bachelor who lived alone. On those occasions when she was coming by, he liked to clean it up to let her know she was someone special. These days Nina was just about the only person who ever darkened his doorway. As best he could recall, the only other visitors he'd had over the past few months were a couple of city cops who came by to ask if he'd killed somebody in the parking lot at Crescent Park.

At ten to four he dragged his Chevy out of Belanger's garage to drive the six blocks down to the Centreville Bank. He easily could have walked to meet Nina, but he knew they'd need the car later to drive over to Warwick for dinner. Besides what kind of self-respecting man picked up his date on foot. He even took a few minutes to throw some of the trash strewn on the floor in the front of the car onto the floor in the back. He parked in front of the bank and smoked a cigarette while he waited for her. At five after four she emerged from the building and carefully walked down the stone steps on her impossibly high heels. That was another reason he was glad he hadn't suggested they walk to the apartment. He got out the car and circled around to the other side to open the door for her.

She smiled at his manners. "Why thank you, Mr. Doherty. You do know I'm old enough to open car doors for myself, don't you?"

"I was just trying to be polite, in my stumbling sort of way."

When he returned to the driver's seat Nina leaned over and gave him a peck on the cheek. "Your chivalry is much appreciated, Sir Galahad." Doherty drove around behind the town center and was in front of his apartment on Crossen Street in less than ten minutes. The walk would've taken at least twenty, maybe even thirty on Nina's high heels. On the short drive to the apartment she chatted about her day at the bank and her relief that it was Friday.

Once they were inside, he took Nina's wool coat and hung it in the hall closet. He then rummaged around in the kitchen, opening every drawer looking for a corkscrew.

"Can I help you with something in there?" Nina asked while relaxing on the sofa in the living room with her high heels kicked off and her stocking feet up on the coffee table.

"No, I'm just trying to find an opener for this bottle of wine I bought. I know I have one in here somewhere," he said as he continued to loudly thrash through the various drawers. Nina came in and held up the bottle of French wine.

"Chateau Latour. Where did you get this fine specimen?"

"Believe it or not at Ryder's."

"Hmm, and I thought they only sold beer and hard liquor there." Luckily Doherty had wiped the dust off the bottle when he first brought it home so she wouldn't know how long it had languished on the shelf at the packie. He

72

finally found a corkscrew buried in the recesses of a drawer where he kept a screwdriver, some pliers, a small hammer, and other hand tools. Before trying to get the cork out he struggled with the seal that encased it.

"Here, why don't you give me that while you find us a couple of clean glasses?" He took two glasses down from the cabinet; they were tumblers not wine goblets, but that was all he had except for some old jam jars he also used as glasses. He apologized but Nina told him she didn't expect a shot and beer drinker like him to have wine glasses. As she expertly removed the seal and opened the bottle with the corkscrew, he put out a plate with some slices of the Swiss cheese and the Laughing Cow triangles in its center with the Ritz crackers arrayed around the edge. Meanwhile Nina sniffed at the top of the opened bottle to make sure it didn't smell like turpentine.

"My, oh my. Hors d'oeuvres to go with this fine French wine. Why are you being such a thoughtful host today? Is this the prelude to you telling me we're breaking up?"

"We're not breaking up. And I will tell you what's on my mind later. For now, why don't we go into the living room and have some wine and cheese?"

"Are you really going to drink wine with me and not your usual double shot of Jameson?" Doherty had poured the wine into the two glasses, being careful not to show his lack of couth by pouring too much in each.

Nina went through the ritual of again smelling the wine and then swirling it around in her glass.

"How is it?" he asked after she swished some wine around in her mouth before swallowing it.

"Surprisingly good. Are you sure you bought this at Ryder's?"

"Swear to God. I had to do some searching to find it. And when I pulled it off the shelf the bottle was kind of dusty. I remembered you telling me that most wine gets better with age, so I figured although it might've been on the shelf at Ryder's for a few decades it would still be good."

Doherty drank some and agreed it tasted all right. He wasn't exactly an expert on wine, but he thought he'd have noticed if it tasted like vinegar. Usually he only drank wine when he was out with Nina. Now he supposed he should get used to it since that's what all the Frenchies drank.

They sat on the sofa drinking wine and nibbling at the cheese. Nina mostly nibbled while Doherty gobbled. The wine got better with each sip. After a few glasses he could tell Nina was feeling its effects. Without warning she stood up, grabbed the wine bottle with one hand, and took his hand with her other one. She led him into the bedroom where he'd been sure to neatly make the bed that afternoon. Without saying a word Nina began to unbutton his shirt; he did likewise with her blouse. Their clothes were slowly peeled off one garment at a time until they created a mixed pile on the floor. They slid into bed and were soon making love in a lazy Friday afternoon sort of way. Doherty had not expected Nina to be so forthright; he had to admit he kind of liked her this way.

After they were finished, they drank more wine, this time directly from the bottle. He lit a cigarette and propped himself up against the pillows.

"That was very nice," he said. "I didn't expect you to be so …" he didn't know what to tag onto this sentence that wouldn't come out sounding crude, so he shifted gears. "It must be the wine going to your head."

"The wine and a long week of work. Since we're not breaking up can you now tell me what's on your mind? You've had me on pins and needles all week."

He took a deep drag off his Camel while assembling his thoughts. "I'm going away for a while."

Nina grabbed his thigh in a tight grip. "Are you goin' to prison, Doherty? I'll wait for ya. Don't worry I'll wait for ya." Her sudden comedic outburst almost caused him to spit his cigarette out onto the sheets.

"Well, it's not exactly prison," he said going along with the gag. "I've been hired to go to France on a case."

"France? Jesus, Doherty."

"Yeah. I'm being hired by none other than the B.W. Royal family to go to France on a mission of mercy. The whole thing might turn into a boondoggle, but I'll tell you the plan and then you can let me know what you think." Doherty spent the next twenty minutes laying out the whole story from his first meeting with Mrs. Royal and her daughter Mary Margaret to his visit to the Royal estate to his interactions with Royal's man Murray. He didn't bother to leave anything out since there was no client confidentiality involved in the telling.

"And you think B.W. is sending you on this excursion just so you can come back and tell the stepdaughter that her father was a hero who died fighting for his country?"

"That's about the size of it."

"What's your take on this scheme?"

"My take? My take is that I'll go over there for a week or so, drink some wine, eat some good food, consort with various mademoiselles, and come back with a wad of Royal's cash still in my pocket. C'est la vie."

Nina punched him on the shoulder. "No, wise guy. What are you really planning on doing once you're in France?"

It took him a few moments to concoct an explanation that would satisfy all parties involved. "First I'll be in Paris where I'm hoping to consult with some fellow my Uncle Patrick is hooking me up with. After that I'll go out to Normandy to see what I can find out about this dead McDonald kid. I'm not expecting to discover much more than that he was killed by some German soldier and is buried in the mass cemetery over there. If I find out the kid was a coward or died under some suspicious circumstances, I'll probably keep that to myself. I don't see what good it would do to put something like that on the daughter's plate. Hell, she never even knew her father to begin with. I think she only wants to prove to herself that her real father was a better man than B.W., although I doubt this McDonald fellow could've provided her with the kind of comfortable life Royal has."

"What will you say to the wife, or to Royal for that matter? They're the ones paying the freight."

"I don't know. It'll depend on what, if anything, I uncover."

"How long do you think you'll be away?"

"A week, maybe a little longer. The briefer the trip the more of Royal's money I get to pocket. He has me booked into a hotel in Paris for three nights. I suppose I'll use some of that time to take in the sights before I head out to Normandy. Right now, this looks like nothing more than a free trip to France. I'm only sorry you can't come along."

Nina shrugged. "That's okay, Doherty. From what you've told me, things didn't work out all that well for some of your previous girlfriends who got involved in your cases. Maybe your time away will do both of us some good."

"What's that supposed to mean?"

Nina was silent for a while - obviously not wanting to answer this question. "Let's face facts. All of this sleeping around stuff is nice. Actually, it's better than nice. And I like you, Doherty. Sometimes I even tell myself I'm in love with you. But you're forty years old and it doesn't sound like you have any plans for getting married. I'm still in my twenties and to be honest with you, I'd someday like to have kids. On top of that my parents don't particularly like or approve of you. Since I'm still living at home I have to hear about that every time I tell them I'm going out with you. I've tried to get them to stay out of my affairs, but they're my parents and they refuse to ignore how I live my life. Maybe a couple of weeks apart will give both of us some time to think about the future."

"Are you breaking up with me?"

"Oh hell no. Come here, you big lug." Nina wrapped him up in a tight embrace and they made love for a second time as the afternoon turned into the evening. When they were done, she took one of his cigarettes and lit it, which was unusual since Nina seldom smoked his non-filtered butts.

"I think we have to get one thing straight before you go over to the other side of the Atlantic. If the opportunity presents itself for you to play around with some cute little French girl, it'll be okay with me. Just don't tell me about it when you get back. I've heard all about those French girls"

"Is that from some article you read in one of your women's magazines? If I do what you say will it mean you have license to find a more appropriate boyfriend while I'm away?"

"Around West Warwick? I doubt that. I'm just saying I don't want to hold anything over you while you're in France. Just consider that you have a free pass when you're over there. After you get home we'll talk some more. As for now, I think I'd like to go eat some chicken."

Chapter Twelve

O n Monday morning Agnes called the apartment to say that she wasn't coming into the office. It was fine with Doherty since he had a number of things to take care of before flying off to France. After a late breakfast he drove into town to do some shopping at St. Onge's; he needed some clothes to take to France as well as some other essentials. Even more important, he realized he didn't have a suitcase since he hadn't gone away anywhere for longer than a weekend since being discharged from the service.

His good friend Ed Nunan was working the men's department at West Warwick's most prominent men's clothing store. After some small talk Nunan took him to the back of the store where they had a number of suitcases piled on top of one another. Doherty perused the stack before prying a mid-sized tan leather valise out from the bottom. It was a little dusty, so he wiped it down with his handkerchief before looking inside.

"You considering buying that old thing?" Nunan asked skeptically. "I think that baby's been here since the war."

Doherty took his time in examining the suitcase. He didn't plan on taking a lot of clothes with him and would probably supplement any bag he took with a briefcase he'd carry most days when he was working. The inside of the valise had a smooth silk lining. All and all it looked like something one of the people in an Ernest Hemingway novel would carry. He was thinking a lot about the Hemingway books he'd read since most of them took place somewhere in Europe.

"I like this one. It's kind of old fashioned, which suits my personality."

That drew a knowing smile from Nunan. "About what I would expect from you. I'm sure Mr. St. Onge'll be glad to get rid of that old thing. I doubt he'll charge you more than about a ten spot."

Doherty blew some more dust off the outside of the case. Nunan then took it upstairs to see what the owner would want for the vintage suitcase. While he was gone Doherty picked out a couple pairs of boxer shorts, some new socks, and a light blue dress shirt still squared away in its package with all the pins and cardboard. When Nunan returned he placed these goods on the counter by the register.

"The old man wanted fifteen for the valise, but I was able to talk him down to twelve when I told him this was gonna be your first trip abroad. He's a big proponent of world travel. He and the wife have been just about everywhere. I guess you can do that when you have big bucks like they do." Nunan's last remark had a touch of resentment in it. All told Doherty's purchases came to twenty dollars and change.

Back at the office Doherty killed most of the afternoon making a list of what he needed to take with him to France. He spent the remaining time trying to figure out how he was going to move on the McDonald investigation. He didn't have much to go on, only some bits of information Royal and his man Murray had given him about the outfit the kid was attached to, where he'd done his basic and combat training, and where and when he'd bought the farm in Normandy. All of this was outlined in some official government documents Mrs. Royal had kept as mementos of her first marriage. Doherty assured Murray that he would be careful not to let any damage come to these papers. Royal's man indicated neither he nor his boss much cared one way or the other.

A few minutes before four Doherty decided to pack things up for the day. He'd bought a paperback of another Hemingway novel at the Arctic News and was anxious to start it. This one was called *The Sun Also Rises*. Apparently a lot of it took place in Paris. It was old but it would give him a leg up on seeing what the place was like from an author's point of view. The last few days he'd been poring over the Frommer book Royal had lent him. Hemingway's novel might give him a different perspective on the so-called City of Lights.

There was a soft knock on the office door. It took Doherty a few seconds to remember that Agnes wasn't in before he got up and opened it himself. Much to his surprise Mrs. Royal was standing in the hallway looking nervous.

"Please, please come in."

"I'm sorry to appear unannounced," she said, no longer adopting the seen-it- all attitude of her first visit.

"I'd offer you some coffee but what's in the pot has been sitting there since this morning."

Charlene Royal breezed by him into his office and sat in the chair across from his desk. She took out one of her long, filtered cigarettes, which Doherty quickly ignited with his Zippo. Not wanting her to smoke alone he torched one of his Camels and brought the large glass ashtray within reach for both of them.

"Before we talk, I need to tell you my husband doesn't know I was coming here today. I would appreciate it if it stays that way. And that includes his boy Murray as well." Doherty thought it interesting that she referred to Royal's forty plus year-old gofer Murray as a 'boy'.

"According to my records you're the client who signed our agreement. So anything you say in that direction today is confidential. Although as far as I can tell, it's your husband who's footing the bill for my retainer."

Mrs. Royal took a long drag from her cigarette and blew smoke in the direction of the ceiling. "That's what Brayton loves more than anything – paying people to do his bidding for him."

"I'd hardly say I'm doing his bidding. Seems to me this is more about doing you and your daughter's bidding."

She gave him a sardonic smile. "I'd like to believe you, Mr. Doherty. But I bet my husband has already instructed you to go over to France, have some fun on his dime, and then come back with some fabricated story about how John died a hero fighting for his country."

Doherty leaned forward and gave the woman a stern look. "A lot of good men died over there during the war trying to stop evil from spreading. It didn't matter what their motives were or how much they believed in what they were doing, they're dead just the same. I think it would be best if you packed up your cynicism and headed back to your gentleman's farm. That way I can do my job like I planned to."

"I did some checking on you, Doherty." The Mr. was now gone from her term of address. "On one of your more recent jobs I understand you were asleep while a girl you were shacking up with stuck a knife into someone's chest. Is that how you usually operate as a private eye?" It was all Doherty could do not to physically escort Mrs. Royal out of his office.

"Listen, Charlene, or should I call you Cheryl, which is who you were when you were married to McDonald." Two could play the insult game. "I know B.W. hired me because, in his words, I would be like a 'fish out of water' over there in France; not knowing anybody or being able to speak the language. But you see I'm not the kind of guy who lets anyone play him. If I thought a client was tooling me for his own purposes, I'd drop him like a hot potato no matter how much money he was waving in my face. Maybe Royal thinks when I get over there and see how difficult this case is, I'll piss my pants and come home. However, I can assure you that's not going to happen. I'm going to find out what happened to John McDonald no matter where the chips might fall. I hope you and your daughter are prepared for that."

For the first time Charlene Royal gave him what looked like a friendly smile. "I'm sorry, Mr. Doherty. I was just testing you. You have to understand something - my husband is not all he's cracked up to be. Ever since the family's mills went bankrupt, he's been living mostly on his reputation."

"That fancy farm you have over in Warwick looked like you were living on more than reputation."

"If you really must know, the farm is mortgaged to the hilt. Brayton is planning to sell almost all the land it sits on to the state so they can build a community college there. We'll be able to continue living in the farmhouse if we choose, but all the other buildings will either be knocked down or transformed by the college into classrooms. I'll be stuck in a house on property where college kids are roaming all over. Meanwhile my husband will be off on business, which is a euphemism he uses when he's meeting up with one or another of his latest girlfriends. None of whom, of course, he thinks I know about.

"This isn't the life I bargained for when I married into the Royal family. Frankly, I thought I'd spend the rest of my life living in the lap of luxury. Most of my husband's business transactions these days are evasions he employs to keep the bill collectors at bay. After he sells the land to the state, he's going to sell another large parcel to some sleazy developer who wants to build a shopping mall on it. That will hardly leave us with much of the *gentleman's farm*. His Aunt Livinia will be spinning in her grave."

"Where does that leave you?"

"My only interest right now is ensuring that my daughter gets through high school and into a good college. Then she'll at least have a chance to spread her wings and fly."

Doherty took a few moments to take in what Mrs. Royal had just spilled to him. "Let me ask you a question: What exactly do you want me to find out about your first husband?"

"I don't know. I guess if you can find out something meaningful about the way he died you can bring a little bit of John back to me and my daughter. He was a good boy, who loved me beyond what I deserved. I've kept most of the letters he wrote me while he was away. I can't bring him back nor can I expect that what you find out about him will bring me any comfort in my present state."

She stopped there as if her words, like the boy's life, had hit a dead end. She shuffled in her purse and withdrew an old photograph of a young man in uniform.

"Please take this so you'll have a bit of John with you when you go to France. While you're there, I'd like you to think of him as a real person, not just some anonymous dead soldier."

Chapter Thirteen

A little after eleven on Tuesday morning a messenger boy dropped a thick white package onto Agnes' desk. She quickly took it into Doherty's office and handed it to him. The return address was an official looking label from the state department in Washington. He fingered the large envelope before taking his penknife and slitting it open. Inside some folded up blank papers was a small, drab green passport, no more than 3½ by 6 inches. He'd expected something more substantial and official looking than the flimsy document he now held in his hands.

On the top of the cover was an identification number perforated all the way through it as well as through the first two pages. The first page required him to fill out some personal info. Facing it was a statement from the secretary of state about the rights of travel of any American holding this passport. The important stuff was on the next two pages, the first of which had all of Doherty's pertinent information including his birth date and place of birth, where it only said 'Rhode Island, U.S.A'.

The next page had nothing more than one of the mug shots Dr. Lague had taken of him with Doherty's signature beside it. Running up one side of his picture was an official government stamp that stated the date the passport was issued. At this point Agnes came into the back office and asked if that was his passport the messenger delivered. Doherty smiled at her and held up the page with his picture on it.

"I've never seen one of those before. All Louie needs to go to some foreign port is his seaman's papers. Jeez, boss, his papers look more official than this here passport. Are you sure that's all you're gonna need to get into France?"

"Well, it says it's an official U. S. passport, so I guess it'll have to do. According to the guidebook Royal gave me, I'm not going to need a visa or anything like that to enter France. What do you think of my mug shot?" he asked, holding that page up for Agnes to see.

She studied it carefully while searching for the right words. "At least it doesn't make you look like a criminal."

"That's good. I suspect the Frenchies have enough criminals of their own." Doherty flipped through the next ten pages of the booklet; they were all blank with only the small word *Visas* printed at the top of each. The last two pages had a heading: IMPORTANT INFORMATION FOR YOU. It was filled with stuff under headings like Customs, Public Health Services, Agriculture, Loss of Nationality, Loss, Theft or Destruction of Passport and a host of other things. He'd take some time later to read all of this information. He flipped back and forth through the document still marveling at how insubstantial it felt for something that would be so vital for his trip. When he handed the passport to Agnes, she skimmed through it slowly, shrugging her shoulders as if she expected the document to be something more impressive than what was in her hands.

"I'm going to call Royal's secretary to tell them to make plans for my departure. When they call back with the details, I'll need you to write them down for me."

"Whatever you say, boss. I wouldn't want you to forget when your plane is leavin'. That wouldn't make you look like the ace detective you are."

Doherty dialed the number B.W. Royal had left with him. His secretary answered after the second ring. When he told her to tell Mr. Royal he had received his passport she said Murray would be in touch with him as soon as he made the necessary arrangements with the airlines. She then hung up without saying anything more. He found it interesting that Royal's secretary did not attach a "Mr." to Murray either.

He put his feet up on the desk and engaged in some conversation with Agnes about the sights he hoped to see while in Paris. As he spoke her eyes expressed a good deal of envy. Still on his mind was yesterday afternoon's visit from Mrs. Royal and what she had imparted to him about both her former and present husbands. In the end he held back telling Agnes about her visit not wanting to violate any client confidentiality. He also didn't want to convey to Agnes what Mrs. Royal had told him because he didn't want her passing judgment about his new client. In the end he figured Agnes would be happy with the bonus money that would come her way thanks to Royal's generous retainer.

Less than a half hour later Royal's man Murray called the office. Agnes answered it with their official greeting and then passed the call on to her boss. Once again, the caller identified himself only as 'Murray' and then very matter-of-factly gave Doherty the information about his departure flights. He was booked onto an Alleghany Airlines plane leaving Hillsgrove on Thursday afternoon at 3:15 p.m. arriving at New York's Idlewild airport approximately two hours later. The flight to Paris wouldn't be leaving Idlewild until seven that evening so he'd have a layover in New York of a little less than two hours. Murray said this would give Doherty time to get to the Pan American terminal, have his bag checked through to Paris, and go through passport control before leaving the U.S. His flight to Paris would be arriving sometime around the middle of the next day French time. That was because it would be in the air for about seven hours and the time in France was six hours later than in New York.

Doherty repeated everything Murray told him out loud so Agnes could scribble it down on her steno pad. Royal's man signed off by saying if Doherty needed help with anything he should feel free to call Royal's secretary between 8 a.m. and 5 p.m. If something needed to be attended to after-hours, he should leave a message on her answering machine, which Murray checked each evening before retiring around 11 p.m. Doherty assumed this meant Murray resided somewhere on the Royal estate.

Agnes retired to the front office to type up the itinerary Murray had given them on the phone. Meanwhile Doherty took one of the traveler's check packets and went out to clean up some last-minute details before putting things together for the trip. As usual he took a quick lunch at the downstairs counter at the Arctic News. While there he had an overriding desire to flash his passport to Mildred who waited on him as she often did, before realizing such an act would look like bragging in a town where few people left the state, let alone the country.

After lunch he walked down Main to Centreville Bank and cashed two of the traveler's checks at one of teller windows. He purposely did this before stopping to talk to Nina at her desk. She saw him at the window and gave him a wry look. Cashing the checks went as Murray had described it should. He simply filled in the date and countersigned his name at the bottom. Since he was a regular customer there, Sylvia, the teller, didn't bother to ask him for identification or look to see if the two signatures matched. She did scrutinize the checks for a few moments. He assumed not too many people cashed traveler's checks at the local West Warwick bank.

With four crisp tens in his hands along with his new passport Doherty strolled over to Nina's space with a noticeably cocky gait. He held up his passport and said, "Look what yours truly got in the mail today."

Nina grabbed the passport and like Agnes flipped through the pages. When done she expressed the same disappointment Agnes had.

"Doesn't seem all that official. Keep a good eye on it. I hear if you lose your passport, you'll never be able to return home."

"Would that bring a tear to your eye?"

Nina gave him her best insincere smile, "Most assuredly, Mr. Doherty. So, when do you leave on this transcontinental caper?"

"Thursday."

"Of this week? That's pretty soon. Hardly time for us to throw you a bon voyage party."

"Oh please, Miss Vitale. You don't have to go to any trouble on my account. I do have a couple of favors to ask of you and I hope they won't cause you any inconvenience. Do you think you could drive me to the Hillsgrove Airport on Thursday? My flight doesn't leave until three; you could drop me on your lunch hour if that works for you."

"You forgot something, Doherty. I don't have a car."

"I know. That's my second favor: I'd like you to take care of my car while I'm away. I'm afraid if I leave it in Belanger's garage unattended for too long it won't start when I get back."

"Please, Doherty, you leave that chariot of yours unattended all the time. Remember you're the guy who prefers to walk rather than drive. It's all I can do to get you to pick me up when we're going to a movie or out to eat."

Doherty shrugged. "I know. I guess what I'm saying is that I thought you'd like to have a car to cruise around in while I'm away. It'll mean you won't have to take the bus to and from work every day. You'll also be able to squire your new boyfriend around as soon as you get over missing me."

"Well that would make perfect sense. Me running around in your car with some new guy. What am I supposed to tell him when he asks where I got such a fine set of wheels?"

"Tell him your boyfriend died and left you his car in his will."

"I'll ask Mr. Lambeau if I can take my lunch hour a little later on Thursday so I can take you to the airport closer to three. I wouldn't want you to have to hang around Hillsgrove for a couple hours. I don't believe there's a whole lot to do out there. And yes, I will babysit your Chevy while you're in France on one condition: you clean it up before you leave. Last time I was in it your backseat looked like a toilet bowl. On another note, what are the chances of us getting together tomorrow evening. I'd like to give you a sendoff gift before you leave." There was a suggestive twinkle in Nina's eye.

"That would be nice. I'll pick you up after work – with the car."

"Fine. I'll see you around four then."

Back at the office he retreated to the back room and started putting his game plan down on paper. Arriving in Paris in mid-day he would first check into his hotel. If he were traveling on his own dime, he would take the Metro from the airport to a stop nearest to his hotel. He'd read in the *Five Dollars a Day* book that the Paris Metro was very efficient and could take you just about anywhere you wanted to go. But with Royal's money already burning a hole in his pocket he decided he'd spring for a cab from Orly Airport into the city.

Depending on the food on the plane he would probably want to catch a late lunch before doing anything else. He read that Parisians ate and drank wine at all hours of the day and night. Nina had given him a tutorial on French food based on the numerous articles she'd read in her women's magazines. Although she'd never been to France herself, she had been to Quebec City and Montreal, which he figured was the next best thing. His plan was to take it easy the first day or so, maybe do some sightseeing before contacting Uncle Patrick's man at the American embassy as the first step in getting his investigation underway. He was booked into the hotel in Paris for three nights. That meant he wouldn't be heading out to Normandy until Monday. Where he would go from there would depend on whether the fellow in the embassy had some good leads for him.

Aside from his passport, plane tickets, and other documents, he would be bringing his PI license and a cover letter he'd have Agnes write up explaining who he was and what his mission was all about. Once in Paris he would try to find someone to translate this letter into French. That might help him grease the way through any foreign interference he might encounter.

With this part of his plan set he left the office around four. At the apartment he began to put things in order there. He did some cleaning and disposed of any food items not in cans that he probably wouldn't be eating in the next two days. Otherwise he checked to make sure all of his bills were up to date. After that he shuffled through his clothes trying to decide what to take with him. Earlier that morning he'd called the weather service at the airport and got a pretty good idea what the weather in Paris would be like over the next few days. When he did this, they reminded him that the temps in France would all be on the Celsius scale so he should figure out how to convert them into Fahrenheit.

He decided to take the clean suit hanging in his closet rather than the rumpled one he was wearing. Along with that he'd throw in a sport coat, a couple of sweaters, a second pair of shoes, some slacks, underwear and socks and a pair of pajamas. Those plus two handkerchiefs would pretty much make up the sum total of his wardrobe. All of that would easily fit in his new valise. He would eschew taking his topcoat and opt instead for his belted raincoat. It would be lighter and give him that Humphrey Bogart look he knew from their movies many Frenchmen had adopted.

The coat and his hat would go on the plane with him. Room would be set aside in his briefcase for the travel book and the Hemingway novel, both of which he hoped would occupy his time in the air - and keep him from thinking about the three-thousand miles of empty water he was flying over. Charles Lindbergh he wasn't. The only other materials he would need were documents and notes relating to the case. For the most part he was all set except for those moments when his nerves got the better of him. He anticipated that a few drinks on the flight would help ease them.

Chapter Fourteen

Nina was noticeably troubled as they drove to the airport on Thursday. He didn't know if it was because he was leaving for an indeterminate amount of time or that she wasn't sure what the separation might mean for their relationship. Everything seemed fine the night before. He'd picked up some steaks at the First National and they ate in at his apartment. They accompanied their meal with the remainder of the bottle of French wine left over from Friday. He was trying his best to acclimate himself to drinking wine on the assumption that it was pretty much what most people drank in France. After eating and drinking he and Nina made love in a familiar manner. When it was time for her to leave, he suggested she take the Chevy home with her so she could get used to driving it. As requested, he'd cleaned out the car earlier in the day.

But now something was clearly eating at her as they crossed over into Warwick on their way to Rhode Island's modest public airport.

"Cat got your tongue today?"

Nina wouldn't look at him and for a long time said nothing.

"Are you angry at me for going on this trip?"

"It's not about you," she replied in a quiet voice. "It's my parents. They were waiting up for me when I came home last night. My father took one look

89

at your car and he exploded. Asked me how long I was going to be your *whore*. That's what he called me - a whore."

"Jeez, Nina, what did you say?"

"I yelled at him. Told him to mind his own business. That's when he slapped me. I think I might've said, 'Mind your own goddamn business.' I was so mad. I told him I was a big girl who could make her own decisions about her life."

"Then my mother started in with Darrell again. She said she couldn't understand why I would break up with such a nice boy like him. That plus the wine I had at your place set me off. I yelled at her too. Told her I didn't break up with Darrell – he broke up with me because he was a goddamn fairy. That's when my father slapped me again. Told me I couldn't use language like that in his house. I think he slapped me the second time because he was upset that his daughter almost married a guy who was secretly a homosexual. You've got to understand something, Doherty, my parents are simple people who live in their own tidy little world. They don't know how to deal with a world where guys are homos and girls sleep with men they're not married to."

Doherty didn't know how he was supposed to respond to this last remark. "What happens now?"

"I don't know. Maybe it's a good thing you're going to be away for a while. At least then I won't have to explain our relationship to them every time we go out. If I get my yearly raise at the bank, I'm thinking of looking for a place of my own. I can't afford one right now, but I can't continue to live with them much longer. Especially now that you're a big part of my life."

They turned up airport road and headed to the small terminal that was the sum total of Hillsgove Airport. Doherty parked the Chevy in the public lot across from the terminal building. Once inside he checked in at the Allegheny counter and was told his flight would be boarding in twenty minutes. He and Nina sat on some plastic chairs and smoked cigarettes until the flight was called.

"At least you'll have my car. If things get uncomfortable at home, you can always go out for a ride." He then handed her a key to his apartment. "Or if you want you can stay at my place while I'm away. You saw last night how I cleaned it up for you."

Nina took the key and thanked him for the offer. "I guess what I'm most upset about is the language my father used. My mother said he only swore like that when he was on the golf course. I know he loves me and only wants what's best, but it's like he's from another era. Still it's painful when I remember how much of a daddy's girl I was when I was young."

"He's an old Italian papa who doesn't like having his daughter running around with an older man - and an Irish one to boot. Hey, at least I'm not an older married man." Nina punched his arm.

The PA announced that the Allegheny flight to New York was now boarding. Doherty grabbed his valise and briefcase and headed toward the boarding gate, one of the few they had at Hillsgrove. Before stepping up to hand the clerk his ticket he dropped his bags and took Nina in a tight embrace.

"You be careful over there, Doherty. France won't be like Rhode Island."

"I'll see you in a week or so. I'll send you a postcard when I get there. Maybe we can work some things out after I get home," he added, purposely keeping it vague. He then rubbed his hand across her cheek and borrowing a line from Casablanca said, "Here's looking at you, kid."

"Thanks, Bogie. It goes with your trench coat." He turned back at the gate and gave Nina a brief wave before crossing the tarmac to climb the portable staircase to the plane. At the door he looked back, but she was already gone.

The two-hour flight to New York passed without incident. The smallish plane was a propeller jet so it made a lot of noise, though not nearly as much as the parachute drop planes he'd flown in when he was in the army. Sitting by the window he was able to see the airport and the houses around it as they slowly receded until they looked like the miniature towns kids built around their toy train sets. When he and his fellow soldiers were transported to Sicily from their embarkation points in England there were no windows on their plane. Instead they sat on benches in the cargo hold the whole time anxiously clutching their equipment. For most of the trip guys were praying they wouldn't be shot down by enemy anti-aircraft fire and that their parachutes would open after they jumped. This flight was luxurious by comparison.

Rather than read the French guidebook or the Hemingway novel, he decided to peruse the morning *Journal* instead. He found he couldn't concentrate on the news as thoughts of Nina and then of his recent meeting with Mrs. Royal swirled around in his head. About an hour into the flight a stewardess passed down the aisle offering coffee and donuts to the passengers. The plane was only half full so the cute blond in uniform gave him two donuts to go with his coffee, along with a sweet smile. He put the paper aside while he ate and drank his coffee. He stared out the window when the plane crossed over what he thought was Long Island on its way toward New York.

As the Alleghany propjet approached Idlewild Airport Doherty was amazed at the number of runways and terminal buildings that made up New York's large airport. It was certainly a far cry from the single terminal at Hillsgrove. The plane circled over at least four different buildings, one of which looked like a Martian spaceship out of a Captain Midnight episode. It finally came to a halt at a modest structure slightly larger than the one at Hillsgrove. It didn't take long for the portable staircase to be rolled up to the exit door so its twenty passengers could descend to the tarmac. He grabbed his valise from the upper rack and briefcase from under the seat in front of him and joined the exiting passengers.

Once inside the terminal Doherty was immediately lost. After roaming around aimlessly for a few minutes he spotted a large electronic board listing all the flights in and out of Idlewild over the next twelve hours. He spotted the flight to Paris he was scheduled to take; it was listed as leaving from a gate in Terminal 3. Looking around he spotted an elderly Negro skycap lugging some-one's oversized suitcase. He stopped him and asked how to get to Terminal 3. The guy pointed to an exit door and informed Doherty he needed to take a shuttle bus to something he called Worldport.

With no idea what that meant he descended to the ground floor on an escalator. There he asked another skycap how to get the shuttle to Worldport. This time the colored boy gave him a big smile and said, "You in for a big treat, mister." He took Doherty's valise and led him to a bus stop where a number of other travelers were standing. "Take the next bus that stops here. You won't miss your terminal; it looks like a flying saucer." Doherty flipped the boy a quarter and thanked him for his help.

Two minutes later a half-sized bus pulled up and everyone piled on, luggage and all. Doherty had no problem finding a seat as the shuttle was only about three quarters full. He tried to not appear bug-eyed as he took in the enormity of the Idlewild terminals. The two skycaps were right about Terminal 3. The Pan American building did indeed look like a flying saucer. It wasn't as tall as some of the buildings in downtown Providence, but it was by far the largest horizontal structure he'd ever seen. As it had looked from the air, it did resemble something from a science fiction movie. During the short ride Doherty noticed that a fair number of his fellow passengers were speaking languages other than English.

Once inside the terminal he found himself rubbernecking at its futuristic features. It looked like something from a World's Fair. Everything was so modern and streamlined. Within the circular structure there were virtually no square corners as everything flowed in a curving fashion. The building was enormous with escalators rising and descending from upper floors. Looking through its massive plate glass windows he saw that several planes had taxied up so close to the terminal that they were sitting under the circular overhang that acted like an awning. Passengers boarding or departing planes at this terminal would be completely sheltered from the outside elements.

In the center of the ground floor was a large round information kiosk with panels that radiated from it like light beams on its ceiling. Everything on the ground floor was designed to be in harmony with the rounded design of the outer building. After absorbing the breathtaking nature of the structure Doherty finally located the Pan American departure counters for international flights. According to the big board there were planes leaving from this terminal destined for London, Paris, Berlin, Madrid and Rome. In addition there were Pan Am flights going to the Far East and other places he'd never heard of.

He carried his bag to the counter where he was asked to produce his ticket and passport. The woman spoke to him in English though he'd heard her speaking to the couple in front of him in perfect French.

"How long will you be staying in France, Mr. Doherty?"

"I'm not sure; maybe a week or two. Depends on how my business goes."

She asked him to place his bag on the conveyor belt beside the counter where she tagged it and sent it on its way.

"First time traveling to Paris?"

"No, I was there during the war. I suspect I'll find it much more pleasant this time around."

She gave him a knowing smile. "Have a nice trip."

Before he left the area, he could hear her seamless slip back into French with the next family that approached. He looked his watch; he still had over an hour before his flight departed. While checking out the terminal on his arrival he'd noticed a bar on the second level. With his briefcase in hand he took the escalator that came up facing a rounded bar that was of the same design as the information kiosk on the ground level, including the light beam ceiling panels that jutted out from its center. Taking a seat at the bar he ordered a double shot of Jameson neat. It was just the tonic he needed before boarding the trans-Atlantic flight.

The bar area was quite busy with a myriad of languages being slung about. Like the attendant at the departure desk, the bartender appeared to be able to fill orders in several different languages. Everything about the Worldport terminal was so splendiferous and airy that Doherty was almost sorry he'd be leaving it to be confined for seven hours on an airplane. Forty minutes and two Jamesons later a loudspeaker announced in both English and then French that his flight was about to board. He slipped the bartender a generous tip and made his way toward his departure gate.

Right away he could tell from the number of people crowding around the gate that the Pan Am jet to Paris was going to be much bigger than the Alleghany plane he'd flown on from Hillsgrove. Boarding was slow as everyone was required to show their passports as well as tickets at the gate. The inside of the plane was quite large with three seats across on either side of the aisle. Two extremely attractive stewardesses greeted him as he entered and pointed in the direction of his seat, which was about three quarters of the way back. He was fortunate it was by the window rather than on the aisle, or worse, in the middle. A heavyset man was already sitting in the aisle seat reading a German newspaper. He smelled of cigar smoke as Doherty slid by him into his window seat. It was nearly ten minutes before a middle-aged woman dropped into the center seat. She immediately took out some knitting and began to work on it feverishly. When one of the stewardesses passed by, she said something to her in French. A quick conversation flew back and forth with the attendant replying to her in kind. A few minutes later she returned to hand the woman a small pillow.

The knitter nodded at Doherty and asked, "Etes-vous Francais?"

"No, American."

"Vous ne parlez pas Francais?"

Doherty knew she was asking if he spoke French. He did not think he wanted to spend the next seven hours trying to converse in his pidgin West Warwick French with someone who might be a chatterbox; he told her he did not speak French.

"C'est dommage." He didn't know what that meant but hoped there would be no more verbal interaction between them for the duration of the flight. It was curious that she did not ask her German seatmate if he spoke French. At first, he thought maybe it was because of the smell the guy was emitting. Then, sizing up their respective ages and his reading of a German newspaper, he thought perhaps it was understandable that she wouldn't want to have anything to do with him.

With that settled Doherty removed the Hemingway book from his brief-case and tried to read. Five minutes in he was interrupted when the plane's intercom came on welcoming them all aboard and outlining the length of the trip, the meal schedule, and other matters of that sort. All of these messages were repeated in French, though so rapidly that he was only able to pick up a few of the words. This was not a good sign for what his time in France was going to be like. A stewardess then set herself in the center of the aisle demon-strating how to attach the seat belts and how to activate their safety equipment, particularly the life vest in case the pilot had to put this aircraft down in the middle of the Atlantic. Doherty was inclined to give this orientation only par-tial attention since he knew from his military training, if this plane went down in the Atlantic, they'd all be dead as soon as it hit the water.

He found it better to occupy his time by reading. In the novel a guy named Jake Barnes was playing tennis with a former college acquaintance named Robert Cohn at a court on the outskirts of Paris. It was some years after the end of the First World War and Cohn was attacking their *friendly* game in a ferocious manner that put Jake off.

Much to Doherty's delight the big jet took off smoothly and without incident. Twenty minutes later a stewardess passed along the aisle pushing a drink cart. The German fellow ordered a beer; it came out sounding more like 'bier.' The knitting lady requested something called pernod, a drink Doherty'd never heard of. He chose to stay in his own lane by ordering another Jameson straight up. She handed him a glass and a small nip bottle of his favorite elixir. By the time he returned to his book, as if by coincidence, two of the main characters were sitting at a café in Paris drinking several rounds of the same pernod drink as the knitter next to him.

So far all he could discern from the book was that the fellow named Jake was smitten with this Brett Ashley woman, who likewise had a thing for him. However, she was married to someone else and there were hints that something else made their chances of a relationship ill-fated. Being the excellent writer he was, Hemingway had a way of implying all this without making the story come off as a soap opera. Before finishing his Jameson Doherty began to nod off.

He was awakened about an hour later as a full dinner was being served including free glasses of wine. Doherty chose the beef over the chicken entrée and was handed a small tray with each helping consigned to its own little niche. He had a hard time manipulating the small utensils as well as opening the tiny packets of salt and pepper. The food itself was acceptable and eating it helped pass the time. After two glasses of wine on top of the Jamesons he was feeling a lot more comfortable about flying at 30,000 feet over the world's second largest ocean. The French woman next to him did little more than nibble at her food. Instead she lit up an acrid smelling cigarette that she'd pulled out of a cardboard box with the name Disque Bleu on it. Fortunately, the oversized German did not spark up an after-dinner cigar. Doherty was pretty sure airlines didn't allow cigar smoking on board, though he wasn't sure about ones going to foreign countries. Dessert came in the form of some sort of apple filled pastry that was accompanied by an equally small cup of black coffee. He found it difficult to manage everything on his tray with his large hands. In the end he was grateful when the attractive brunette stewardess took the whole mess away.

Now he was just waiting for the hours to pass. He tried reading more of the Hemingway book, but found the characters to be nothing more than a bunch of idle Americans drifting around Europe looking for god-knows-what. Basically, they spent most of their time drinking, while the main guy Jake pined after the Lady Brett, who in turn slept with a number of other men including Cohn and a Spanish bullfighter half her age. Robert Cohn, who would regularly reappear throughout the book, turned out to be an obnoxious bore that some of the others attributed to his being Jewish. Doherty didn't like this association since he'd become more familiar with Jews from the war and his work on the Meir Poznansky case. In that investigation he'd even come into contact with some Israeli operatives chasing down ex-Nazis in the U.S.

Sometime around hour three into their ocean crossing he put the book aside and began to map out his plans for after he got to Paris. Once he was settled into his hotel, he would try to contact the Michael Shanahan fellow who worked at the U.S. Embassy. Where he would go from there would depend on the kind of information Shanahan was able to pass on to him. In any case, he would at least pay a visit to the Normandy battlefield sights. It was something he needed to do to honor his fellow soldiers who fought and died there. Maybe when out in Normandy he would be able to scrape up something about John McDonald other than that he was buried there.

He spent some time flipping through the chapter on Paris and other parts of France in the *Europe of Five Dollars a Day* book trying to get a lay of the land. From the city map in it, he could tell that the older sections of the Paris were very densely settled as he suspected a place that old would be. The Normandy beachheads did not look like they were more than a day's journey away. The book mentioned several busses and trains that went there each day from Paris. His plan was to rent a car and drive out to Normandy at his leisure, assuming he could find his way through the French countryside without getting lost.

For the balance of the trip he slept fitfully. Sometime early the next morning he was aroused again when the interior lights were turned on indicating another meal was being served. He checked his watch and saw that they'd been in the air for a little over five hours. The food cart made another journey up and down the aisle distributing something that looked like breakfast. This time his little tray contained a crescent shaped roll he would later learn was a French croissant, a small glass of some orange juice made from concentrate, a cup of yogurt – a substance he'd never eaten before - and a coffee cup that another stewardess following the food cart filled for him. He was glad he didn't take cream or sugar in his coffee, as the little packets they came in would've proven hard to open in this confined space. Sometime later the pilot came on the PA to announce in a laconic English voice that they would be landing at Orly Airport in about an hour. A few minutes later a female voice made roughly the same announcement in French.

As they approached the Paris airport Doherty tried to see if he could spot any Paris landmarks through the plane's small plastic window. As it turned out, Orly was located ten miles south of the city so he wouldn't have been able to see anything notable through the early morning cloud cover. It was a good-sized airport compared to Hillsgrove, though only about half the size of Idlewild. Most of the terminals they passed while taxiing to their destination looked old and pretty shabby – especially in comparison to the Pan Am Worldport in New York. When the plane finally stopped and the interior lights were turned on there was a mad shuffle among the passengers to retrieve their small bags so they could exit the plane as fast as possible. It wasn't long before Doherty understood why as the passport control lines seemed to stretch on forever.

He lit a Camel and used the time he was standing in line to loosen up his back after being folded into a tight airline seat for over seven hours. When he reached the front of the line a stern looking official with a mustache similar to that of General DeGaulle took his passport and looked at it for an inordinate amount of time.

"How long will you be staying in France, Mr. Doherty?" he said in English tinged with a nasally French accent.

"A week, perhaps more. Depends on how I like your country."

"Where will you be staying in Paris?" Doherty gave him the name of his hotel. From the expression on the official's face it was apparent he'd never heard of the Hotel Wetter.

"Your first time in France?"

"No I was here on leave during the war. I was with the American army at the time." Although he wasn't exactly expecting the fellow to thank him for liberating his country, he didn't expect the sullen look he got.

"You are here as a tourist now?"

Not wanting to muddy the waters he said, "Yes, I am here as a tourist."

With nary the trace of a smile the customs officer took a big hand punch and marked Doherty's passport with the entrance stamp. "You may go," he uttered – no welcome to my country or have a pleasant stay – just, "you may go."

The next order of business was to change some of his traveler's checks into French money. He inquired at an information counter where he could do this. The friendly female guide offered him his first French smile before pointing to a money exchange counter nearby. Repeating the process he'd followed at the Centreville Bank, he dated and countersigned two checks and produced his passport. After fingering an adding machine the clerk at the exchange doled out a fistful of large, colorful French bills and some coins. He also handed Doherty a lengthy receipt for the transaction.

In handling his newfound currency, he was surprised at how much larger in size the bills were compared to American greenbacks. Their design was very lavish as well with much brighter colors than his home currency. He didn't recognize most of the faces on the bills but could tell from their familiar names that they weren't all political figures like the dead presidents that emblazoned American money. Shoving the oversized cash into his wallet he went off in search of the area where he could retrieve his valise. Like everything else at Orly Airport, locating his bag took an inordinate amount of time. Obviously, the French did not operate at the same fast pace as Americans. He passed through one more customs check where his bag tag was checked against his ticket. Thankfully they did not ask him to open his valise. Now he was officially on his own in France. He followed the signs that said taxis. It was his good fortune that the French word for taxi was the same as at home. Once again, he found himself in a line, though this one moved more rapidly than the custom's checkpoints.

Within minutes a burly fellow wearing a beret took his valise and tossed it into the trunk of his small cab. Doherty handed him a slip of paper with the name and address of his hotel on it.

The man laughed. "Ah, Le Quartier Latin." The cabbie zipped out of their parking space and wove his small vehicle both left and right around double-parked vehicles and stalled traffic. This was going to be a trip worth remembering.

"Etes-vous Anglaise?"

"American."

"American. Ah, I like Americans. Very generous people, no."

Doherty didn't know what to answer so he kept to himself. He thought the cabbie said this to gin up his tip. The guy continued to weave through traffic with reckless abandon. There didn't appear to be many stoplights in the city, so every intersection was an every-man-for-himself confrontation. Most of the cars seemed like miniatures from go-cart tracks compared to the much larger vehicles driven back home. Twenty minutes into this demolition derby cab ride they passed into the old city, the Paris Doherty had always seen on travel posters. There appeared to be at least a half dozen open-air cafes on every block with people sitting outside despite the chilly temperatures.

As they approached the center of the old city the streets grew narrower, which was occasion for his cabbie to lean on the horn whenever a small truck or another car blocked his way. They soon turned into a warren of even narrower streets where it would have been impossible for two vehicles coming in opposite directions to get by one another. Many of the buildings lining the street looked like they were built before the United States was a country. Halfway up one of these paved entirely of cobblestones the driver stopped the cab. He turned to Doherty and said, "Hotel Wetter."

He looked out the window at a small sign plastered on the front of a building that very easily could have passed for someone's home. The cabbie spit out a number in French and Doherty paid the fare adding a modest tip. Perhaps it should have been more substantial given that the driver had taken him on a hair-raising ride without killing anyone. When the cab pulled away, he stood on the narrow sidewalk giving the hotel and the narrow street a good going over. The place certainly wasn't anything fancy. Since B.W. Royal was paying for his stay who was he to complain.

Chapter Fifteen

The entrance to the hotel was through a doorway just wide enough for Doherty and his valise. A desk clerk was leaning on a counter reading a newspaper with a cigarette dangling from the corner of his mouth. His longish hair hung down over his forehead. He looked to be about thirty and from his pale complexion apparently didn't spend much time outdoors.

"Bon jour," Doherty said in a weak attempt to act like a native.

"You have a reservation?" the man asked in a disinterested tone.

"Yes, the name is Doherty," he said waving his passport under the guy's nose. "I believe I have a room booked for three nights."

The clerk casually examined a large book that rested on the counter in front of him.

"Mais qui. You are to be in room 234 on the third floor. In Paris the ground floor is the premier étage, the second is the first, and so on," he explained. "You will need help with your baggage?"

"No, I think I can manage. Do you have a key?"

The man handed Doherty a key that looked like one of the skeleton keys he used to play with when he was a kid. It was connected by a small chain to a large piece of wood with the room number on it. "Le petit déjeuner is from 7 to 9 hours in the morning in that room," the clerk said pointing to a shuttered space off the miniscule lobby. "Please, the stairs are to the back. I am sorry we have no elevator at the Hotel Wetter."

Doherty took the key and mounted a narrow staircase. On each landing was small table with a lamp and some dusty antique piece next to it. The walls in the hallways were covered with prints of the French countryside. Judging from the way people were dressed in them, they were obviously from earlier times. The hotel smelled old and musty. Once he found Room 234 he had a little trouble getting the door unlocked.

Inside he detected the same musty smell as in the hallway. The room was small with a single bed, an armoire to hang his clothes in, and an undersized dresser that wouldn't hold much more than his underwear and socks. A small bathroom slightly larger than a walk-in closet had a tub, no shower, a sink, a commode and another fixture that Doherty would later learn was called a bidet. It was intended for washing your lower regions only. All of this was squeezed into a very cramped space that made it difficult for him to even turn around.

In order to let some air into the room he pushed open a window that swung to the side. He was immediately greeted by a magnificent view of the upper towers of the Cathedral Notre Dame. It was easy to recognize as a poster of it had adorned one of his classrooms at St. James school.

After unpacking his valise, he began to feel lightheaded from lack of sleep. He could've crashed out right then but remembered Murray's recommendation that he try to get himself acclimated to Parisian time as soon as he could. Instead of sleeping he picked up the Hemingway book and headed back downstairs. The guy at the desk was working on the same newspaper along with a new cigarette.

"Excuse me, is there somewhere nearby where I can get a quick bite to eat?"

The clerk motioned with his cigarette hand. "Just down the street there is a café. If you want something more, you will have to walk over to Place St-Michel." He said this last part without indicating where Place St-Michel was located.

"Do you happen to have small map of the city? I wouldn't want to get lost on my first day in Paris."

The clerk reached under the counter and pulled out a colored map of

Paris. With a pen he circled the small street where the hotel was located. Doherty thanked him though the guy had already gone back to his paper.

It was colder outside than Doherty expected it to be, so he belted up his trench coat and pulled his hat down low. Out on the street he noticed many Frenchmen went hatless though almost all of them wore scarves around their necks. Most of the women were young and well dressed. It sure didn't feel like Main Street in Arctic. The café was about a block down on the right. It was painted red and had a large awning that stretched almost all the way across the sidewalk to the street. Several tables were lined up outside, but no one was sitting in them. He decided he'd rather be inside out of the cold.

The tables were covered by red tablecloths, a few with noticeable holes in them. He took a seat and tried to make sense of the menu mounted high on the wall above a counter where various coffee machines resided. Naturally all of it was in French. A blond woman wearing tight pants and a long gray sweater that hung down almost to her knees approached his table brandishing a pad and pencil.

"Bon jour, monsieur," she said and then rattled off a whole lot of French he didn't understand.

"No comprends," he said feeling stupid. She smiled at him and let out a little giggle. Her blond hair was tied up into a ponytail in the back while in front it hung down on her forehead in bangs. She looked to be somewhere in her thirties and was very pretty in a French sort of way.

"Parle pas Francaise? You are English maybe."

"How could you tell?"

She smiled. "Monsieur, you are carrying an English novel."

He looked down at the Hemingway book and then back at the girl. "You are very perceptive," he said before he realized she may not've known what perceptive meant. "Actually I'm American, not English."

"It is okay. I speak English some. Perhaps better than you parlez Francaise. Would you like something to eat or drink?"

He looked up at the menu on the wall knowing full well he did not understand most of it.

"Un café, s'il vous plâit." At least he was trying.

"Blanc ou noir?" He knew noir meant black so he stayed with that.

103

"And to eat?" She could tell he was confused by the menu. "What would you eat for le déjeuner at home? Sandwich, soup, omelet – what do you like?"

"I like cheese sandwiches," he said deciding to play it safe.

"Bon. Hot or cold?"

He gave her an uncertain look. "Hot, I suppose."

"I will make you something nice. Are you very hungry?"

"Yes."

"D'accord. I will bring you something you will like. Please to wait. I will get the coffee tout de suite."

While she was gone, Doherty flipped open the Hemingway novel. The crew of wandering expatriates were now in Spain in some town where the fighting bulls ran through the streets chasing drunken Spaniards and foreigners. He found this part interesting since he knew little or nothing about Spain or bullfighting. Hemingway apparently was quite the connoisseur of that blood sport, so his descriptions of it were very moving.

The woman returned with a large cup of black coffee; it was twice the size of the small cup of weak coffee he'd had on the plane.

"My name is Yvonne," she said holding out her hand.

"I am Doherty."

"Doherty? A very strange name for an American."

"It is my surname. My given name is Hugh, but everyone where I live calls me Doherty."

"And mine is St. Pierre, but you can call me Yvonne." They exchanged smiles before she went back to the kitchen. Five minutes later she returned with a plate that had a large piece of French bread with some ham and a lot of melted cheese on it. There was a pile of French fries accompanying the sandwich.

"What is this called?"

"It is a Croque-monsieur; French for Mr. chop chop," she said smacking her teeth together.

"Aw, Mr. Crunch, my favorite."

Doherty dove into the oversized sandwich. It was just about the best grilled cheese he'd ever had. There was a dressing on the bread that tasted like a mix of mayonnaise and mustard. The fries were cooked to perfection. When

Yvonne saw that Doherty had finished his coffee she returned to the table with a bottle of red wine and a glass.

"You are eating a Croque-monsieur in Paris so you must have some wine with it. Is only right."

"Will you join me?" She looked around. The only other patrons in the café were two old gents who looked like they'd been nursing the same cup of coffee for the last few hours.

"Thank you for asking." She retrieved another glass from behind the counter and took the seat across from him.

"Do you own this café?"

"Non. My papa owns it, but he seldom works anymore. He was injured in the war and cannot be on his feet for long. My husband used to run it with me, but he is now gone."

"I'm sorry. When did he die?"

She laughed but it was not one of amusement. "He is not dead. Some days I pray he was. He left me for another woman. She is younger and prettier than me, but not so smart."

"That's hard to believe. You're awfully pretty yourself."

Instead of thanking him for the compliment she pulled out a pack of cigarettes. He studied the label – they were called Gauloise. She offered him one, but Doherty did not like to smoke while eating. It was a habit Millie St. Jean had broken him of when they were dating.

"Are you here to be a tourist, Monsieur Doherty?"

"Not really, though I hope to spend some time seeing the sights. Mostly I'm here on business."

"Ah so you are a businessman. Maybe importing and exporting, non?"

"Hardly. I'm a private investigator. I've come to France to find someone." He decided to leave his mission purposely vague knowing that offering any more details would make it sound ridiculous.

"A private eye, eh - like Sam Spade in Le Fauchon Maltais?"

"You know that book by Dashiell Hammett?"

"Non, but I know the movie with Humphrey Bogart – I have seen it four times. He wears a trench coat just like yours. I have the poster of it on my bedroom wall upstairs in our apartment. I love Humphrey Bogart – even in

Casablanca. Many French people do not like that movie because it makes us look not so good."

"I happen to be a big movie fan myself. Do they show many American movies here in Paris?"

"Oh yes, very many. The old ones are very popular in the Quartier Latin."

"Are the American movies shown here dubbed in French?" he asked, thinking of the foreign movies he was exposed to at the Avon Cinema in Providence when he was dating Rachel Katz. Most of them had subtitles.

"Some are dubbed, but many have the words on the screen at the bottom. So, we read them in French as the actors speak them in English. What is this book you are reading?"

"It's called *The Sun Also Rises*. It's by Ernest Hemingway. Much of what I've read so far takes place here in Paris in the 1920s."

Yvonne smiled again. "Ah, Hemingway. You know he used to live in this very neighborhood in two or three different places – before I was born. My father remembers seeing him in the cafes and the bars. A big man with a very loud voice. You must go to Shakespeare and Company while you are in Paris."

"What is that?"

"It is a bookstore. Must be the most famous English language bookstore in France if not all of Europe. Your Hemingway, James Joyce, Henry Miller, and many other authors used to visit and even live there sometimes. It was run for a very long time by Madame Sylvia Beach. She brought many English language writers from U.S. and U.K. to Paris. It is one of most famous bookstores in the city. You must go there."

"Do you read books in English?"

She shrugged. "I try but my English reading is not so good. Many words I must look for in a French dictionary, so it takes a long time. It is easier for me to read English books in French translation."

Yvonne poured them each another glass of wine. The two old timers at the other table trundled off leaving the cafe all to them as the afternoon light began to fade.

"What else will you do while in Paris, Monsieur Private Detective?"

"I don't know. I guess I'll visit the usual sights: the Eiffel Tower, the Louvre, Notre Dame. I can see the spires of Notre Dame from my hotel room.

It is quite magnificent."

"I will tell you where else to go, yes."

"Whatever you say. I have a map here so you can circle them on it." He pulled out the folded-up map that he'd tucked inside the Hemingway book and spread it out on the table.

Yvonne leaned forward and studied it closely trying to get her bearings. "Do you like art?"

"I suppose so."

"Then you must go to the Jeu de Paume. It has the most beautiful collection of impressionist art you will ever see. It is here," she said as she circled a building alongside a strip of green called Les Jardins des Tuileries. If you go to Notre Dame you must also visit Sainte-Chapelle; it is here," she said circling a cathedral not far from Notre Dame on the same island in the middle of the River Seine. "You must also go up to the Montmartre – it is a different neighborhood - very famous for the artists who lived there. The famous nightclub Moulin Rouge is in Montmartre, though now only popular for the tourists. While you are there you will see Sacré-Coeur, one of the most beautiful churches in all of France.

"From this cafe you can walk up the Boulevard St-Michel to the Jardins du Luxembourg," she said as she drew more lines and circles on his map. "It is a very nice place to take a rest. Very beautiful flowers, though not so much this early in the spring. And as much as you can, Monsieur Doherty, you must walk along the banks of the Seine to see the many lovers embracing there." Doherty didn't know what Yvonne meant by this last remark and decided not to pursue it.

Chapter Sixteen

After leaving the café Doherty returned to the hotel. He stopped at the check-in desk and asked pale face if he would put through a call for him to the American Embassy. The fellow did so at a leisurely pace while Doherty stood by nervously waiting to take the phone. The guy said a few things in French to whoever answered then handed him the receiver. A female voice on the other end spoke perfect English albeit with a noticeable French accent. He asked if she could put him through to Michael Shanahan's office. The hotel clerk did not appear the least bit interested in his phone call. He was too busy reading a magazine called Paris-Match.

Another woman came on the phone whose English was decidedly American. He asked to speak with Shanahan but was told that he was in a meeting and would be for at least another hour. Doherty gave his name and made an appointment to meet with Shanahan the next morning at eleven. Before hanging up he got the address of the embassy. When he asked the clerk to show him where it was, he looked at the address and then circled an area on the map beyond the far end of Tuileries Gardens on the other side of a large open space called Place de la Concorde. It was a good distance from the hotel though Doherty thought a brisk morning walk would give him a chance to see some of the old city.

He hopped up to the room and swapped the Hemingway book for the travel guide and set off in what he thought was the direction of the river. He was already dog-tired and the two glasses of wine at the café hadn't helped. Still using the map he headed north toward the Seine. He'd read in the book how the river divided Paris into the Left and Right banks. The Left Bank where he was staying had a long history of being the more Bohemian section of Paris whereas the Right Bank was historically a wealthier part of the city with broad boulevards and large department stores. In the middle of the Seine were two large islands, Ile de la Cité and Ile St- Louis. Apparently, the cathedral Notre Dame was located on the former.

When he reached the river directly across the water from where he was standing was the backside of Notre Dame. It was by far the largest church he'd ever seen. There were two large towers in its front and a large spire at its center. He walked slowly along its flank on the far side of the river taking in its majesty as he did. There were some fairly large Catholic churches in Rhode Island, even in West Warwick, but Notre Dame dwarfed them all by a long shot. Tour boats and small commercial craft plied the river that ran alongside the cathedral. Crossing over the first bridge he hit, Doherty soon found himself standing in a large plaza directly in front of the church. Statues of what he assumed were saints and apostles lined the edge of the roof and gargoyles with hideous heads stuck out from the upper level. He remembered seeing these gargoyles up close in the Charles Lawton film *The Hunchback of Notre Dame*. He didn't think it was filmed here, though the gargoyles in the movie matched up well with the ones he could see today.

Groups of tourists mingled in the square in front of the church. They were joined by several hawkers flogging guidebooks or their own personal services. Several of them accosted Doherty, pitching multiple languages his way hoping one of them would stick. Dressed in his trench coat and fedora he didn't exactly look like a soft touch American tourist. He rebuffed their entreaties and entered the cathedral on his own. He removed his hat and looked up at the massive interior with its high vaulted arches. He had to admit he'd never seen anything quite so majestic in his life.

His mouth must have been hanging open as he was approached by another tout who immediately launched into an unsolicited description of the history of the building in proper English. Without thinking Doherty handed the man two francs and they were off on a tour. Maybe it was because he liked the fellow's looks or because he spotted Doherty as an English speaker and launched into his spiel without tossing any Spanish, Italian, or heaven forbid, German his way.

His guide explained how it took nearly 200 years for the original cathedral to be completed, how it was plundered during the revolution in 1790 and then restored 23 years later. Like a lot of important sights in Paris, Notre Dame had not been damaged when the Nazis occupied the city in the 1940s. The guide said this was because the Germans wished to preserve much of Paris' art and attractions for their own benefit once the city was under their control. He knew from his wartime briefings that many German soldiers and civilian hangers-on enjoyed their time in Paris and were most reluctant to return to their bombed-out homeland after the allied forces liberated the city.

Without the guide accompanying him, Doherty climbed the bell tower as a way of paying homage to the poor hunchback who inhabited the church before meeting his death at the end of the film by falling from there. Returning to the main floor they circled the nave, the choir area and the sanctuary, paying particular attention to the beautiful rose window in the wall above the main entrance. As part of the tour his guide pointed out various statuary and inscriptions on the walls and in the floor of the cathedral. Doherty eventually dismissed him, though not before handing him another one-franc coin.

He sat for a long time in one of the pews letting the grandeur of the building waft over him. He thought about the countless sculptors, stonemasons, and other workmen who had labored in anonymity for centuries creating this magnificent structure. He knew from his history classes at school that religions of all stripes throughout time had used their belief systems to conquer, persecute, and murder thousands of "non-believers" and those they deemed to be heretics. Still, he had to give them credit for creating some of the most impressive buildings in the world – often in homage to their particular God.

Doherty had been raised in the Irish version of Catholicism in West Warwick. Throughout most of his young life he attended Mass with his mother and sister at the St. James church. His father seldom accompanied them as most Sunday mornings he was sleeping off a hangover. Doherty was educated at St.

James' school adjacent to the church up through the seventh grade before transferring over to the town's public junior high. After being drafted he assumed his expected role of fighting in Italy and Germany. Somewhere along the way his religious beliefs began to die along with many of his fellow GIs. He could never understand how the merciful God he'd been taught about in catechism and his son Jesus could allow such wholesale carnage. Even the splendor of Cathedral Notre Dame could not bring his Catholicism back. Nevertheless, on his way out he put a 50-centime coin in the box near the exit and lit a candle for his dead mother. He did not say a prayer for her; praying was no longer in him.

Outside, free of the smell of frankincense he took in the fresh late afternoon air. He dropped down to walk along the quay that ran close by the river. As Yvonne had said, there were many young people walking arm in arm as well as other strollers walking alone or with a dog on a leash. Paris was a busy city with more people out in the light of day than Doherty was used to. After a while he ascended back to street level and found himself facing a large series of buildings his map told him was the Louvre Museum. He had expected Paris' largest and most famous art museum to be smaller and more contained than the edifice he was now facing.

Too tired to take in any art today, he decided to cross over a wooden pedestrian bridge named the Pont Neuf that took him back to the Left Bank. Meandering along at street level he passed dozens of open-air kiosks where books of various shapes, sizes, and languages were being hawked. In addition there were old magazines, art prints, maps, and artifacts of various quality including just plain junk on display. Elsewhere men were selling movie posters, pictures of famous actors and actresses, many of whom were American, along with phonograph records. What was most surprising was the number of obviously native Parisians who were picking through this material. Interspersed among the book and art print kiosks were vendors selling all manner of tourist trinkets from miniature Eiffel Towers and Notre Dames to prints of the Mona Lisa encased in cheap metal frames.

Feeling lightheaded from lack of sleep he stopped at a busy outdoor café in what he soon learned was Place St-Michel. There was a large fountain in the square with a statue that from the French inscription he was able to identify

St. Michael, or Michel to the French, slaying a dragon. He was familiar with the tale of St. George and the dragon but not St. Michael. He made it a point to look up the statue in his guidebook only to find out the fountain had been built under the rule of Napoleon III as a warning against rebellious locals. Apparently, the dragon was supposed to represent Satan – who Nap III believed the rebels worshipped instead of the Catholic God. For what it was worth the fountain now seemed to serve mostly as a meeting place for young people, many of them students from the nearby universities.

He ordered a double espresso and settled into what he learned was the chief occupation of many denizens of the outdoor cafes in Paris – people watching. For the next hour he sipped the strong coffee, smoked a couple of Camels, and flipped through the guidebook planning how he would spend the following day. He saw that the museum of impressionist art Yvonne had told him about was on the way to the American Embassy. He thought he might stop there prior to his meeting with Shanahan. After that perhaps he would wander over to where the Eiffel Tower was located and climb it if he was equal to the task. It was, of course, Paris' number one tourist attraction. But what the hell, he was a tourist himself who might never have a chance to return to this city. As twilight turned into nighttime, lights went on all over the square. He could even see that the Cathedral Notre Dame was now bathed by spotlights.

He left the café and wandered up the Boulevard St.-Michel passing numerous small shops and take-out food counters. He came to an intersection where it was crossed by another large street called the Boulevard St-Germain. He turned left on that and walked several blocks in what he thought was the direction of his hotel. Hunger overcame him along the way so he stopped into a small restaurant that had a menu posted on a sign outside that said Prix Fixe. Using the food glossary in the back of his guidebook he was able to translate it. The set menu consisted of some kind of soup, steak with fries, a vegetable, and dessert. It all came with a complimentary carafe of wine. At twenty francs it seemed like a bargain.

The soup turned out to be lentil and the steak was thin and a little tough, but the fries were excellent as they'd been at Yvonne's café. The vegetable was a small lump of something that tasted like squashed eggplant with some other herbs thrown in. It was tasty but not very appealing to Doherty's palate.

After two forkfuls he pushed it aside. A generous piece of the wonderful French bread with butter accompanied the meal. His waiter was very efficient and unobtrusive. After gobbling down the fruit tart dessert with a cup of coffee Doherty waited patiently for his check. Although the restaurant was only three quarters full no one approached his table until he finally signaled the waiter by making a writing sign with his hands. He remembered reading that French waiters never brought the check unless it was asked for. As a result if a customer chose to, he could sit at a table in a French eating establishment until it closed.

Using his map Doherty made his way with some difficulty back to the Hotel Wetter. A different, dark skinned man was behind the desk when he asked for his key. This fellow was much friendlier than pale face. In broken English he reminded Doherty that the petit déjeuner was served between 7 and 9 in the morning. By the time he got up to his room Doherty was so tired he practically fell asleep before getting his clothes off.

Chapter Seventeen

He woke early enough to make the breakfast before everything was cleared away. It was a lavish spread by American standards, consisting of fruit, boiled eggs, a variety of smoked meats, the crescent rolls the French called croissants, and breads and other pastries. He ate hardily and washed it all down with two large cups of dark French coffee. While sipping his coffee he consulted his guidebook and located the art museum Yvonne had suggested he visit. If he stepped on it, he could walk there from the hotel and have an hour or so to look at the paintings before crossing the Place de la Concord to the American Embassy.

After a bracing walk along the left bank of the river Doherty crossed over the Seine on the same wooden pedestrian bridge he had the day before. From there he passed through a large ceremonial arch into a park called the Les Jardins des Tuileries. It wasn't much of a garden, more like an open area park where one could stroll free from the city's noisy traffic. There were a number of outdoor cafés along the way where folks drank coffee in the chilly morning air. The gardens were also lined with numerous benches on which locals sat reading newspapers or just watching the morning walkers.

The museum was housed in a large rectangular stone building that Doherty read had once contained indoor tennis courts, hence the name Jeu de

Paume, which roughly translates in English to "game of palm." He paid six francs at the concession desk and took a small pamphlet with a map of the museum. Fortunately, it was in English. He didn't know much about fine art; it wasn't exactly on the curriculum in the West Warwick schools. The only art museum he'd ever been in was one at the Rhode Island School of Design where his eleventh-grade class was taken on a field trip. They had to write an essay about some piece of art they saw there. He chose a painting of a bunch of people clinging to or falling off a crowded raft in a tempestuous sea. As a joke on the teachers some of his wise guy friends chose to write about statues of naked women.

He had no idea what Yvonne meant when she said this museum had the world's greatest collection of impressionist art. It didn't take long for him to figure out that in this form of painting the artists used heavy brush strokes to create the impression of a scene, rather than depicting the scene itself. He could see clearly what the artists were trying to paint when he stood away from the pictures. However, when he examined them up close, they just looked like a collection of random brush strokes in many different colors. He wondered how an artist standing within an arm's length of a canvas knew what his painting would look like from ten or twenty feet away.

In some of the paintings the colors were magnificent while in others they were dark and brooding. A number of the paintings had plump, well-endowed, nude women in them. Doherty had never seen nudes in paintings before and thought these art works were more erotic than the naked women he'd seen in smut magazines. What struck him most was that except for the portraits of some prominent upper-class people, most of the art was of ordinary people, sitting in cafes or bars, or doing menial labor. A series of paintings of a cathedral at Rouen struck his fancy. They were all painted in a highly impressionistic style from the same view at different times of the day. Although the cathedral itself never changed, the painter's use of color showed it as it passed from daylight into nighttime.

Near the end of his tour he came across two painters whose work were extraordinary in their difference from those of the impressionists. Several in one room were by a Vincent Van Gogh, whose name sounded more Dutch than French. His images were clear but painted with vibrating swirly lines as if the objects themselves were in motion. He wondered if the artist was in a trance or having some kind of hallucination when he painted them.

The other painter whose work really struck him was a guy named Paul Gauguin, who had several early paintings of people in Brittany. Others were brightly colored ones of naked and semi-naked women in a place called Tahiti. From the pamphlet he learned that Tahiti was somewhere in the South Pacific where this fellow Gauguin spent his later years after leaving France. The women looked a bit like American Indians though they wore much less clothing. The world this artist painted was very exotic compared to anything Doherty'd ever seen. He wondered why someone would go to a place like Tahiti especially back in the last century. For now France was strange enough for him.

He sat in this room with these mysterious paintings and read about the museum. Apparently during the Nazi occupation Hitler's right-hand man Hermann Goering made ten trips to Paris to gather up as expensive works of art as he could from museums and the homes of rich Jews who were deported to concentration camps. His plan was for all of these valuable pieces to be transported back to Germany where he and his boss would divvy up the loot. In the end they would make off with hundreds of pieces of priceless art.

While in Paris on leave Doherty had heard about teams of American and French art experts who were poised to go into Germany after the surrender to reclaim much of this stolen art. The French had done their best to squirrel away a lot of their more famous art works before the Nazis came and looted museums like the Louvre and the one he was in. It was a nasty business and the art experts were never sure all the precious works that had been hijacked were retrieved. The Nazis also destroyed a lot of art they thought was either decadent or produced by Jewish artists.

When Doherty stepped outside of the museum all of Paris looked to him like an impressionist painting. He was running a little late, so he hotfooted it across the Place de la Concord, dodging the crazy French drivers as he did. A large obelisk rose up in the center of this busy square – apparently a gift from Egypt in an earlier time. On the far side of the square was Paris' largest street, a boulevard called the Avenue Des Champs-Élysées. At the upper end of this avenue far in the distance he could see the famous Arc De Triumph. One of

France's lowest moments was when the Germans, after taking Paris, hung the Nazi flag from this arch in 1940. He'd seen film footage on the newsreels of this event at the Palace Theatre. The camera scanned the crowds of Parisians watching this event, many with tears streaming down their faces.

The American Embassy was located one street north, parallel to the Champs-Elysees. There were three buildings in the complex. Doherty assumed the one with two fully armed marines standing out front was where official business was conducted. As he approached the entrance one of the marines stepped in his path and asked for his passport. After he flashed his green booklet the soldier stood aside and Doherty passed into the lobby. A young woman with horn-rimmed glasses was sitting at a desk across from the main door. Behind her were an American flag on one side and a French flag on the other. Between the flags was a large photo of President Eisenhower in civvies. In most official photos he'd seen of Ike he was usually in his military uniform with the whole spread of scrambled egg patches and medals arrayed across the left side of his chest. It was odd to see him posing in a plain suit.

Doherty flashed the girl his passport and told her he had a meeting with Michael Shanahan at eleven. She asked him to sign the guest book and then made a call upstairs.

"You may go up, now," she said after she put down the phone. "You'll find Mr. Shanahan's office on the second floor to the left. We don't do things French style here, so the second floor is only one flight up."

Inside the embassy appeared to be like any other office building even if from the outside it looked more like a classic Parisian mansion. He had no trouble finding the office at the end of a long hallway with Shanahan's name in black lettering on an opaque glass door.

Another young woman greeted him, this time a blond with hair that ended in a flip at her neck. She told him he could go right in; Mr. Shanahan was expecting him. As soon as he passed through the door, he was met by a small man with dark hair greased and swept back from his forehead. Shanahan was obviously black Irish like himself and looked like he couldn't have weighed more than 140 pounds. His handshake was firm though his hand was small and soft.

"Glad you could come, Mr. Doherty. So nice to meet you. I got a letter just the other day from Patrick McSweeny singing your praises."

"Well as an Irishman, my uncle Patrick is known for his singing. In this case, however, I'm glad you were the one he was singing to. How did you come to be acquainted with him?"

"Please come and sit down over here." The two men pulled up some comfortable chairs on the side of the room away from Shanahan's cluttered desk. On the wall behind the desk was a copy of a famous painting of Benjamin Franklin, America's first ambassador to France.

"Would you like something to drink? Coffee or perhaps something stronger?"

Shanahan spoke in a clipped manner with bit of a New York accent.

"Coffee would be nice – black please." Shanahan picked up the phone and asked the woman named Betty from the outer office to bring them some coffee.

Shanahan leaned back and spoke in a more unhurried fashion, "I met McSweeny in Washington at the tail end of the war. He was working for the war department and I was with state. I couldn't serve on active duty because I have a bit of a heart murmur. My father was friendly with our congressman, so he was able to wangle me a job in the capital. I was very anxious to do my share as best I could. I'd studied languages at Yale and spoke very good French. After I was sent to England I worked as a liaison with the Free French, whose leaders were still mostly headquartered there. This was before the Normandy landing. I later came over here once we and our allies had cleaned out the Germans. You could say one thing led to another and I stayed on. Married a French girl in '52 and have been working on the reconstruction of France and the rehabilitation of the French people ever since."

"What do you mean by rehabilitation?"

Shanahan took the occasion to light a cigarette. He offered one to Doherty, but he opted for one of his Camels instead. "Well you know the Nazis were here for nearly four years. During that time many French people collaborated with them; most because they were afraid of what would happen to them if they didn't, especially if they were people of some importance. You know, men who were government officials, those connected to important industries, and various businessmen. There were others who did it for self-interest, happy to help the Germans remove certain *undesirables*."

"By undesirables do you mean Jews?"

"Jews, homosexuals, gypsies, communists, you name it. But occasionally just people they had grievances against that had nothing at all to do with politics, religion, or race. It gave them an opportunity to take their neighbors' goods once those neighbors were arrested or deported. Don't get me wrong, Doherty, there are many fine people here, especially now that we're all buddy-buddy with the French. Below the surface, however, there's still a great deal of prejudice among them that the Germans did their best to encourage. I've felt this a lot more when I've gone out to the provinces. Don't forget, in our efforts to liberate France from the Germans, we killed a fair number of French people and destroyed a lot of their property.

"One of my jobs after the war was to help restore property to those people who'd had it taken from them when they fled or were deported. To make matters worse some of this property belonged to Free French soldiers who'd been evacuated to England along with General DeGaulle. When they came back, they often found someone else living in their homes. Like I said it was a difficult time. The people in my department made a lot of enemies as a result of this restoration work. The fact that we Americans were foreigners to the French didn't help. Despite what people in the U.S. saw on the newsreels, not all Frenchmen greeted us as liberators. A lot of that heroism stuff shown back home was primarily for domestic consumption."

"How do things stand now between us and the Frenchies?"

Shanahan shook his head. "Things were going along fine until about five years ago. That's when the Cold War between us and the Russians began to heat up. For a while now the French have been lukewarm about playing a big a role in our undeclared conflict with the Soviet Union. Part of it is that they've seen two world wars fought on their soil and they're not particularly anxious to see another one. Many Frenchmen rightfully saw that the Germans were defeated, to a great extent, by the Russians. There's always been this curious historical bond between the French and the Russians going back to the time of the Czars. Adding to that is the fact that there's a pretty strong Communist Party here in France. Communism isn't outlawed over here like it is at home. Many Frenchmen don't see the Soviet threat on quite the same terms as we do.

Leaders like DeGaulle want to see France play the role as a third force in the conflict between the east and the west."

"I assume that means these folks don't see communist boogeymen under their beds like folks at home do. I appreciate your providing me with all this background info. Can we put politics aside for the time being to talk about why I'm here and what you can do to help me?"

"Sure." At that moment the young woman named Betty appeared carrying a tray of coffee cups. Shanahan took his with some foamy milk on top. A plate of crunchy pastries accompanied the drinks.

"This may sound kind of loopy, but I've been hired to go out to Normandy to find a dead soldier who's buried in the American cemetery there."

Shanahan smiled over the rim of his coffee cup. "You're right, it does sound like a strange reason for someone to pay you to come all the way to France. The list of American soldiers buried at Normandy is in the public records. Maybe you should give me some more details."

Doherty spent the next fifteen minutes describing the mission the Royal family had hired him to undertake, leaving out only the details about their unpleasant family dynamics. All the while Shanahan shook his head in wonderment.

"How exactly can I assist you in this quest?"

"Well I was hoping you might know someone out in Normandy who could help me find my way around out there. Preferably a person who speaks English as well as French."

Shanahan spent a few moments considering Doherty's request. "I do know a man who I think is stationed out in Rouen that might be of help. His name is Walter Bogdanovich; he's a captain in the U.S. Army. Last time I saw him he was working with the Economic Cooperation Administration on a variety of reconstruction projects in Normandy and Brittany."

"What is this Economic Cooperation Administration?"

"It's the agency that directs programs under what used to be called the Marshall Plan."

"I didn't know the Marshall Plan was still in operation."

"Well, we no longer refer to it by that name. But you have to understand something, Mr. Doherty. Although it takes only a short time to destroy things in war, it takes years to rebuild them afterwards. I'll try to reach the captain by phone this afternoon. If I can't get ahold of him, I'll send him a telex to let him know you'll be coming out his way. Do you have any idea when you'll be heading to Normandy?"

"Right now I'm planning to leave Paris on Monday. In the meantime I could use your help in scraping up any more information you can about this dead soldier."

Doherty reached into his suit jacket and took out the official papers on John McDonald Mrs. Royal had given him. "I can lend you these if they'll help. The dead guy's wife would like them back when you're done."

"No problem. Is there anything else you need?"

"I can't think of anything right now. If I do, I'll call your office before I leave Paris. Like I said I'll be here at least until Monday."

"How do you plan on getting out to Normandy?"

"Either by train or maybe I'll rent a car."

Shanahan gave him a concerning look. "Renting a car over here can be a huge pain in the neck. Especially if you don't have an International Driver's License, which I have a hunch you don't. I can requisition a car for you from the embassy motor pool. Hardly anyone stationed at the embassy uses one of our cars unless they have to go out on official business. On a daily basis most of the employees who live here in the city take the Metro. Or else if they live outside of town like I do they drive their own cars. For the most part our cars just sit in the lot collecting dust. I'll have my secretary put together the necessary papers that will make your usage of one of the embassy's cars sound official. That way you won't have any trouble if you get stopped by the police. Without a car you'd find it pretty hard getting around Normandy."

Shanahan stood up at this point. "I don't mean to rush you, but I have a meeting across the courtyard in ten minutes and I need to relieve myself beforehand. Give me the name and phone number of your hotel so I can call you when I get some information."

Doherty wrote down the necessary address and phone number for the Hotel Wetter. Shanahan looked at the note. "Wetter, huh. Never heard of it."

"I believe it's in an area called the Latin Quarter."

This brought a smile to Shanahan's face. "You better be careful over there. The Latin Quarter is a favorite spot for some of Paris's cleverest pick-pockets. By the way, you never told me what Patrick McSweeny is up to these days."

"He's acting as one of the finance chairmen of the Kennedy-for-President campaign. Works out of their headquarters in Boston."

"Wow, the Kennedy-for-President campaign. Do you think our boy has a chance of winning?"

"Right now, I'd say it's fifty-fifty."

"Spoken like a true diplomat. Perhaps you should think of pursuing a career with the diplomatic corps."

He shook his head. "I don't think so. I'm too much of a small-town guy." The two men shook hands before Doherty left. He liked Mike Shanahan but did not envy him his work over here in France.

Chapter Eighteen

After leaving the embassy Doherty found his way across the Place de la Concorde without getting hit by one of the French drivers who zipped around the broad plaza as if they were in the La Mans speed race. He could see the Eiffel Tower on the other side of the river and thought it would be a short walk. The sun was out for a change and the temperature had climbed up at least ten degrees since the day before. He saw a couple of thermometers along the way, but since they only measured it on the Celsius scale, he had no idea how warm it really was.

He sat on a bench on the other side of the river in front of a large building complex called Les Invalides. Flipping through his guidebook he discovered that this was originally a soldier's home where injured, sick, and old soldiers could live out their final days in peace. Somewhere in this building was the tomb of Napoleon that Doherty promised himself he would visit after climbing the Eiffel Tower. The book also informed him that the Place de la Concorde was where the revolutionaries had cut off the heads of King Louis XVI as well as that of his young bride Marie Antoinette, setting off the Reign of Terror. The king and queen were not alone as the uniquely French killing machine, the guillotine, severed the heads of many French aristocrats deemed to be enemies of the people. Nowadays the French apparently did all their killing there with their cars.

Once he reached the plaza where the Eiffel Tower rose high above him, he was assaulted by a gaggle of hucksters like the ones who'd approached him outside of Notre Dame. He ignored all of their multi-language pitches and quickly made his way to the long line of visitors, intent on climbing the stairs to the top or ascending via a rickety elevator. When he saw that people were being packed into the lift like sardines into a can, Doherty opted to take the winding staircase to the top. It was a 1700 step climb just to the third floor. About halfway up he had to stop to catch his breath. Perhaps it was time for him to rethink his two-pack a day Camel habit. Nevertheless, he pushed on to the observation platform at the third floor that provided a spectacular view of the city. He might've taken the elevator all the way to the top, but the line was still too long. His burning lungs made any further climbing out of the question. After admiring the views from all sides he prudently opted to take the lift for the descent.

Once on solid ground he retraced his steps back in the direction of Les Invalides. Along the way he stopped at a café for a ham and cheese sandwich on their delicious bread and another cup of café noir. He was starting to feel a little more comfortable throwing around his pedestrian French.

Still a hero to many Frenchmen, Napoleon had at one time conquered most of Europe and some outlying countries as well. Then he ceremoniously crowned himself emperor. His tomb was housed in a building that had a grand collection of French armaments going all the way back to medieval times. There was a large array of armored suits as well as hand weapons of all shapes, sizes, and killing capacities. Further on there were firing weapons from primitive musket loaders through to more sophisticated gunnery pieces. In the end none of them prevented Napoleon from being soundly defeated at Waterloo. Nor later did more complex and efficient killing machines save the French from taking horrendous casualties in the trench warfare in the First World War or allow them to repel the Nazi invasion in the second one. Weaponry was sometimes no match against opponents with massive numbers of men willing to fight and die for their cause, no matter how ugly that cause might be.

Napoleon's tomb was the centerpiece under the dome of one of the two churches on the grounds of Les Invalides. It was protected by six coffins, one inside the other. The outside one was gigantic and made out of red quartz. Along the walls in this circular space were statues symbolizing Napoleon's conquests throughout Europe and parts of the Middle East. It was all a curious tribute to France's dictatorial emperor whose career ended in ignominious defeat and exile. Given France's military humiliations in the twentieth century, perhaps it was fitting that they would have a nostalgic longing for that single moment in history when France dominated the continent.

He bid farewell to the dead emperor and started the long walk back to the area where his hotel was located. Along the way he could not help but think of the fellow everyone called Napoleon, who used to live in an apartment above him with his fat wife Peaches on Crossen Street in West Warwick. Napoleon was not his real name, but everyone called him that because he was short. One weekend he'd taken off with Peaches' slenderer and more attractive sister. Doherty was hired by the wife to find her lost husband and convince him to return to her plump arms. After some persuasion the man did return of his own free will. It struck Doherty as strange that he would be jokingly referred to as Napoleon by so many of his acquaintances simply because of his size, when the real Napoleon was a man of enormous ambition, who, despite his size, ruled over a great deal of the western world.

Doherty wandered slowly along the Left Bank of the river. There were many more people camped out on the quays enjoying the sunshine and the pleasant spring temperatures. He mused about someday strolling along the Seine with Nina on his arm. He passed by a large train station obviously built in another era. It was called the Gare D'Orsay and had an enormous glass and strut roof that brought sunshine into the building. He ventured in to see the interior's glow. Hundreds of people were milling about, some in haste to catch a train while others were disembarking from ones that had already arrived.

To rest his weary dogs, he sat at a café inside the pavilion, ordered a beer, and wrote out a postcard to Nina that he'd purchased earlier at one of the kiosks along the river. He didn't bother to ask for a specific brand of beer and the waiter never offered him a choice. In time a small glass arrived holding some tepid suds. Still it was nice to take a load off after walking so many city blocks. He read in his guidebook that this station was only one of the several that took travelers out of Paris in all directions depending on where they were located. The Gare D'Orsay was primarily for passengers going south as far as Marseilles and the French Riviera. He wondered if this was the station where Ilsa Lund left Rick Blaine standing in the rain in the movie *Casablanca*.

After leaving the Gare D'Orsay Doherty ambled along some of the narrow backstreets of the St. Germain neighborhood until he came to the broad boulevard which bore that name. From there he had no trouble finding his way back to the area where his hotel was located. Heeding Shanahan's warning about pickpockets in the Latin Quarter, he found himself repeatedly touching his inside pocket of his jacket where he kept his wallet and passport. It was a strange sensation for as far as he could recall no one had ever had their pockets picked in West Warwick.

Passing by Yvonne's café en route to the hotel he saw her through the large window facing the street. She was wiping down tables as there were no patrons in the place at this late afternoon hour. He peaked in to see if she had a few moments to talk. She gave him her welcoming smile and waved him inside. After he crossed over the doorway, she flipped a sign facing the street that said *Ferme'*. From his limited knowledge of French he was aware that she'd just closed the café for the day.

"You look very tired, my friend. Have you been out sightseeing today?"

Doherty took a seat and watched as Yvonne put the final touches on locking up her café.

"Yes. I saw many sights and also did some business at the American Embassy. This is a rather remarkable city to walk around in."

"As remarkable as New York? I would so like to go there someday."

Doherty had to laugh at himself. "To be honest with you, Yvonne, I've never been to New York. In fact, I've hardly ever been anywhere, even in the U.S."

She went behind the bar and soon returned to his table with a bottle of red wine and two glasses. She poured each of them a healthy amount. "Tell me about your day, Mr. Private Eye."

He gave her a detailed a rundown of his trek around Paris and the various sights he'd seen. She interrupted occasionally to ask questions or to get his impressions of the places he'd visited. It was nice to have someone he could talk to since just about everyone else he dealt with here, except for Mike Sha-nahan, spoke nothing but French. When their glasses were empty, she poured some more wine. It was just what he needed after a long day of touring around Paris. Some lovely music was playing on a phonograph near the cash register. A woman was singing in French, and although Doherty could not understand what she was saying, her voice was quite beautiful.

"Who is this singing? It's quite nice."

"Her name is Françoise Hardy. She is new and very young. Do you know what she is saying?"

"Not really."

"She mostly sings of love. But sad love. France is all about love – even sad love. Is not the same with music in the U.S.?"

"It was but now most of the popular music at home is rock and roll; teen-age music. About dancing and driving cars very fast. I prefer older music. Songs by people like Frank Sinatra and Ella Fitzgerald."

"Oui. They are very popular here too, but not so much among the young. I am thirty-six, so I am, how you say, captured in between. My son likes this rock and roll music - French as well as American."

"You have a son?"

"Mais qui. Julian. He is fourteen and goes to a school where the students live. My husband did not want him to grow up living above a café in the Quartier Latin. He pays for the school. His new wife's family has much money so they can send him there. I don't argue because it is a good school near Lyon. Julian comes to Paris often. He so loves my papa."

"And your mother?"

"My mother is dead. She died two years ago from cancer of the breast. My papa has been very sad ever since. My mama was his second wife. His first wife died when she was very young. He is much older than my mama – almost like a grandfather to me. I love him just the same. This has always been his café, but he cannot run it by himself anymore."

They both were quiet for a while letting the sorrowful songs of Francoise Hardy wash over them. More wine was poured and Doherty found himself sliding into a sorrowful mood himself.

"What will you do tonight, my tourist friend? You know there will be much merriment in the streets because it is Saturday. No one in Paris works on Sunday."

"I don't know. Perhaps have a late dinner and go to sleep."

Yvonne slapped Doherty on the arm, though not in an aggressive fashion.

"Then you must come with me tonight. I will show you a part of Paris that is not like any place you have ever been. I will take you to the Montmartre to see things that will astound you. Before that you must come to dinner with my papa and me. Every Saturday night he makes the finest Boeuf Bourguignon you will ever eat. Please will you come?"

"I will on one condition; you must tell me what this Boeuf whatever is."

Yvonne gave him her best knowing smile. "It is a stew with meat. Nothing special except that is made with much wine. And we will drink more with it. My papa is a wonderful cook. You will love him."

"Well, that sounds like an offer I can't refuse. What time should I come to your apartment?"

"Come at seven. The door is just to the right outside of the café. Ring the bell and I will let you in."

After one more glass of wine Doherty returned to the Hotel Wetter. The friendly dark-skinned man was at the desk when he asked for the key. Doherty inquired where he might buy some wine to bring to Yvonne's. The guy directed him to a shop nearby. He decided he needed to take a nap and bathe before taking up the dinner invite.

Chapter Nineteen

It was a half past six when he roused himself from his nap. He immediately cleaned up as best he could with a washcloth and soap, having no time to run a full bath. He then donned some clean casual clothes. It was still somewhat chilly so he wore a sweater under his sports coat, thinking this look would be more French than the suit and trench coat he'd been wearing all day. There was no problem finding the wine shop around the corner. It emitted a wonderful fragrance the moment he walked in. In addition to wine and other liquors, it also sold a variety of different kinds of cheeses, cold cuts, and canned items. In France he learned they call such stores <u>charcuteries</u>. He had no idea what kind of wine to buy so he simply chose a bottle of red with a nice label that was not the cheapest but far from the most expensive.

Yvonne greeted him at the door dressed in a blue and white striped sweater with buttons along one shoulder, tight black pants that ended just below her knees, and flat shoes that looked like ballet slippers. She'd let her hair down so that her blond locks reached well below her shoulders. A small amount of make-up had been added to her already lovely face. When they reached the second floor, she took his arm and escorted him into a parlor where her father was ensconced in an easy chair with a cigarette dangling from his mouth. Wonderful food smells wafted into the room from a nearby kitchen.

She introduced her father to Doherty. His name was Henri with a last name different from hers. He assumed this meant she was still using her ex-husband's second name. Yvonne's father rose uneasily from his chair. He was heavyset and wore suspenders to hold up his baggy pants. Traces of cigarette ash marred the front of his wrinkled white shirt. Although his face drooped with heavy jowls, he had a pleasant smile and greeted Doherty warmly. She wasn't kidding when she described him as being more like a grandfather than father to her.

"My father speaks no English but very much likes Americans. He was a messenger in the First World War running cables between the French and American troops. He worked too with the pigeons that were used to send messages back and forth. He has loved birds ever since – even the ones that shit on our awning from the rooftops," she added with a chuckle. "He would get so mad at my mother for poisoning the pigeons."

The older man said something in French that Doherty did not understand.

"He wants to know if you would like an aperitif. It's a drink before we eat. Maybe a pastis or a pernod?"

"Those are the ones that are licorice flavored, right?"

"Oui, made from anise."

"Do you have any whiskey?" She asked her father and the old man smiled. He trundled over to a cupboard and pulled down an unlabeled bottle with something brown in it. He filled half a juice glass, which he handed to Doherty and made a motion for him to drink. It was whiskey all right. It agreed with him more than any of the liquor made from anise would have. Yvonne and her father had glasses of pernod dissolved in water that produced a murky yellowish green liquid. They clinked glasses and the old man said, "salute."

After some awkward three-way conversation, most of which involved Yvonne's father asking Doherty about his time in the war, while he responded with his own stories of being a messenger in the Great War. In time they made their way to a small table that sat in the kitchen not far from the stove. The apartment was tiny and cramped yet cozy, nonetheless. Art prints lined the walls and each window was decorated with a printed valance. Doherty was getting the sense that the French were much more into decorating the interiors of their homes than Americans. It seemed as if every wall had a piece of art or a mirror on it and every table had a decorative piece sitting atop it. Apparently in France no surface was to go unaccompanied.

Yvonne brought three bowls to the table accompanied by a bottle of white wine. Each bowl was filled with blue-shelled mussels soaking in a broth that emitted a wonderful garlic smell.

"You know this dish, les moules?"

"Yes. At home we call them mussels. When I was young, I used to pick them off the rocks by the beach."

"Muscles, like these?" she asked raising her arms and flexing her biceps. She quickly translated and they all had a good laugh, with her father punctuated his with a deep cough. Yvonne and her father ignored the forks on the table and ate their mussels by using the shell of one as a caliper to pry out the others from their homes. Doherty tried to follow suit. At first, he found this method awkward and kept dropping his prey into the broth. In time he got the knack of it. They each broke off pieces from a long baguette and dipped it into the broth. Meanwhile the bottle of white wine was quickly disappearing. When they finished the mussels, Yvonne cleared the bowls and dumped all the shells into a waste bin.

She handed Doherty the wine he had brought and a corkscrew and asked him to open it. Her father meanwhile smoked a smelly Gauloise cigarette, coughing as he did. He spoke to Doherty in French; he just smiled and nodded his head in return. For all he knew the old man could've been asking him if he was going to screw his daughter after dinner.

Yvonne returned with a large black pot that she set down in the middle of the table. She handed each of them a shallow bowl and ladled a helping of the wonderful smelling stew into each. Doherty poured red wine for everyone and more toasts were made – some in French, some in English and a few in unintelligible guttural sounds her father made. Yvonne's papa would periodically interrupt his dinner to light up another cigarette. Neither Yvonne nor Doherty followed suit. He had broken himself of the habit back when Millie St. Jean told him she thought smoking while eating was poor etiquette. It was not his place, however, to say anything to the old man. He'd already noticed that smoking while eating seemed to be a national pastime in France.

The dinner was delicious. He complimented his two hosts on the fine meal. In turn they complimented him on the wine he'd brought. He smiled and thanked them, not daring to tell them that he bought it simply because he liked the design of the label. When the dinner was completed Doherty helped Yvonne clear the table and clean some of the dishes. She told him not to bother, she would clean the rest up in the morning. Since the café did not open on Sundays, she would have plenty of time then.

Yvonne made coffee, which she brought to the table along with some crunchy pastries. In addition, she set down an after-dinner liqueur in some small fluted glasses. When she lit up a cigarette, he decided it would be okay to spark up a Camel of his own. He offered one of his cigs to the old man who accepted it with a big smile. The Camels certainly were less pungent than the smelly Gauloises the old man had been smoking all evening.

While he and Yvonne drank their coffee and liqueur her father excused himself and returned to his easy chair. Within minutes he was snoring like a foghorn. They both tried to ignore the noise and then broke down in laughter, acknowledging they'd been self-consciously trying to overlook her father's snoring.

"I shouldn't laugh," Doherty said. "I've been told I can snore with the best of them at times."

"By your wife?" He wondered if this was Yvonne's way of poking into his personal life.

"I don't have a wife. I've never been married."

She leaned her head on her cupped hands and gave him a sympathetic smile. "Ah, so sad."

"I don't know. It doesn't sound like your marriage worked out all that well."

She shrugged. "It was good for a time. We were so much in love. Then like a typical Frenchmen he found someone else to be so much in love with. Sometimes I think we French too easily fall in love with being in love."

He didn't know what to say to that and wasn't really interested in going down that road. He looked at his watch. "Are we still going to Montmartre? If so, maybe we should get the show on the road before we've had too much to drink."

"Très bien. Before we do could you please come into my room. I want to show you my Humphrey Bogart poster."

Her bedroom was small, tidy and not particularly feminine. The only hint of a mess were the clothes bursting out of her closet. The poster for the *Le Faucon Maltais* was large and appeared to be an original. Bogart's face dominated the graphic as a sultry, full-bodied Mary Astor in a red dress leaned backwards on a stool in the foreground. The two were given equal billing on the poster. Below them the names of the supporting players Sidney Greenstreet and Peter Lorre along with that of the director John Huston were listed. It was a lovely piece of art. He could see why she took him for a Humphrey Bogart wannabee when he first walked into her café in his trench coat and fedora. He wondered if she was disappointed he wasn't wearing that outfit tonight.

Yvonne emerged from her closet with a scarf and a black beret. She took another scarf, a woolen one, and handed it to Doherty.

"You should take this. It will be cold up at the Montmartre. It was my husband's. It was one of the few things he left behind when he ran off with *her*."

Chapter Twenty

They walked to the Metro at St. Michel where Yvonne led him through the turnstile after dropping fifty-centime pieces into the coin slot for each of them. They took two of the only available seats in a car marked *deuxième classe* as the Metro was quite crowded. It seemed as if everyone in their car was a young person smoking a cigarette. The train made many stops along a red line route before Yvonne grabbed his hand and led him out of the car and onto another train; this one was the blue line. Two stops later they exited onto a platform that was outside rather than underground. The first thing that struck Doherty was the sight of a magnificent church all lit up sitting on a hill high above them. The sight literally took his breath away.

Yvonne stood looking at Doherty, pleased that this vision left her companion dumbfounded.

"That is Sacré-Coeur. She looks down over all of Paris like a maiden aunt. She is most beautiful at night, n'est-ce pas?"

"I have never seen a church so lovely. It doesn't look at all like a cathedral though, more like a wedding cake."

"It is not a cathedral. It is a basilica."

Below the hill the church was perched upon were a series of narrow twisty streets with garish lighting. The area looked a bit like the Latin Quarter only different in some ways. The streets were all paved with cobblestones, which made walking a little difficult.

"Where to now?" he asked Yvonne.

"Come this way. I am taking you to a club like no club you have ever been to, my American friend. Please try not to be too shocked by what you see inside. They call it Le Chat Noir. Do you know what that means?"

"Yes. The Black Cat."

She took his arm. "Come this way." She led him down a wide street with much traffic. Up ahead a large crowd was gathered on the sidewalk.

"What's going on over there?"

"That is Le Moulin Rouge. It is very famous club but much too touristic now. Many know of it because of the posters by Toulouse-Lautrec and the American movie. It is no longer authentic like Le Chat Noir."

Yvonne led him down a narrow alley where a small neon sign of a cat surrounded the words Le Chat Noir indicated the club's entrance. They descended a flight of steps and pushed through a red door that opened into a large, smoke filled room. Inside were the sounds of gaiety along with jazz like music playing somewhere in the background. Doherty craned his head in all directions taking in this Parisian underground establishment. It reminded him of a folk club called the Café Medici that Rachel Katz had taken him to on the East Side of Providence. This place had more smoke and French was the language of choice. A waiter escorted them to a table off to one side, far enough from the band so they could talk, but not so far that they wouldn't be able to see the acts that would soon appear on the small stage.

Before leaving the waiter asked Yvonne what they would like to drink, or so Doherty assumed. She asked for two absinthes.

"I don't know what that is," he said.

"It is like nothing else you have ever drunk. It is made with anise too, but we will put it into water so you can drink it. If it is good absinthe it will make you feel most high."

"High like from marijuana?"

Yvonne gave him a knowing smile. "You have smoked marijuana?"

"Yeah, a time or two."

"Absinthe is more like hashish. That is what the French smoke. But only when the police are not around."

The drinks arrived in two shot glasses. Much to Doherty's amazement, the liquor was green. Two tall glasses of water accompanied them. Yvonne tossed her absinthe into the water and suggested that he do the same. Like the pernods she and her father had drunk earlier, the absinthe dissolved into a milky substance. Still, when he tasted it the anise flavor was quite prominent.

A minute later a spotlight clicked on the now darkened stage and a small man in a tuxedo came to the microphone. His dark hair glistened so brightly under the light it looked like it had been painted onto his scalp. He had a thin mustache and spoke very rapidly in French. Whatever he was saying drew much laughter from the crowd. Yvonne leaned in his direction and told Doherty he was telling many jokes about sex.

The MC's monologue gave Doherty a chance to scan the room. A couple of jovial fat men were seated near the stage with two scantily clad women with lots of makeup sitting on their laps. The four of them were laughing boisterously. Behind them sat a couple of young men holding hands with each other atop the table. Young bohemian types sat at the tables further back casually smoking their cigarettes and talking through the monologue. More women wearing a great deal of rouge and lipstick occupied some stools at a small half round bar near the back of the room. Standing beside them were two large men in dark suits with greasy hair. They looked like gangsters. Behind them in a dark corner two women were kissing very amorously. Doherty had never witnessed such an exotic crowd before.

The MC finished his off-color monologue and introduced a small band at the corner of the stage. The trio consisted of a skinny man wearing an equally skinny tie playing a violin, a sallow looking fellow playing a gypsy sounding tune on an electric guitar, and a tall black man with a mustache and goatee strumming a stand-up bass. The music had a nice bounce to it and Doherty found himself tapping his toes along with it.

"What is this music?" he asked Yvonne.

"It is the music of the Manouche Romani. Made famous in Paris by Django Rheinhardt and Stephen Grappelli."

"What are the Romani?"

"I think in English they are what you call the gypsies. Gitane in French.

This is a special kind of jazz music to you, non?" Doherty was a fan of more traditional jazz, though he had to admit he liked the beat of this music. The three bottles of wine at dinner, the absinthe, and the company of a beautiful woman certainly enhanced his mood.

Soon the stage went dark again and some soft mood lighting came on. A thin but well-proportioned man in a sailor's outfit began to dance around the stage. In time a very attractive young woman in a short dress and no shoes joined him. She had very long hair tied back in a ponytail that hung down her back to her waist. She cavorted about the stage while casting innocent looks and gestures toward the crowd. The sailor boy approached her with a menacing smile and pulled her cruelly toward him. He held her tightly until the music grew darker and then he threw her violently across the stage. Approaching to retrieve her, he once again pulled her into a strong embrace. Then just before their lips met, he spun her around and again hurled her violently to the ground. Each time she hit the floor the audience broke into cheers. There was something very sadistic about the dance, though also mesmerizing as she returned time and again for more punishment at his hands. Her legs were bare and occasionally one could spot her underwear under the short dress. No words were ever spoken between them. At the end of their routine he picked her up into his arms and carried her off the stage. The crowd gave them a loud ovation. They returned, holding hands and bowed deeply. Many patrons, including the fat men in front of the stage, threw flowers at them in appreciation.

The next act was a mime, one of Doherty's least favorite forms of entertainment. He'd seen clips of the famous mime Marcel Marceau and may have seen him or someone like him do a mime routine on the Ed Sullivan Show. Using this act as an excuse, he told Yvonne he needed to visit the men's room. He asked the bartender for the "toilette" and the man stuck his thumb out over his right shoulder. The washroom was cramped, and he had to squeeze his way to the urinals, several times uttering "pardon" as he did. When he looked in the mirror that lined the wall above the urinals, he saw the reflection of two young, pretty faced men embracing against the opposite wall. Doherty returned his attention to his business at hand. On the way out he couldn't help but notice that one of the pretty boys had slipped his hand down the front of the other boy's trousers.

While he was gone Yvonne had ordered them two more glasses of absinthe. These, combined with the alcohol they'd had with dinner, were starting to go to his head. But it did not distract him from the next act, which was a line of can-can girls doing the traditional cabaret number but with a lot of obviously planned mishaps. In mid-act Doherty realized that the dancers were actually men dressed in traditional female can-can outfits. The crowd loved it and the dancers played to them, often flipping up their dresses to show their manhood bulges and to the crowd. The audience was clearly becoming drunker and rowdier. Yvonne was having a gay old time and kept flashing smiles Doherty's way. She was taking great pleasure in his obvious discomfort.

After this act finished the MC returned to the stage. From what Doherty could infer there would be an intermission from the show while the band played dance music. Without much prompting a large number of people in various forms of coupling hit the small dance floor where they could do little more than shuffle around in one spot while bumping into each other. He took this occasion to make a trip to the bar to get himself a beer. The absinthes had made him a bit wobbly; he thought a beer might help him regain his equilibrium. He didn't notice the two disheveled characters at the end of the bar giving him a hairy look when he peeled some francs to pay the barman from the fat roll of bills he was carrying.

Returning to the table he saw a slimy looking fellow holding Yvonne tightly by the arm trying to induce her onto the dance floor. She was resisting as politely as she could. Doherty put a strong hand on the fellow's shoulder and indicated without saying a word that the guy should get lost. Their unwanted guest leaned close enough for Doherty to smell the liquor on his breath. He blathered something in French at him; Doherty had no idea what he was saying. To relieve the tension between the two men Yvonne dragged Doherty onto the dance floor.

"I don't dance very well," he said with an apologetic chuckle.

She shook her head. "It does not matter. There is only small room to move anyway."

"Who was your friend back there?"

"He is a nobody. A drunk only. But he is friends with those two by the bar in the dark suits. They are, how you say, gangsters. Bad men who deal in

138

contraband goods. They make much money on the black market. Stay away from them. They can be dangerous – even to you, Mr. Sam Spade."

On the dance floor Doherty held Yvonne for the first time. Although she was light on her feet, she was substantial to hold. When the band played a slow number, the crowd thinned out and she rested her head on his chest as they shuffled around the floor. Over her shoulder he could see the man who'd been pestering her conversing with the two suits. Although he was pretty drunk Doherty's antenna was up in case there was some trouble down the line.

After they returned to their table the MC reappeared on the stage. With much enthusiasm he began to prepare the crowd for the headline act. The only words Doherty could pick up from his intro were "Negro" and "America." The lights then went almost dark save for a lone spot that focused on the center of the stage. The band broke into an up-tempo tune and a woman pranced into the light holding two large white feathery fans that hid all of her except for her head and feet.

The crowd went wild, stomping and cheering as this single woman slowly twirled her way across the stage, each time positioning her fans so that no parts of her body were revealed to the audience. She was a light skinned Negress wearing a headband with white feathers that matched the ones she was holding. A golden chain necklace surrounded her exposed neck and gold high-heeled slippers covered her feet. Her erotic dance drew an enthusiastic response from the crowd. She smiled from a highly made-up face set off by bright red lipstick. The music soon turned as sultry as the performer's moves. As she pranced about the stage skillfully waving her feathery fans in time to the music, in subtle ways it became clear that her headband and shoes were the sum total of her clothing.

Doherty glanced at Yvonne who flashed him a smile that had a touch of a leer in it. Meanwhile the woman on the stage turned her back to the audience and revealed a well-rounded and completely naked buttocks. The crowd went wild. As she turned, she let one of the fans slip slowly down her front exposing one of her large breasts. The nipple area was quite dark compared to most breasts Doherty'd ever seen. Yvonne reached out and took his hand and gave it a squeeze. It was apparent this act was getting her very excited. As he sipped his beer the performer waved her fans in front of her giving the crowd a quick glimpse of the hairy triangle between her legs. He'd been to strip shows before but had never seen an act quite so artistic as the one this black woman was putting on.

The stage lights brightened ever so slightly revealing two plastic palm trees in the background. The band picked up the tempo once again, mimicking some kind of jungle music. The dancer shimmied more erotically and moved the fans in such a way that with each twirl she flashed more of her naked body. Finally, she turned her back to the crowd, wiggled her abundant, now naked hips furiously, and then in time with a loud crescendo from the band, the stage went dark.

When the house lights came on the crowd was stomping their feet and chanting, "Josie, Josie." She walked back out onto the stage, her front totally covered by the fans and made a deep bow. Dozens of flowers were thrown in her direction. They were quickly gathered up by some bus boys who emerged from the wings. Josie did not reappear for a second curtain call. The MC returned to inform the crowd that the stage show was over.

The band continued to play though many of the patrons began to slowly leave Le Chat Noir. Yvonne finished her third absinthe and suggested they too should depart if they were to catch the Metro back to St. Michel. Doherty swallowed the last of his beer and took her hand as they made their way to the exit. Before leaving the club, he eyeballed the guy at the bar who'd given Yvonne a hard time. He was embroiled in a heated conversation with the two suits giving them nary a glance. Outside the air felt fresh and clean after being in the smoky cabaret. Yvonne took his arm, leaning into him as they stumbled down the cobblestone alley. Doherty's mind was filled with images of the fan dancer's act; it was like nothing he'd ever witnessed before.

A short distance from the main drag two men approached them from the opposite direction and blocked their way. They had been at the bar when Doherty ordered his beer but had barely registered with him until now. One of them was very thin with blonde hair. He was waving a thin stiletto knife in their faces. His white shirt was buttoned to the neck under a black leather jacket. The boy's hand shook as he spoke through clenched teeth. All Doherty could pick up was the word "argent" which he knew meant money.

In an anxious voice the fellow kept saying, "Donne-moi ton argent." His cohort was stockier and wearing an oversized black trench coat. He hung back and didn't say anything.

Yvonne tugged at Doherty's arm. "He wants you to give him some money. Please, we do not want trouble."

He looked hard at the skinny guy with the knife. Despite the cool night air, a noticeable sweat had broken out on his brow. That plus his shaky hands gave him away as a hophead. As Doherty continued to stare at his assailant the guy grew more insistent with each passing second. Doherty raised his hands in a peace gesture and reached inside his jacket pocket where he kept his billfold and passport. He slowly removed some bills from his wallet and held them just far enough away that the thief would have to reach for them. When he did Doherty slapped down on the guy's knife hand with his leather wallet and the blade went clattering to the pavement. When the junkie stooped to pick it up, Doherty kicked him hard in the ribs. Their would-be assailant crumpled to the ground like a paper bag.

Doherty snatched up the knife and turned his attention to the sidekick. Everything had happened so quickly that the buddy was frozen in place. Doherty grabbed him by the throat and smashed his head up against a nearby wall. The fellow blubbered something in French. For good measure Doherty hit him in the gut, then stood over him as he slid down the wall and vomited on his pants.

Yvonne knelt down and examined the one who'd been brandishing the knife. He'd gotten himself up into a sitting position while holding his ribs and moaning. She reached into her handbag and took out her billfold. She slipped a ten-franc note into their assailant's shirt pocket.

"Why did you do that?"

"He is an addict. He needs money only for his fix." She looked up at Doherty. "You should make yourself more careful when you show so much cash in a place like Le Chat Noir. There are thieves and desperate junkies everywhere in the Montmartre."

Doherty didn't know what to make of her gesture. "Let's take a cab back to the hotel. Do you know where we can get one near here?"

"Oui. There are always many taxis near to Le Moulin Rouge."

Chapter Twenty-One

The taxi dropped them in front of the Hotel Wetter. Still feeling flushed with Royal's money Doherty gave the cabbie a generous tip. He and Yvonne stood awkwardly on the sidewalk for a few moments, looking at each other. Despite passing by a lot of loud activity in other parts of the Latin Quarter, it was rather quiet on the narrow street where the hotel and her café were located. She took his arm and said, "Can I stay with you at the hotel tonight? I am much upset about what happened on the street in the Montmartre."

Doherty didn't know what to say so he led her into the lobby without uttering a word one way or another. The dark-skinned man was at the desk listening to something scratchy on a radio. As soon as he saw Yvonne, he came around the desk and kissed her on both cheeks, as was the French style. They conversed in French while Doherty stood idly by, surprised that Yvonne was so friendly with the clerk. After a while she took Doherty's arm and he led her up to his tiny room on the third floor. Once inside he opened the side-swinging window that afforded them a beautiful view of Notre Dame all lit up. She stood beside him and wrapped her arm around his waist.

"You seem very friendly with the boy downstairs."

"Who Ahmed? He comes into the café many times each week. He is from

Algeria. I dated with his cousin for a while. But he was too much of an Arabic lover, so I ended our time together."

"What does 'too much of an Arabic lover' mean?"

"The Arabs always want to control the women they are with. It is how it is in their countries. That is not the way we are here in France."

"So, instead you just invite yourself up to the hotel room of a man you hardly know. Is that how it is in France?" These words came out sounding much harsher than Doherty'd intended.

Yvonne gave him a frown. "If you want, I will go home to my apartment. I just thought you would like my company for the night. After all you did rescue us from some desperados on the street. You should have a reward."

"And the reward is to spend the night with you?"

"Mais oui."

Doherty shook his head, realizing he didn't know at all how things worked in France. He did recall that Nina had more or less given him free rein to follow his heart, or more appropriately that other part of his anatomy, while he was over here.

"I'm sorry. I would be very pleased if you would spend the night with me. This whole day has already been strange enough."

Yvonne slipped into his arms in a tight embrace. "Oui. That is how Mr. Sam Spade would have answered."

Doherty excused himself to go into the small bathroom to wash his teeth and relieve himself. When he returned only soft light filled the room. Yvonne was already in the bed. He stripped down to his skivvies and slid in beside her. She was naked save for a pair of silk underpants. They eased off these last garments and made unquiet love. Yvonne was a most passionate lover; not at all self-conscious like most American girls he'd been with. While he was inside her all Doherty could think about was the Negro woman in the stage show, briefly flashing her nakedness from behind her fans.

After their coupling Yvonne slithered out of bed into the bathroom. He heard water running and knew she was using the bidet as well as the sink. When she returned, she said, "I used your toothbrush. I hope you don't mind." Doherty thought about this for a few seconds. Somehow her using his toothbrush was almost more intimate than them having sex. In time the aperitifs, wine, after dinner liqueur, absinthes, and beer got the better of them and they each fell into a deep sleep. Sometime in the middle of the night, or perhaps early morning, she aroused him again and they made love a second time.

The next thing he knew morning sunlight was filling the room. Yvonne was standing beside the bed slipping into her tight black pants. She was already wearing the striped sweater.

"Where are you going?"

"To my apartment. I always have le petit déjeuner with my father on Sunday. It is our custom."

"He won't mind that you were out all night?"

She sat down on the bed and placed a hand on Doherty's cheek. "I am no longer his little girl. I am a woman as I'm sure you are aware. It will not be the first time I will be out all night - or the last. My papa is French; he understands the amour. He will still be asleep when I get home and not know that I was out to the morning. And if he did, he would not care."

Doherty pulled Yvonne down toward him and kissed her deeply. He could tell she was weighing the option of having sex one more time, then said, "Ah. I must go. I have a favor to ask of you – two favors really."

"Okay, shoot."

"Will you come to Mass with me at Sainte-Chapelle. The small chapel there is most beautiful when the sun is shining in."

Doherty took some time to offer a response. He hadn't been to Mass since his mother died and had more of less broken all ties with the Catholic church of his youth. But this was Paris and he'd wanted to see Sainte-Chapelle. It was already in his mind as a necessary tourist stop, so he agreed.

"What is the other favor?"

"Will you let me take you today to see the real Paris. Places you would never go on your own. I will make it a very good day for you."

"And night?"

Yvonne gave him a sly smile. "Peut-être."

"Then you must do me a favor."

"Oui"

"Let me escort you to a very nice restaurant tonight for dinner. This will be my last night in Paris and you have been so kind to me. It is the least I can do in return."

She gave him a soft slap punctuated by an equally soft kiss. "Come to the apartment in one hour and we will go to Mass."

Doherty took a relaxing bath, shaved, and dropped down to the ground floor to catch a bit of breakfast before swinging by Yvonne's. He pocketed two jam filled croissants from the buffet table to give to her and her father as an offering. Passing through the small lobby on his way up to his room he was interrupted by a new person manning the hotel desk. This one was older and a bit more obsequious than the pale-faced fellow.

"Pardon. Are you Monsieur Doherty?" He said that he was. "There is a message for you." The clerk handed him a folded piece of paper. The note simply said, 'Come see me at the embassy at 10 tomorrow morning.' It was signed M. Shanahan. Doherty slipped it into his pocket, retrieved his sport coat from the room and headed to Yvonne's. It was a beautiful sunny day. Though the air was still somewhat brisk, he decided to go with a sweater under his sport coat and a pair of clean slacks. He even slung Yvonne's ex-husband's scarf around his neck.

Yvonne answered the door with a sweet smile. She wore a print dress of a pale violet design. Her hair was up in a ponytail and she wore only a hint of lipstick. As usual she gave him the two-cheek kiss before ushering him upstairs. He handed her the two croissants wrapped in paper napkins. As a thank you she gave him another soft kiss, this time on his lips.

"My papa is still in bed. He is not feeling so good today. We will have a quick cup of café au lait and then be off to Sainte-Chapelle. If we wait too long the pews will all be filled." Before leaving Yvonne freshened up her face and put a light sweater over her shoulders. She then grabbed a thin, lacy white scarf, which she theatrically threw over her head.

They walked quickly to the river then along the bank past Notre Dame. They crossed near Place St. Michel and soon arrived in the square facing the cathedral Sainte-Chapelle. It was much smaller and less impressive on the outside than Notre Dame, and fortunately had none of the hucksters who latched onto tourists like they did outside Paris' better-known attractions. Once inside the main doors Yvonne took Doherty's hand and led him up a narrow spiral staircase to the upper chapel. For what seemed like the hundredth time in the past few days his mouth dropped at the spectacle before him. The space was narrow with high vaulted ceilings of the gothic style. What really set the small chapel apart from any church he'd ever been in were the incredible stained-glass windows. And with the sun shining through them it gave the space a glow that was almost heavenly.

Doherty had been taught about heaven and hell throughout his parochial school years. He'd been shown many images of each; one being a place where those saved floated with angels and the beloved Jesus on clouds up in the sky. The depictions of hell, on the other hand, were full of graphic scenes showing all manner of human suffering in frightening detail. For the moment the light reflected in those windows at Sainte-Chapelle was as close to his image of heaven as he could imagine. As far as hell was concerned, he'd already seen it in all its gruesome glory during the war.

They squeezed into a small space on the edge of one of the remaining pews. Soon a priest intoned in Latin indicating the Mass was about to begin. Although words of French were occasionally interspersed, the Latin service was very familiar to Doherty from his days at St. James. When the congregants were asked to rise, he rose. When they were expected to kneel in prayer he desisted. One elderly woman sitting near him gave him a nasty look when he failed to slump to his knees. His days of kneeling before God or Jesus or who-ever he was supposed to be praying to had deserted him in the mud at Anzio.

Yvonne had placed her white scarf over her head and pulled it forward as she prayed. He watched her close her eyes and silently move her lips. He wondered if she were asking God's forgiveness for what they had done last night. Then he remembered she was French; only Irish Catholics like himself were raised to think sex outside of marriage was sinful. He didn't think such proscriptions were taken seriously by the French.

When the service was over, they exited by the narrow staircase, took a brief look in at the larger main sanctuary of Sainte-Chapelle and then were out on the street.

"Where to now?"

"Now we will walk for some time to the Marais. It is the oldest part of the city that is still as it was. What did you think of the chapel at Sainte-

Chapelle?"

"It was magnificent. Such wonderful arches and the windows gave it an explosion of colored light."

"It was built by Louis IX to house a once large collection of relics he stole from the emperor at Constantinople. He claimed he had acquired Christ's Crown of Thorns, a sliver from the true cross, and some of Christ's blood. Of course, no one believes that now since Louis was king over a thousand years after Jesus was crucified. I think those who collected relics were just superstitious men who wanted to brag about having such things. Like people who buy priceless paintings to put in their dining rooms where no one else can see them. If all the churches in Europe that claimed they have a piece of the true cross put their pieces together they could build a railroad from here to Moscow."

"I suspect it was their way of attracting travelers in medieval times. Like the art museums do now."

They walked along the opposite side of the river in the direction they had come before turning north into an old part of Paris. Soon they arrived at a large square with a covered walk surrounding it.

"This is the center of the Marais," Yvonne said. "Marais meant marsh, and it was that until one of the kings built this whole structure around us as his Palais Royale. When Louis XIV moved the center of the court to Versailles this area became for commercial use until it fell into a poor state. It was a collection of narrow streets where the revolutionaries built up barricades during their revolt. When Louis Napoleon came to power to get at the revolutionaries, he destroyed many of the old homes and warehouses on the narrow streets. After that the Marais was the Jewish quarter. It remained as that until all the Jews were sent away after the Germans came. There are still many remembrances of the Jewish life around here – but not so many Jews."

They roamed through the Marais for some time, stopping once for a refreshing drink. Yvonne chose to have sparkling water, claiming that her head still hurt from the night before. Doherty had a beer. Heading further north they came to a large and somewhat busy square. The fact that it was Sunday meant that the usual crazy city traffic was quite mild by Parisian standards. Soon she directed his attention to a large, imposing stone building that Doherty thought looked somewhat like an older version of the armory in South Providence.

"Do you know this place?" she asked.

"Can't say that I do."

"in some ways it is where modern France began. It is the Bastille. You know about the Bastille?"

Doherty smiled and gave Yvonne a light squeeze. "Of course, I know what the Bastille is. Along with the Eiffel Tower, D-Day and the Normandy beaches, it is about the only other thing most Americans know about France. And, of course, the Queen who said, 'Let them eat cake.'"

"Ah, Marie Antoinette. She and her husband, Louis XVI, had their heads cut off in the revolution."

"I believe it was in Place de la Concorde, where you can now meet your maker getting hit by a crazy French driver."

After visiting the Bastille, they agreed to stop for lunch at one of the few cafes open on Sunday. Yvonne assured him by the evening most of the eateries in the city would be opened for business. She chose something called a salad Nicoise, while Doherty opted for a ham and cheese omelet. The usual delicious bread arrived along with a carafe of wine Yvonne had ordered. Apparently, her hangover had dissipated. His omelet was, of course, delicious and accompanied by a salad half the size of Yvonne's. He could see that a salad Nicoise was one garnished with tuna, boiled eggs, string beans, and anchovies. She spooned some across the table so he could have a taste. It too was a delight on his palate.

They wandered slowly back in the direction of the river, sometimes holding hands. Sometimes with her taking his arm. An hour into their walk Doherty picked up on a smell that grew much stronger as they approached another square.

"This is Les Halles, the central marketplace for all of Paris," Yvonne said proudly.

"I should've known by the smell."

"If today was not Sunday it would be a madhouse, with all the most delicious and disgusting food smells you could ever imagine. You have places like this in the U.S.?"

He shook his head. "Not where I live. People there buy most of their food at supermarkets. Those are indoor food stores. Some of the bigger cities have these kind of open-air markets, though I think they're now mostly a European thing." Although he did recall the lunch he'd had with his Uncle Patrick recently in the restaurant near Boston's Haymarket. Knowing the French, he figured when fully operating Les Halles would be a much bigger version of that.

"Come with me, I want to take you to one of my favorite places to go on Sunday." She took his hand and dragged him down a narrow street that eventually opened up into another large square, where all kinds of goods were being sold right out on the street.

"What is this?"

"It is a marché aux puces."

"You mean like a flea market?"

"Oui."

As they meandered around the square, he could see that all manner of devices, clothing, military surplus, musical instruments, household goods, books, records, old maps, shoes, boots, scarves, and whatever else you could imagine were on sale. Doherty sidled up to a rack where a variety of men's shirts, pants, coats, jackets, and even ties were hanging. The barker there was filling the air with French words of which Doherty could understand about one out of every twenty. He was fingering a leather bomber jacket when Yvonne came up beside him. He looked at the tag, which said 100 francs.

"You like this jacket?" she asked.

"I think I sort of do," he answered, not exactly sure why. He removed it from the rack and tried it on. It fit well enough though was a mite short in the sleeves. Otherwise it was in good condition. While he was working the zipper up and down, Yvonne engaged the seller in some conversation.

"He says it was worn by a French pilot in the war."

"Did he live or die? No, don't ask him that. I was just being facetious."

"Facetious," she said mispronouncing it. "I do not know this word. How much are you willing to pay?"

"I don't know what things like this are worth here."

"Please wait I will bargain with him." Yvonne launched into a protracted discussion with the vendor about the leather jacket. While she did, he checked all the pockets. Inside one he found the stub of a train ticket to Marseilles. Like his stop at the Gare d'Orsay the day before he took this to be an omen from the movie *Casablanca*.

"He says he will sell it to you for seventy francs. I told him you were a soldier for the Americans during the war. He believes you helped to liberate Paris. I did not tell him something different."

"Then I will give him 70 francs. He peeled the francs from his bankroll and handed over the cash.

They shook hands and the sellers must have said. 'Merci monsieur' at least six times.

After another loop around the flea market square they decided they were tired of walking and made their way back toward the river. Doherty swapped out his sport coat for the heavier leather jacket and wore his new acquisition all the way back to the Hotel Wetter.

Chapter Twenty-Two

Before heading to the restaurant he sat with Yvonne and her father for an aperitif. She and the old man had glasses of Pastis while Doherty chose a shot of the whiskey he had the night before. Yvonne's father seemed distracted and was clearly not feeling very well. Still, it didn't stop him from smoking a couple of his smelly Gauloises with his drink.

She was wearing a simple black dress but with shoes that had a heel to them rather than the flat ballet style slippers from the night before. It was a brisk night so she accompanied her outfit with a jacket with wide shoulders that pinched in at the waist. It was not the type of outerwear you would see women around West Warwick wearing. Her outfit was set off by a small strand of pearls that may or may not have been real. For his part Doherty eschewed the leather jacket and returned to wearing his suit and trench coat. He chose to go hatless since he never knew what to do with his hat in French restaurants, as many of them didn't have cloakrooms.

Yvonne had chosen a place not too far from the hotel and her apartment. It was off the Boulevard St. Germain and just far enough for them to have a nice evening stroll. The place was called Le Procope, which according to Yvonne was one of the oldest restaurants in the city. It had first opened nearly a hundred years before the United States became the United States. Rumor had it that among the luminaries who had dined there were Benjamin Franklin and Napoleon, though not with each other. Yvonne warned him it was a little touristy and fairly expensive. Doherty did not mind the former since he was a tourist himself. As for the latter, he still had quite a bit of Royal's money he was more than happy to toss around.

They were escorted to the second floor – the premier étage to the French - and seated at a table by a window overlooking the street. Since it was a Sunday night the pedestrian traffic was fairly minimal by Parisian standards. Yvonne was looking particularly beautiful tonight so he reached across the table and took her hand. When the waiter came by, she ordered them a bottle of white wine to get started. They perused the menu, though since it was all in French, Doherty couldn't really make heads or tails out of it. The wine arrived and the waiter opened it in a perfunctory manner without the flourish many waiters at home have adopted when serving wine. They drank it slowly while he recounted some of the highlights of his time in Paris. He kept trying to repress the fact that he would be leaving in the morning and might never see this lovely woman again.

She translated the menu for him, telling him that Le Procope was famous for its Coq au Vin. She explained this was a staple French dish of chicken cooked in red wine. They both chose that selection. Doherty opted for the onion soup as an appetizer, while Yvonne ordered *escargot*. When the waiter left, she explained that escargot were snails. In his mind's eye all Doherty could envision were the tiny snails that clung to rocks by the beaches in Rhode Island. They didn't strike him as very appetizing.

They'd nearly finished the first bottle of wine before the first courses arrived. The soup had a cheesy crust on its top and a piece of bread floating in it. It was thick and tasty. Yvonne's snails proved to be rather different from what he expected. They were tucked into large shells, which sat on a plate with sculpted out crevices where each shell rested in pool of garlic butter. The aroma was powerful but not displeasing. She lifted each shell with a claw-like device apparently designed specifically for holding snails. Once she had a grip on each, she used a small fork to extract the snail from inside. It was an intricate process that he found intriguing.

"Would you like to try one?" she asked.

"I don't know. What do they taste like?"

She gave him a quizzical look. "I don't know. They taste like escargot." She then released one of the small mollusks from its resting place, dipped it in the butter, and held it out for him. The snail felt rubbery in his mouth, but the flavoring of the garlic butter overcame any qualms he might've had about eating it.

"What do you think?"

"Interesting. But I think I'll stick with the soup. The cheese and bread floating in it makes it about as exotic as I get with my food." This elicited a laugh from his companion.

In time their main dishes arrived. Before the waiter could depart Yvonne ordered a bottle of red wine. She didn't bother looking at the wine list, just ordered something she was familiar with. The Coq au Vin came in a shallow bowl and was more of a stew-like concoction than any chicken dish Doherty was familiar with. It had bits of carrots and small onions floating in the wine sauce. Like her father's Boeuf Bourguignon it was more substantial than some of the other dishes he'd eaten the last few days in Paris. The food stood in contrast to the elegant décor of the restaurant. Despite her earlier warning, the prices weren't bad either.

They ate slowly, savoring each bite, the ambience, and each other's company.

"Do you come here often?"

She let out a puffing sound. "No, I cannot afford to eat at Le Procope so often. For me it is much too expensive. Tonight, I am your date, so."

He smiled at her and to himself. It was with pleasure that he could take such a beautiful woman out for this nice dinner on B.W. Royal's dime. After consuming only half of her chicken Yvonne admitted she was too full to eat any more. She would confine herself to drinking the wine.

"You could take it home and have it for another meal."

She gave him a stern look. "You do not take food from a French restaurant to your home. It is not done."

He was confused. In Rhode Island he took many a dish home from an eatery to have for lunch or even dinner the following day. "Why not?"

She laughed. "If you ask to do that in a restaurant like this the chef may

153

come out for you with a kitchen knife. In France we believe food is to be eaten when served. Not to be taken home and eaten later in another form. During the war when food was short it was acceptable, but not now. To do so here tonight would be an insult."

He sighed and poured them each another glass of wine. The waiter soon returned to retrieve their plates. And he did not ask if they'd like to take their leftovers home with them. Instead he handed them some small dessert menus.

"I do not want dessert for myself, but perhaps I can have some of yours." From her slurred speech he could tell Yvonne was a little tipsy. He ordered a fruit custard and coffee for both of them. She added two glasses of cognac to that order. He assumed this meant she wasn't so drunk after all. The three arrived at the same time. They alternated between the coffee and cognac, while also passing the small dessert fork back and forth. As with everything else in this meal, the custard was absolutely delicious. Doherty had to hand it to the Frenchies; they sure knew how to cook food well. Eating at restaurants in Paris was a far cry from his basic meat and potatoes fare at home.

They smoked while they sipped the cognac. She asked him some questions about his impending trip out to Normandy. He gave her the same stock answers he had earlier, though the looks that passed between them made it obvious they had other things on their minds. As was the case in all French restaurants, the bill, or l'addition as it was called, was not delivered to their table until they asked for it. Yvonne seemed a little unsteady as they made their way down the staircase to the ground floor and the street.

"Are you going to be able to walk home?"

"Oui. I will be fine. The air will make me more sober. I am not so used to walking with high heels. Because I am on my feet all day at the café, I always wear the flat shoes." There was a slight slur in her speech, but he didn't mind. Doherty wasn't exactly sober himself. He was hoping no thieves would approach them like the two up at Montmartre. He wasn't sure he'd be able to fend them off tonight.

Yvonne did not bother to make a pass at returning to her apartment. She took his arm and accompanied him straight to the Hotel Wetter. The boy Ahmed was at the desk and she conversed with him for a few minutes. Then they walked, though it was more like a stagger, up to the third floor. As soon as they were inside, they embraced and kissed hungrily. The black dress slipped off Yvonne's shoulders without much effort. Doherty dispensed with his suit in no time. He loosened his tie just enough to pull it over his head and removed his shirt in the same fashion. They made love atop the bedspread, not even bothering to slip between the sheets until they were done.

Afterwards they lay on their respective pillows and stared at one another.

"Do you have a sweetheart back home on your little island?"

Doherty wasn't sure how to answer this question. Things between Nina and him had been left pretty much up in the air before he left.

"I don't know if I do right now. I have been with someone for a while, but some events in a case I was working on may've changed that."

Yvonne reached out and touched his face. "Tell me about it."

"It's a long story."

"I am here, not going anywhere. I will listen to your long story."

After a few moments of silence, he gave her an abridged version of how things in the Grimaldi case had played out, including his presence at Doris Donahue's apartment the night she stabbed Brian Willis to death. Yvonne winced when he described how Doris had plunged her kitchen knife into Willis' chest.

"Your girlfriend is not sure of you because you were in this woman's apartment when she killed the dangerous man?"

"There's more to it than that. My presence at the murder scene was all over the news. We live in a small town where stuff like that will be fuel for gossip for months on end. It put my lady friend in a very bad position. On top of that her parents do not like me. They think I'm too old for her and will never ask her to marry me."

"Will you one day ask her to marry you?"

In light of his present circumstance, it took Doherty a few seconds to come up with a good answer. "Well, lying here with you is a good indication that I'm not exactly being faithful to her."

Yvonne shook her head and gave him an uncomfortable smile. "You Americans are always, how you say, always so prudish. Passion is passion and love is love. They do not have to be the same thing."

"I've always had trouble making that distinction – at least until now. It is comforting to know I can sleep with you without offering up a promise of marriage. That's not so easy back home."

"It does not matter. I would not marry you anyway. The man I saw beating those two boys in the Montmartre is scary to me. I love being for a while with a dangerous man. But to marry one…" Once again she let out her puffing sound. "If I marry again the next man will be gentle; the kind of man who is fond of children and animals. Not someone who carries a gun and gets into fistfights."

"I hope that's not the sum total of how you see me."

"I don't know who you are, Doherty. I only know that you are a good lover, and that is all I've needed these past two days." With that they crawled into each other's arms and soon fell dead asleep.

When he awoke in the morning Yvonne was gone. After he cleaned up, he packed his valise, deciding to squeeze his trench coat in with his other clothes. The breakfast room was empty save for one elderly man who was smoking a cigarette and reading a French language newspaper. Doherty ate deliberately, trying as best he could to get his mind past Yvonne and onto the case of the dead soldier he was originally in France to investigate. Before retrieving his bags, he stopped at the desk where Pale Face was at the controls. He told him he'd like to settle up his bill, which only amounted to few incidentals and some taxes as B.W. Royal had paid for his hotel stay in advance. Then Doherty requested that the clerk order him up a taxi in the next hour.

He carefully packed the rest of his goods, putting most of the pertinent notes relating to the case in his briefcase along with the Frommer travel book and the Hemingway novel. Once done he lugged his bags down to the lobby and asked the clerk to store them behind the desk while he ran some errands.

Things were jumping at the café as Yvonne and another, younger girl moved through the tables, chatting with customers and picking up tips. She gave him a sweet smile as he stood by the coffee bar. When she caught a break, she came up to him and they exchanged a two-cheek kiss.

"You are leaving today?"

"I have a cab coming for me in twenty minutes. I wanted to return this to you," he said holding out her ex-husband's scarf.

She smiled. "Please, you keep it. He will never come back for it. Let it be something to remind you of me." They stared at each other for a few moments.

"I guess we'll always have Paris."

Yvonne hesitated for a moment and then chuckled. "Yes, yes, from the movie *Casablanca*. You are my Humphrey Bogart after all."

"Though not exactly the real thing."

"But good enough, mon cherie." She gave him a soft full mouth kiss and then returned to her customers.

There was nothing more to be said. He made his way back to the hotel where a taxi was idling out front. While the cabbie put his valise in the trunk, he told the driver he wished to go to the American Embassy. As they passed the café, he looked through the back window to get one last glimpse of Yvonne St. Pierre.

Chapter Twenty-Three

After flashing his passport to the marine guards out front, Doherty entered the main hall of the embassy. Michael Shanahan was waiting for him in the lobby. He fingered Doherty's leather jacket.

"Nice jacket. Along with your scarf it makes you look like an authentic Frenchman. Please come with me."

He led Doherty out of the embassy and around the corner to a small parking lot. "He pointed at a vehicle slightly larger than a lawn mower masquerading as a car.

. "These are your wheels for the next week or so. I hope it suits you."

"What the hell is that?"

"It's called a Deux Chevaux. I'm sure you've seen them around the city. You'll find it very inexpensive to run. Petrol, I mean gasoline, is very expensive here in France. This little buggy will take you a long way on one tank."

"Who makes these things?"

"Citroën. They are very manageable in narrow streets and you can park them just about anywhere."

"Is it safe?"

Shanahan shrugged his shoulders and laughed. "As safe as any car is given the way the French drive. It doesn't go very fast, so you'll probably find many cars passing you, even on narrow country roads. Be patient with it and drive carefully."

Doherty continued to look skeptically at the little vehicle. Peering inside to examine the interior, he saw that it was about half the size of his Chevy Bel Air back home. This made him feel even more insecure.

"I also have these for you," Shanahan said as he handed Doherty a couple of manila envelopes. "This is all I could scrounge up about your dead soldier, Corporal John MacDonald. They're in here along with the documents you gave me the other day. It isn't much but at least it will tell you where his burial plot is at the American cemetery in Collevile-sur-Mer. I'm not sure the people there will be able to give you any more than what's in here. The other file is all about his unit in XIX Corps. From what I can tell your boy was killed along with a lot of other American soldiers in the battle for Saint-Lô. This file will show you the route his outfit took all the way from their crossing over the channel to the Siegfried Line and into Germany. I don't know if any of that will matter since Corporal MacDonald was killed just over a month after landing in France."

He handed Doherty a smaller envelope. "This contains the documents you will need to prove that you work at the American Embassy and are using the Deux Chevaux under our auspices. I embellished a little bit on your role, just enough to confuse the police if they stop you for any reason. Trust me, Doherty, no one in France ever gets stopped for speeding. Occasionally the police will stop foreigners merely to harass them. If that occurs a handful of francs will make them go away."

Shanahan spent the next quarter hour showing Doherty how to operate the midget vehicle, which didn't take long since all that appeared on the dashboard were switches for lights and windshield wipers. It also contained a choke, which he hadn't seen on a car in years. Shanahan had written out some directions on how to get out of the city and onto the road to Rouen. He told Doherty he'd spoken by phone to Captain Bogdanovich in Rouen, and he would be expecting Doherty's arrival later that day.

With some trepidation Doherty sandwiched his valise into the Deux Chevaux's small trunk and set off for Normandy. From his limited French he knew Deux Chevaux meant two horses. He was hoping the car would have a little bit more power than that, but soon found that it didn't. It took him nearly an hour for him to get out of the city and onto a country road toward Rouen. Apparently the most important accessory on most French cars was the horn, a tool they used quite liberally. He had to steel himself into ignoring the epithets hostile drivers slung his way as he made a myriad of wrong turns.

Once outside of Paris driving on the smaller roads proved to be just as harrowing as motoring in the city. Cars would zoom up on his tail and at the merest opening whisk past him at a breakneck speed, often swerving back into his lane seconds before colliding head on with an oncoming vehicle. What made things worse was when a large truck coming from the opposite direction occupied a portion of his side of the road. Luckily the Deux Cheavux was small enough to ride partially off the road without careening into a ditch. The speedometer topped out at 80 kilometers an hour. Doing the quick math in his head that meant the vehicle's maximum speed was about 50 mph. Given his uneasiness with driving in France this was probably a good thing.

It was almost noon by the time he reached the first good-sized town, a place called Vernon. Judging from the map Shanahan had provided for him he was about halfway to Rouen. Wanting to reach his destination before it was too late in the day, he elected to stop at a small market along the roadside to get some food. For only a few francs he was able to purchase a block of cheese, some smoked sausage, a bottle of cold beer, and a baguette. A few kilometers outside of Vernon he stopped at a pullover off the road where a picnic table sat. Using the switchblade knife he'd taken off the would-be thief in Montmartre, he cut up some sausage and cheese and made a sandwich from a section of the bread. He used the door handle of the car to open the beer bottle. It was an old trick he learned as a kid when he and his pals found themselves with some stolen beers but without a church key.

While he ate, he spread out the documents on John McDonald and read as much of his bio as Shanahan was able to pull together. As he already knew, McDonald was from Warwick, Rhode Island, had graduated from high school in 1941 and had enlisted in the army a year later. He had a wife named Cheryl, but no other info was provided about when they were married or what his wife's maiden name was. McDonald had done his infantry training at Ft. Bragg and was assigned to a signal corps as part of XIX corps. He had been an exemplary soldier and was promoted to corporal in September of 1943. His unit had been mustered at Camp Kilmer in New Jersey in early 1944 and transported by ship from New York City to England for advanced training in April. On June 10 they crossed from Portsmouth to the port of Isigny-sur-Mer near Cherbourg, three days after the initial Normandy landings at Omaha and Utah Beaches. The men in XIX corps marched south to a place called Castilly where they met significant German resistance and then onto St- Lô. The battle for that town lasted almost a month before the Germans were finally subdued. It was somewhere around St-Lô that Corporal McDonald met his death. The material Shanahan provided went on to enumerate the many subsequent battles that McDonald's unit engaged in, but none of that was relevant to Doherty's mission.

He knew from stories he'd heard that the battle for St-Lô was one of the worst engagements of the entire Normandy campaign. It had ended with an American victory, though at a very high price for the GIs who fought and died there. Doherty figured he would get more details about St-Lô from Captain Bogdanovich once they hooked up in Rouen. The beer did little to alleviate the bad taste left in his mouth from reading about McDonald's death. For now, all he'd have to report back to his former wife and daughter was that he was killed in an intense battle along with many other American and German soldiers.

Back on the road he continued to push his two-horse vehicle to its maximum speed. Though that didn't stop the French racecar wannabees from pulling up inches from his rear bumper before flying out at the smallest opening to pass him. Several went by and gave him a sneer as they did. By now he was getting used to this French roadway behavior. When he got close to Rouen, he followed signs to the Centre-Ville. Within minutes he could see the ornately decorated spires of Rouen's famed cathedral. He continued in that direction until he was mere blocks from the church. He squeezed the Deux Chevaux into a small parking space and made the last two blocks to the center on foot.

The Rouen Cathedral was everything Monet had depicted it as in his murky paintings - and then some. Whereas Notre Dame was impressive by its size and Sainte-Chapelle by its ornate windows, the cathedral at Rouen was notable for its elaborate design, especially on its massive façade. Doherty had

161

never seen carvings so intricate. It was a wonder that it hadn't been damaged during the war. He circled the massive structure before entering into what was the very essence of a gothic church. The vaulted ceiling seemed to reach to the heavens. He took a seat in one of the pews. The rest did him some good after the three-hour journey in the rattletrap vehicle. If he were a religious person, he might have lit a candle or said a prayer of thanks for his survival on the narrow country roads. Instead he used the respite as an opportunity to rest his aching back.

Leaving the cathedral, he noticed a small storefront across the plaza that featured a sign that said Tourist Office. He wandered in and a nice young woman who spoke perfect, though accented, English was helping a British couple plan a walking tour of the city. When she was free, he flashed her the address of Bogdanovich's office and asked for directions. She took out a city map and circled where they were now and the street where he wished to go. It turned out Bogdanovich's office was a short walk down that same street under an archway with a clock in its center. From there it was only two side streets further on.

Following her simple directions, he easily found the address he'd been given. On the outside wall was a metal plaque that read Administration de la Coopération Économique. The door was unlocked so Doherty walked into the building. To the left immediately inside was a half glass door through which he could see a busy office. Signs pointed up the stairs to other businesses. The one in front of him had an English sign indicating it was the U.S. Economic Cooperation Administration.

Once inside a young man in a white shirt, bow tie, and horn-rimmed glasses approached him.

"Can I help you, sir?" he said in American English.

"I'm here to see Captain Bogdanovich."

"Your name?"

"Hugh Doherty."

"Follow me, Mr. Doherty. My name is Dan Gentile. I'm just an underling with the ECA," he said self-deprecatingly.

Without knocking they entered a small office where a large man in an American army uniform was sitting at desk speaking in French with a decidedly American accent to someone on the phone. Gentile stood beside Doherty as Bogdanovich spoke angrily to whomever was on the other end of the line. The captain had broad shoulders and still featured a military brush cut. His face was large and had a tough guy look to it. In time he slammed the phone down and rubbed one of his large hands across his close-cropped head.

"Trouble again, captain?" Gentile asked.

"Goddamn fucking construction people. I know they're loading every project up with extra costs just to line their pockets, but I can't prove it. These voleurs think all Uncle Sam has to do is go down into the cellar and print more money. I'm dealing with a bunch of thieves here." It was only then that Bogdanovich acknowledged Doherty's presence.

"I'm sorry, you'll have to excuse me. It's been a rough coupla weeks."

Doherty stepped forward and introduced himself. Bogdanovich stood and buried Doherty's hand in his big mitt. He smiled and said, "Nice to meet you, Mr. Doherty."

"You can call me Doherty; everyone back home does."

"And you can forget the captain shit and call me Walt. I'm talking to Doherty here, not you Dan. To you I'm still Captain Bogdanovich."

"Aye, aye, sir," the young guy saluted before making his exit.

"Please sit down," Bogdanovich said pointing to a chair. "Would you like a smoke?"

"I'll have one of my own if you don't mind. Can't take the smell of those French cigs."

"Neither can I. That's why I have my boys bring me back cartons of Rothmans every time they cross the channel. So, what can I do for you, Doherty? Mike Shanahan said I should treat you like a state department VIP."

"Oh I don't know if I deserve the VIP treatment. But any help you can give me will be most appreciated."

Doherty lit one of his Camels and reached across the desk to torch Bogdanovich's Rothman. The captain admired the inscription on his Zippo and said so.

Doherty began, "First of all what can you tell me about the ECA and what it does?"

"The ECA is the agency set up by what folks back home used to refer to as the Marshall Plan. Mostly what I do is some portion of whatever money the Congress is willing to appropriate for rebuilding projects in Western European countries. Once it's sent over here we decide where and on what to spend that money in France."

"I've got to say I'm surprised the Marshall Plan is still in operation. Hell, the war's been over going on fifteen years."

Bogdanovich shook his head, "I know, I know. Problem is once we start a project here it can take years to finish it. Did you see the cathedral when you came into town?"

"Yeah. I even stepped inside to check it out."

"Did you admire the stained-glass windows?"

"I guess. Didn't pay them much attention."

"You should've. That's your tax dollars at work. Took ten years and a lot of Yankee dough to get them replaced. Now they look really nice. Do me a favor before you leave Rouen; stop in there again and admire the glass. Consider it your patriotic duty."

"Doesn't the French government contribute to their own rebuilding projects?"

"Sure they do and private donors as well. Right now, there are a couple of philanthropic Americans pumping a lot of money into rebuilding St-Malo further west from here. One of them is a friend of mine – a vet who inherited a bundle of cash while he was still in the service. Problem is the more we shovel into this place the more the French want. I don't want to sound like Scrooge, but you know the old story – whenever there's free money around every grafter is going to want his share. Same as back home. My job is to separate the chickens from the turkeys. Let me tell you something, Doherty, when it comes to construction kickbacks and labor racketeering people in the States have nothing on the guys over here. There's just too much money floating around and everyone who's anyone wants some of it. You could say it's one of the ways some French people compensate for their deprivations during the war. Look, there's some stuff I gotta finish up here before the day's over. Where are you staying?"

"I don't know yet."

"I'd invite you to my house, but with my kids running around you'd never get a moment's rest. There's a nice little hotel in town called the Vieux Carré. Tell the guy at the desk that you're a colleague of mine and he'll give you a nice room at a good price." Bogdanovich looked at his watch. "Why don't I meet you there, say around seven, and we'll go to dinner at one of my favorite restaurants; it'll be on me. Then over a bottle of wine you can tell me more about your mission." Bogdanovich then wrote out some directions to the hotel.

Chapter Twenty-Four

The Vieux Carré was a pleasant little place where the proprietor couldn't do enough for Doherty once he dropped Bogdanovich's name. Like his stay in Paris, the room was small with little closet or dresser space. That was fine with him since he didn't have much by way of clothing and wasn't going to unpack most of what he did have anyway. After washing up he took the occasion to catch a few zees before meeting with the captain for dinner. As was his habit Doherty was in the hotel's miniscule lobby a good fifteen minutes before Bogdanovich was due. He spent the time smoking and foolishly looking through a French newspaper where he understood virtually nothing. The paper had no photos and the messages in the two political cartoons on the editorial page eluded him.

Bogdanovich arrived at seven sharp and warmly greeted his friend at the hotel desk. After exchanging a few more pleasantries he quickly ushered Doherty out to the street.

"Louie is a good fellow, but he can talk the skin right off your face if you let him. In case you haven't noticed one of the national pastimes among the French is to sit in cafes and talk for hours, often while smoking a never-ending series of smelly cigarettes. Their habits stand in sharp contrast with those of us Americans who like to get things done without wasting too much time. But you know the old adage, 'when in Rome'. Sometimes in order to avoid pro-longed discussions I simply tell approaching Frenchmen I don't understand their language. *Comprends pas* can be a very useful term in situations like that."

"You don't have to tell me. In the time I've been here I've hardly been able to understand anything people were saying to me. Fortunately, I met a very nice woman in Paris who took me around and showed me the sights."

Bogdanovich laid one of his large hands on Doherty's shoulder and said, "I bet that wasn't all she showed you." He didn't respond and the big fellow didn't throw out a follow-up comment.

A few blocks from the hotel they ducked into a charming little restaurant that was the very essence of a French bistro. Bogdanovich knew the owner who doubled as the maître d, and they exchanged warm greetings.

Once they were seated, he said, "François knows enough not to occupy too much of my time when I'm here with a guest. I use this place to do business with some of my French counterparts. Sometimes they are men he doesn't approve of."

"Why would that be?"

"Because, my American friend, they are men who tend to operate on both sides of the law. I've been told some of them openly cooperated with the Krauts when they were here; others bought and sold goods on the black market during the war, often gouging the locals."

"Why are you having dinner with the people like that?"

"Because they happen to run almost all of the construction companies in Normandy and parts of Brittany. If we don't deal with them, they'll tell their people not to work for us. Like I told you at the office, the construction busi-nesses back home would seem as pure as snow compared to some of the char-acters I've had to deal with here. My job requires me to get things done. Some-times in order to do that, I have to engage with some unsavory characters. It ain't pretty, but I remind myself that large swaths of this country were the killing fields during the last few years of the war. And I don't need to tell you, we Americans did some serious damage in our efforts to drive the Germans out. People back home have no idea how much death and destruction occurred near to where we're sitting right now. So, Doherty, why don't you shut me up and tell me your war story?"

At that moment they were interrupted when the owner delivered two bowls of soup and a bottle of red wine to their table. The pause gave Doherty a chance to recall what of his wartime experiences he would be willing to share with someone he'd only met a few hours ago.

"I was working at Quonset Point in Rhode Island where I was raised when the Japs bombed Pearl Harbor. At first, I thought they'd pass me by because I had a defense related job. It's not like I wasn't ready to fight if I got called up. I just thought my chances of staying alive were better at Quonset than in Italy where I ended up." This brought a knowing smile to Bogdanovich's broad face.

"I got drafted in the summer of '42 and was sent out to Ft. Sill in Oklahoma to learn how to jump out of airplanes. It wasn't my first choice since I'd never been off the ground before. After a few months there the next thing I knew I was on a troopship on my way to England; only we didn't dock in England, but in Wales instead. A godforsaken place if there ever was one. After a few weeks of more practice jumps, they herded us onto planes one night and told us we were off to Sicily. Most of the guys in my outfit didn't even know Sicily was part of Italy. I happen to know because a lot of Sicilian Italians live in Rhode Island.

"They dropped us somewhere outside of Palermo in the middle of the night; it took us quite a few hours to reconnoiter with the men in our outfit who survived the jump. After that it seemed like we were engaged in constant fighting across the island and then up the boot. By the middle of '43 it was mostly against the Germans as the Italians we encountered along the way had already come over to our side. Every place we fought over and won, the Italians greeted us as heroes. Except we knew many of them had been all for the Fascists not that long before we arrived."

"Yeah, it was the same here. All the girls came out and kissed us and did other things as if the Germans had merely been an inconvenience before we landed. I think the thousands of Jews and other undesirables the French helped deport would disagree with that wartime narrative."

"Anyway," Doherty continued, "by the time we got to Rome it was all but over for Mussolini and his crew. He was overthrown that July. From then on it was us, the Brits, and some Italian partisans against the Krauts. But it was tough fighting all the way up the peninsula. Lots of good American boys bought it at Anzio and Monte Casino. Casino was the worst. After that the fighting felt more like a mopping up operation as the Germans began to retreat north."

"Shanahan told me you were awarded a silver star." Doherty was taken aback for a moment realizing the embassy officer had obviously checked out his military records as well as McDonald's.

"Lots of guys got medals in the Italian campaign. And lots of other guys rightfully deserved them except they were dead. Getting a medal for killing other young guys no matter what their nationality is nothing to celebrate. It only meant that they wouldn't get to live a full life and I would. What we did there had to be done just like here. But that still doesn't make it any easier to accept."

Bogdanovich raised his wine glass. "I'll drink to that. Here's to peace"

"To peace and crooked construction companies."

They drank in silence for a while, using the break to spoon up some delicious lentil soup. In time Doherty broke the silence. "Okay, captain, now it's your turn to tell me about your war."

As was his habit, Bogdanovich rubbed his big hand over his bristly scalp before starting in. "I enlisted in '39. Grew up in Buffalo and went from one thankless job to another after graduating from high school. I'd played football and hoped to play at Buffalo College, but my folks didn't have any money and the school didn't offer enough for me to go there. So I went into the army. I thought at least Uncle Sam would provide me with a more interesting life than the mills in Buffalo. Besides what with the news coming out of Europe, I thought it was only a matter of time before we got into the war. I wanted to be ready and not be one of those officers we referred to as '90-day wonders'.

"There were a lot of openings in OCS back then, so I applied and got in right away. Over the next few years I was transferred from here to there and back, but I didn't mind. Hell, I wasn't married or nothing then. It's not like I had any kind of a home base. I expected to be sent overseas soon after Pearl Harbor but that didn't happen. I was older so they wanted me to stay stateside to train less experienced men. I didn't get over here until the summer of '44. I was afraid the war would be over by the time I did. I was assigned to a tank destroyer battalion. Our job was to disable as many Jerry tanks as we could. The Panzer 2s were quick and mobile; much more versatile than our heavier Shermans. However, the armor on the Panzers wasn't as thick so a direct hit from one of ours or from a bazooka would put them out of action.

"Our unit landed at Cherbourg in late September after the main invasion. It was easy going from there up to Paris and Riems. After we crossed into Belgium it was a whole other story. The Battle of the Dykes outside of Brussels was brutal as was our entry into Antwerp. From there we were chasing the Jerries all the way to Achen, Cologne, across the Siegfried line to the Rhine, and into the heart of the fatherland. By then the fabled Wehrmacht was on its last legs. Some days we would round up as many as a thousand German POWs – a good number of them as young as fifteen. The Prussian officers were a nasty bunch, still looking for a fight. But most of the other soldiers were done.

"Our battalion spent months occupying parts of Bavaria and Austria after the surrender. My unit liberated Herrenchiemsee Island where Goering had stashed a lot of his ill-gotten loot. I was instrumental in returning some of the lost art you might've seen in Paris. When my unit was scheduled to return to the states my commanding colonel asked if I'd be interested in staying over here to help with resettlement issues. Frankly I didn't know what that meant. By then I'd already been promoted to captain and had nothing to go home to. Over here I was somebody important. Back in Buffalo I'd just be another vet and maybe be remembered as the Polack who'd once been a football star in high school. So I stayed.

"When they stationed me in Paris, I took classes and learned the language. Later they sent me to Zurich to help recover some of the stolen cash the German leaders had salted away in private Swiss bank accounts. Dealing with those crooked Swiss bankers was something else. When I returned to Paris, I met my wife, Héléne, and we were married within the year. That was twelve years ago. Since then we've split our time between Paris and Rouen. I love the capital though sometimes it's nice to be out here where it's quieter. My kids aren't so crazy about Normandy.

"In Paris it feels like most people have put the war behind them. Not so much here where it still weighs heavily on the minds of a lot of French people.

But I can't complain. Between the army and the ECA, life has been good to me and my family. Way better than things would've been if I'd returned to Buffalo. However, it's only a matter of time before the ECA winds down its operations in France. Then the army will send me somewhere else. Germany is a likely place given how many bases we have there now. I guess that would be all right, though I'm not sure I'll ever get over my hatred for the Krauts."

Their meals arrived and they ate in silence, trying their best to leave the war behind them. Doherty had a steak with fries, while Bogdanovich ate some kind of chicken dish. The steak was leathery and couldn't compare to a good old American T-bone; the fries, as always, were excellent. Somewhere along the line they finished the bottle of wine and Bogdanovich ordered up another one. With the small bistro now cleared out except for them, the owner, François, sat down at their table bringing his own wine glass with him. Since he didn't speak any English and Doherty spoke little French, they engaged in an awkward three-way conversation like the one he'd had with Yvonne and her father. In this case Bogdanovich served as the middleman. A few times François spoke at length while Bogdanovich only bothered to translate a small part of what the Frenchman was saying.

With the second bottle of wine nearly empty, the owner returned to the bar where he grabbed a bottle of brandy and some glasses. The conversation continued over the after-dinner drinks. At one point an exchange between Bogdanovich and François grew rather heated, with the Frenchman raising his voice and pounding the table with his fist. Doherty had no idea what the argument was about, though François kept repeating the name of René somebody. Bogdanovich was doing his level best to remain patient, not an easy task considering how much they'd had to drink. For his part Doherty was straining to stay focused though his head was spinning, more from all the words flying back and forth than from the alcohol.

Finally, in a burst of anger Bogdanovich pushed away from the table. He dropped two twenty-franc notes in front of François and dragged Doherty by the arm out of the restaurant. Neither man spoke at first as they stumbled down the street in the direction of the Vieux Carré.

"What the hell was that all about? Your pal François seemed pretty pissed off."

"François is a hot headed Normandian. It's an old argument that comes up every time I eat at his place with a certain individual."

"Would that be the René fellow he kept referring to?"

Bogdanovich stopped and gave Doherty a daggered stare. "Look, my friend, I think the less you know about what's going behind the scenes here the better off you'll be."

"This wouldn't have to do with one of your construction contracts, would it?"

Bogdanovich put his hands on his hips and steadied himself in place. "René Depardieu is a big wheel in this part of France. Little of any value gets done here unless his hand is greased. I don't like it and neither does anyone else who has to do business with him. But if we don't, all our efforts will suddenly grind to a halt. I had a meeting with Depardieu at the restaurant recently. François has a stick up his ass about him because of certain things that happened years ago that don't involve you or me."

Now it was Doherty's turn to give the hard stare to the man who'd just bought him dinner. "Come on, Walt, you can't leave me hanging like that. What's the story? And don't jerk me around. I don't like being jerked around even by a guy who just stood me dinner and a couple of bottles of wine."

"François' younger brother Marius was seeing this Jewish girl back before the war," the captain began. "I guess you could say he was courting her. They were planning to marry. That was until the roundup of the local Jews occurred. She and her family were sent to the East. According to François, Marius never saw her again. When the Germans occupied this area, Marius joined the resistance. That was Marius' way of getting back at them for what happened to his girlfriend and her family.

"Shortly before the invasion he was captured and killed when the Germans found out he was doing reconnaissance work for the Allies. François believes it was Depardieu who betrayed Marius to the Gestapo. For the last sixteen years he's let that idea fester in him. He says he will never forgive Depardieu. And he holds a grudge against anyone like me who has to deal with him. I didn't know the whole story until after my first meeting with René at François' restaurant. That's the long and short of it. And if I were you, Doherty, I'd file that away and forget about it. This is not your place and you don't have to interact with these people like I do."

Chapter Twenty-Five

Bogdanovich picked up Doherty at his hotel a little after nine the next morning. He was driving a green Renault sedan that proved to be a much more comfortable than the Deux Chevaux. It took about an hour for them to get out to the beaches where the invasion of June 6, 1944, had taken place. Along the way they talked about different aspects of the war and its aftermath. Nothing was said about René Depardieu or the dust-up at the restaurant the previous night.

They drove first to Juno Beach where a small pavilion provided some information about the landing there of the combined British and Canadian forces. What initially caught Doherty's eye was a large diorama of the invasion made up of miniature ships, landing crafts, tanks, and hundreds of tiny soldiers hitting the beaches. It showed how most of the machinery used in the invasion was off-loaded onto temporary pontoons sunk out in the water that were then attached to floating rafts. That was how the heavy vehicles were brought ashore. He'd always been fascinated by such dioramas, but this one was detailed in the extreme.

Above the miniature display was a picture window that covered almost the entire wall looking out at the sea. This was the same patch of coastline being depicted in the diorama. Bogdanovich explained that the rubble they saw floating out in the water was the last vestige of the pontoons used for the invasion. Now they were just permanent reminders of what transpired at Juno beach.

Above the window was a gigantic wide-angle photo of the invasion itself. It too stretched the length of the wall. Doherty found himself moving his gaze up and down trying to take in the entirety of three depictions he was seeing. Although the water was rough out at sea, the only signs of life today were the flocks of seagulls flapping back and forth across the sky.

The rest of the pavilion was filled with cases of other D-Day pictures accompanied by explanations of how this part of the invasion unfolded that day. Neighboring cases covered the Allied planning that went into the preparations for the massive landing. Sprinkled among them were artifacts picked up off the beach or from out in the water that attested to the events of that day. Many of the display cases also contained commentaries by the British and Canadian soldiers who landed at Juno or Sword Beach and lived to tell about it.

After nearly an hour at this site Walt tapped him on the shoulder and said, "C'mon, lets mosey on up the coast and see where our guys landed." They drove inland and then turned onto a road that ran alongside the shoreline. Everything was so peaceful and quiet it was hard to believe that less than sixteen years ago this place was the site of the largest amphibious invasion in history.

They parked in a small lot that a sign indicated was the place the Americans called Omaha Beach. A few people were walking their dogs along the sandy shore. Otherwise nothing about the beach indicated it was a special place. A monument at the center of the walkway above the beach said that this was the spot where "The Allied forces landing on this shore which they called Omaha Beach to liberate Europe on June 6, 1944." There was a French message also carved into the monument that Walt indicated said pretty much the same thing.

As Doherty and his companion walked along the beach all he could think about was the vast amount of blood that had sunk into the sand here on that fateful June day. What struck Doherty was how normal everything seemed given what had once happened here. He walked down to the water's edge and looked back at the beach trying to imagine what the men saw and felt when they first disembarked from their landing craft. He wondered how many of them were killed even before they reached dry land.

Walt indicated that it was time to move on. They drove up through the countryside past stone houses surrounded by high walls. "Normandy was always being invaded by some enemy or another," Bogdanovich explained. "That's why the houses and villages are often protected by those high walls,".

He soon turned down a narrow road that led back out to the coast. They parked in a lot where there were perhaps a half dozen other cars. After a ten-minute walk they came to a high crest that provided a panoramic view of the Normandy coastline.

"This is Pointe du Hoc," Bogdanovich said. "It was here that a small band of U.S. Army Rangers scaled these cliffs with grappling hooks and rope ladders in the teeth of enemy fire." The entire hillside around them was pitted with large bomb craters, all now filled with wild grasses. Concrete German bunkers, many of them constructed long before the invasion, were carved into this high position. "The navy unloaded a massive bombardment on this hillock before the Rangers mounted their ascent. Looking down that cliff it's hard to believe that the first American soldier made it to the top in five minutes," Bogdanovich said with admiration.

Before visiting the American cemetery at Colleville-sur-Mer, they stopped for coffee and some breakfast pastries. Doherty was excited by what he had seen so far and asked Bogdanovich a hundred questions about the Normandy invasion and the subsequent campaign. His host very patiently tried his best to answer them.

Entering the cemetery sight, they passed through a visitors' center where several ledgers were available to search for the specific grave of a soldier who died in one of the Normandy battles. It didn't take long for Doherty to find the entry for Corporal John McDonald. He was one of a dozen McDonalds logged into the book. The description said he died on or about July 12, 1944 at the battle of St-Lô. Otherwise his entry simply listed his hometown of Warwick, Rhode Island, his religion as Catholic, the unit and battalion he was attached to, and his age. Below his name was a letter and number designation. This was how one could locate McDonald's cross among the many that appeared to cover acres on the hillside overlooking the sea.

The only activity within the confines of the cemetery was of people placing flowers next to identified crosses. Sprinkled among the crosses were graves with Jewish Stars of David on them. Each grave was identified only by the soldier's name, rank, and country. Walt informed him that the dead soldiers, or what was left of them, were indeed buried in the grass in front of each memorial. Doherty spent a few minutes studying McDonald's cross, which had Cpl. John S. McDonald, U.S.A. etched into it. Otherwise it looked no different from the thousands of other gravesites covering the hillside.

It was a quiet ride back to Rouen. They stopped for lunch and drank some wine, though all the while each man was lost in his own thoughts about war, life, and death. It struck Doherty how events so momentous could happen in this place less than two decades ago, and now the world around them had simply moved on. War leaves nothing behind it except death, destruction, and sad memories.

Back in Rouen Bogdanovich invited Doherty to have dinner that night with him and his family. He politely declined, not wanting to spend the evening trying to put on a happy face for strangers after what he had seen today. He thought it best to spend some time by himself. He wanted to write a letter to Nina in which he would try to describe everything he'd witnessed that day and what it meant to him. As far as his clients were concerned, all he'd be able to report to them was what they already knew – that Charlene Royal's husband and Mary Margaret's father had died in battle "fighting to liberate Europe."

When Doherty came down for breakfast the next morning, he was surprised to find Captain Bogdanovich waiting for him at one of the tables, sipping a café au lait and smoking a cigarette.

"How did you get in here?"

"Louie agreed to let me have breakfast with you on the condition that I listen to fifteen minutes of his tales of woe."

"What all is bothering him on this bright morning?"

Bogdanovich smiled and shook his head. "I don't know. I already forgot most of what he said." He then reached into his breast pocket and removed some folded-up paper.

"When I looked up your boy's unit yesterday in the ledger at the cemetery something about it rang a bell. So I put in a call to our mutual friend Shanahan at the embassy in Paris. Actually, I called him at home because I knew he would've already left work at five like all good bureaucrats do here in France. Remember when I told you about how some big American muck-a-mucks were putting a lot of their personal wealth into the rebuilding of some structures and towns destroyed in the fighting out here? Well one of those guys turns out to be a fellow I've met a on a couple of occasions named Andrew Pettigrew. Shanahan discovered Pettigrew was a lieutenant in the same outfit as your dead soldier. Not sure if he actually knew Corporal McDonald, but it might be worth your while to take a trip out to St-Malo to see if he can give you some more info on your guy that you don't already have. From what I know about him, Pettigrew came into a fair amount of money through an inheritance. Since then he has dedicated a great deal of it to rebuilding the citadelle within the walls of old St-Malo."

"Is that close to here?"

"Not really. It's out along the coast in Brittany. Maybe a two-hour drive from Rouen. St-Malo took a beating when General Patton's forces bombarded it for a couple of weeks before the German forces there finally surrendered. To make matters worse, just for spite the Krauts burned a lot of the old buildings within the town. From what I've heard the weird part of the story is that even though Pettigrew got mustered out in late '45 like most of the American military personnel in France, he never went back to the states. Just hired some lawyers to settle up his business back home and had most of his money transferred over here. If I were a betting man, I'd hazard to guess a lot of it is salted away in some Swiss bank accounts so he doesn't have to pay taxes on it in the U.S."

"Sounds a little shady to me. Is that all you know about this ex-pat?"

"Only that he's married to some Swiss gal, has a couple of kids and lives in a chateau outside of St-Malo. Seems Pettigrew has maintained a low profile where other Americans living over here are concerned. However, I do know someone who would know a lot more about Andrew Pettigrew than anyone else."

"Oh, yeah. Who would that be?"

"You're not gonna like it."

"Try me."

"René Depardieu. I understand they do business together."

Chapter Twenty-Six

Before he left the hotel Doherty thanked Bogdanovich for the heads-up on Andrew Pettigrew. He would've liked to have the captain accompany him to St-Malo, but the big guy had to beg off given his busy work schedule. Now Doherty was on his own. At this point he very well could've return to Paris for a flight back to the U.S. having more or less completed his mission for the Royal family. Yet there was something about this Pettigrew fellow that piqued his interest. Besides he still had three quarters of a tank of gas in the Deux Chevaux so a jaunt out to Brittany might prove to be interesting. Along the way he could stop at Mont-St-Michel, the famous abbey built out on an island that Sister Mary Aloysius, one of the nuns back in his elementary school at St. James, used to wax poetic about. She even pinned up a print of it in her classroom that Doherty often found a pleasant diversion from whatever subjects were being drilled into them that day. Apparently, the old crone had once made a pilgrimage to Mont-St-Michel.

After checking out of the Vieux Carré and thanking Louie for the pleasant accommodations, he drove west, initially toward the town of Caen. Along the way he stopped to pick up some road food: a can of paté, a baguette, a piece of cheese, and a couple of bottles of beer. He was finding it easier to stop at some serene spot for lunch rather than having to go into a café and wait out

180

the inevitably slow service. Everyone he encountered was courteous enough in helping him with his language issues, but sometimes the long wait in restaurants and the equally long wait to pay was just plain annoying. Caen was a bustling town about as busy as Rouen, though it lacked any attractions on the scale Monet's famous cathedral.

He drove on in a southwesterly direction following the signs to Mont-St-Michel. He could see the high steeple of the abbey from a long way off before he got out to the coast where it sat on an island at the end of a long causeway. Signs indicated by symbols as well as French words said that pedestrians should not attempt to cross the causeway when the tide was coming in, less they be stranded out on the island.

He parked the Deux Chevaux at a pull-off on the causeway and leaned over the railing to check the tides. Luckily the water appeared to be flowing out to the sea and not in. He found a bench at the far end of the causeway that provided him a splendid view of the abbey. Taking the foodstuffs from the car he satisfied his hunger by eating a hearty lunch while admiring the spectacle of the abbey. The old nun in his third-grade class had been wrong about a lot of things, but not about the majesty of Mont-St-Michel.

After putting the remnants of his lunch back into the car he walked toward the island. Along the way he considered how he would move on Andrew Pettigrew and possibly René Depardieu once he got to at St-Malo - or even if he had any moves to make at all. A fair number of tourists were lined up waiting to enter the abbey grounds. Since they were all part of a single group, Doherty slipped ahead of them, paid a small admission fee, and crossed onto the island complex. He followed a narrow cobblestone street that was lined with the usual shops selling cheap tourist goods; mostly postcards, trinkets, and miniature depictions of Mont-St-Michel.

The street rose higher and higher until he reached the church cloisters and the Great Hall. The interior of St-Michel was dark and foreboding so he chose to spend most of his time there walking along the several perimeter paths on the ramparts that afforded a fine view of the adjacent gulf and the English Channel Islands off in the distance. To the west he could make out a town that one of the shopkeepers told him was St-Malo. From Mont-St-Michel it looked like the drive along the coast to that town wouldn't take him more than an hour.

Although he had some trouble finding his way from the causeway to the main road to St-Malo, the trip took less time than he anticipated. He read in the Frommer book that St-Malo had once been a walled city, though now many sections of the wall that surrounded the old town inside called the *intra-muros* were under repair. From what he could discern from the signs, motorized vehicles were not allowed within the citadelle unless they were on official business.

He left the car in a parking lot across from the main gate. Toting his valise and briefcase he entered the old town. Turning to the right he passed a number of restaurants and cafes but saw no signs for hotels or guesthouses. He mounted a narrow cobblestone street and stopped at a news kiosk that sat on a corner to ask where he might find a hotel. The mustachioed proprietor came out from inside his stand and took Doherty's hand and led him to an even narrower side street. The man was heavyset and wore a black beret that was tilted on his head at a jaunty angle.

A small sign indicating the Hotel Cartier was nestled inside the walls of a stone façade. The hotel took up a narrow space within the stonewalls, but otherwise seemed neat and clean. No one there spoke English so in his halting French Doherty asked to see one of the *chambres*. He was led up two flights of stairs to a room that looked out over the walls of the citadelle. The bathroom was located two doors down the hall, but the proprietor indicated for the present he would be the only one staying on this floor.

Returning to the foyer he gave the news seller a one-franc coin for his help and thanked him profusely. He then handed his passport to the proprietor and registered for the room. After some awkward back and forth he realized the hotelier was asking him how long he would be staying in St-Malo. The best Doherty could do was make a motion with his hands indicating he wasn't sure. Since the hotel did not seem to have many occupants the proprietor didn't seem bothered one way or the other.

After unpacking his valise, Doherty changed into some more comfortable walking shoes and pulled on his leather jacket. Retrieving his passport at the desk downstairs he went out for walk around the town. He started on the perimeter walkway along the upper walls of the city. At several spots he was

182

forced to descend where the ramparts were under construction, or rather re-construction. At one far corner looking out over the sea he came upon a statue of Jacques Cartier. Hence, from which his hotel got its name.

Doherty knew from his American history classes that Cartier had been one of the earliest French explorers to Canada. From the French inscription on the pedestal he could deduce that Cartier was a native of St- Malo, who sailed out of this town on his several voyages to North America. In West Warwick, given its large French-Canadian population, the schools had always put more emphasis on the French explorers than the English ones when they covered the early exploration of North America. As best he could remember, Cartier may have been the first Frenchman to sail up the St. Lawrence River.

Further along on his walk he came upon a site where a sign indicated that the work on a building was being done by P&G Construction. He approached one of the workers and asked if he spoke English. The man gestured with his fingers indicating he only spoke it a little. But he held up his hand indicating Doherty should wait as he sought out someone who could. In time a young, good-looking fellow no older than his late twenties, wearing a yellow vest and a hard hat approached him.

"Parlez vous Anglais?"

"I should think so," the guy said with a smirk. "I was born in Baltimore. How can I help you? Are you lost?"

"Baltimore, huh. No, I'm not lost. I'm an American visiting St-Malo. I was curious about this P&G Construction. Who exactly are P&G?"

"There is no G. The name stands for my boss, Mr. Pettigrew. He thought calling it P&G would make it sound more like a typical American construction company."

"He wouldn't happen to be Andrew Pettigrew, would he? If I remember correctly, I may have served with someone by that name in XIX Corps during the war."

"Really? That's quite a coincidence."

"Not really. There were a lot of soldiers in XIX Corps. I was told by someone working for ECA over in Rouen that an Andrew Pettigrew headed up one of the reconstruction companies working on St-Malo. I'm here on a bit of a vacation. You know, visiting the battlefields and the cemeteries. Paying my respects to some old buddies who didn't make it home."

"What's this ECA?" the guy from Baltimore asked, skepticism entering his voice.

"It's the agency that dispenses money from what we used to know as the Marshall Plan. I reckon some of the money Mr. Pettigrew is using on this project comes through the ECA. The rest I've been told is his own. In any case, do you know how I can get in touch with Pettigrew. It might be fun to get together with a fellow vet to talk over old times."

"He doesn't come up here all that much. He's got three or four other projects going along the coast."

"Does he have an office I could check in at?"

"Not that I know of. He does most of his business out of his home. He lives in a big chateau outside of town. I've only been there once and wouldn't be able to tell you how to get there."

Doherty could hear the suspicion seeping into Baltimore's voice and thought it best not to belabor the point. He would have to find Pettigrew on his own. If Pettigrew was the remote character Bogdanovich indicated he was, Doherty'd have to rely on his wits as a detective to track him down.

Back at the hotel he put in a call to Walt Bogdanovich and luckily the big fellow was at his desk. They spoke for a few moments about his drive to St-Malo and his stopover at Mont-St-Michel. The captain was pleased that Doherty had found the abbey worth the side trip. Then Doherty got down to business.

"I met one of Andrew Pettigrew's workmen today; a young American guy from Baltimore. He told me Pettigrew did most of his business out of a chateau he lives in somewhere outside of St-Malo. I thought you might be able to give me a heads up on this chateau." He purposely spoke in a low voice not wanting the hotelier to hear him mention Pettigrew's name.

He could hear Bogdanovich breathing hard on the other end of the line. Though he couldn't see him he was sure the big fellow was rubbing one of his large mitts over his short bristly hair. "There are a couple of chateaus on the outskirts of St-Malo. I know that a few of them have been converted into hotels. You might want to check out the Château du Colombier. If I remember correctly, it was built sometime in the 1700s by managers of the British East India Company. Its English pedigree would've appeal to someone like Pettigrew. Otherwise I wouldn't know what else to tell you. If you give me an hour or so, I'd probably be able to track down his homestead."

Doherty said he'd look into this Colombier place. He gave Bogdanovich the name and phone number of his hotel and suggested he leave a message there when he had something more substantial. In the meantime, he would try to locate the Château du Colombier on his own.

His first inclination was to ask the man at the hotel desk about the chateau, but there was something about the way he'd surreptitiously listened to Doherty's conversation while acting like he wasn't that set off his suspicious antenna. Instead he walked down to the news kiosk and made his inquiries there with the fellow who'd helped him find the hotel. Their conversation was a bit awkward with Doherty at best understanding only about a third of what the man was telling him. In the end, the news dealer took out a pad and drew some directions on it, indicating landmarks Doherty should follow to get to the small village where the Château du Colombier was located.

Doherty shoved the scraps of paper with the vague mapping into his pocket and wandered down through the old town out the main gate to his car. The Deux Chevaux did not look any better in the afternoon sunshine. After a short coughing fit the little vehicle sprang into action. Between trying to wind his way out of the town, consulting the news dealer's map in his lap, and incurring the wrath of the French drivers, he eventually found his way out into the countryside. There were no vehicles out here except for the occasional tractor taking up the entire width of a narrow country road. He passed through a series of small villages with stone houses that hugged tightly by the road. Seeing few signs of life, he thought he was lost since he couldn't find anyone to tell him otherwise. Eventually he saw a farmer ambling along the roadside with a haying rake over his shoulder. Doherty pulled up beside him and simply said, "Château du Colombier, s'il vous plait." The fellow gave him an unpleasant look and thrust his arm out straight ahead.

Surrounded on either side by fields full of high corn stalks, he drove a couple kilometers along the same road until he came to an ornate sign for the chateau. He passed through a stone gate and over a small wooden bridge that traversed a narrow creek. A hundred yards or so down a hard-packed dirt track he came to a large mansion, a chateau by French standards. It was painted a pale pink with a couple of towers on either side. Two good-sized autos were parked out front; one was a luxury Citroën, the other a Rolls Royce. He pulled his midget car in beside them on a gravel patch. He briefly took in the majesty of the place before extricating himself from the Deux Chevaux.

Across from the chateau a large field spread out a couple of hundred yards before encountering a tall stand of trees. Two men were at the near edge of the field hitting golf balls out toward the tree line. It was a wholly incongruous sight. One of the men was wearing a flat golf cap, like the ones Ben Hogan and President Eisenhower wore; the other had on an all-black outfit. A black sport coat hung from one of the clubs in a golf bag by his side.

Doherty walked slowly toward the two men, each of whom gave him a good going over as he approached. The shorter of the two was wearing black pants, a black turtleneck sweater, and black shoes. He was short and stocky with a dark goatee and an equally dark mustache that connected with it in a semicircle around his mouth. He did not look like someone to be trifled with. The taller fellow was wearing plus fours to go with his golf hat. He had on dark rimmed glasses and his face featured a bushy moustache, whose color matched the dirty blond hair that was sticking out of the sides of his cap. He gave Doherty a quizzical but not unfriendly look.

Doherty smiled and raised his hand in a hello gesture. The two men kept staring at him.

"I'm looking for a fellow named Andrew Pettigrew. I was hoping one of you two gentleman might be him."

"I'm Pettigrew," the one in golf outfit said. The other man just snarled.

"My name is Hugh Doherty. I'm an American veteran over here doing some sightseeing. I've been told, Mr. Pettigrew, you may have served in the army with someone I knew from back home in Rhode Island. I believe he died in the battle for St- Lô. Does the name John McDonald mean anything to you?"

Everything was awkward for a few moments until Pettigrew stepped forward and took Doherty's hand. "Always glad to meet another ex-GI. This grumpy fellow here is my friend René Depardieu. René, say hello to Mr. Doherty, an American comrade from the war." René gave Doherty a hard look and then went back to hitting golf balls. His swing was awkward and the balls he hit went everywhere but straight.

"René," Pettigrew said. "You're holding the club too tight. You need to relax your grip to let your right hand turn over." The man ignored this advice and continued to lash wildly at the golf balls.

Pettigrew turned his attention back to Doherty. "Please come inside. I'd like to show you around my chateau."

The main hallway of the chateau was large with a high ceiling that looked all the way up the three-story stairway. The floor was a large checkerboard design in some sort of stone tiling. To one side in the hall was a full set of medieval armor holding a lance in its right glove while the left one rested on the hilt of a long sword. Everything about it looked aged and completely authentic.

Pettigrew escorted Doherty into a study where several comfortable couches sat. A number of portraits of men wearing costumes from previous centuries looked down on them from the high walls. Pettigrew flipped open an ornately carved box and removed a thin cigar. He offered one to Doherty, but the detective preferred his Camels instead. When he pulled them out Pettigrew stared at the pack with the noble looking dromedary on it.

"God, I haven't seen a Camel's package since the war. Are they still popular in the States?"

"Not so much anymore. A lot of people, particularly women, have moved over to filtered cigarettes. Camels and Luckies are still pretty common, though mostly with guys. You hardly ever see packages of Chesterfields anymore."

"Hard men like you, right Doherty?" he said with a crooked smile.

Doherty nodded in agreement. "Scientists now say cigarettes will kill us – and that Camels will kill us faster. Warnings about the dangers of smoking don't seem to bother the French very much."

"No, smoking cigarettes is a way of life over here. That and drinking red wine, preferably together. Ever since that Belmondo movie came out all the young guys in France walk around with their cigarettes dangling from the corner of their mouths. I tried on that look for a while but kept getting smoke in my eyes."

Pettigrew took a clippers out of his hand carved wooden humidor and snipped off the end his cigar. Doherty held out his engraved Zippo and torched his host's smoke. Pettigrew took a few seconds to admire the emblem of Doherty's outfit from the army that was embossed on the lighter.

"Were you here or further south during the fighting?"

"I was mostly in Italy. Then later as part of the final push into Germany. The only time I was in France was when I took liberty in Paris. Thought I should see the sights there once the Krauts were out of the way. And you?"

"My unit crossed over on D-Day plus three. By then the Germans were slowly retreating south and to the east. The worst of it was at St-Lô.

"I believe that where McDonald bought the ranch. I have to be honest with you Mr. Pettigrew."

"Please call me Andy. It'll feel nice hearing my name pronounced with an American accent for a change. No more Andy, with a broad 'a' and a heavy accent on the 'y'. "

"Okay, Andy. I wasn't being square with you before. I never really knew this John McDonald. Never set eyes on him in my life." Pettigrew appeared to relax at this admission.

"Back home in the States I'm a private eye. I used to be a cop but gave it up to go into business for myself. Turns out McDonald was married before he was sent over - to a wife who was already pregnant before he left. Anyway, to make a long story short, the baby, who's now a teenager, wanted to find out more about the father she never knew. Apparently, she and her stepfather don't get along all that well, despite, or perhaps because, he's one of the wealthiest men in Rhode Island. Or at least his family was for a few generations. They owned a string of textile mills all over New England. At the behest of the daughter, the family hired me to come over here to find out what I could about her dead father. So far you're the only person I've met who might've known him."

Pettigrew motioned Doherty over to some pictures on the walls of the study. One in particular on the mantle over the fireplace was of a platoon of GIs posing for an informal group photo. Some of the men were only wearing sleeveless army issue undershirts and shorts. Six men knelt in front making funny faces while an equal number of guys standing in back were also clown-ing it up. A few held up fingers representing donkey ears over the guys in front. Doherty's first impression was how young they all looked.

"This picture was taken a few days before we disembarked from England to cross the Channel. Half these guys would be dead within two weeks. I was their looey, fresh out of OCS." Doherty moved closer to the photo. He recognized one of the guys kneeling as possibly a younger version of Pettigrew, without the glasses or moustache. "That's me," Pettigrew said pointing at the guy Doherty'd been focusing on. Without his uniform shirt, Doherty couldn't tell if Pettigrew was a lieutenant or not.

"Which one is McDonald?"

Pettigrew looked closely at the photo. "I really couldn't tell you. I didn't know most of these guys all that well before they were killed. I only took command of the platoon a week before we left for France."

"Is there anything you remember about McDonald? Anything at all I can take back to his former wife and kid."

"They were so young and innocent," Pettigrew said sadly. "All I remember is that most of them spent time talking about their wives or girlfriends back home. Guys would also mention their folks from time to time, but I don't recall anything specific they said. For the most part none of these soldiers had ever been away from home before they went into the army. It was my job to make sure they didn't dwell too much on being homesick. I couldn't afford to have them forget about our mission."

Doherty looked closely at the photo of Pettigrew's platoon. It was too hazy for him to pick out anyone who matched up with the photo McDonald's wife had given him.

"I know what you mean. It was the same with a lot of the guys I served with. I wasn't married and my family wasn't close so what I was homesick for were things like a T-bone steak and a healthy shot of Jameson. It was better that way; kept me focused on being a soldier."

"I wish I could tell you more about Corporal McDonald. But as an officer I tried not to get too close to the enlisted men. Last thing I remember is that he, along with several others, got ripped to shreds by German machine gun fire somewhere outside of St-Lô. The battle for that town was terrible, though probably no worse than what you experienced in Italy.

"Let me show you the rest of the chateau. I'd like to invite you to dine with my wife and me tonight if you're free. It's not often that I get to spend time with a real veteran. I should tell you as an added bonus my wife is a big fan of mystery novels. So perhaps you can regal her with stories about some of your cases. Don't be afraid to embellish on them if you have a mind to. The gorier the tale the more charming she'll find you."

"Will your golfing buddy René be joining us?"

"Oh God no. My wife Celeste can't stand him. You know, he's something of a gangster around these parts. But not an appealing one like the villains in her mystery novels. Unfortunately, people like René are a necessary evil if you want to get any reconstruction projects off the ground in this part of the woods."

Doherty shrugged. "Hey, this isn't my world so far be it for me to pass judgment on what goes on here in France."

Chapter Twenty-Seven

The rest of the chateau was as splendiferous as the rooms on the ground floor. It looked more like a museum than a place where people actually lived. The kitchen was as large as one in a restaurant. Two women from the work staff were busy leaning over a hot stove. Pettigrew did not bother to introduce Doherty to either of them. Outside there was a small pond fed by a stream that ran under a bridge that the drive traversed. A number of white and black swans glided through the water or rested on the riverbank. It was a pastoral setting of unsurpassed beauty.

Pettigrew took Doherty on a short tour of the grounds, pointing out different plantings along the way. The field where the men had been hitting golf balls was now empty. The gruff fellow named René had departed in what was apparently his Rolls Royce. Back inside Pettigrew ushered Doherty onto a screened-in porch that looked west to where the sun was about to set. It was a bit chilly, so his host set up a couple of electric space heaters to warm the area. They sat and smoked and talked about French customs versus those in the U.S. One thing Pettigrew said he could never get used to was how late the French took their evening meal. He insisted that he and the missus dine no later than seven, which pleased the kitchen staff, though it often put off guests who regularly ate an hour or two later.

While they were talking a tall willowy woman wearing a plain black dress with long sleeves and a high neck drifted into the room. She was very beautiful with dark hair that fell to her shoulders and almost alabaster skin. Her red lips punctuated her pale face. Both men rose and Pettigrew put his arm around the woman's waist and introduced her as his wife Celeste. He described Doherty to her as a fellow army vet. Doherty took her slender hand in his and for a second thought of kissing it, as it seemed that was what such a beautiful hand required.

"Doherty here is a private eye like the men in those books you read, my dear. I thought he might entertain us with his tales of crime solving while we ate." He uttered this last remark as if his guest was a trained seal.

The wife sat down with them and gave Doherty a smile that spread her red lips exposing teeth even whiter than her flesh. "Do you do investigate murders, Mr. Doherty?" she asked hopefully, in English tinged with a French accent.

"Not really. Most of the time I leave those to the police. The bulk of my work involves tracking down men or women sleeping with someone they're not married to."

Celeste gave Pettigrew a funny smile. "Well you wouldn't get much work doing that en France. Here having illicit affairs is practically a way of life. Isn't that right, Andy?" Pettigrew did not answer, nor did he make eye contact with his wife.

In order to cut the tension in the room Doherty blurted out, "Actually I have been involved in a few murder investigations lately. Though they didn't start out that way. I guess you could say I stumbled across some dead bodies."

Celeste placed her hands under her chin and gave Doherty a killer look. "Oh, pray do tell us about these murders."

The conversation was interrupted by one of the kitchen girls bringing out a large tureen containing a soup that was white in color. Some words passed between the wife and the servant girl that Doherty couldn't follow.

"Sandrine says the soup is cream of cauliflower. I hope you like it, Mr. Doherty," she said, once again flashing her stunning smile. The girl then ladled portions of the soup into shallow bowls for each of them.

"I have to confess I don't usually eat cauliflower at home, but since I've been over here, I've decided to suspend judgment and indulge in the local cuisine. I must say the French certainly have a way with cooking. However, I have drawn the line at snails and frog legs."

"It's because the French eat frog legs that people, particularly the English, call them *frogs* or *froggies*. Being Swiss I never took it as an insult. Andy has never eaten frog legs either, have you dear?"

Pettigrew mumbled something, though he seemed to have momentarily checked out of their dinner conversation.

"Well, Mr. Private Eye, will you tell us about some of the murder cases you've been involved in."

Doherty started with the Spencer Wainwright murder and how it had been the result of his involvement in a real estate deal with gangsters. He didn't use the word Mafia because he didn't know if that term had any currency in France.

"Andy knows all about gangsters, don't you dear? He's had to cuddle up with some of them here including that disgusting René Depardieu. I believe I saw him and his Rolls Royce in our drive just this afternoon."

"He wanted to come out to hit golf balls. What could I say – you know how he can be," Pettigrew said weakly.

Once again Doherty took the lull in their brittle repartee to describe his role in the Meier Poznansky case. He spent a lot of time describing the Polish ex-Nazi and his collaborators who were living in Providence and threatening his client's life. Talking about Nazis walking around free in the U.S. definitely perked up Pettigrew's interest. Doherty purposely left out the part the Israeli agents played in the death of Antonin Bradz. That, of course, was the deal he'd made with the Israelis when he took responsibility for killing the despicable Pole. He did emphasize that in the end the police chalked up his killing of Bradz as self-defense.

By this point the dinner had arrived. A good-sized whole fish cooked perfectly with a crispy skin was placed in front of Pettigrew. His host carefully filleted it with the skill of a surgeon. He then passed plates to his guest and his wife. Before he did, he coated each piece of fish with a sweet lemony butter sauce. Bowls of carrots, potatoes and green beans accompanied the fish as side dishes. The host opened a second bottle of white wine as they commenced to dive into this delicious meal. Pettigrew joined the conversation again, mentioning with some pride how the fish was a grouper caught in these very waters this morning.

At the wife's prompting Doherty moved onto the case that brought down the big-time political operative Kevin O'Shaughnessy. As he had earlier when he left out the Israelis and Rachel Katz's rape, he chose while describing this case that involved some incriminating smut films to leave out the part where his pal Gus Timilty murdered two Boston hit men. Doherty had to admit that in telling these stories while being fueled with wine and delicious food, he was beginning to see his work as a small-town detective in a totally new light.

"You should write up your cases in novel form, Mr. Doherty. Like that Ellery Queen fellow does," Celeste Pettigrew suggested.

"I'm afraid Ellery Queen is a fictional character. And the men who created him were never private detectives. What I've recounted for you, Mrs. Pettigrew, are murders that really happened."

"All the more reason why you should write about them - for their realism. And please let's not be so formal. You may call me Celeste."

"Darling, I don't think Mr. Doherty is interested in becoming an author of his own life. In fact, he is here in Normandy working a case right now. He's trying to piece together the life of a young man who served in my platoon and was killed at the battle of St-Lô. That's one of the reasons I invited him to dine with us. Why don't you tell Celeste about Corporal McDonald and your mission here in France?"

While they ate their fish, he spun out the whole tale of how the Royal family hired him to find out what he could about John McDonald. How the gist of his case was to uncover anything about the biological father of a young girl who wasn't even born when her father died.

"My lord, that is fascinating. How is your investigation going so far?"

"Well, aside from seeing the sights in Paris and Normandy while drinking a lot of fine wine and eating good food, I've found out very little I didn't already know about the boy I'm supposed to be investigating. So far, your husband is the only person I've met who had any acquaintance with him at all. And from what he's told me the young man died a little over a month after arriving in his platoon. As of now all I can tell the family is that he died in Normandy defending freedom."

"Defending freedom," she spit out as if they were curse words. That put a definite chill over the conversation.

Nothing more was said about Corporal McDonald or the war. After dessert and coffee Mrs. Pettigrew excused herself from the table and retired to some room on the upper level of the chateau. Pettigrew invited Doherty to accompany him back to the study for cigars and after dinner drinks. He passed on the cigar but accepted what Pettigrew described as a very old and rare Armagnac. Under most circumstances Doherty wouldn't have known the difference until this liqueur glided down his throat like a soft breeze. Pettigrew flashed him a pleased smile when Doherty commended him on it.

"I did a lot of talking about myself at dinner. Why don't you tell me about yourself, Andy? How does a guy like you end up living in a place like this?"

Pettigrew skillfully clipped the end off of his cigar and torched it with his own slim lighter. Doherty'd had too much to drink to bother raising himself off the comfortable leather sofa to light his host's smoke.

"I was born and raised in Wisconsin," Pettigrew began. "I came east in thirty- seven to go to school at Dartmouth. That's in New Hampshire."

"I know where Dartmouth is," Doherty retorted. "I also know where Wisconsin is. My sister Margaret lives in Minnesota."

"Yes, it's our neighboring state. Have you ever been there?"

Doherty shook his head. "No. I keep intending to go out for a visit, but something always gets in the way." Pettigrew appeared to relax knowing that Doherty had never been to his part of the Midwest.

"Like one of your murder investigations?" Pettigrew said in a snide tone. Doherty chose to ignore the remark. Clearly his host was a bit put out by his beautiful wife's keen interest in Doherty's cases.

"I graduated in 1941 and returned to Wisconsin and went to work for my father. He was in the farm equipment business. To hear him tell it he started out as little more than a peddler driving a beat-up old pick-up truck from town to town hawking his goods. By the time I came of age he owned one of the largest businesses of its kind in the upper Midwest. You could say I grew up with a silver spoon in my mouth. But there were also troubles along the way. After I was born my mother had several miscarriages. In time they caused havoc with her mental health. When I was fourteen, she took an overdose of sleeping pills. It was never clear whether it was an accident or she took them on purpose. My father was devastated. He'd spent so much time and money trying to help her get healthy that after she died all he had left was his business. He had few friends, and because he was an only child like myself, by process of elimination I became his only living relative."

Pettigrew returned to the bar area where he retrieved the ornate bottle of Armagnac and poured two more glasses for each of them.

"When the war broke out my father worked some of his rich man's magic to get me into OCS. He was thinking if he pulled a few strings he could arrange a cushy wartime job for me either with the draft board in Milwaukee or in Washington."

"What happened that landed you over here?"

"I wanted to get into the action. I was young and foolhardy, and I wanted to get away from Wisconsin and my father. My original plan after graduation was to go to work on Wall Street, but my father would have none of that. He insisted that I come into the business with him. When the war came that changed everyone's plans. Once I got my lieutenant's stripes, I volunteered to lead a combat unit. Although I was commissioned in late '42, I didn't get sent overseas until the winter of '43. After the landing and our battles in Normandy we headed north into Belgium and then Holland. Fought the Krauts at the Battle of the Bulge, and then, like you, pushed our way into Germany. Many of the original men under my command were lost along the way. I was lucky; I never even got a scratch."

Doherty listened with rapt attention, though he couldn't help but feel

that Pettigrew's narration of his wartime experiences somehow sounded rehearsed.

"What about this chateau? How did it come into your possession?"

"My father died right before the armistice. He was pleased that I survived, but his heart gave out anyway. It probably had more to do with his efforts to keep his businesses on track during the war. I didn't feel any responsibility for his death even if he did spend the last two years of his life worrying about the fate of his only son. When I was discharged, like a lot of other GIs, I decided to do some touring around Europe before going home. My old man had salted away some money in a Swiss bank account that only he and I could draw on. It was while I was in Zurich withdrawing some of our money that I met Celeste.

"The next time I came back there we became a couple. After that we traveled around Europe together. On one of our tours I insisted that we come out here to Normandy because I wanted to show her some of the places I'd been during the war. Once we saw how much damage had been done, much of it caused by the Allies, she convinced me I should use some of my wealth to help rebuild places in this area. I then arranged with my father's lawyers back in the States to sell most of his holdings to his business managers. It was easily done since many of them were more than happy to get their hands on it after I'd made it clear I had no interest in running his operations. I still own a lot of property in Wisconsin and thereabouts that I collect rents on. Some of that money goes directly into various accounts I have here in France and in Switzerland.

"For the most part I was able to have the bulk of my father's estate transferred to me over here without having to go back home. All I had to do was prove my identity and sign a slew of documents that were notarized by various officials here and in Switzerland. Celeste had worked for a bank in Zurich so she was able to help me with a lot of the red tape. Once that was done, Celeste and I, and later our children, were able to live the good life over here without ever having to return to the States. A large part of our money now goes into a variety of philanthropic efforts in this part of France. The main one right now is the reconstruction of the medieval citadelle at St-Malo."

"And you have no desire to go back to the States?"

Pettigrew shook his head then took a long drag on his cigar. "I did at first, but then that whole business with Joe McCarthy happened. The fact that he was from Wisconsin and an acquaintance of my father's kind of soured me on returning home. After Celeste and I were married and had the boys, I realized my life was over here. Our sons have been educated in French schools and speak English only sparingly. They would be out of their element in the U.S. Celeste isn't exactly a fan of our homeland either, in case you didn't catch her drift at dinner."

"I guess. Though she does like American mystery novels."

"And movies as well. I think she would find the real thing very disappointing, especially if I took her out to Wisconsin. Besides there is no one there for me anymore now that my father's dead. My mother's people were a bunch of hicks from Oklahoma. I met a few of them at her funeral. They were pretty plain spoken in holding my father responsible for her breakdown after the miscarriages. They might've had good reason to. Even so, I had no interest in developing a relationship with any of them."

"Is there anything you miss about home besides eating dinner at a sensible hour?"

This brought a small laugh from Pettigrew. "You may find this a bit trivial, but I do miss baseball. When I was a kid, I used to regularly study the box scores in the newspaper every day."

"All the more for your loss. As you probably know the hapless Braves moved from Boston to Milwaukee in '53 and became a championship team. They even beat the Yankees in the '57 World Series."

"I knew about that. I pick up the *International Herald Tribune* whenever I'm in a city big enough where it's sold. My boys aren't the least bit interested in baseball. They play and follow soccer, or football as the French call it. Personally, I find their games rather boring because there is so little scoring. However, you run the risk of bodily harm to say such a thing out loud in France. The French of all ages and classes worship at the shrine of their football stars. Plus, betting on the games is endemic in the culture."

Noticing that Doherty had drained his second snifter of Armagnac his host replenished his drink with a mere flick of the wrist.

"Is your friend Depardieu involved in the betting game as well?" Doherty asked, hoping to poke that hornets' nest a little.

"René is hardly a friend. He is someone I have to work with to get certain projects underway in and around St-Malo. Regrettably, he often takes inappropriate liberties with my property here whenever he feels like it, as you saw this afternoon. Celeste loathes him, which I think is one of the reasons he likes to hang around the chateau knowing that she doesn't welcome him here. I have no doubt he would like to screw my wife, though I'm sure she would just as soon slit his throat as climb into bed with him. You see, René is the kind of man who always wants what he cannot have. So, in some cases he simply takes it by force."

"What about the police? Can't they help you get him out of your hair?" This comment elicited a loud laugh from Pettigrew, the first of the evening.

"Doherty, don't be so naïve. The police are all on René's payroll. His wishes are their commands. Things out here are not all that they seem. But let's not talk about René Depardieu. It will only make it more difficult for us to digest the wonderful meal we just had."

Doherty rose to leave but found that his legs were not being all that co-operative.

"You don't look like you're in a good frame of mind to wend your way back to town. It's a tricky drive even under sober circumstances. Why don't you stay the night here at the chateau? Lord knows we have plenty of rooms."

Doherty agreed to take up Pettigrew's offer. His host then escorted him to the second floor; all the while Doherty kept thinking of it as the *premier étage*. A lovely guest room was already set up to receive any drunk unable to drive back to town. Pettigrew showed him where the nearest bathroom was and provided him with a towel, a bathrobe, a toothbrush, and paste.

"It is not uncommon for us to have dinner guests who stay too long and drink too much to find their way home safely. Celeste makes sure the maid keeps a couple of rooms prepared for just such occasions," Pettigrew explained. With that he bid Doherty a good night.

He was tempted to flop onto the bed fully clothed, then thought of how disgusting he would feel in the morning if he did. With a certain unsteadiness he made his way to the bathroom, washed his face and teeth, and returned to the guest room. Stripping down to his skivvies he was in the sack before another thought about Andrew Pettigrew, his wife Celeste, and the detested René Depardieu could pass through his mind.

He didn't know how much later it was when he heard the door to his room ease open. If he were at home, he might've reached into the bedside table for his .38. However, he was in France and his trusty piece was three thousand miles away. Slowly he pried his head off the pillow only seconds before Celeste Pettigrew sat on the bed mere inches from his face. She gently placed her hand under the covers on his naked thigh and smiled at him. Through the slits where his eyes usually were he saw that she was dressed in a sheer nightgown that left little to the imagination. He could see the nipples of her breasts as they pushed against the fabric.

"To what do I owe this unexpected visit?" he mumbled still tasting the Armagnac on his breath despite the tooth brushing.

"I heard Andrew setting you up down here and thought you might like a little company." Her French accent got him before she reached 'company'.

"I try not to make it a habit of sleeping with another man's wife. Especially when her husband is occupying the floor above us."

"You don't have to worry about him. He went out less than an hour after he tucked you in."

Doherty had no idea what time it was. Still he said, "Where would he be going at this time of night?"

A dark expression crossed Celeste Pettigrew's face or what he could see of it in the lightless room. "I suspect he went to visit one of the trollops he has waiting for him at some cheap hotel in town."

"And why would a man with a wife as lovely as you be seeking solace with other women?"

"Andy has a propensity to slum it with girls who will do things with him that I won't." Doherty knew the polite thing here was not to ask what those things were. Before he could gather his thoughts, Celeste Pettigrew let her gown slip from her shoulders. For a brief second in the dim light he took in her beautiful white form before she slipped under the covers with him. They made love with her assuming the dominant position; Doherty did his best to get his alcohol-addled mind in touch with his current circumstances. It took quite a while for each of them to be satisfied, though he was in no position to complain about it.

When they were done Celeste rested her beautiful naked body next to his while Doherty tried not to fall asleep. He craved a cigarette, though had neither the energy nor the wherewithal to search out his pack of Camels. In a short time Morpheus got the better of him and he fell into a deep sleep.

Chapter Twenty-Eight

Needless to say, when he awoke shortly before dawn his nighttime companion was gone. His first gesture was to have that cigarette he'd craved hours before. When he finished it, he rolled over and went back to sleep, thinking of Celeste Pettigrew's alabaster body atop him as he drifted off.

Sometime later he awoke ready for the day. The bathroom lacked a shower, but it did have a nice large, old-fashioned bathtub that sat up on a pedestal. While occupying himself shaving and brushing his teeth he ran himself a hot bath. Before sliding into the tub, he thought of what a shame it was to wash off the lovely scent from Celeste's body.

Once bathed and dressed he made his way to the ground floor where he was immediately greeted by one of the women from the kitchen staff. She spoke no English, yet he understood enough of what she was saying to seat himself at a small table in the dining space where she began to bring him various breakfast goodies. Le petit déjeuner was becoming one of Doherty's favorite French meals. The girl poured him a cup of rich dark coffee that she added some hot milk to. Before she returned to the kitchen, he asked in his halting French the whereabouts of Monsieur and Madame Pettigrew.

With a wave of her hand the girl indicated that Madame had gone off somewhere. In parsing her words as best he could he concluded that Monsieur Pettigrew was ensconced in his office. The girl brought him a large basket full of French pastries of various kinds as well as a bowl with some fresh cut peaches and pears in it. He ate well, washing it all down with several cups of the strong coffee. A copy of the *Herald Tribune* was stuffed into a magazine rack near the breakfast table, so he retrieved the week-old journal. For the first time since he'd arrived in France he caught up with news from around the world. Most of the stories were about events going on in Europe - things that he had little or no interest in. The American stories were primarily about the campaign for president, with Jack Kennedy drawing most of the press attention. The sports page was filled with pieces about tennis tournaments and auto races around the continent. There was nothing about baseball.

Once he was finished with his petit déjeuner Doherty took the liberty of venturing through the foyer to Pettigrew's office-study. The door was shut so he knocked and then walked in without being summoned. His host had a pair of reading glasses stuck on the end of his nose and he was hunkered down over a mass of papers spread out before him. When he saw Doherty at the door, he slipped off those glasses, replacing them with his dark rimmed ones.

"Ah, Doherty. So nice to see you this morning. I trust you had a good sleep?"

Without mentioning that he'd spent part of the night with his host's wife he replied, "I slept like a lamb. Must have been that fine Armagnac you sent me off with."

"Yes, yes, nothing like a good digestif to insure a solid night's sleep."

"Was it my imagination or did I hear a car drive off sometime after I went upstairs?"

"I confess, that was me. I had no business driving after all we'd had to drink. Unfortunately, there was some pressing business in town that I had to attend to right away." Pettigrew said nothing more and Doherty wasn't about to pursue the issue.

"Well anyway, I think I'll be making my way back to St-Malo town. If you could give me some rough directions, I may be able to drive back to town without getting lost."

Pettigrew wrote down some intelligible directions that he assured

Doherty would get him safely to the old town gate.

"Thanks for your hospitality. Maybe we can get together again before I leave this part of the country."

"Do you have any idea how long you'll be staying in St-Malo?" The question came out weighted with more than mere curiosity.

"I don't know yet. It doesn't seem like I'm going to be able to dig up much more about Corporal McDonald than I already have. I suppose I'll spend a few days doing some touristy things and then head back to Rouen before returning to Paris. If you think of anything else that might be of value in my quest, I'm staying at the Hotel Cartier. Do you know it?"

"Yes, I know it. A small hotel not far from the old gate. We are doing some reconstruction on the citadelle close by. Perhaps if you're still around the day after tomorrow, Celeste and I can meet you in town for a dinner. And I assure you it will be no later than seven," he added with a wink.

With only one missed turn Doherty found his way back to the parking lots across from the old gate. The early morning chill helped bring some clarity back to his thinking. A younger version of the hotel's proprietor was at the desk when he finally made his way into the small lobby of the Hotel Cartier. He gave Doherty a suspicious look until he informed the fellow that he was registered at the hotel but had spent the night at a friend's out in the country. The guy apologized in as obsequious a manner as a Frenchman could, which wasn't very much. Doherty told him he would be going up to his room to change. When he came down, he would like the desk clerk to help him put through a call to Paris.

Upon returning to the lobby he gave the fellow Shanahan's number at the American Embassy and asked him to ring it up. The phone in the lobby appeared to be the only one in the hotel. After some back and forth in French the clerk handed the headset to Doherty.

"Parlez vous Anglais?" he asked of the woman at the other end.

"Yes, of course."

"I would like to speak with Mr. Shanahan. It is on a matter of some urgency."

"Could I have your name please?" Doherty gave her his name. He was informed that Shanahan was in a meeting and would not be back in his office for at least thirty minutes. Holding the phone away from him Doherty asked the fellow at the desk if he would arrange for a call back to be made to the hotel. The clerk took the phone and slung some more French with the woman on the other end. After he hung up, he told Doherty she assured him that his desired party would call back *a très vite.* He assumed this meant as soon as possible.

He decided to wait in the miniscule lobby for Shanahan's call. There was a small bookshelf behind the two easy chairs that made up the sum total of the lobby waiting area. He fingered through them looking for something to occupy his time. They were all well-used paperbacks, most in French. One in English was a collection of stories by the author J.D. Salinger. Doherty'd read his novel *The Catcher in the Rye* a few years back. He came away from that book thinking the main character was an egotistical prep school kid who could have used a good slap upside the head. Yet he was aware that a lot of young people loved the book and took it as their personal bible. Doherty was willing to chalk that up to generational change.

He was halfway through a story called "A Perfect Day for Bananafish," about a supposedly damaged war vet who takes up a peculiar relationship with a very young girl on a beach somewhere in Florida. Before he could reach the end of the tale, the phone at the desk rang loudly, causing him to jerk in his chair. The clerk spoke some French into the mouthpiece before handing it to Doherty. Michael Shanahan's familiar New York accent was on the other end.

"Having a good time out in the provinces, Doherty?"

"Yeah, to some extent. I will say it's been interesting. I'm going to need a very big favor from you, Mike. It might even require you to contact my uncle Patrick if you can't get me what I need on this side of the Atlantic."

He could hear Shanahan audibly hemming and hawing at the other end. "Why don't you tell me what you're looking for before I put in any calls to Boston. The embassy frowns upon us using the phones here for private long-distance calls. If I do have to call your uncle, I'll file it under official business. What are you looking for?"

Doherty pulled the phone cord as far away from the hotel desk as possible. He didn't want anyone in St-Malo, including the clerk, to know what he was up to. "I need anything and everything you can find about a fellow named Andrew Pettigrew. He's a wealthy American doing…"

"Jesus, Doherty. I know who Andy Pettigrew is. I don't think there's anyone over here connected with the U.S. government who doesn't know about him and what he's been doing to help with the rebuilding of France."

"Good. That'll give you a head start. Could you send me anything you can find about him? I'm staying at the Hotel Cartier in St-Malo. And if someone can scratch up an old photo of him, like on his enlistment papers or even sometime before that it would be helpful as well."

"Do you mind if I ask what this is all about?"

"Let's just say that I don't think Pettigrew is all that he's cracked up to be."

"You're making this sound awfully mysterious."

"That's my game, Mike. Remember, I'm a private investigator."

"Swell. Look I'll do what I can. How long do you plan on being in St-Malo?"

"As long as it takes until I hear back from you." With that Shanahan rang off. Doherty had spoken into the phone in a quiet voice. Still, he wasn't sure how much the young guy at the desk heard of his conversation, or what he would do with it if he had.

Doherty spent the next few hours exploring the nooks and crannies of St-Malo. The old citadelle that sat out over the water was a small walled-in part of the larger town, or intra-muros as they called it. Its ramparts commanded a rather spectacular view of the English Channel to the north and the Rance basin to the south. St-Malo could trace its origins back to a monastic community founded there by Saints Aaron and Brendan in the 6th century. In time, a succession of pirate-mariners controlled this part of the Brittany coast, exacting tribute from many passing cargo ships, especially those of the English. The wealth these brigands brought to St-Malo helped fund voyages of exploration such as those of Jacques Cartier to North America.

Another famous brigand, Robert Surcouf, was also immortalized by a statue in the same area as Cartier's. After all the saints he'd been exposed to in France, Doherty found it somewhat gratifying for a place to celebrate its history by venerating a band of what were essentially outlaws. For a while the fortified town was even able to declare itself an independent republic. Clearly with the wealth it accumulated by extorting tribute from foreign vessels it could afford to do so. In time the corsairs of St-Malo passed into history and the area was taken over and officially incorporated into France.

Because of its location the Germans found it a perfect spot to garrison 12,000 troops in anticipation of a cross-channel invasion by the Allies. Once the combined Allied forces landed at the Normandy beaches, some German soldiers from there retreated west along the coast to St-Malo. As a result of their presence there, the town took a tremendous pounding from American artillery shelling and aerial bombing along with British naval bombardments. Patton's army assaulted St-Malo in early August of '44, just two months after the D-Day landings. By early September the final three hundred German soldiers defending the citadelle were forced to surrender due to the lack of drinking water. But not before they burned a number of ancient wooden buildings in the old town just for spite. In the end the Allies took nearly 10,000 German prisoners in the battles there and in neighboring towns along the coast. Their surrender of this strip of land freed the English Channel for the landing of more Allied troops and heavy equipment. However, the battle also left much of the medieval citadelle of St-Malo in ruins.

Since then a massive amount of aid through the Marshall Plan and other similar Allied projects as well as from philanthropists like Andrew Pettigrew have helped to physically restore the town to its former glory. In that time St-Malo has slowly become a popular tourist destination for French as well as foreign travelers. He read that the beaches at nearby Dinard and other spots along the coast are now desirable destinations for sun worshippers. Being a person with white on white Irish skin, Doherty never saw the need to travel anywhere to sunbathe. He could easily pick up a homegrown sunburn on the beaches in southern Rhode Island.

While circling the ramparts he briefly ducked into the Musée d'Histoire de la Ville to see the self-aggrandizing exhibits of the exorbitant riches the town once accumulated through piracy, colonialism, and slave trading. Despite his inability to comprehend most of the French inscriptions below the items on display, he could tell that the slave trading part was only mentioned in passing. But who was he to criticize? He lived in a state where many wealthy families in the pre and post-Revolutionary period made much of their money buying and selling humans transported unwillingly to the Americas from their homes in West Africa. These men, having grown rich through slave trading, donated some of their wealth to fund schools and other public institutions that bore their names to this day. He recalled how many Rhode Islanders celebrated these men for their business acuity, never for their trading in human flesh. That part of his state's noble history had been effectively swept under the rug.

The museum also displayed some Nazi handbills reminding the locals of the terrible damage the English had periodically rendered to their picturesque town, especially when they blew up its port in 1693. That was one thing that struck Doherty about his time in France. Memories of events and lingering resentments of those events that had transpired centuries ago were conjured up as if they'd happened only weeks before. National, regional, and even familial animosities continued to fester long after those who'd initiated them were dead and buried. Consequently, German propaganda reminding the denizens of St-Malo of the damage the Brits had perpetrated on them nearly three centuries earlier might indeed have had some effect in the 1940s. Of course, it wasn't as if the Germans were merely tourists who chose to stay in Normandy and Brittany for a fortnight to enjoy the beaches along their coasts. What made the more recent history of St-Malo complicated is that almost all of the serious damage visited upon this quaint little town in the war was at the hands of the Allies, mostly the Americans. He was sure a good many of the locals hereabouts did not welcome the Yanks who entered St-Malo in September of 1944 as heroes bringing the blessings of freedom where only tyranny had prevailed before.

Everywhere Doherty ventured through the old city he came upon construction equipment, much of it bearing signs of P&G Construction. At least Pettigrew was doing his level best to account for the damage his country had inflicted upon this town. Feeling pangs of hunger, Doherty stopped into a little café. Without too much trouble he was able to order a ham and cheese omelet accompanied by a bottle of French beer. Along with the eggs came a delicious salad dressed with oil and vinegar and a hint of mustard. As was typical for any French meal, half of a baguette accompanied it as well.

While eating Doherty mused about America's role in the so-called liberation of France. He wondered what the Frenchies out this way thought of the occupying Krauts and their Allied liberators in light of how much death and destruction was visited upon them. What complicated things even more is that the French now did quite a bit of trade with neighboring West Germany, while trying their best not to get involved in the Cold War imbroglio between the U.S. and the Soviet Union.

It was nearly three o'clock by the time Doherty returned to the Hotel Cartier. He was hoping to catch an afternoon nap given how his sleep the previous night had been interrupted by Celeste Pettigrew's unexpected visit. The younger man was still at the desk when he strolled into the pint-sized lobby. Before he could hit the stairs, the fellow indicated that there was a message for Doherty. He thought it would be too soon for him to be receiving anything of substance from Mike Shanahan, so he wasn't surprised when the clerk handed him a small envelope.

The note inside read: *Meet me at the Hotel de France et de Chateaubriand at five. Room 28. C.* He did his best to find out from the clerk where the Hotel De France at de Chateaubriand was located without raising any suspicions. His question made the man uncomfortable.

"You are not happy at the Hotel Cartier?" he asked in stilted English.

Doherty smiled. "No, I am very pleased with the Cartier. I am meeting a friend at the Hotel de France."

The young guy pulled out a small map of the citadelle area and marked the other hotel. It was not far from the main square. He checked his watch figuring it wouldn't take him more than fifteen minutes to walk there. Once in his room he set about washing and changing into some more fashionable looking clothes on the assumption that the Hotel de France et de Chateaubriand was a classier joint than the Cartier.

He wasn't mistaken. When he approached the grand hotel, a doorman swept the glass entry door open for him and offered up a smiling "Bonjour." The place must have had at least six times the number of rooms as the Cartier, though the latter certainly fit Doherty's style more than this place. At the main desk he asked for room 28 and the young woman pointed him to the elevator down the hall. The lobby was much grander than one at the Cartier and very

inviting with several easy chairs and couches scattered around it. A large ornate table stood in the middle of the space with an enormous vase of fresh cut
flowers resting on it. Even the corridor walls on the path to the elevator were
lined with what looked like original watercolors of the French countryside.

The lift was small, barely room enough to carry four people provided that
they weren't toting any luggage. Both sidewalls were mirrored so he could
look at himself from both front and back in the small space and see an infinite
number of self-images while he did. He checked his teeth in the mirror to make
sure no lettuce from his lunch salad had lodged itself in them. The elevator
stopped at the third floor, which Doherty reminded himself would be the second in France. Room 28 was halfway down the hallway on the left-hand side.
He paused before knocking, wondering for a second if he'd be walking into an
unexpected trap. Celeste Pettigrew answered right away and pulled him
quickly into the room while looking down the corridor in either direction.

"Don't worry, no one's followed me. And there was no one else in the
elevator other than a thousand continuing images of myself."

Without responding she slipped into Doherty's arms and gave him a very
deep kiss. He did his best not to offer any resistance.

"I ordered some champagne. I hope you don't mind," she said as she
handed him the bottle to remove the cork. He did a competent job of removing
the cork so that it didn't bounce off the ceiling.

"What are we celebrating?"

She slid into his arms and kissed him again, nearly as a deep as the first
time. "How about this," she said with her irresistible French accent. She was
wearing a tight blue dress with a high neck. It was bisected around her waist
by a silk sash that was on the turquoise side of blue. She'd already kicked off
her high-heeled shoes and stood in stocking feet. Doherty poured them two
glasses of champagne and returned the bottle to its nesting place in a silver
bucket filled with ice. They clinked glasses as if they were toasting his cuckold
of her husband.

The room had a couple of French doors that led to a small balcony that
afforded a beautiful view of the sea beyond the walls of the citadelle. It sure
beat Doherty's view at the Cartier of a stone wall under repair. For obvious
reasons they chose not to appear on the balcony like the king and queen of

England.

They were only two glasses of champagne in when Doherty took the liberty of relieving Celeste of her sash and blue dress. Much to his excitement she was wearing a black brassiere and a black garter belt attached to nylon stocking on the blacker side of neutral. It was an outfit he'd only seen worn by models in the men's magazines at Harry's Barbershop back home. Sensing the titillation she was bringing to this American rube, Celeste offered him a brief provocative pose. The black against her creamy white skin was enough to get him aroused. When she whispered some sweet nothings in French and breathed softly in his ear, he knew he was a goner. His clothes came off as fast as they ever had in a barracks inspection and the two of them were atop the bed in short order. He took his time removing her undergarments, pleasing himself with her get-up as a form of foreplay. Once she reached inside his boxers it was the beginning a one-way trip to the pleasure dome.

This time their lovemaking was slow and as erotic as anything he'd ever been involved in. He had to wonder what Pettigrew's cheap sluts did that his wife wouldn't since she seemed to be up for just about anything. Perhaps Andy's sideline girls dressed him in a diaper and paddled him like a baby. His wife might not have been interested in those kinds of kinky fantasies, although she was eager to engage in everything else. By the time they finished that afternoon he thought he might have to send his member and the body it was attached to off to a health spa for rehabilitation.

Apparently at one point he slipped into a kind of slumber because the next vision he saw was of Celeste standing before a mirror in her sexy undergarments combing out her long dark hair, which flowed almost to her waist when it wasn't tied it up.

"I hate to interrupt this erotic adventure with some mundane questions. What exactly is going on between you and your husband that caused you to invite me up here today?"

"Let's just say our relationship has evolved into something more platonic than intimate."

"Does that mean you and he don't engage in sex anymore?"

She turned and looked at Doherty. "No, we do sometimes; after all this is France. One can have sex here with whomever one wishes. But my husband is a man of many secrets. I have chosen not to know what some of them are."

"What does that make me? Just an interesting diversion?"

She came over and sat beside Doherty on the bed. Her perfume combined with the smell of sex was getting him aroused for perhaps one more go-round before he checked himself into a hospital.

"You Americans are always looking for romance and meaning along with the sex. Can't you only enjoy what is before you when it is there?" Her explanation was not dissimilar from what Yvonne had said to him in Paris. Celeste reached over to the table and poured them two more glasses of champagne.

"Please Doherty, let's enjoy what we have now without looking too far into the future."

"Sounds good to me," he said as he reached up and unsnapped her black bra.

Chapter Twenty-Nine

D oherty returned to the Hotel Cartier about as satiated as one man could be after his evening tryst at the Hotel de France et de Chateaubriand. He and Celeste had elected to leave separately so as not to draw attention to themselves as a couple. Since the room was registered in her name, or perhaps some fake name she chose for the occasion, he exited first. She mentioned something about staying on to bathe. Pettigrew had gone to Caen on some business that day and told her he wouldn't be back at the chateau until quite late. Doherty didn't want to speculate as to what her husband's business was.

After some cleaning of his own at the Cartier he decided what he really needed was something substantial to eat. An evening of love making can do that even to the best of men. He wandered down to the street that circumvented the town just inside the main gate. There were of host of small restaurants along this strip. Without much effort he found one that had a prix fixe menu posted outside. This would save him the task of having to engage in a labored conversation with a waiter about what was on a menu he couldn't read. The prix fixe offered a bifteck with frites as its main course. By now Doherty was able to recognize the various names the French used to describe what was essentially a piece of beef masquerading as a steak.

213

The meal came with a carafe of red wine, which was welcomed as Doherty's mouth was still sore from mugging with Celeste Pettigrew. What he hadn't anticipated was that the *huitres* listed as the entrée were raw oysters. Doherty had seen these ugly morsels on other people's plates back in Rhode Island but had never indulged in the slimy bivalves himself. He initial thought was to send them back. Then the phrase 'when in Rome' got lodged in his head. After dousing them with lemon he slid one into his mouth. At first, he was put off by their texture, which frankly reminded him of a glob of spit. Yet when he bit into it, it tasted rather good. Using the wine as a means of washing his mouth between each oyster, he found himself eating the whole half dozen with a modicum of pleasure.

The steak proved to be just on the edible side of shoe leather, though the lemony cream sauce it was covered in at least made it palatable. The sauce reminded him of the covering Pettigrew had put on their grouper the night before. Although he couldn't stop thinking about his rendezvous with Celeste, he was determined to get his mind back on the case he was supposed to be investigating. A lovely piece of chocolate cake with some cream sauce atop it finished off the prix fixe menu. He ordered a cup of café noir to go with it.

Halfway through his coffee and dessert, two men plopped down in the chairs on the other side of the table from him. The place was about half full, so their abrupt entrance caught the attention of just about everyone in the restaurant, particularly the waiter and the proprietor. The one who took the chair across from him was René Depardieu; the other, larger man was a tough looking pug with a face that had fifty miles of bad road on it. When this guy put his hands on the table Doherty noticed his paws were a series of swollen knuckles covered in scar tissue. He had a look about him that would've scared the cape off of Count Dracula. Depardieu clicked his fingers at the waiter. When the fellow drew closer to the table, René ordered some cognac and circled the table with his index finger to indicate glasses for all three of them.

Doherty took a hard look at Depardieu. He was a singularly unattractive man with dark acne scarred skin, a black van dyke beard, and matching greasy hair combed back from his forehead. On looks alone he could see why Celeste Pettigrew found him loathsome. The waiter seemed noticeably uneasy as he brought a small round tray carrying three snifter glasses to their table. His hands were shaking as he placed each glass down on the table. Depardieu exchanged some French in a raspy voice with their server, who withdrew as quickly as he'd appeared. He then gave Doherty a smile through teeth that would have looked better on a ferret.

"Bonsoir, mon ami," he said as he raised his glass. Doherty knew *ami* meant friend. He couldn't imagine any world in which René Depardieu would be his friend.

"Please to introduce my bodyguard, Bruno. Bruno meet Monsieur Doherty. He works as a private detective over in the States." The large bundle of meat named Bruno didn't appear to understand Rene's description of Doherty's profession. He translated it to *détective privé*. From his expression it was apparent Bruno had no use for anyone who detected anything.

"My friend Bruno was a middleweight boxer. He once fought for the French national title."

"How did that work out?"

"Not so good," Depardieu said with a shrug. "The smart money was bet on his opponent. He was made to lose the match. After boxing I put him to work for me. Today he makes more money than he would've if he continued getting hit in the head. No matter, his head was already a little cuckoo," René said as he circled the side of his own head with his index finger.

Doherty took the opportunity to give Bruno a good looking over. From the expression on the ex-pugilist's face it was clear that at best he was only drifting in and out of their conversation. Doherty chalked this up to the language barrier as well as too many left hooks to his skull.

He and René sipped their cognacs and gave each other inquiring looks. Bruno didn't seem aware that there was a drink sitting in front of him until Depardieu signaled for him to pick up the glass. When he did the boxer drained the cognac in one gulp. This brought a pitying smile to Depardieu's face.

"So, René, to what do I owe the pleasure of your company?"

Depardieu emptied his glass and signaled for the waiter to bring them another round even though Doherty'd barely touched his.

"I understand you have been asking questions about my partner, Mr. Pettigrew of P&G Construction." Doherty recalled the phone call he'd made from the Hotel Cartier that morning. He wondered if the young guy at the desk was on Depardieu's payroll.

"My questions have been in relation to an American soldier who died over here sixteen years ago. My only interest is in what Pettigrew knew about this boy who was under his command during the war. What you and P&G Construction are up to out here is none of my business."

He was hoping this explanation would satisfy Depardieu and his bulldog. The second round of cognacs arrived and as before Bruno ignored his as if he hadn't seen it placed in front of him. Rene´ stared at his sidekick and shook his head in disgust. Doherty finished his first drink but let the second one sit untouched.

Depardieu leaned in and asked, "How long do you plan to stay in St-Malo, Monsieur Doherty?" His question was dripping with menace.

"I don't know. Maybe a day or two more. I have some business to attend to in Rouen before returning to Paris and then home to the U.S."

Depardieu lit a cigarette and let it dangle from the corner of his mouth like all the French film stars did. "I think it would be better for everyone if you left St-Malo as soon as possible. I am most worried about the health of my friends, Monsieur and the beautiful Madame Pettigrew."

This last remark drew Doherty's attention. "What does Mrs. Pettigrew have to do with any business you have with her husband?"

"Information has come to me that she likes to sleep with random men at the Hotel de France et de Chateaubriand. I can understand this. I would not mind biting off a piece of her myself one of these days. But she is putting her husband's work here in danger. That, mon ami, would not be good for anyone. Do I make myself clear?" Depardieu nudged Bruno, who as if on command, flashed Doherty his meanest look. It was enough to scare the bejesus out of anyone.

"I don't understand. I thought you were the big wheel around these parts. I've been told you even have the local police in your hip pocket. What is there for you to be worried about?"

"Certain Americans in Paris frown upon how we do things out here away from the capital. They have expressed some unhappiness with the way their money is being spent. There is only so much we can do here in St-Malo with Monsieur Pettigrew's money alone. If the Americans who give us aid for our projects grow unhappy, their money could disappear. That would not be good for me or the men who work for me. You see, the rebuilding of St-Malo would stop without me."

Doherty did not know how to respond to this last statement, nor was he interested in learning more about the construction *costs* in St-Malo than he was already aware of. However, he now felt obliged to pass Depardieu's threats on to Pettigrew and his wife. Beyond that he didn't know what else, if anything, he could do.

Back at the hotel he lay awake for the longest time trying to understand what exactly the message was that Depardieu was sending him. There was definitely an implicit threat against Doherty as well as the Pettigrews. He was also trying to figure out if Captain Bogdanovich and the ECA were behind the investigations into Depardieu's business methods that René had alluded to. His worst thought was that perhaps Bogdanovich was also bilking money out of the very agency he was in charge of. He quickly discarded this idea, wanting to believe that above all else the American captain was a stand-up guy. However, with so much aid money floating around it was understandable that many different people would want a piece of the pie. Given how government business was done back home in Rhode Island, there was no reason for him to believe things in France were any different. Nevertheless, a man in Depardieu's position would not be above using blackmail, extortion, and even violence to protect his fiefdom out here in the coastal provinces.

The sensible thing for Doherty to do would be to hop into his little Deux Chevaux tomorrow morning and hightail it back to Paris. After all, what was happening businesswise out here was not his problem. He'd already learned all he could about the sad demise of Corporal McDonald. Once he returned to Rhode Island he could report to the Royals that the dead soldier had died nobly in battle *fighting for freedom*. In order to satisfy the Royals that their money was well spent, he might even embellish upon Pettigrew's observations of McDonald.

It was Depardieu's threat against Celeste Pettigrew that stuck in Doherty's craw. Was René's comment about her bedding down at the luxurious Hotel de France with random men something real or was it his way of letting Doherty know he was aware of their earlier liaison? Before he fell asleep, his mind was clouded by two conflicting thoughts: leave town for his own safety or stay long enough to insure the well-being of Celeste Pettigrew. As far as her husband was concerned, he would have to fend for himself.

Chapter Thirty

He arose later than usual the next morning, having decided to temporarily postpone his planned exit from St-Malo. If nothing else, he thought it was his duty to apprise the Pettigrews of his dinner conversation with Depardieu along with the presence of his man Bruno. While taking his coffee and breakfast in the small room off the lobby he was interrupted by the hotel proprietor. "There is a currier for you at the desk, Monsieur Doherty."

A boy who looked like he was barely out of his teens was standing at the front desk wearing a bicycle racer's outfit. He handed Doherty a large manila envelope and said something in French. Doherty looked to the deskman for help.

"He is telling you this came to the telex office here in St-Malo from Rouen this morning. He needs for you to make a signature to say you received it."

Doherty did as instructed. He handed the boy two francs and watched as he strutted out to the street and hopped on a speed bike.

The desk clerk lingered, no doubt wanting to know what had been sent to his guest with such haste. Trusting no one, Doherty elected to retreat to the breakfast area to finish his meal without opening the packet. When he was done, he climbed the stairs to his room, where he purposely locked the door before unsealing the envelope. He was concerned the hotel proprietor might already be on the phone with René Depardieu describing the urgent telex delivery.

From the cover letter it was apparent that the enclosed documents were sent from Paris via Walter Bogdanovich's office in Rouen. This meant Bogdanovich had seen the material before he sent it on to Doherty. If the captain were on Depardieu's payroll, which as the worst-case scenario he had to consider, then the content of this packet might bring Doherty into deeper danger.

The first three pages were a brief bio of Andrew Pettigrew, following the outline of his life as Pettigrew had narrated it to him two nights ago. He was indeed the only child of a rich midwestern industrialist, who had used his influence to get his son a cushy job in military intelligence during the war. As Pettigrew had indicated, he rejected his father's connections and wangled himself a combat assignment. What Pettigrew didn't know was that his father continued to use his influence to delay his son's transfer overseas right up until a larger number of additional troops were needed for the cross-channel invasion. Once those plans went into effect, the army required many more combat trained soldiers be sent over to England as quickly as possible.

The details of how Andrew was able to transfer so much of his father's wealth over to himself in France without returning to the States were a bit murky. What the American authorities didn't know was that Pettigrew's old man had deposited a great deal of his money in Swiss bank accounts, mostly to avoid the heavy burden of U.S. taxation. Apparently there were limits to the patriotism of Pettigrew's father as well as the son. The remainder of the report had to do with Pettigrew's marriage to Celeste Bonard, a Swiss national, and the birth of his two sons, André and Leon. The last page listed approximately a dozen projects Pettigrew had invested his money in, or used his construction company to complete, on the restoration of towns in Normandy and Brittany damaged during the Allied offensive. A paragraph at the bottom of the page enumerated several honorary awards Andrew Pettigrew had received for his generous service over the past ten years from various organizations and politicians from towns in the region. Nothing was said about the role René Depardieu played in any of these projects. There was, of course, mention of the ECA and Pettigrew's work in obtaining vital funds through that U.S. government agency.

Separate sheets, unattached to the previous biographical material, contained a copy of Pettigrew's enlistment papers and combat orders. Everything was as it should be except for the grainy photo on the second page. Despite the haziness of the facial image, it was readily apparent that the Andrew Pettigrew Doherty'd been consorting with for the past few days didn't appear to be the same person shown in this photo. Although he would have to take a closer look at the one of Pettigrew's platoon on the mantle in his study, Doherty had a hunch one of the men he'd seen in that picture was the real Andrew Pettigrew and the man Pettigrew had identified as himself was someone else altogether.

He carefully stuffed the contents of the packet into his briefcase. With the case securely tucked under his arm, Doherty headed down through the town to the main gate and out to the parking lot where the Deux Chevaux sat. Today the old two-horse wagon sputtered to a start without an argument. While driving out of town he periodically checked his rearview mirror to assure himself that he wasn't being tailed. Just in case, he took a few detours down country roads before doubling back in the direction of the Château du Colombier. Despite the sidetracking, for once he completed his journey to the chateau without getting lost.

Only a dark green Citroën was parked on the crushed pebble lot out front After banging the door knocker, he was greeted by one of the servants who flashed him a smile as if he were now one of the regulars at Colombier. As best he could he asked about the whereabouts of the monsieur and the madame. The maid indicated Andrew was out of town while the madame was upstairs dressing. She read Doherty's body language and understood his pidgin French enough to know he was asking her to fetch the mistress of the house.

While waiting for Celeste he took a seat in what looked like a replica of a Louis XIV chair, or perhaps it was the real thing. Ten minutes passed before Celeste Pettigrew descended the staircase. She was wearing a riding outfit of light gray jodhpurs, knee high black boots, and a tight black jacket over a white jersey. She was holding a black riding cap, which she twirled nervously.

"Why Mr. Doherty, this is indeed a surprise," she said holding out her hand. He didn't know if he was supposed to kiss it or shake it. He opted for the latter. Acknowledging the maid's continued presence Celeste was doing her best not to give any indication she was greeting the same man with whom she'd had several hours of torrid sex the day before.

"I was on my way out to go riding," she said trying to cover her nerves.

"I wouldn't have guessed from your outfit."

She turned to the maid and said something in French that clearly meant for the woman to get lost.

"Why don't we go into the sitting room and have a little chat. I'll have Lynette bring us some coffee."

Like the rest of the house the sitting room was busy with art prints, pieces of bric-a-brac on every flat surface, and ornate table lamps with equally decorated shades. It was as if the French could not stand to see any empty space devoid of some piece of art, real or faux.

Once the sitting room door was closed Doherty told Celeste about his visit from René Depardieu and the goon named Bruno.

"My God, that must have been a revolting experience! Did they threaten you?"

"Not in so many words, though he did strongly suggest that I leave St-Malo as soon as possible. He said it would not only be good for my health, but also for that of you and your husband."

"Me. Why me?"

"Because, to use his words, he is aware that you often spend time entertaining random men at the Hotel de France et de Chateaubriand."

"He actually said that?"

"Yes. He also said he wouldn't mind taking a bite of your sweet favors one of these days."

"And you believe him?"

"I certainly believe Depardieu would like to indulge in your sexual favors. I mean who wouldn't? Beyond that, I don't know what to believe. He could've been saying those things just to stir me up. For all I know it might've been his way of letting us know that he was aware that we'd met up at the hotel yesterday. Do you think he would say something about us to your husband?"

Celeste interrupted the conversation to ring a little bell. When the maid named Lynette entered the room, she jabbered something in French of which Doherty recognized only his name and the word café.

"I don't think Andy would give a fig if I slept with another man. In light of the bevy of tramps he copulates with he would have no standing to criticize me. However, neither of us would want to hear about it from that dreadful man. What do you think René's up to?"

"From what I could gather, he seems to be running scared. Someone has leaked to him that the ECA is taking a hard look at his role in the projects they and your husband are funding. I think he's afraid the American gravy train is going to dry up. He may be able to bribe the local constabulary and key members of the town councils, but the American government is a different story. They like to keep their corruption to themselves."

"Is this why you came out here today? To warn Andy and me that Depardieu is worried about losing his portion of their money?"

"That's one reason. The other is a little bit more sensitive. Before I give you a fuller explanation, I was curious if you have some photos of you and Andy when you were younger. Maybe wedding pictures and anything else you might have from that time or before."

"There are a few albums upstairs in my bedroom. I'll bring them down and we can look at them together. It'll be fun. I haven't seen our old photos in quite some time." If nothing else, Doherty knew this activity was not going to end up being *fun*.

After Celeste left the room Doherty sparked up a cigarette and pulled over an ashtray on an elaborately decorated stand that looked like it was left over from the Napoleonic era. The maid brought in a large tray with two cups of café au lait, a sugar bowl, a variety of small finger pastries, and the necessary silverware.

Celeste soon returned with two thick photo albums. She signaled for Doherty to join her on a little settee where they could sit side by side while rubbing their legs against each other. The first album contained early photographs of Celeste and Andy in the Swiss Alps, on a canal in Venice, at the Parthenon in Greece, and other grand sights throughout Europe. They both looked predictably young and happy with each other.

"These were our best years together. We met in Zurich in 1947. I was working at a mid-level job in one of the big banks. I'd grown up in a small town near the Austrian border and was able to attend university in Geneva during the war because my country did not participate as you know."

"Yeah, the Swiss were too busy laundering money for the Nazis to get their hands dirty with the actual fighting." Celeste ignored his snide remark and turned the pages of the album.

"In '48 when he returned to Zurich, Andy convinced me to leave the bank and travel with him. Many ex-soldiers and other young people were aimlessly wandering the continent in those years after the fighting. It was different for us because Andy was so wealthy. He took me to places I never would have been able to go to on my own. It was as if a whirlwind had swept me up."

"What happened to end your idyllic travels?"

Celeste gave him a wry smile. "I got pregnant with André. That's what Andy wanted to name him, supposedly after his father. At first, I was afraid he would leave me when he found out. Instead he insisted that we get married. It was very hurried because I was already starting to show. I didn't tell anyone besides my family about the baby. My mother was very upset at first, but she got over it when Andy started lavishing expensive gifts on them. He even offered to buy them a new home. They were a little leery of him because he was a foreigner. But in time they came to accept him and his money."

Celeste next opened an album that contained their wedding photos. She rattled on about this relative and that one, but Doherty was only interested in the close-ups of Pettigrew. He didn't have his bushy moustache nor did he wear the dark rimmed glasses back then. As would be expected, he looked very boyish. Almost all of the guests at their nuptials were Celeste's friends and family. As the only child of an only child, Andy, she explained, had only a few business acquaintances as guests. Still, it was an extravagant affair held in a lakeside village with the Swiss Alps in the background. Doherty didn't ask but was sure Pettigrew paid for the whole thing.

"A few months after we were married, we moved to Paris. That was where André was born. Two years later I had Leon. The boys kept me busy though I always had an au pair to help out. But I could see that Andy was restless. Having too much inherited money can do that to a person. He started going out at night with friends and staying out to all hours. The next morning,

I could smell the perfume of other women on his clothes.

"After a while he didn't bother trying to hide it from me. I told him he had to find something other than cheap women to spend his money on. Otherwise I would leave him. He knew if we divorced, I would go after the money he had hidden away in Switzerland. A few months later one of his business acquaintances told him about the ECA and its reconstruction work in France. Before long he was throwing himself and our money into these building projects. That was when he established the P&G Construction Company"

"And René Depardieu?"

"René did not show up until later. We first moved to Caen, but that city had no charm. Much of it had been destroyed during the war and what replaced it was modern and characterless. A year later Andy started on the St-Malo project, which was more in line with his historical interests. While spending time out here he discovered this chateau. At the time it was owned by an elderly Frenchman who could no longer pay the taxes on it. So, in Andy's words, he bought it from him for a song. That's how you Americans say it, isn't it?"

"Only if they have money that sings loud enough to buy a French chateau. What about your boys? How did they like living in a chateau?"

"Oh, they came to hate living here. At first, they thought it was great fun for us to own a mansion. But there are few children their age nearby. André was not happy about having to be driven to school each day. When Leon became old enough, we sent the boys to a boarding school near Bayeux. They love it there and now only come home on holidays. They will be here next week for the Easter holiday. I do miss them so. On the other hand, because he is always working Andy has become like a stranger to them."

"When did René Depardieu start horning in on Andy's construction projects?"

"As soon as he found out how many local men were needed to do the work. You see, he has gained control of the labor unions in this part of France. Don't ask me how. You will have to discuss that with my husband. I try to stay out of his business. You must understand, Doherty, here in France nothing can be done without the cooperation of the labor unions. Almost every day one or another of them is on strike. In my husband's business when that happens everything grinds to a halt. It is a matter of necessity that he work with men like

René. As Andy tells it, René Depardieu has his ways of keeping the workers in line."

"I'll bet he does; with men like Bruno and others to enforce his rules. I suppose that's the cost of doing business over here."

Celeste pushed her wedding album aside and gave Doherty the look that made him fall for her the first time he saw her. He wanted to kiss her right then and there yet needed to get some other business out of the way first.

"If the American aid agencies are taking a closer look at the way their money is being spent here, they will pry into Andy's business practices as well as his relationship with Depardieu."

"Does that mean they think my husband's is a corrupt businessman?"

Doherty shook his head. "I can't answer that. However, it is vitally important to find out what René thinks of your husband. So far, he has probably seen Andy as nothing more than a cash cow. If he suspects Andy is passing information onto the ECA about the tactics Depardieu uses to control the labor market while simultaneously pocketing a fair amount of their aid dollars, they might decide to diminish their role in the restoration of St-Malo. That could leave you and your husband in the lurch. If René suspects Andy has double-crossed him, he wouldn't hesitate in taking his revenge out on the two of you. Once he gained control of the construction unions, Depardieu was clearly intent upon playing for much bigger stakes. Andy's interest so far has only been in these rebuilding projects. Someday they will come to an end. But there will always be the need for manual labor. As long as René controls them he will be someone people in power will have to reckon with. The last thing he wants is to be the subject of a criminal investigation. He won't be able to control the unions if he's in prison."

Celeste leaned over and put her head on Doherty's shoulder. "What you are saying is scaring me," she murmured. "Will you help us?"

"I don't know what I can do. Don't forget, I'm a foreigner over here in your adopted country. My PI license doesn't mean squat in France."

"But you are an American. Can't you speak with the Americans and find out what they are looking into? Will you find out if my husband is under investigation? Everything he has done is because he loves the French and feels that his country has an obligation to help them to rebuild what was destroyed in the war. Andy has had to deal with René because it was the only way to get things done."

"I'll do what I can. Do me a favor, when your husband comes home tell him what I've told you. Suggest that he and I meet again before I leave St-Malo so that I can give him the lay of the land. In the meantime, I will call my connection in Rouen to see what I can find out about their investigations."

Celeste stood and Doherty rose beside her. She fell into his arms and gave him a deep kiss. He lingered for a moment then broke away, afraid the maid might barge in at any moment to retrieve their used coffee cups.

"You said you wanted to see pictures of us when we were younger. Is there something about Andy's past you are most interested in?"

Doherty hesitated, not sure he wanted Celeste to know where his investigation was headed. "Let me talk to your husband first. It may be nothing, though I'd feel a lot better if he cleared up a few matters for me. Right now, it doesn't seem all that important," he lied.

Chapter Thirty-One

When Doherty returned to the Hotel Cartier the young clerk was manning the desk. He gave him the number and asked if he would put through a call to the ECA office in Rouen. Once the connection was made the fellow handed the receiver to Doherty.

"*Parlez vous Anglais?*" he asked the man at the other end.

"Yes, of course," he answered in a slightly accented voice.

"I need to talk with Captain Bogdanovich on a matter of importance."

"I'm afraid he's on another line. I will have him return your call as soon as he's free."

The connection was broken. Doherty decided to wait in the miniscule lobby for the return call. He waded through the bookshelves looking for the Salinger short story collection he'd been reading the day before. He resumed the story about bananafish at the part where the man was pushing the young girl on her raft out into the water while telling her about the life of bananafish. Doherty was finding this fellow's relationship with the kid a little bit creepy. Thankfully when they return to shore the girl leaves the man named Seymour alone on the beach. He decides to go back up to his room where he apparently left his wife napping. For no good reason he gets into an argument in the elevator with a woman who he accuses of staring at his feet. Back in their hotel room he retrieves his old army pistol and goes into the bathroom where he blows his brains out.

In a fit of pique Doherty hurled the book across the room, which immediately got the attention of the desk clerk. The guy gave Doherty a confused look, but he was too angry at the story's end to pay him much attention. He'd heard many tales of war veterans who returned home from combat only to kill themselves in civilian life. Some were broken by what they had seen and done overseas. Others simply couldn't adjust to civilian life, where the stakes seemed so small compared to the ones they faced in the war. For some soldiers the end was more traumatic than the war itself. He knew vets who suffered from what was later identified as "survivor's guilt," the idea that they survived for no good reason while others were randomly killed. Doherty understood all this, though for him he could have kissed the pavement in front of his family's house when he came home after going through the most horrific experiences of his young life. He would never again take walking the familiar streets of West Warwick for granted.

A few minutes later the phone rang; the desk clerk indicated that the call was for him. As before Doherty stretched the phone cord as far away from the desk as it would reach. He knew the young man's English wasn't all that good, but he wasn't taking any chances. Bogdanovich's gruff voice called out to him on the other end of the line.

"I may have to speak to you in a kind of code, Walt. Things out here have gotten a bit dicey," he said in a low voice.

Bogdanovich didn't respond right away. "Okay, whatever you say pal. But make it snappy. I've got to go out on a site inspection in a few minutes."

"I've made contact with a certain construction company owner. The fellow you told me your office has been working with. I need to know if he has been passing some confidential information on to you."

Again, there was an uncomfortable silence at the other end of the line. "I'm afraid I can't answer that question," Bogdanovich said, his flat voice not revealing anything.

"Well, it turns out that the other fellow, the one your friend who owns the restaurant we ate at isn't particularly fond of, has been making threatening comments to some people including yours truly."

"Jesus, Doherty, what the hell have you gotten yourself into. I thought you were only interested in finding out if Pettigrew knew some soldier in his outfit who was killed at St-Lô?"

"I'm afraid things have gotten a little more complicated out here through no fault of mine."

"Look, pal, it's vitally important to this agency that nothing bad happens to Andrew Pettigrew or any member of his family. Do I make myself clear?"

"If that's the case you better send some reinforcements to St-Malo. I'm afraid the second person I mentioned might decide to pull the plug on the first one if he becomes any more suspicious. And that, Walter, will be on your head, not mine."

The pregnant pause at the other end of the line left Doherty feeling most unsettled. "All I can say, Doherty, is for your own good you should get your ass out of St-Malo as soon as possible."

"I'm afraid I can't do that. I've made some promises to people here I need to keep."

"Then you're on your own, pal. I can't protect you if you're intent upon playing the fool." Bogdanovich then abruptly ended the call.

Doherty took himself up to his room to think things over. His first impression upon entering was that something about the room didn't seem right. On closer inspection he saw that his space had been tossed but in a very meticulous way. His goods weren't thrown around and nothing appeared to be broken or missing. Aside from his clothes and the valise that he'd grown so attached to, he'd left nothing of real value at the hotel. As always, he'd taken with him his passport and his money belt containing the balance of the thousand bucks from B.W. Royal – some of which was now in denominations of francs as well as dollars and traveler's checks. He'd only removed the belt once outside of the hotel and that was when he was in bed with Celeste Pettigrew at the Hotel De France. Under the circumstances he thought the money belt might get in the way. The papers Shanahan had sent him about Pettigrew had never left the inside pocket of the jacket he was wearing.

He was certain that his room had been searched by someone looking for the contents of the packet he'd received that morning from Rouen. What he didn't know is if whoever had gone through his room was specifically looking for info about Andrew Pettigrew or if it was a broader search for whatever was in the packet without having a clear idea what it might contain. In either case since Doherty had taken the material with him to the chateau there was nothing to be found.

He lay down to take a short nap but was soon interrupted by a knock at his door. At home he might've grabbed his .38 before answering. However, here his only weapon was the switchblade he'd taken off the junkie robber at the Montmartre. Before opening the door, he slid the knife into his pocket where he could easily reach it if necessary. The young clerk was standing in the darkened hallway. He mumbled something in French and handed Doherty a note. He gave it a quick glance. All it said was *Dinner at the chateau, 7 p.m. sharp, Andrew.* He wanted to ask the kid who delivered the message, but knew his French wasn't good enough to get that question across. Instead he handed him a few centimes as a thank you.

At a half past six he meandered down to the town gate and across the plaza to his car. As before he swiveled his head to and fro to make sure he wasn't being followed. No strange moves by other pedestrians indicated that he was. Rather than taking the elaborate diversions he had earlier in the day he began to drive straight to the chateau. A few kilometers outside of town he spotted another vehicle's lights in his rearview. Doherty slowed hoping the other car would pass him as most Frenchman would of a car moving at less than racecar speeds. However, this one pulled up on his rear and made no attempt to pass. He floored the accelerator on the Deux Chevaux, knowing this was a futile ploy, as the toy car would max out at 80 kilometers per.

The chase car hit its high beams, which they hoped would blind him, as they did at first. It also had the unintended consequence of allowing Doherty to see some narrow passages between the buildings in the small town he was approaching. Without hesitating he slid his vehicle through one of these narrow spaces between two stone houses. As he did, he heard his car scape against one of them. He knew the big car on his tail would not be able to make this same maneuver. He soon found himself driving through someone's backyard down a dirt path. Somewhere along the way he took down a clothesline with sheets still hanging on it. He was now driving through a planted field on a path designed for a tractor. At the far end from what he could see around the torn sheet that now covered half his windshield was a low stone wall with a tall stand of trees beyond it. Looking behind him he could see the chase car stopped on the main road where he'd cut between the two buildings.

He shut off his lights and moved slowly along the stone wall, hoping the noise from the Deux Chevaux's engine wouldn't give away his whereabouts. Before long he came to a break in the wall that was yet another dirt path that took him through the trees. In time he came out to a narrow, paved road. He pulled to the side and looked back across the field he'd just traversed. There was no sign of the car that had been tailing him. He removed the sheet from the Deux Chevaux's windshield and continued on.

Not knowing which direction he should take on this new road he elected to turn right. A few kilometers along, he came to an intersection with a couple of road markings. One of them pointed in the direction of St-Malo. He chose to carefully retrace his route back toward the town. It wasn't long before he came to a more familiar intersection where one of the roads headed in the direction to the Château du Colombier. With his eyes peeled in all directions he slowly made his way to the chateau. He did not encounter any other cars before turning through the stone gate at its entrance. Despite the cool night air Doherty could feel sweat trickling down his back. Two Citroëns were parked out on the crushed stone patch in front of the mansion. He hoped both belonged to the Pettigrews.

Before using the ornate door knocker, he took a few moments to regain his composure. He decided not to tell the Pettigrews about the car chase until after the evening meal. There was so much to unload on them he thought it best to do it in one conversation. The maid met him at the door; he handed over his hat, trench coat, and briefcase before being escorted into the dining room. Pettigrew greeted him in a gregarious fashion before indicating that Doherty was late for dinner. He remembered his host's obsession with his seven o'clock dinner hour.

"I had some car troubles. You know how a Deux Chevaux can be."

Pettigrew gave him a droll smile. "Can't say that I do. Never had the pleasure of driving one." Of course, a man of his wealth would never stoop so low as to drive something that was a mere facsimile of a car. "Please come in.

Celeste and I were just finishing our cocktails. What can I get you, Doherty?" he asked placing a firm hand on Doherty's back as he did.

"I could use something strong. Some bourbon would be nice."

"I'm afraid, despite its French name, bourbon is a little hard to come by over here. I do have some wonderful hundred-year old single malt scotch I brought back on my last trip to Scotland." He wandered off to his study and returned with a bottle of something whose label began with Glen. He poured Doherty a good-sized tumbler of the brown liquor and ushered him into the dining room where Celeste was sitting at the table sipping a glass of clouded Pernod. She didn't bother to stand but accepted Doherty's greeting by exchanging a kiss on each cheek. He could smell the familiar perfume from the Hotel de France.

She looked as gorgeous as ever, wearing a light brown dress with a halter-top that wrapped around her neck. A fair amount of cleavage was on display, which Doherty hoped was for his benefit. Her dark hair was tied up behind her head showing what looked like some very expensive diamond earrings. Her lips were painted as red as a rose.

"I had the cook prepare something special for us tonight. I hope it will remind you of home," Andy said proudly.

He was trying to pay attention to what Pettigrew was saying but his eyes kept being diverting by his beautiful wife. When she slipped off one of her shoes under the table and slid her toes up Doherty's pantleg he knew this was going to be a memorable meal. They started off with a dish of cold herring nestled onto some greens surrounded by small cuts of raw vegetables. The Pettigrews were drinking from a bottle of white wine. As soon as Doherty had finished his Scotch he joined them. When the first course was completed, the maid swooped in and cleared their plates. A short time later she reappeared carrying a large serving tray with a standing rib roast as its centerpiece. It was placed in front of Andrew who stood admiring it. Meanwhile the servant used the occasion to open a bottle of red wine.

"I'm sure you haven't had beef this good in all the time you've been in France. This meat comes from a special breed of cows raised only in Provence. I have a side of it shipped up here every six months. I save it for special occasions like this. I hope you like your meat on the rare side."

"Rare is fine with me. It'll be nice to have some beef that doesn't take twenty minutes to chew," Doherty said.

Pettigrew shook his head. "Good beef is still hard to come by in France. Most of what they serve in restaurants is an inferior cut because that's all they can afford to put on the menu. If they prepared beef like this, they would have to charge so much most Frenchmen would be unable to afford it. They only serve meat this good in the finest restaurants in Paris, and even then in small cuts. It's not like in the States where steak is the national dish."

Pettigrew took the carving knife and sharpened it by slashing it back and forth on a honing rod. He did all this with great ceremony before cutting into the meat. After slicing the beef he set a large juicy piece on a plate for Doherty and then a smaller one for his wife.

"Celeste is not too fond of beef. She has a soft spot in her heart for the poor cows. Isn't that right, dear?"

Without cracking a smile she replied, "Whatever you say, Andy. I doubt Americans like Mr. Doherty think much about the cows when they sit down to a good steak." It was a sarcastic remark neither man bothered to honor with a reply.

The meat was the best Doherty'd had since crossing the Atlantic.

"Our youngest, Leon, has decided to eat as a vegetarian. It seems foolish to me since he's one of the few French boys who could indulge in beef of this quality."

"I believe he is doing it for ethical reasons," Celeste said as a challenge.

"Ethics. What the hell does an eight-year old boy know about ethics? Am I right, Doherty?"

"I wouldn't know, I don't have any children. When I was eight, we ate whatever my mother put on the table or we didn't eat at all. Neither my sister nor I had the privilege of deciding what we would or wouldn't eat." He slipped the word *privilege* in to remind the Pettigrews just how fortunate they were.

The meal continued with inconsequential conversation. Doherty was anxious to bring up the threats René Depardieu had leveled at all of them. Instead he decided to let the evening's meal play out peacefully for a while. He drank more than he should have trying to block out the harrowing car chase from earlier. Halfway through a second bottle of red wine the maid cleared away the dinner plates. Pettigrew lit a cigarette.

"I think we should wait a bit for dessert. Give us a chance to digest the fine beef. Is that all right with you, my dear?" he asked his wife.

"Yes, darling. Whatever you say," she responded like an automaton.

"Doherty, Celeste tells me you're thinking of leaving St-Malo. Had too much of the country? Anxious to get back to Paris?"

"Yes, I am planning on leaving soon. Truth is I would like to get back to the States. At this point I think I've seen enough of France to last me a lifetime. But before I go, we need to talk about René Depardieu and his threats."

"Oh. I wouldn't take René all that seriously. Sometimes he's just trying to act like the gangsters he sees in the movies."

"Well it didn't sound to me like an act when he and his moose Bruno threatened me last night. And to add insult to injury his thugs tried to drive me off the road on my way out here this evening. That was the real reason I was late."

"Mon Dieu! Why didn't you say so when you first arrived?" Celeste asked in a shaky voice.

"I guess I was too busy listening to Andy wax poetic about his roast beef."

"Look here, Doherty, I think you may be wading into waters you don't want to be in. Perhaps it would be a good idea for you to leave St-Malo. That way we can all get back to business as usual."

"Fine. I can go home with a clear conscience - leaving you to clean up the mess you're making."

"What mess?" Pettigrew asked putting a perplexed look on his face.

"I have a hunch Depardieu is being investigated by the ECA for labor racketeering and corrupt business practices. I also think he believes you are cooperating with them. Whether that's true or not, it's conceivable he now sees you and all your money as a liability – a liability he needs to rid himself of."

Holding his wine glass close to his mouth Pettigrew's whole body shook with laughter. "Don't be ridiculous. Are you implying that René would try to kill me? That's absurd. That would be like slaying the goose that lays the golden eggs."

"Maybe not you. Maybe a member of your family to throw a scare into you."

Celeste shuddered at this last remark.

"I think you're blowing this way out of proportion. How dare you come into my house, drink my wine, eat my food, screw my wife, and then toss these preposterous allegations in my face? Yes, Doherty I know all about your assignation with Celeste at the Hotel de France et de Chateaubriand yesterday. Guess who told me – our mutual friend René. So, don't think you can use him to threaten me."

"I'm not threatening you. Why would I do that? Frankly I wouldn't care if he hung you up by your balls and cut your liver out. But I do want to make sure no harm comes to Celeste. She didn't create these problems, you did. Why don't you tell us if you've been passing information on to the ECA that could lead to the arrest of René Depardieu?"

"Glad you're so concerned about my wife's health. Tell me, Doherty, why would I want to cooperate with some American investigators?"

"For one simple reason - to save your own ass. If they are onto him and were able to get you to spill what you know, then that means they're onto you as well."

"Me? I have nothing to hide."

"That's a conversation I think I'd rather have with you in private."

Everyone was now uncomfortably eyeing each other around the table. Luckily the tension was broken when the maid brought in the dessert and coffee. It was beautiful looking chocolate tart, with a whipped cream and berries added to each serving. Without taking a bite Celeste stood and said, "I think I'll skip dessert. I seemed to have lost my appetite. If you'll excuse me." With that she quickly left the room. Andy Pettigrew and Doherty kept looking at each other but said nothing. Instead they ate the delicious dessert in silence.

When they were finished Doherty said, "I think we should go into the study and talk things over." Pettigrew rang the tiny bell on the table and the maid appeared forthwith. From the gestures he made it clear he wanted her to finish up with the dinner dishes and then go home.

"The help doesn't live here in the chateau?"

"No, they live in the village just down the road." From his several trips out this way, Doherty knew the village he was referring to was nearly a kilometer away. He thought it inconsiderate of Pettigrew to make the women walk home in the dark at 10 o'clock at night. But he wasn't paying them, Pettigrew was.

Before going to the study Doherty asked the maid if she could bring him his briefcase. Pettigrew gave him a quizzical look but withdrew to the study. Once inside Doherty carefully closed the door, which Pettigrew also found curious.

Andrew poured the two men snifters of his favorite Armagnac, which he presented with almost as much ceremony as his roast beef. He then clipped and lit a cigar before parking himself in an easy chair.

'Why all the secrecy, Doherty? Afraid René and his thugs are going to burst in at any moment?"

He ignored Pettigrew's comment. "I need to know if you're acting as an informer for the ECA or some other investigative agency." Pettigrew gave him a noncommittal look.

"Andy, all I have to do is call Walter Bogdanovich to find that out for myself," he bluffed. "I'd rather hear what's going on from you."

Pettigrew nervously chewed on his cigar end. "Let's put it this way, Doherty. It's not like they gave me much of a choice."

"I'm listening."

"The ECA and the French Sûreté Nationale; that's their equivalent of the FBI, are trying to build a case against René."

"Why? For grafting and a little labor racketeering? I thought that was how business was done here in France."

Pettigrew took a large gulp of his Armagnac and quickly refilled his snifter. Doherty had barely touched his.

"I'm afraid it's a little more serious than that. They're trying to pin extortion, kidnapping, and possibly murder charges on René as well."

"Well murder certainly makes it more serious. Who was he supposed to have killed?"

Pettigrew hesitated to answer right away. "Two men that they know of. One was a union chief who apparently didn't see eye to eye with the way René was treating the work force. He died in a terrible accident; fell off a high wall at a worksite here in St-Malo and broke his neck. The other was a disgruntled worker who was beaten to death in bar brawl. I have it on good info that it was Bruno Tourneau who delivered the killing blows. The local police dismissed the first death as an accident and the second as self-defense. I'm pretty sure René greased a few palms with the local constabulary to get those investigations thwarted."

"How did the ECA get you to cooperate? I thought you and they had reconciled yourselves to Depardieu's business tactics."

Pettigrew rose from his easy chair and began to slowly pace around the room; snifter of Armagnac in one hand, cigar in the other. "People at the ECA along with the French National Police have been trying to build a case against Depardieu for some time now. In order to facilitate things, they threatened to deport me if I didn't cooperate with them."

"I thought you were a French citizen."

"I never took out the necessary papers. As long as I was contributing my money to operations over here they were perfectly willing to let me to stay in France. That went for Celeste as well even though she's still technically a Swiss citizen. Our boys are French because they were born here. So you see, Doherty, my situation right now is complicated."

Doherty said, "Worst case scenario, you'd have to go back to the States. I shouldn't think you'd find life there all that hard with the kind of dough you've got."

"You don't understand, it's not that simple."

At this point Doherty reached into his briefcase and removed the copy of Andrew Pettigrew's enlistment papers. He handed the two sheets to his host who read them very carefully. When he looked up all he said was, "Not a very flattering photo is it."

Doherty then removed from his briefcase the photo of John McDonald that his former wife Charlene had given him. "You look a little better in this one. Though I have to say your mustache and glasses had me fooled."

While Pettigrew was studying the photo of McDonald, Doherty walked over to the mantel to examine the photograph of Pettigrew's platoon. One of the men in the hazy picture bore a close resemblance to the man sitting in front of him, another to the fellow whose picture was attached to the enlistment forms. His host slumped down in the easy chair, his face now ashen.

"I'm assuming this is why you can't go back to the States. Turns out you're not really Andrew Pettigrew. And all the money you inherited has not come to you legally. I believe at least one of your crimes would be fraud. I won't bother mentioning impersonating an officer or tax evasion."

Pettigrew leaned forward and said with some vigor, "What would've happened to old man Pettigrew's money if no one inherited it? It would've gone to some useless charity, or worse into the government's coffers. Look at all the good I've done with that money out here. No one would've done what I've done, not even Lieutenant Pettigrew. He was just a rich bastard who spent all our time together bragging about his wealth and all the things he would buy when he got home. To be honest with you, I never really liked him."

"Well that was mighty white of you, John. You don't mind if I call you that, do you?"

"Nobody's called me that in fifteen years. As far as the world's concerned I *am* Andrew Pettigrew. Right now, Doherty, you're the only one who knows otherwise."

"Not even your wife?"

"Who Celeste? Do you think she would've married me if I was some poor slob from Warwick, Rhode Island? Hell, when I met her, she didn't even know that Rhode Island was in the U.S. She thought it was some island in Greece."

Doherty had to shake his head at this sudden turn of events. In the back of his mind he was contemplating the idea that he was the only one who knew Pettigrew's true identity. It certainly would be to McDonald's benefit if he got one of Depardieu's thugs to get rid of him. From this point on Doherty knew he was skating on thin ice. But that still wouldn't relieve McDonald of the pressure the ECA was putting on him.

"Why don't you pour me another Armagnac and tell me the whole story?"

Pettigrew, or McDonald as Doherty now thought of him, did as suggested. He settled back in his comfortable chair in his lavish chateau and began to spin out his tale.

"I was assigned to Pettigrew's platoon. He was a green looey when he arrived in England. Most of the men in our unit had either seen some action or at least been overseas for a while. I learned from him later that his old man kept pulling strings to keep him stateside. In the end Pettigrew would've been better off staying out of the action. When one of our sergeants was killed outside of Caen and the other wounded, I became the next ranking member in our platoon. I could tell Lt. Pettigrew was scared most of the time we were in combat. Who wouldn't be - the fighting was that bad. Since he didn't know what he was doing, the men hardly ever listened to his orders. That left me in charge. Back then I wasn't all that book smart, but I was plenty street smart – and that's what paid the bills in the war.

"Some officer screwed up calling in an air assault outside of St-Lô and most of our platoon was wiped out by friendly fire. Nice expression, huh - friendly fire. That's what they call it when some jackass gets the coordinates wrong and his own men have bombs dropped on their heads. Next thing I knew me and Pettigrew were the only ones still alive and we were cut off from the main American forces. Pettigrew was terrified. That's when he started to tell me his life story. It was as if he wanted somebody to know who he was before he met his maker. I have to admit I started feeling sorry for the rich bastard. He had nobody. At least I had a wife back home with a kid on the way. Then I got to thinking about my life if or when I returned home. I married Cheryl because she got pregnant. At the time I didn't really know her all that well. If I survived the war what did I have to look forward to: a forty hour a week job and a wife who maybe I wouldn't even like once we started living together. And a kid to boot.

"While we were trying to get back to St-Lô we ran into some German stragglers. They saw us before we saw them. They opened up with some rounds before we could respond. I wasn't hit but Pettigrew got torn up pretty bad; it was all I could do to hold his parts together. I carried him some distance back the way we came. Thankfully the Jerries headed in the opposite direction. That night I thought the only decent thing to do was bury the lieutenant. I took his dog tags and his papers. Aside from his order sheets that was all he had on him along with a fistful of Francs. It wasn't as if he had anybody back home who would miss him. There was nobody to tell that he was dead.

"It took me three days to find any semblance of an American force. Everybody I talked to didn't know a thing about the other platoons in our outfit. For all I knew the other guys in ours were dead. That's when I got to thinking:

if I ditched my uniform shirt with my name and corporal stripes on it, I could pass myself off as Lieutenant First Class Andrew Pettigrew. I mean a lot of uniforms were in tatters after the assault on St-Lô so it wouldn't be that hard to do. Without any guys from our platoon around to tell anything different, it would be a cinch for me to become Pettigrew. He'd told me enough about Wisconsin and what a big deal his old man was, I figured I could fake it in case I ran into anyone from up that way. Once we caught up to some American forces, I was assigned to a new unit where they were more than happy to have another looey in their ranks. At the time first lieutenants were dropping like flies in Normandy. Over the next few weeks I worked on my accent, remembering as best I could that broad Midwestern way Pettigrew talked.

"It didn't take long before I convinced myself I was Andrew Pettigrew. For further cover I wrote letters under his name to my wife and parents back in Rhode Island telling them their husband and son John McDonald had died heroically fighting at St-Lô. I typed them at headquarters knowing that if I wrote them they'd recognize my handwriting. When I learned that the other guys from our platoon had died in combat, I wrote letters to their families as well, signing all of them Lieutenant Andrew Pettigrew. You see, I was being thoughtful. Pettigrew would've never done that. He was too full of himself. For all practical purposes you could say Lieutenant Pettigrew survived while the other men in his platoon died.

"Once the Germans surrendered, some of us got sent back to Paris. I found a stack of mail there waiting for Pettigrew. Almost all of it had to do with his father's death and legal questions about the dispensation of the companies he owned. I was smart; I consulted with a law firm in Paris that did a lot of work in the States. Little by little they helped me unravel and then sell Pettigrew's father's businesses. They even wrote letters to the Bank of Switzerland in Zurich in reference to his secret bank accounts there. Until I met Celeste getting ahold of the money in the Swiss accounts was proving to be difficult. She knew some higher-ups in the bank where she worked who could help me. In time as the only heir of Andrew Pettigrew Sr. I got access to most of his private accounts. And the rest you might say is history.

"So, you see, Doherty, I can't go back to the States, especially if I'm deported. Not only would I lose access to the Swiss money, but I'd also run the risk that someone over there would recognize me for who I'm not. Lord knows, I can't ever show my face in Wisconsin or Rhode Island. Who knows what the law would do with me if they found out I was an impostor."

"Who or what is buried in John McDonald's tomb in the cemetery?"

"Whatever was left of my stuff. My uniform shirt, my dog tags, and whatever papers I had on me when I decided to make the switch. I turned them all in at headquarters to be added to the remains of all the other poor fellas who bought it in the campaign out here. I suspect a lot of those graves don't contain much more than McDonald's does."

"What happens now?"

McDonald, as Doherty now thought of him, smiled and said, "That depends on the actions of three people: René Depardieu, Walter Bogdanovich, and you.

"What's Bogdanovich's role in this whole affair?"

"Who do you think is leading the investigation of Depardieu? He's the go-between for the ECA and the French national authorities. From what you've said I guess I have good reason to be leery of what René may be thinking about me right now. Then there's always you. You can blow the whistle on me anytime you want now that you know my whole story. You could even spill the beans to Celeste, though I doubt she'd be inclined to leave me and all that money behind. If she sues for divorce, then it's possible my true identity could come out. If that happens, she wouldn't get anything. And as for you, Doherty - if you disclose who I am all the money I've been pouring into the rebuilding of St-Malo and other places out here will disappear. I'll leave it up to you to make the right decision.

Chapter Thirty-Two

D oherty needed time to think and knew he couldn't do it while ensconced in the lap of luxury at the Château du Colombier – especially
with Celeste sleeping a floor above him. Despite the late hour and the
ample amount of liquor he'd consumed, he was determined to return to his
hotel in town. By doing so he knew he'd have to be on the lookout for Depardieu and his henchmen.

He arrived at the lot outside the town gate without incident. Moving
stealthily up through the citadelle he made it to the Hotel Cartier unmolested.
Once inside his room he immediately double-locked the door. After retrieving
the switchblade knife from his jacket, he slipped it under his pillow before
hitting the sack. Sleep did not come easily as he spent time mulling over
McDonald's story about how he'd blithely stolen the identity of the wealthy
dead Lieutenant Andrew Pettigrew. For Doherty the path of least resistance
now would be to pack his bags and leave St- Malo first thing in the morning.
One peculiar thought that kept nagging at him was what he would tell Charlene
Royal and her daughter Mary Margaret when he returned to the States. Would
he tell them that he found John McDonald alive and well living the good life
in a French chateau as an impostor, married to another woman, and with no
intention of ever returning to the U.S.? For the moment Doherty, like

McDonald, was also caught in a complex web of deception.

He had no idea what he would do with the information McDonald, as Pettigrew, had passed onto him. Perhaps he should put a call through to Walt Bogdanovich, except he had no idea exactly what he would say to the ECA captain. Anyway he looked at it he could not in good conscience leave St-Malo until he saw how McDonald's situation with René Depardieu played out.

After breakfast he took a stroll around the town for what he hoped would be the last time. As far as he could tell no one was following him. No matter how he tried to reconcile things to himself, he felt the burden of being the only person besides McDonald who knew his true identity. At the far end of the town he stopped in at a café to think things over. When he was leaving to return to the hotel, he was greeted by two unsavory looking characters. One was short and stubby with the dark end of a cheroot sticking out of the corner of his mouth. The other one was taller and wider through the shoulders. These guys were clearly not people Doherty wanted to mess with without having a gun handy. Just in case he slid his hand into his jacket pocket where he put a firm grip on the switchblade knife. Then, in a saner moment, realized he should see what these guys wanted before initiating any kind of a physical encounter.

"Monsieur Depardieu wants to talk with you," the tall goon said in crooked English.

Doherty took a step backwards. "I'm not going anywhere in a car," he responded, as if that was some kind of sensible reply under the circumstances.

The two thugs looked at each other and exchanged sinister laughs. "No car. An office near to here. Please to come with us." Fortunately, neither man attempted to strong-arm him, so Doherty allowed himself to be escorted a few cobblestone streets away to a building with a sign outside reading Le Syndicat de Travail Brittanique. Ushered into a dimly lit office he saw René Depardieu sitting behind a large desk sipping coffee from an espresso cup. A cigarette occupied his other hand. As usual he was dressed all in black. The office was well appointed and antiseptic – hardly the digs one would expect of a crooked racketeer.

Without bothering to get up Depardieu gave Doherty a gap-toothed smile indicating he should take a seat on the other side of his desk. Doherty scanned the room eyeing a number of photos along the wall of Depardieu holding a ceremonial shovel at various construction sites as well as others of him shaking hands with men Doherty assumed were civic leaders. John McDonald, posing as Andrew Pettigrew, was also present in a few of the photos. In addition, there were a couple of pictures of René standing beside two small children. A series of certificates in French likewise adorned the office walls.

"Would you like some café, Monsieur Doherty?" Depardieu asked.

"No thanks. I've already had my morning fill." Instead Doherty took out his Camels and sparked one up. "What can I do for you, Depardieu?"

"Your French pronunciation, it is not so good."

"I've only been here a little over a week. Give me some time and I'll get the hang of parlez vousing."

Rene gave him as kindly a smile as he could muster, which wasn't very kindly to say the least. "I am afraid you will not have the time to learn our language. It is my wish that you leave St-Malo, and France, as soon as possible. That is a statement of fact, not a request. You have become an interference with our work here."

"By our, are you referring to your and Andrew Pettigrew's construction projects?"

"Exactly, my friend. It can be very difficult to do reconstruction business here in St-Malo without my help. I'm sure Monsieur Pettigrew has explained that to you. Your leaving will make things much easier."

"I don't know what my being here has to do with your business. I have no desire to stay in St-Malo any longer than I need to. I will be happy to leave on one condition: that no harm comes to Pettigrew, his wife, or his children."

René smiled and lit another cigarette from the butt end of the one he was already working on. "Monsieur Doherty, look around this room. You see me in the photos on the walls. I am a man of great importance in my part of France. And with that importance comes much power. Now look at the men standing behind you." He pointed his finger in a menacing gesture toward Doherty. "To me you are nothing but an *escarboucle* on my behind. You do not make demands on me. Do you understand? I am the one who makes the demands. My dealings with Monsieur Pettigrew are none of your business. Comprenez vous?"

"Yes, I understand. But you're forgetting something, René. I'm an

American and it's American money flowing to you through the ECA that pays for much of your work here. If I were to call their office in Rouen and suggest to Captain Bogdanovich that you have threatened me as an American, the ECA may decide to take a closer look at your business practices and some of the people who work for you. My experience with American businessmen is that money always talks louder than words."

René let out a fiendish laugh, one in which he was joined by the two thugs standing behind Doherty. "You Americans are so like children. You think you can use your high-minded principles to tell others how to behave. I don't have to tell you that the war has taught us all that life is cheap over here. What does it matter if one, or even two Americans die from bad accidents? Things like that happen all the time."

"If that's meant as a threat you've missed your mark. I don't scare easily. And I don't think Pettigrew does either. We both did our share of killing in the war. It may not have been pleasant, but it was something we had to do. We American vets don't scare easily."

Depardieu rocked back in his chair and laughed again, though this time with less confidence. "So now it is you who is threatening me, no?"

"Look, I don't have any skin in the games you guys are playing here. What you and Pettigrew get up to with the aid money that comes your way is no concern of mine. My only interest is that nothing bad happens to the Pettigrews or me. I understand that you and Andrew can't operate without one another. If you give me your word that he and his family will remain safe, then I'll give you mine that I'll stay out of your affairs and leave St-Malo as soon as I can." Doherty rose and stuck out his hand offering Depardieu a shake on this agreement. The Frenchman gave him a sinister smile but shook hands anyway. Despite the cool temperature outside Doherty was sweating profusely when he left the office of Le Syndicat de Travail Brittanique.

On his way back to the hotel it dawned on Doherty that Depardieu may suspect him of being a functionary of the ECA. It was entirely possible that he saw Doherty's presence in St-Malo as something other than a mere tourist excursion. By demanding that he leave town René was testing to see if Doherty was there to gather information for the ongoing investigation the ECA and French authorities were carrying out into his criminal business practices. If he thought Doherty was working for the ECA he would probably be reluctant to harm him for fear it would bring the authorities down on his head. Or maybe not. After all in St-Malo accidents could always be arranged.

The older man was at the desk when Doherty returned to the Hotel Cartier. He stopped him before he could climb the stairs to his room.

"Monsieur, you had a phone message. A Monsieur Pettigrew called saying you must call him at once. He used the word 'urgent'." The Frenchman pronounced that word with emphasis on the second syllable.

Doherty gave the man Pettigrew's number and asked him to ring him up on the house phone. One of the servants answered. In his stilted French Doherty identified himself and asked to speak with Monsieur Pettigrew. When Pettigrew came on the line, he sounded nervous.

"I've just had a call from René. He insists upon meeting with me tonight."

"What does this have to do with me?"

"I'm calling you to see if you would accompany me as back-up. I don't have anyone else else in St-Malo I can trust right now."

Doherty had to think for minute, weighing what Pettigrew, er McDonald, had just told him. He also had to be aware that the deskman was obviously listening just a few feet away. Putting the palm of his other hand over the receiver, Doherty whispered, "I don't like it; it sounds like a trap."

"A trap? For what purpose?"

"I don't know. I can't talk about it now. Why don't I come out to the chateau so we can work out a plan?"

"No, I will come to you. Tell me where your hotel is." Doherty gave him the address of the Hotel Cartier and hung up. When he looked at the deskman the fellow was busily trying to act as if he hadn't been eavesdropping on the phone conversation. Damn, Doherty thought, this town is a nest of vipers.

He climbed the narrow staircase to his room on the third floor. He needed some time to think things out. He knew the smart move would be to call Walt Bogdanovich to fill him in on Depardieu's suspicions. However, the content of any calls he made from the front desk would be quickly translated to Depardieu soon after he got off the phone. If René thought the ECA was circling in on him and that Doherty was part of it, then a phone call to them would only confirm his suspicions. The other thought that was bouncing around in his head was whether Pettigrew/McDonald, and Depardieu were conspiring to do him in. Now that he knew McDonald's true identity it might be in all of their best interests to have him eliminated. The problem with that scenario was that Bogdanovich and the ECA were already squeezing the guy they believed was Andrew Pettigrew. If anything untoward were to happen to Doherty, Pettigrew would become a suspect in their investigation along with Depardieu. If that occurred McDonald might not be able to keep up his pretense of being Andrew Pettigrew.

Chapter Thirty-Three

H e tried to sleep, though under the circumstances no rest would come. He slipped out a little after five and bought a baguette, some cheese, and cold meat at a nearby charcuterie. He wanted to accompany them with some wine, or perhaps something stronger, but knew he needed his wits about him when he and McDonald had their powwow with Depardieu. Back in his room, as a precautionary measure he slipped his money belt and passport under the mattress, not wanting to have them with him when they went to the meeting.

A little after six there was a hard knock at his door. He opened it a crack and peered out. McDonald was standing in the hall wearing a topcoat and fedora.

As soon as the door was unlocked he quickly swept into the room. He looked around the small space and sniffed his disapproval. "Where did you find this flea bag place?"

"A news vendor recommended it. I don't think he sized me up as a rich American tourist. It's not exactly the Hotel de France and de Chateaubriand, is it?" he added to see if mention of the hotel where he'd slept with McDonald's wife would get a rise out of him. McDonald's expression remained unchanged. Maybe he didn't know, or care, that Doherty and his wife had bedded down in the town's plushest hotel.

"I'll be frank with you up front. I don't like us walking blindly into this meeting with René. I think it's some kind of trap. Is he expecting you to come to his office where I had my sit-down with him earlier today?"

"No. He wants me to meet at one of our construction sites up along the west wall near the old guardhouse."

"I think you should call it off."

"I can't. I spoke with Bogdanovich this afternoon. They want me to brace René about some electrical contractor who he'd had a confrontation with that subsequently disappeared. He told me René threatened this guy when he refused to kick back the money he was demanding. The ECA is leaning on me pretty hard. If I don't give them something of substance soon, the jig could be up for me."

Doherty sat down on the bed and lit a cigarette. He offered one to McDonald who refused and remained standing.

Flashing a German pistol he said, "I brought this Mauser I took off a dead Jerry near Amiens. I have a smaller piece for you if you want it".

"I can't be caught with a gun here. I don't have a permit and have no desire to spend time in a French jail."

"It could save your life."

"That's what I'm depending on you to do, John." McDonald shuddered for a moment as Doherty realized no one had called him that in a decade and a half.

"Whatever you do, Doherty, when we're with René don't let on that I'm anyone other than the rich American philanthropist Andrew Pettigrew. He was already sounding suspicious in our conversation this afternoon." McDonald took a small flask out of his coat pocket and swallowed a large mouthful. He offered it to Doherty, but as much as he wanted a drink he took a pass.

"What time is the meet?"

"Seven."

"I think we should leave now."

"Why? It's only ten after six."

"Because as an investigator I make it a habit of getting to meeting places early. Gives me a chance to case the area before the other party arrives."

Without objection, McDonald agreed, though not before taking another shot of booze from his flask. The deskman gave them a sidelong glance as they left the hotel. Doherty had a good mind to circle back to see if the guy was already on the horn with Depardieu apprising him of their departure. Instead they walked slowly up the ramparts heading in the direction of the guardhouse at the west corner. It was quiet when they arrived; only a few evening strollers were in evidence. McDonald stood rigidly at the meeting site while Doherty did his best to examine all nooks and crannies around the locale.

At ten to seven René Depardieu and the pug Bruno appeared out of the shadows. Both men approached McDonald and Doherty with their hands dug deep into their coat pockets. As was his style René was dressed all in black, which now included a black overcoat and a similar colored scarf wrapped tightly around his neck to ward off the cool night air. Bruno Tourneau was wearing a dark oversized tan trench coat and a round brimmed hat pulled low over his eyes, though not so low as to mask his scar tissue mug.

René spoke first. "What is he doing here?" he said in reference to Doherty.

"Why don't you tell me what all this hocus pocus is about first? Why are we meeting up here instead of at your office? I thought we had an understanding." Doherty didn't know what he meant by this last remark but didn't want to interrupt things by asking.

Depardieu's gaze shifted back and forth between the two of them; he didn't offer anything by way of an explanation. Bruno stood firmly behind him, though from his expression it looked like he wasn't entirely sure where he was or what was going on. McDonald had his right hand crammed into his coat. Doherty assumed his knuckles were wrapped around the handle of the Mauser.

"I am afraid I have lost my trust in you, my friend," René said. "My people in Rouen have informed me that the ECA and Captain Bogdanovich are now trying to pin the disappearance of one of our electrical contractors on me. I have reason to believe you are helping them, Andrew. Now is that any way to treat an old friend?"

McDonald didn't speak. He and Doherty stood beside each other trying as best they could to size up the situation.

Doherty said, "What's the disappearance of one contractor to you, René? Just this afternoon you told me life is cheap out here. If I remember correctly you mentioned that you could arrange for two Americans to meet untimely accidents without causing any alarm."

Depardieu stepped forward and pointed a crooked finger at Doherty. "You, monsieur, are making me very angry." Bruno moved closer as well in a menacing fashion.

McDonald pulled out the Mauser and leveled it at Bruno. "Better tell your bulldog to back off René before I have to put him down."

"Bruno," René said, though it wasn't exactly clear what he wanted his man to do – attack or back off. With surprising speed, the ex-boxer came at McDonald and unloaded a left hook that would've floored a smaller man. Instead McDonald stumbled backwards, his back hitting the wall of the ramparts very hard. Bruno stepped in for another combination but not before McDonald pulled off two shots that hit the former boxer dead center. To everyone's astonishment Bruno kept coming forward. He grabbed McDonald by the lapels of his topcoat. In one motion he lifted him over the ramparts and dropped him onto the rocky outcropping fifty feet below.

"Merde!" René screamed, as everyone stood frozen in shock. Bruno staggered backwards and then for the first time noticed the dark spot blotching the front of his coat. He looked at Doherty and then at René before he fell to his knees. He toppled over onto his face. It was only then that Depardieu and Doherty noticed that in the skirmish McDonald had dropped the Mauser. They both dove for it and wrestled on the cobblestone pavement for the gun. René came up with it but Doherty had him wrapped around the middle so tightly he couldn't raise the weapon to get off a clean shot. They struggled in this fashion for a few minutes until Doherty was able to get the switchblade knife out of his coat pocket. Depardieu raised the Mauser but before he could pull the trigger Doherty plunged the knife blade directly into the wrist of the hand holding the gun. He must have hit an artery because blood immediately started spurting out of the wound like river. René dropped the gun and grabbed his wrist but couldn't stop the blood from flowing through his fingers. He looked at Doherty in desperation. For a few seconds Doherty watched as a look of fear spread across Depardieu's face. They both knew he might bleed out if nothing was done.

Doherty unfurled Rene's scarf from around his neck and then carefully slid the coat off the shoulder of the bleeding arm. He used the scarf to tie a tight tourniquet around his arm just above the elbow to stop any more blood from being pumped from his heart out through the wound. Depardieu looked like he was about to go into shock. By then a few people who'd heard the shots came out from their houses and were edging closer to the fight scene. When he saw them, Doherty screamed "La police! La police. Appelle la police!"

It took some time for the cops to arrive at this remote part of the citadelle. Doherty had propped René Depardieu up against the ramparts where he was now breathing heavily. Fortunately, the blood from his wrist wound had abated somewhat. Doherty used his handkerchief to craft a makeshift bandage that he wrapped around the wounded man's wrist. When that was done, he stepped over to the wall to peer down at the body of John McDonald lying inertly below. A number of people had waded across the mud flats to inspect the remains of the dead man. Returning his attention to the immediate vicinity he examined the equally lifeless body of Bruno, the former boxer. He was unable to detect a heartbeat either at his throat or wrist. He lifted Bruno's head and put his fingers just below his nose and mouth. There was no sign of breath coming from either orifice.

By this time a large crowd had gathered encircling the dead and wounded men. There was much loud jabbering in French, of which Doherty understood very little. He heard some sirens and looked over the ramparts as three police cars neared one of the smaller gates further down the wall by the causeway that circled this part of the citadelle. It took a good ten minutes before a squad of five uniformed policemen reached their part of the ramparts. René spoke to them in a weak voice as one of them grabbed his legs and another his arms. They hoisted him up and began to carry him down to the lower part of the wall. Two other cops pushed Doherty up against the wall and roughly patted him down. Satisfied that he had no weapon on him they cuffed his hands behind his back and escorted him through the crowd. Although he had no idea what anyone was saying, he was sure from the expressions on their faces that the locals were jeering at him, tossing French expletives his way as he and the policemen moved through the crowd.

When they reached the small gate where the cop cars were parked, he was shoved into the backseat of one of them. He could see René standing by another police vehicle while a medical person was rebandaging his cut wrist. When he saw Doherty, Depardieu threw him a spiteful look. Within minutes they were moving quickly along the road that circled the exterior of the citadelle with the uniquely sounding French siren splitting the night air. Less than fifteen minutes later they reached an antiseptic building that he assumed was police headquarters. He was then dragged from the car into the building, along a long corridor, and up a flight of stairs where his shins smashed against the cement steps. After he was forcibly escorted down another corridor he was violently tossed into a barely lit cell. Throughout this ordeal the arresting officers screamed at him in French. He had no idea what they were saying. His only hope for rescue would be a call to Walter Bogdanovich. Since it was now nighttime there was no way of reaching the American captain even if the French cops allowed him to make a phone call.

Several of the adjacent cells were occupied. He could hear some men snoring and at one point a guy in the cell next to his said something to him in French. Doherty understood that the fellow was trying to communicate with him. However, having no idea what the guy wanted he didn't bother to answer. Instead he laid down on a stone platform that was supposed to serve as a bed and assessed his physical condition. Except for the scrapes on his shins from being dragged from the police car he was otherwise all in one piece. At least he had avoided being dropped from the citadelle ramparts like McDonald or having Depardieu put a bullet in him. Nevertheless, it was certainly true that his French vacation had taken a decided turn for the worse.

He must have fallen asleep because the next thing he knew the cell door was dragged open and a tin tray left just inside it. He picked up the tray and sipped lukewarm coffee from a metal cup. Beside it sat a piece of a stale baguette. He consumed both without hesitation. A few hours later the cell door creaked open again and he was unceremoniously escorted by two uniforms down the stairs he'd been dragged up earlier. Words were tossed his way though he had no idea what either cop was saying. He was taken into a well-lit but sparsely furnished room without windows. Along the way he'd had the chance to glance at a clock that indicated it was a few minutes after nine a.m.

No one entered the room for at least an hour until a plainclothes officer accompanied by one in a uniform strolled in. The one in the civilian suit was carrying a thick folder under his arm. He was overweight, bald, dark eyed, and seemingly disinterested in his work.

"Parlez vous Français?"

"Un petit peu. Je parle Anglais seulement."

"You are English?"

"American"

"Ah, American. You have a passport, Monsieur…"

"Doherty. Je m'appel Huge Doherty. My passport is at my hotel."

The fat cop smiled for the first time. "As a foreigner it is not safe to go out without your passport. I am Deputy Inspector Fournier. Do you know why you are here?"

"I assume it's because two men are dead, and another man was stabbed in his wrist."

"Monsieur Depardieu is saying you killed his man Bruno Tourneau when he tried to stop you from throwing Monsieur Pettigrew over the wall. He says too that you stabbed him when he was wishing to use Pettigrew's gun to stop you. I must say, monsieur, this all looks very bad for you."

"I would like to make a phone call."

The inspector rubbed his chin and shook his head. "We are not like in American movies. Here in France you do not get a phone call."

"In that case I have nothing more to say to you until I speak with a lawyer."

The fat cop stood up and slapped Doherty hard across the face with the thick folder. Doherty's first impulse was to retaliate, and he raised his hand without thinking.

"I would not if I were you. In France it is most serious to strike a police officer."

"How about that phone call?"

"Maybe in an hour or two. After we talk again with Monsieur Depardieu." He then signaled the uniform cop to take Doherty back to his cell.

Sitting on the cement slab he could still feel the sting of the inspector's slap on his face. He laid on his back and stared at the ceiling, trying to figure out how he was going to get out of this jam. While contemplating things he cursed out the Royal family, John McDonald, René Depardieu, and even Walter Bogdanovich and Mike Shanahan. He thought about the tender flesh of Yvonne St. Pierre and Celeste Pettigrew, and his girlfriend back home, Nina Vitale. He wondered how long it would be before he was able to touch a woman's body again. A few hours later a guard clanged on his bars.

"Hey, Americain, vous avez une visiteuse."

The next thing he heard was some wild whistling and puckering sounds coming from the neighboring cells. A few moments later Celeste Pettigrew was standing on the other side of the bars. The guard stood a few feet away leering at her. He did nothing to stop the catcalls and animal sounds coming from the other prisoners.

"Oh, my god, Doherty. What has happened? All they will tell me is that Andrew is dead and you are in jail. That he somehow fell over the ramparts."

Celeste reached out to touch Doherty's face. The guard made a sound indicating touching was not allowed.

"He didn't fall, he was pushed by Depardieu's ape Bruno. But not before your husband pumped two slugs into the fighter's chest. Andrew dropped his gun when he was lifted up. René and I then fought over it. When he tried to shoot me, I stabbed him in the wrist. I think I hit an artery because blood was gushing everywhere. He might have bled to death if I hadn't saved the sonofabitch's life. Now he's trying to pin both murders on me. I need you to help me, Celeste. I'm helpless not knowing the lingo or what the legal procedures are here in France. If I don't act quickly Depardieu is going wrapped me up like a slaughtered pig and serve me to the cops."

"What can I do, Doherty? Do you need a lawyer?"

"The first thing I need you to do is call the ECA in Rouen and get ahold of a guy named Walter Bogdanovich. Tell him what I just told you about how things went down last night. He'll need to get his ass out here before they release Depardieu. After that things could get out of hand for me. If I stay in here much longer my life might be in danger."

"Sure. I can call this man as soon as I leave here."

"Celeste, I'm truly sorry about Andrew. Despite everything, he was a good man and a good soldier."

"Yes, I believe he was. The boys will be home tomorrow. Then I will have someone to grieve with."

Chapter Thirty-Four

Hours went by with nothing happening except for Doherty's fellow prisoners making noises and continuing to say things about Celeste Pettigrew's physical attributes. For once he was happy he didn't understand French, knowing that whatever they were saying wasn't complimentary - unless they were praising her beauty, which he doubted. He understood enough French to hear them exchanging ideas of what they'd like to do with her. Finally, a different guard appeared at his door and left a bowl of watery soup and another piece of a stale baguette. Doherty was disappointed his meal wasn't accompanied by the requisite carafe of house wine.

It must have been sometime around mid-afternoon when two uniforms opened his door and ushered him out of his cell. On the way downstairs Doherty had a chance to take whiff of his rank body odor. It was a combination of fear sweat and the odors acquired from spending the night in a station house jail cell. After descending a flight of stairs, the three of them moved down a long corridor to a meeting room that contained a long table with cushioned chairs all around it. Arrayed at the table were Walter Bogdanovich, to Doherty's surprise Mike Shanahan, a man in plain clothes he didn't recognize, the fat Inspector Fournier, another cop in a white shirt with epaulets and a lot of decorations on its chest, and a policeman wearing a totally different style of uniform than he'd seen on anyone at the St-Malo station.

"You'll have to excuse my smell," Doherty said off the bat. "My accommodations here aren't exactly on par with those at the Hotel de France et de Chateaubriand."

There was some nervous laughter from everyone except Inspector Fournier.

"Perhaps I should introduce the people here that you don't know," Shanahan said in English. "This is Adrian Tourette; he is an agent of the French Sûreté Nationale and the main liaison between the French government and the Economic Cooperation Agency," he added, indicating the man sitting to his left in the gray pinstriped suit. "The Sûreté is kind of like our FBI. At the head of the table is Capitaine Martin, the chief of the St-Malo police, and next to him is Colonel Longiel of the French National Police. Of course, you know Captain Bogdanovich of the ECA and the U.S. Army. And I believe you've already made the acquaintance of Inspector Fournier." Doherty took the opportunity to scan the table wondering where the discussion would be going from here.

"Monsieur Tourette is going to ask you a series of questions concerning your dealings with René Depardieu and Andrew Pettigrew. I suggest you answer them slowly as Chief Martin and Colonel Longiel are not entirely fluent in English."

Doherty took it as a good sign that Shanahan was leading the proceedings.

"Now, Monsieur Doherty, could you please tell us why you are here in St- Malo in the first place?" Tourette began. Doherty looked at Shanahan and then Bogdanovich to see if they had fabricated some official role for him with the American embassy. Neither changed their neutral expressions. He figured he'd have to wing it, being careful not to say anything out of line.

Very slowly Doherty spun out his tale of how he was hired by the Royal family to come to France to find out what he could about the fate of John McDonald, an American soldier killed sixteen years ago in the battle for St-Lô. As he spoke Shanahan dropped in some French here and there to clarify what he was saying. By their facial expressions it appeared that the Frenchmen around the table either didn't entirely believe his story or thought if it were true his trip was a colossal waste of the Royal family's money. The chief stated at one point that only rich Americans could afford to pay for such adventures.

That drew a knowing snicker from Inspector Fournier.

"Was your mission successful, monsieur?"

"Not entirely given that this McDonald fellow was already dead. But I did make the acquaintance of Andrew Pettigrew, who was briefly Corporal McDonald's commanding officer. He at least knew the dead man and had some complimentary things to say about him that I can bring back to the family." He uttered this last remark on the assumption that at some point he'd be allowed to leave St-Malo.

"Was it through Monsieur Pettigrew that you made the acquaintance of Monsieur Depardieu?"

"Yes. We were informally introduced to one another. I came to understand that Depardieu and Pettigrew were business partners engaged in several reconstruction projects in and around St-Malo. Pettigrew indicated to me that he was not entirely pleased with this arrangement. He knew he had to accept Depardieu's help because otherwise he would not've been able to employ a work force large enough to get the jobs done. According to Pettigrew, Depardieu controlled the construction unions in this part of France."

"Excusez moi," interrupted the police chief. "Why did Monsieur Pettigrew make you his ...," he hesitated here obviously searching for the correct word. "Confidant?"

"I first heard about the possible connection between Pettigrew and the dead soldier I was investigating from Captain Bogdanovich. The captain thought Pettigrew may have served with McDonald, which in fact he had. When I arrived in St-Malo, I looked Pettigrew up to see if he could remember anything about Corporal McDonald. As a courtesy to a fellow American veteran he invited me to dinner at his chateau. Afterwards we had drinks in his study. We got to talking about the war as one old soldier to another. He told me that McDonald had briefly served under his command. Later Pettigrew explained how he had fallen in love with France and chose to remain here after the war. According to him that is what led him to invest some of his wealth in the restoration of St-Malo and other places in this part of France. It was during that conversation that he began to complain to me about having to work with René Depardieu. He told me he did not like Depardieu's business tactics."

"What were those tactics?" Tourette asked.

Doherty knew he had to be careful here, not wanting to step too heavily on the feet of the local constabulary, which according to McDonald, were on Depardieu's payroll. "He believed René Depardieu was being unfair with the workers, ignoring their complaints about safety, hours, and wages. In addition he suspected Depardieu of having some of his men physically injure those who complained too loudly."

At this point Inspector Fournier let out an exasperated sound that drew everyone's attention. Doherty continued, "He told me that René had his bodyguard Bruno and some other men physically assault a few of these disgruntled workers - and even a few unhappy contractors. He also said he suspected that Depardieu might be involved in a couple of murders."

At this point the chief pounded the table and shouted, "Where did he hear such absurdité?" That certainly drew the attention of everyone else.

"From me," said Bogdanovich. "My office has been taking a serious look at Depardieu's behavior for some time now."

"And so has my office," Tourette said in a calm voice. "We have been investigating René Depardieu's business practices for over a year now. I have reason to believe he has been involved in labor racketeering, extortion, bribery, and possibly murder."

"Why has none of this come to my attention?" the chief protested. His question hung in the air, the very asking of it all but indicting him and the entire St-Malo police force.

"Can we get to the events of last night, Monsieur Doherty?" Tourette asked, breaking the ice in the room that was now the size of a berg. "Why is it that you and Monsieur Pettigrew went to meet Depardieu and his man last night on the ramparts?"

"At first I thought it was because Pettigrew wanted to have it out with Depardieu and needed my backing. He told me he had no one else he could rely on." Doherty was not going to mention the part where he thought Pettigrew might've have been setting him up because he'd discovered Pettigrew's true identity. "Before we left my hotel, he told me the ECA was leaning on him to get evidence of René's role in the very crimes you just mentioned."

"Why was Pettigrew so willing to cooperate with the ECA if he knew he was putting his safety and the future of his projects in jeopardy?"

"From what he told me the ECA was colluding with the French government to have him deported if he refused to cooperate. By your appearances here today it looks as if that might've been the case."

Shanahan leaned forward and looked angrily at Bogdanovich. "Is this true Walter? Were you really threatening to have Pettigrew deported if he didn't cooperate with your investigation?"

"It was only partially true," Bogdanovich said weakly. "We needed something to hang over his head to get him to help us take down Depardieu. Pettigrew was not a French citizen, so using the threat of deportation proved to be advantageous for us."

"Would you really have deported him after all the good work he's done here and the money he has donated to the rebuilding of France?" Shanahan said aghast.

"It was only a threat, Mike. We probably wouldn't have actually gone through with it," Bogdanovich added in a low voice.

"Jesus, Walt. If you did threaten him and somehow Depardieu found out about his cooperating with your office, then that very well could be why he was killed."

"Now wait a minute. You can't pin Pettigrew's death on me!"

"Gentlemen please. Let us sort out the events of last night before we start accusing one another," Tourette interrupted, temporarily defusing the tension between the two Americans. "Now, Mr. Doherty, tell us again why you went to this meeting between Pettigrew and Depardieu."

"It was obvious Pettigrew was scared and wanted some back-up. I also knew Depardieu had gotten it into his head that my presence in St-Malo had changed Pettigrew's behavior in terms of their partnership. I believe René thought I was playing a much different role than that of an old war vet looking to find out about a dead soldier. When I consider now how he acted toward me he might've believed I was an agent of the ECA."

"And how do you know that?"

"Depardieu all but told me so. Earlier yesterday he sent two of his goons to escort me to a meeting at his office. It was clear from our talk at that time he blamed me for Pettigrew's change of heart. I knew he was way off base, but it made me feel even more responsible for Pettigrew's safety."

"You didn't do a very good job, did you, monsieur?" Inspector Fournier broke in.

"Nor did you inspector – and you're the police. "

Fournier rose as if he were about to say something more but his boss grabbed his sleeve and made him sit back down.

"So, you and Monsieur Pettigrew went to the ramparts near the guardhouse at the west end of the Citadelle, am I correct?"

"Yes."

"Did you bring a weapon?"

"Only a switchblade knife I took off some kid who tried to hold me up in Paris. I do not have a permit to carry a gun in France like I do back home."

"Did Monsieur Pettigrew bring a weapon?"

"Yes, a Walther P.38. He said it was a souvenir he took off a dead German during the war."

"And that was the gun used to shoot Bruno Tourneau?"

"Yes. Pettigrew shot Depardieu's goon when he came at us with malicious intent."

"That's not how Depardieu is explaining things," the chief interrupted. "He claims you shot Bruno and then threw Pettigrew over the wall. He says you would have shot him too if he had not wrestled the gun from you."

"And you believe that?" Shanahan said challenging the chief. "Why would Monsieur Doherty have reason to kill Andrew Pettigrew? He was there to help protect him not kill him."

"Monsieur Depardieu is a respected businessman in our community," the chief replied, sticking his chin out as he did. "We are more willing to believe him than this American and his ridiculous story about why he is here."

"Yes, Chief Martin. But this Depardieu you are so willing to protect is a hardened criminal who I am personally going to escort in handcuffs to Rouen to stand trial," Colonel Longiel announced. "If I were you Chief Martin, I wouldn't say anything more in René Depardieu's defense unless you wish to join him as our guest in Rouen." That shut the St-Malo chief up pretty quickly.

After a few awkward moments, Tourette continued his questioning. "Now Monsieur Doherty, can you please tell us exactly what occurred at the ramparts once Monsieur Depardieu and his accomplice arrived for your meeting?"

Doherty spent the next ten minutes explaining in detail how things played out right up to the point where the local cops showed up. Inspector Fournier let out a few snorts of derision at various points in Doherty's narrative, while everyone else listened attentively. When he was done there was an eerie silence in the room.

"You want us to believe this fairy story?" the chief asked dismissively.

Shanahan stood up and proclaimed, "Monsieur Doherty is an American citizen and a member in good standing in our diplomatic corps. As a private investigator he was brought over here to help the ECA look into corruption in this part of France. As a result, we believe he is immune from French prosecution. I will personally be escorting him to Paris where he will board a plane to return to the United States as soon as possible."

"What about Monsieur Depardieu? What about his témoignage?"

At this point Colonel Longiel rose and said, "As far as we are concerned René Depardieu's testimony is nothing but a series of self-protective lies. He is a career criminal who should have been placed in prison a long time ago. As soon as he is able to travel, he will be taken to Rouen in the custody of my team. There he will be made to stay in jail until a trial date is arranged."

Shanahan took Doherty by the arm and walked him out of the conference room and to the front desk where he retrieved his possessions. Then the two of them hurried out of the police headquarters to a waiting car. "We will stop at your hotel to get your things. I think it best that we get out of town before they find out you are not and have never been a member of our diplomatic corps."

They returned to the Hotel Cartier where Shanahan remained in the lobby while Doherty stuffed his possessions into the leather valise. He gathered up his money belt and passport, which were still safely under the mattress where he'd left them. When he returned to the lobby to settle his bill the deskman and Shanahan were engaged in a lively discussion about *footbal*, the sport Doherty knew only as soccer. After leaving the hotel Mike informed Doherty that assuming the deskman might be on the cuff to Depardieu, he thought it best to occupy him with conversation to keep him from calling René's people about Doherty's sudden departure.

At the parking lot Doherty shoved his bags into the Deux Chevaux.

"Why don't I follow you out of town," Shanahan suggested. "That way I can give you some cover in case Depardieu sends some of his men after you."

"That would be okay except I have to make one more stop before I leave St- Malo. It's important that I have a few words with Pettigrew's widow."

Shanahan shuffled his feet. "Do you think that's wise under the circumstances?"

"Wise or not it's something I have to do before I leave."

"I'll follow you there. For the time being I can't let you out of my sight."

Shanahan tailed him at close range, though he didn't have much choice given how slowly the Deux Chevaux puttered along. When they arrived at the Château du Colombier, only one of the Pettigrew cars was parked on the crushed stones out front. Shanahan accompanied him to the door. One of maids greeted them with a sad face. He didn't know if her sorrow was the result of a genuine feeling of loss for her employer, or at possibly losing a prestigious job. Roaming around the chateau all day had to be a lot better than slinging hash at some roadside truck stop or cleaning dirty hotel rooms.

Shanahan hung back while the woman ushered Doherty to the sitting room. "I'll wait out here," he said. "Make it snappy. I'd like to get to Rouen before dark."

Celeste Pettigrew was lying on her divan when Doherty quietly entered the sitting room. She was already wearing widow's black but had kicked her shoes off of her black stockinged feet. When she rose, there was something about the contrast between her alabaster skin and the black clothing that inappropriately excited him.

"Why, Doherty. I thought the police were keeping you in that horrible jail. I'm so glad to see you're out."

"That makes two of us." He related as much as he could about the meeting in the conference room that sprung him from the hoosegow.

"I wish you could stay and help me with the funeral arrangements. I never realized how much there is to do when your spouse dies. My boys are expected on the six o'clock train. Do you think you could stay for a couple of days?"

"Afraid not. The embassy in Paris is insisting that I leave the country within the next forty-eight hours. They're anxious about the St-Malo cops figuring out that they pulled a fast one on them by saying I was part of the diplomatic corps."

"Does that mean you've come here only to say au revoir?"

"I suppose so. Though I did want to thank you for helping to get me out of jail. If you hadn't contacted our man in Rouen I'd probably still be festering in that dank cell. I also wanted to see how you were holding up. What are your plans once the funeral is over?"

"I don't know," she said shaking her head sadly. "I've thought about selling the chateau and taking the boys back to Switzerland. They'd most likely object now that they've settled in at their school. Oh, I just don't know what to do," she said with a heavy sigh.

"I think it might be a good idea if you left St-Malo and maybe even France as soon as you can. I'm not sure it's safe for you and your sons to stay here. As I suspected, your husband was snitching about René to the ECA. If they withdraw funds from the rebuilding of St-Malo because of your husband's death and René Depardieu's imprisonment, it's going to make a lot of people around here very angry. Some of them, especially if they're cronies of Depardieu, may decide to take their anger out on you. From what Andrew told me there's quite a chunk of change involved in these projects. I'm sure there are a lot of people in St-Malo who have come to depend on that money for their livelihood."

"You're frightening me, Doherty," she said as she nervously tried to light a cigarette. He rescued her by torching it with his Zippo.

"Look, Celeste, I wish I could stay to offer you some protection. However, my keeper out in your foyer is insisting that I accompany him to Paris as soon as possible."

"I understand," she said in a despondent tone. "I suppose this means we'll never see each other again."

"That's pretty certain unless you come to Rhode Island someday. And by the way that's in the U.S. not in Greece. Before I go, I should give you these," he said as he took Pettigrew's military records out of his briefcase.

Celeste carefully unfolded the hazy copies of the documents Doherty had received only a few days before.

266

She looked through the pages though didn't seem at all sure of what she was supposed to be seeing. "What are these?"

"They're Andrew Pettigrew's enlistment papers. I think you should take a close look at the last page."

After doing as was suggested, Celeste looked up with a blank expression. "I don't understand."

"Maybe this will help," he said as he removed John McDonald's photo from his jacket pocket.

"Oh, my god. Is this Andrew when he was a teenager?"

"Not really. It's a picture the former wife of John McDonald, the dead soldier I've been inquiring about, gave me before I left the States."

"I still don't understand." Her voice now sounded anemic.

"It turns out your husband Andrew Pettigrew was once a boy named John McDonald, the very man I was sent over here to find out about. He served under the real Andrew Pettigrew in the army. He and Pettigrew were separated from their men in the battle of St-Lô. After Pettigrew was killed McDonald took on his identity so he could leave his old life behind and live a new one with Andrew's vast wealth."

"Did my husband kill the real Andrew Pettigrew?"

"Not according to him. He told me Pettigrew was shot when they accidentally ran into some German stragglers. He buried Pettigrew and took his dog tags and papers. At first, he was going to turn them in at headquarters so that Pettigrew's artifacts would have a decent burial at the American military cemetery. Sometime later he apparently had a change of heart. He figured if he played his cards right, he would have McDonald's goods buried in Normandy while he took on the identity of Pettigrew. And until the other night it all worked out the way he planned. With your help he got Pettigrew's money, and then he got you as his wife. For all practical purposes, Celeste, you've been married all these years to John McDonald.

Celeste Pettigrew fell back onto the divan clutching the enlistment papers and the photo Doherty had given her. "I don't understand. What does this mean for me? Does it mean that all of Andrew's money, even the accounts in Switzerland, are not rightfully ours?" She started to sob. Doherty hoped it wasn't solely because she saw all of the Pettigrew's ill-gotten wealth slowly disappearing.

He sat down next to her on the divan and took her hand. "Right now, there are only two people in the world who know the truth about your husband, you and me. Andrew, or rather John, obviously knew, but he's now dead. It's not like his family back in Rhode Island would be entitled to any of this money, or even need it. All these years later, I'm sure they'd rather hear that McDonald died a hero in the war rather than being a guy who stole another man's identity and inheritance and deserted them. Besides, in the end McDonald used that money to do good works over here. It's not like you ever knew the real Andrew Pettigrew. And from what your husband told me, the real Pettigrew was just some spoiled rich guy who turned out to be a coward in combat."

"What do I do now that I know the truth?"

Doherty reached into his pocket and took out his Zippo. He handed it to Celeste. She looked at him, at the lighter, and then the enlistment papers.

"I would like the photo back. I promised the family I'd return it."

After she handed over the photo she snapped on the lighter and put the flame to the edge of Pettigrew's papers. When they burned down almost to her hand, she dropped them into the fireplace. Doherty kissed her softly on the forehead and quietly left the room.

Chapter Thirty-Five

S hanahan's plan was for Doherty to meet up with him and Bogdanovich at the ECA office in Rouen. Doherty was very careful along the way to make sure he wasn't being followed by any of Depardieu's cohorts. He assumed that René was in the custody of the federal police, though you never knew who was susceptible to bribes in France. It was almost dark by the time he wheeled his little chariot into the city made famous by the burning of Joan of Arc and Monet's paintings of its cathedral. By the time he found his way to the ECA office on the narrow side street both Shanahan and Bogdanovich seemed anxious about his arrival.

As soon as he walked through the door Shanahan said, "We've decided you should leave the Deux Chevaux here in Rouen and drive back to Paris with me."

"Why?"

The embassy honcho gave him a tired look. "Because we'll make better time that way and I'll know where you are. I also have a license to carry this," he said revealing a small pistol in a shoulder holster under his suit. "In case we run into any trouble."

"Should we be expecting trouble?"

"Walt has been briefing me on Depardieu's operation. It sounds like his reach is longer than we initially suspected. Things are still tough out here; there's no telling what some people will do for a fistful of francs."

"When do we leave?"

Shanahan looked at his watch, "In about fifteen minutes. Why don't you give Walt the keys to your putt-putt while I make some calls to Paris?"

Bogdanovich accompanied Doherty the few blocks where he'd left the Deux Chevaux. The big fella agreed that he'd fetch the car up later that evening. Doherty was disappointed he wouldn't get to see a guy Bogdanovich's size try to squeeze himself into the little car.

When they returned to the ECA office Shanahan was already packing up his gear. "We got you on a flight tomorrow morning just before noon local time. I trust you'll be able to stay out of trouble until then?" Doherty didn't bother to answer this question. "Do you have a place to stay tonight?"

"Well I am a little partial to the Hotel Wetter down in the Latin Quarter. It's where I stayed when I first arrived in Paris last week."

"If you give me the number, I'll set it up for tonight." Doherty fished in his valise and found the card the proprietor had given him. Shanahan phoned the Wetter to make the necessary arrangements.

Doherty shook hands with Bogdanovich and said politely he hoped he'd never see him again, least not on this side of the Atlantic. Walt gave him a knowing smile along with a solid pat on his back that would've qualified as an assault on a smaller recipient.

Shanahan's car was parked just around the corner. It was twice the size of the Deux Chevaux and blocked most of the narrow street. And it certainly felt plush inside.

"What kind of car is this?"

"It's a Mercedes-Benz sedan."

"You're driving a Kraut car?"

Shanahan laughed. "Say what you will about our former enemy, they sure know how to make good cars. Better than anything the Frenchies turn out."

"That doesn't make it any less German."

"Grow up and smell the coffee, Doherty. The war's over and we won. Now it's time for us to have good relations with Germany, or at least with half of it anyway. For the present our fears are all about the Reds. Take my word for it, we'll soon be making nice with the Japs now that the commies have taken over in China."

"So, what are you saying, Mike, we now have to pal around with Nazis?"

"Ex-Nazis, my friend. Many of them already have their denazification certificates. If we eliminated all of the former Nazis from the German government and economy, there wouldn't be enough Krauts left to run the choo-choo trains let alone the country. Germany was a civilized country before the war and it's our aim to help make sure it becomes one again – at least the part of it that agrees with us.

"You've got to understand, Doherty, things over here aren't always what they seem. This is not the simple world of good and evil that people back home think of. You take Normandy for instance. We practically destroyed the whole damn province in order to drive the Germans out. What do you think the locals out here remember: a bunch of German soldiers digging bunkers along their coastline while trying to fuck their daughters or an allied invasion that blew whole towns to smithereens? Maybe our GIs were greeted like heroes when they marched into Paris, but that's not how a lot of people out in the countryside remember us, or the Brits. My whole job since coming to France has been to bind up those wounds."

"How's that going?"

Shanahan chuckled. "Slowly, very slowly. Of course, spreading a lot of Uncle Sam's dough around has made my job a lot easier. Many people in France were starving during the war. Things are better now thanks to our aid through the Marshall Plan. It's ironic that because of our help in getting things back up to speed here, the Frenchies are starting to act like they no longer have to play the game like we want them to. From my work I can honestly say they don't fear the Rooskies like we Americans do. Who knows? Maybe that'll be good for everyone in the long run."

"Hey what do I know? I'm just a simple guy from a small American town," Doherty said sardonically.

"Yeah a simple guy who played a big part in getting two guys killed and a third one nearly so. You seem like a nice fellow, Doherty, but I'll be happy to see that plane of yours lift off from the runway tomorrow. If I were you, I wouldn't plan on coming back to France any time soon."

"It isn't exactly on my future itinerary," he said, although he did think it might be nice to take Nina Vitale to Paris someday.

It was dark by the time Shanahan slid his big German car down the narrow streets of the Latin Quarter to the Hotel Wetter. Before Doherty could retrieve his valise and briefcase Shanahan reached under his jacket and handed Doherty his pistol.

"What's this for?" he asked.

"Just in case Depardieu has some cronies operating here in Paris."

"Won't you need it to protect yourself?"

Shanahan shook his head and smiled. "Only if my wife is angry that I'm late

for dinner. You can give it back to me in the morning when I pick you up to take you out to the airport.

He reminded Doherty to keep his head down and his eyes peeled if he ventured out of the hotel that night. It reminded him of what all his friends back home used to suggest while he was in combat – as if a low head would save your life.

After checking in at the hotel he was offered a room on the second floor, which in France, of course, meant the third. The first thing he did was kick off his shoes and lie down on the bed. It certainly felt better than the metal rack in the St- Malo jail. It had been a wild thirty-six hours. Like Shanahan, he too would be glad to look down on Paris from an airplane. He was trying to make sense of everything that had happened out at St-Malo. Crowding in on those thoughts were ones about how he was going to explain things to the Royal family when he got back to Rhode Island.

He must've fallen asleep because the next thing he knew it was late and he was hungry. His last meal had been some watered-down coffee and a piece of stale bread in a French jail that morning. With a good amount of B.W. Royal's cash left in his money belt, he decided to take himself out for a nice dinner. On his way in the direction of the Seine he passed by Yvonne St. Pierre's café. It was dark and closed up tighter than a mousetrap. He figured he'd stop by in the morning to bid her au revoir.

Notre Dame was lit up in all its glory as he passed by on the opposite side of the river. All of the cafés were noisy with people enjoying the early spring air. There was a joviality, especially among the young, that'd been lacking out in Normandy. Perhaps Shanahan was right – people in Europe, or at least Paris, had moved on from the death and destruction of the war. They wanted to live again and look to the future with hope.

Doherty found a cute little restaurant on the Île De La Cité that overlooked the river. He could sit and watch the lights on the river boats as he enjoyed his last meal in France. With thoughts of Yvonne floating through his head he chose the escargot snails as an appetizer. His waiter appeared surprised by this choice as he clocked Doherty as an American right from the get-go. He followed this up with a roasted half duck, a bird he'd only tasted once while he was wining and dining Nina at the Greene Inn in Narragansett.

As usual that night he'd ordered a steak while Nina selected something called duck a l'orange. He'd never tasted duck before and didn't like the sweet sauce hers was bathed in. Tonight, it came with a berry sauce that was as tart as it was sweet. Accompanied by a bottle of red wine the duck was surprisingly tasty and not nearly as gamey as Nina's had been. The thought of how he could be rotting away in a cold jail cell in St-Malo instead of having this fine meal in a Parisian restaurant only enhanced his appetite. The duck and roasted potatoes were followed by a simple salad with a very tasty vinegar-based dressing. For dessert he ordered a chocolate souffle. It practically melted in his mouth.

Having finished a bottle of wine all on his own, he wound things up with a glass of fairly expensive cognac. It wasn't quite in the class of the Armagnac Pettigrew, or rather McDonald, had served up at the chateau, but it was plenty good enough. He still couldn't get his head around the fact that the highly cultured denizen of the Château du Colombier was once just a simple kid from Warwick, Rhode Island. Doherty smoked two Camels as he lingered over the cognac. When he saw the waiter eyeing the pack sitting on the table, he pulled out a half dozen butts and gave them to him. The fellow lavished several *mercis* on Doherty. Still holding a pocketful of francs he wanted to get rid of before flying out, he paid the bill and left a hefty tip on the table.

His legs felt a little wobbly as he made his way back to the Hotel Wetter. A night in jail followed the next night by such a rich meal, a bottle of wine, and some excellent cognac can do that to a fella. It was past eleven but the cafés in the Quarter were still jumping, mostly filled with students, other young people, and street corner philosophers in berets and beards. Despite carrying Shanahan's pistol in his coat pocket, he knew he was probably too drunk to effectively protect himself from any attack by cronies of Depardieu. In his present state he'd probably shoot first and ask questions later. Yet it felt so good just to be alive and free on this night. After having eaten one of the best meals of his life, he didn't really care so much about his safety. In the end the only real chore he faced at the moment was making it up to his second-floor room, which is actually the third floor in France.

After scarfing down the hotel's generous breakfast offerings the next morning, Doherty strolled up the street to Yvonne's café. Much to his disappointment the place was shuttered and as dark as it had been the previous night. The "Fermé" sign was turned out to the street and a hand-written message below it was taped to the door. He couldn't decipher all of the words but was pretty sure the word *funérailles* meant funeral. The deceased was apparently Yvonne's father whose name was Michel Gravénele. The rites were being held in the town of Reims, a place Doherty'd only vaguely heard of. He remembered that Yvonne's last name of St. Pierre was a leftover from the ex-husband who'd left her for another woman. Saddened Doherty bid the girl a quiet au revoir and returned to the hotel. He was waiting patiently with his luggage in the small lobby when Shanahan's big car pulled up out front. He parked it with two wheels up on the sidewalk due to the narrowness of the street. Doherty thanked the hotel proprietor and pressed an extra handful of francs into his hand. The fellow actually bowed in appreciation. Then they were off at break-neck speed to Orly Airport. Along the way Doherty discreetly returned Shanahan's small pistol.

Chapter Thirty-Six

They all sat in a semi-circle in the farmhouse living room. B.W. Royal was in a large easy chair, Charlene and her daughter Mary Margaret side by side on a sofa, while Doherty was offered an uncomfortable straight back chair. Royal's man Murray lingered standing in the background. Despite the warm temperatures a fire ate at some logs in the nearby fireplace. He'd only been back in Rhode Island a day and a half but decided to meet with the Royals as soon as possible to get his business out of the way. He'd rehearsed what he was about to say all the way back on the flight from Paris. Later he would write up a report that Agnes would neatly type up and send to them.

"So, Mr. Doherty," the wife began. "I trust you had a successful journey to France. It can be a lovely country, can't it?"

Doherty nodded, not sure if his budget trip really measured up to the trans-Atlantic voyage she and her moneybags husband had taken to that country a few years before.

"Let's just say it was interesting. I'd never been out of the country before except during the war, so the touristy part felt a little odd. However, I did meet a number of interesting people and discovered some intriguing facts about your late husband – and your father, Mary Margaret."

"Enough of the travelogue chit-chat," Royal said brusquely. "What exactly did you do with my money over there besides have some good times with the mademoiselles?"

"Brayton, don't be such a boor," his wife snapped at him.

Ignoring B.W.'s comment Doherty said, "Okay, I guess I'll get started. The first thing I did when I arrived in Paris was make contact with a fellow named Michael Shanahan who is assigned to the American Embassy there. I'd gotten his name from my uncle Patrick McSweeny, who I believe you know Mr. Royal."

"Oh yeah, I knew your uncle back in the day. He was one of those crooked Irish politicians who are now running the government here in Rhode Island." Doherty was keenly aware that old Yankees like the Royals resented the stranglehold the Irish, and now many Italians, had on the seats of power in southern New England.

"Actually, my uncle is currently located in Boston where's he's working on the Kennedy-for-President campaign. If the senator wins the presidency then those crooked Irish politicians you mentioned could be running the country by this time next year."

Royal let out a sound of disgust. "Who is this Shanahan character anyway and what did he have to do with the job we hired you for?"

"Well Michael Shanahan serves as a kind of a liaison between the American embassy and the Economic Cooperation Administration, the ECA for short, which is a U.S. agency in France created by the Marshall Plan to help with their rebuilding in the post-war period." Turning his attention to the teenage girl Doherty said, "The Marshall Plan was a program created by our government after the war to help rebuild the economies of various Western Europeans countries seriously damaged in the fighting."

"It was a giveaway program dreamed up by Truman and some of his socialist pals," Royal broke in. "It was intended to pay the Europeans to be our friends, so they wouldn't become commies. If you ask me it was a waste of good money that could've been better spent here at home."

Again ignoring his host's remarks Doherty continued, "The way it works is that we give them financial aid and they in turn buy American goods and services with that money. It has done a great deal to help the European countries ravaged by the war get back on their feet. Meanwhile their spending helped keep us from falling into a depression like the one we were in before the war."

"Yes, I remember reading about the Depression in my history book," the girl said enthusiastically. Royal, his wife, and Doherty all eyed each other, aware that the Great Depression they had all lived through was now just part of the history kids like Mary Margaret studied in school.

"Anyway, this Shanahan fellow put me in touch with an army captain named Walter Bogdanovich, who heads an office for the ECA out in Rouen, which is a mid-sized city in Normandy."

"Where is this Shanahan from anyway?" Royal interrupted.

"Originally from New York, but he's been stationed in France since the end of the war with our diplomatic corps. He's married to a French woman and for the past decade has lived in Neuilly, a town just outside of Paris. Most of his work seems to involve public relations."

"I'll have to look him up. See who his people are," Royal said.

"In any case I then drove out to Rouen to meet up with this Bogdanovich fellow who knew a lot about the battles that were fought on the Normandy-Brittany front. Brittany is the province just west of Normandy. It was through Bogdanovich that I was able to acquire some information about your father, Mary Margaret, Corporal John McDonald. While I was out there Shanahan was searching through military records in Paris to see what else he could scrape up about John."

"All this trouble for a dead man," Royal said dismissively.

"Hey, I didn't want you to think I spent all my time in France on wine, women, and song," Doherty said as a quick retort. "Bogdanovich took me out to where the American cemetery is located at a place called Colleville-sur-mer. It's a beautiful spot that sits on a hill right alongside the sea. Thousands of crosses and some Jewish stars cover several acres of land there. There's a ledger in the pavilion where you first enter the cemetery that lists all of the persons buried there and some information about each of them. Alongside every entry is a number where their graves are located. That was how we found John's. As you're already aware, your father was killed less than a month after the cross-channel invasion in the battle for the town of St-Lô."

"Great end to the story," Royal said cynically. "So basically you didn't find out anything more about McDonald's service time than what we already knew."

"That would be true if all I was supposed to do was find out where he was buried. But you see, Mr. Royal, I'm a private investigator, and for Mary Margaret's sake I took it upon myself to find out as much about this particular dead soldier as I could. Excuse my reference, Mary Margaret."

"Is there more?" Charlene asked hopefully.

"Yes, quite a bit more. It turns out when Bogdanovich found out what outfit John was assigned to, he was sure he knew someone living in the town of St-Malo who may have served with him. Knowing this I decided to venture out there. It was only about a two-hour drive west of Rouen. Technically St-Malo is in Brittany, but not far from Normandy. Without a lot of effort, I located this American, whose name was Andrew Pettigrew. It turned out he was John's commanding lieutenant." Doherty realized that he'd referred to Pettigrew in the past tense though none of his listeners apparently picked up on this. "Does that name ring a bell with you, Mrs. Royal?"

She shook her head looking confused. "I don't think so. Should it?"

"Well maybe I'm getting a little ahead of myself here. I eventually made the acquaintance of this Pettigrew, whose story is at the heart of my investigation. He is a very wealthy American, originally from Wisconsin, who like Michael Shanahan, has chosen to put down roots in France. Pettigrew was indeed McDonald's commanding officer and due to some strange circumstances they became well acquainted."

"Does that mean you met somebody who actually knew my father in the army before he was killed?" Mary Margaret asked enthusiastically.

"To be honest with you their relationship was much more than just knowing each other. As you will see their lives became intertwined. Before John died the two sergeants in his platoon were removed from duty – one because was killed and the other due to a serious injury. By the time their unit embarked on the assault at St-Lô your father was second in command working alongside Lieutenant Pettigrew."

The girl was now on the edge of her seat, her face aglow with pride.

"Then somewhere in the allied attack on St-Lô McDonald and Pettigrew became separated from the rest of their platoon. According to Captain Bogda-novich, the attack on that town was so brutal and chaotic that it took several weeks before they had a complete accounting of which soldiers had died there and which could only be listed as missing in action." Doherty chose here not to mention the errant U.S. bombing that may have been the actual cause of the platoon's destruction. He wasn't sure the kid could stomach the notion of *friendly fire.*

"At one point it was just your father and Pettigrew alone trying to find their way back to the main American forces. Unfortunately, while trying to regroup they ran into a pack of German soldiers, also separated from their main force. A firefight ensued and that's when your father was killed. Accord-ing to Pettigrew your father died saving his life – something he will forever be beholden to him for. As a result, Pettigrew felt responsible for ensuring that John's remains be delivered to a field hospital once he made contact with other American troops. That's how he came to be buried in the military cemetery at Normandy. Lieutenant Pettigrew told me he wrote a personal letter to John's family explaining the circumstances of his death. That's why I asked you, Mrs. Royal, if you remembered his name."

"I don't know. I may still have that letter, or I may have given it to John's parents. I remember getting some typed letters. I thought they were just form letters *regretfully* telling me my husband had died in combat. Everything was so painful back then," she said as she began to tear up.

"Oh please, mommy, can you find that letter. I would so much like to read it."

"If McDonald was such a hero how come Charlene never received any medals for his role in saving his lieutenant's life?" Royal asked.

"You know in wartime medals are sometimes given out in such a random ways. St-Lô was such a vicious battle every soldier who participated probably should've gotten a medal. Pettigrew claims he put in such a request for John, though by then the army was more interested in awarding medals to those who survived rather than posthumously."

"Is that why you got your medals, Doherty? Because you survived?" Royal asked snidely.

"Getting those medals wasn't my call. But I don't have an intention of giving them back. I'm not finished with my story yet. Your father's saving of Lieutenant Pettigrew's life is only part of the tale. Like I said, Pettigrew chose to stay in Europe after the war. His father was a very rich man. He'd made a lot of money selling farming equipment out in Wisconsin where Pettigrew grew up. Like a lot of parents of rich kids, his old man tried to pull strings to keep him out of the action.'' This was an intentional dig at Royal. "However, Pettigrew insisted upon serving in combat. After the war, while he was still in Europe, his father passed away leaving him, as his only heir, a small fortune. With his father dead Pettigrew had no interest in returning home. He sold most of the family's business interests and traveled throughout Europe. Eventually he settled in Paris with a woman he'd met in Switzerland and they were married. They now have two boys being raised as French citizens.

"But living a life of leisure did not suit him, so he decided to use some of his newfound wealth to help repair the damages caused by the allied invasion of Normandy and Brittany. He founded a construction company called P&G Construction that has been working with the ECA on a number of projects restoring destroyed medieval towns along the French coast. He has also purchased a chateau, which, Mary Margaret, is a very old and very large mansion outside of St- Malo. I had the pleasure of eating dinner and sleeping there one night. It was like staying in a palace.

"So, you see your father's saving of Andrew Pettigrew's life has led his lieutenant to do much philanthropic work rebuilding destroyed towns in France. At some point in the not too distant future he's convinced St-Malo will be the kind of place tourists and others interested in medieval history will be flocking to. Perhaps someday, Mary Margaret, you will visit there to see what your father's sacrifice helped to build. All of the good works Lieutenant Pettigrew has done with his money would not have been possible were it not for your father saving his life."

B.W. Royal gave Doherty a disingenuous look, though he was wise enough not to say anything that would upset his stepdaughter.

"Oh, Mr. Doherty, I would so much like to write a letter to this Lieutenant Pettigrew. Do you think you could help me with that?"

"I bet you're capable of writing such a letter on your own. Just write what you feel. When you're done you can bring it by my office; I'll make sure it gets to him at his chateau."

Royal rose indicating that their meeting was over. Everyone stood around awkwardly for a few moments until Doherty turned to Charlene Royal and said, "I'll have my secretary write up a full report of my findings and mail it to you in a few days. Thank you all for your support. This trip was a real eye opener for me." He fully expected Royal to make another crude remark about French mademoiselles, but this time his host thankfully kept his mouth shut.

"Thank you so much, Mr. Doherty," the wife said offering him her hand. "You've given Mary Margaret much to think about."

The girls left first and as Doherty was edging out the door when Royal grabbed him by his arm. "How much of that story you spun in there was true and how much of it was a load of horse manure you piled up just to please my stepdaughter?"

"It was all true," he lied. "And I'd appreciate it if you let go of my arm. Before today John McDonald was nothing more than a ghost to your step-daughter. All I did was put some human flesh on him. As someone who sat on his fat ass during the war and never had a bullet fly by his head or heard the screams of dying comrades, you would do well not to say anything more about her father's death. That is if you're still interested in repairing your relation-ship with her. Now if you don't mind, I'll bid you a kind farewell."

Chapter Thirty-Seven

Two days later Doherty was putting the finishing touches on his report of the John McDonald affair for the Royal family when Agnes interrupted him. "There's a young lady in the outer office who'd like to talk with you."

"Please send her in." Mary Margaret McDonald was soon standing in the doorway wearing her parochial school outfit including the dark blue blazer with the St. Mary's Academy patch on it. He looked beyond her but there was no sign of either of her parents.

"My mother is downstairs in the car. She didn't want to come up," she explained.

Doherty invited the girl into his office and asked Agnes to accompany them.

"My mother found that letter Lieutenant Pettigrew wrote to her about my father's death. It was so thoughtful of him to do that."

"Yes, it was. He told me he wrote a letter to every family of the men in his platoon he knew for certain had died. He's quite a man," Doherty added, purposely leaving this last remark ambiguous.

"I wrote to him. I was hoping you would read my letter." She removed a folded-up missive from her school bag and handed it to Doherty. It was scripted on what was obviously her mother's best stationary.

Dear Lieutenant Pettigrew,

My name is Mary Margaret McDonald. Corporal John McDonald was my father. I never knew him since my mother was expecting me when he went off to war. For many years I have looked at his pictures and wondered what kind of man he was and what kind of father he would have been if he lived. Mr. Doherty, the private detective we hired, went to France recently to find out about my father and met you. He told me how my father saved your life. Now I understand you are using your own money to do good works in France. I would like to think that my father contributed to that in some small way by saving your life. I am thinking of writing an essay for my English class about my father and you. I hope you will not mind. Thank you so much for living a useful life since the war. I wish all rich Americans would do the kind of things you are doing. So much is destroyed in war. I hope people my age will grow up to make sure there is always peace in the world.

Yours truly,
Mary Margaret McDonald

The letter was written in the kind of flourishing script only a sixteen-year old girl would use. Still Doherty was moved by the sentiments in it. He showed it to Agnes who he thought brushed away a little tear when she finished reading it.

"I will make sure to send this by air mail to France as soon as I can. It is a beautiful letter, Mary Margaret. One that I'm sure Lieutenant Pettigrew will be very happy to receive. I like your idea of writing a story for your class about your father. It will do a lot to keep his memory alive."

"I don't know how to thank you, Mr. Doherty," the girl said as she stood on tiptoes and kissed him on the cheek.

"Just do your best to keep the world at peace."

When she left the office, Agnes gave him a knowing look. "Underneath that hardened exterior you know you really are a sentimental slob."

"Yeah, maybe. Just don't let on to our clients. It could be bad for business."

Doherty retreated to his office where he read Mary Margaret's letter for a second time. He neatly folded it into an envelope, which he addressed to Celeste Pettigrew c/o Château du Colombier, St-Malo, France. He'd stop by the post office in the morning and send it off via airmail. He was banking on Andrew Pettigrew's murder not making it into the news in America.

THE END

Author's Notes

Durgin-Park Restaurant, where Doherty dines with his uncle, was a staple of the Boston eating scene from its opening in 1827 to its much-regretted closing in 2019. It was always located in what was locally referred to as the Quincy Market adjacent to Boston's historic Faneuil Hall. For many years Durgin-Park was a destination dining spot for locals and visitors to Boston alike. In 1969 the city arranged with private developers to reenergize and reimagine Quincy Market and transform it from a barely operating food market into a place that would contain a variety of food stalls, bars, and eating establishments. This renovation made Durgin-Park even more of a destination for tourists until its closing.

The Pan American Worldport terminal from which Doherty departs for Paris did not open until May 1960, two months after Doherty leaves from there in the book. I took some license here because the space age building with its flying saucer style roof has always intrigued me and I wanted to get it into this novel. In 1991 Pan American Airlines declared bankruptcy and the terminal became the new home for Delta Airlines, which acquired most of Pan Am's assets as well as the lease on the building that was henceforth referred to as Terminal 3. It was demolished in 2013 despite strenuous efforts on the part of preservationists to have it placed on the list of the National Registry of Historic Places.

The Hotel Wetter in the Latin Quarter where Doherty stays in Paris is a hotel my then girlfriend and now wife Jeanne Berkman and I stayed in 1975 on our first trip to Paris. We have been unable to find it on our subsequent visits to France. Therefore, I have to assume it is no longer in operation. My description of it is based on slides I took while there and our collective memories.

The Château Du Colombier is now the Château Hotel Colombier or Hotel Colombier. My wife and I stayed there on a recent trip to France in 2018. Part of the intent of that trip was to do research for The Dead Soldier. It was one of several places we visited on this excursion also mentioned in Doherty's travels. We had also visited many of these same places on an earlier trip in 1975. Whether they looked the same in 1960 is mere conjecture on my part. However, given how few historic places in France have changed over the centuries I think I was on solid ground in describing them as I did.

One final note has to do with office telephone answering machines. There is some dispute as to how widely used such devices were in 1960. Since I had mentioned such a device in another office in a previous book set a few months before The Dead Soldier, I did not think I was being anachronistic in having Doherty employ such a device in The Dead Soldier. If I was at least I was being consistently anachronistic.

Acknowledgements

First and foremost I must thank my wife Jeanne Berkman for her sage advice, criticism, and editing skills that helped me bring The Dead Soldier to life (excuse pun). I would also like to acknowledge old West Warwick friends Arn Lisnoff and John Barba for adding color and insight about West Warwick from back in the day. Along the same lines was the additional help I got from a long-lost West Warwick friend Dick Lague, who I connected with on Facebook. Dick gave me much useful information about his father, the optometrist Dr. Maurice Lague, who plays a small role in the novel. I may have embellished a little in his scenes, and if so my humble apologies to Dick.

In terms of sections in the novel set in France I have to give a shout out to Barbara Forte of the Travel Collaborative in Cambridge, Massachusetts for putting together our French itinerary at the last minute that featured several of the places that Doherty visited in his quest to find out about the deceased soldier. My old friend Stephen Suffern, an American ex-patriate who has lived in Paris for many years with his family was very helpful in providing some basic information as to how much things cost and what Paris was probably like in 1960. Finally I would like to thank the Association of Rhode Island Authors (ARIA) and especially their former president Steven Porter for helping me to get exposure in Rhode Island and reach readers in that state who love mysteries and nostalgia.